Crybaby of the Western World

[A Novel of Petit Guignol in Long Beach, California]

ALSO BY JOHN LEONARD:

Wyke Regis
The Naked Martini

Crybaby of the Western World

[A Novel of Petit Guignol in Long Beach, California]

by John Leonard

Doubleday & Company, Inc.
Garden City, New York
1969

For my brother, Ken

"They say the drowning man relives his life as he drowns. Well, I was not drowning in water, but I was drowning in West. I drowned westward through the hot brass days and black velvet nights. It took me seventy-eight hours to drown. For my body to sink down to the very bottom of West and lie in the motionless ooze of History, naked on a hotel bed in Long Beach, California. . . . For that is where you come, after you have crossed oceans and eaten stale biscuits while prisoned forty days and nights in a storm-tossed rat-trap, after you have sweated in the greenery and heard the savage whoop, after you have built cabins and cities and bridged rivers, after you have lain with women and scattered children like millet seed in a high wind, after you have composed resonant documents, made noble speeches, and bathed your arms in blood to the elbows, after you have shaken with malaria in the bushes and in the icy wind across the high plains. That is where you come, to lie alone on a bed in a hotel room in Long Beach, California. Where I lay, while outside my window a neon sign flickered on and off to the time of my heart, systole and diastole, flushing and flushing again the gray sea mist with a tint like blood."

[ROBERT PENN WARREN, *All the King's Men*]

"Barring war or catastrophe, the next five years indicate a steady rise in the public works program of the City of Long Beach."

[*1965 Report of Public Works,*
DEPARTMENT OF ENGINEERING, CITY OF LONG BEACH]

"What is it like below, Charidas?"
"Very dark."
"And what about the resurrection?"
"All lies."
"And Pluto?"
"A fable."
"Then I am done for."

[CALLIMACHUS]

Cast of Characters

STANHOPE CRONOPIOS . . . the poet of Long Beach

JOHN THE OSSIFIED MAN . . . a tourist attraction on the Pike

GONGOR . . . a representative of Cucking Stool & Sons, New York publishers

MAUD CRONOPIOS . . . Stanhope's mother

ARBITER AIDOS . . . a professor of intellectual history

BETHESDA . . . Stanhope's one true love

RENALDI HARUSPEX . . . a Long Beach motorcycle cop

SVAM SPADE . . . a leading member of the Now Generation

DOKHMA KOAN . . . a Sikkimese exchange student with a secret

ONALRED . . . a Soviet agent with several secrets

OTTO UNAMUNO . . . a blind dwarf who runs Media, Rare & Well-done

PATHER PARTURIENT . . . a lapsed physicist who works for Otto

GNATPAPPA . . . an Australian aborigine who works for Otto

DR. LANGWEIL . . . Parturient's psychocatalyst

SAHASRARA CANNIBIS . . . another member of the Now Generation

DASEIN CAMEMBERT . . . a former Trotskyite, now working for the FBI

SYNECDOCHE WESSEL . . . the heavyweight champion of genital organization

Plus

Arrow Truex and the Water-polo Lettermen . . . the Surfrajets . . . the Iowa Avengers . . . the Pigstickers of Islam . . . the Nobblies . . . the Acid-Heads . . . Ali-Whoops

And

CAPTAIN HAPPEN

Now [1]

*On the beach, a mysterious summons . . . John the Ossified
Man introduces Stanhope to Gongor . . . persiflage about Long
Beach . . . Gongor and Stanhope leave for Cimarosa Street
. . . Stanhope remembers his mother.*

The wick was low, the gorge was high. The sea sighed through the
vents of the weatherized Neoprene beach tent. The grunion-hunter
said: "Mr. Cronopios?"

"That depends."

"*Are* you Stanhope Cronopios?"

"All right."

"I was sent with a message from John the Ossified Man. He wants
to see you."

"Really? Did he send you collect? I can't imagine John's paying a
messenger out of his own pocket."

"There's a rhomboid with him, who flew all the way out from New
York to find you. The rhomboid pays my freight." His eyes went
click, photographing the contents of the beach tent; his mind decided
not to develop the negative impression.

Even the grunion-hunters are judging me now, thought Stanhope.
He looked at the messenger's Sassoon haircut and Captain Happen
button. By what right did such a person make judgments?

"Thank you," said Stanhope. The grunion-hunter effaced himself.

Well. Who in New York could possibly be interested in Stanhope
Cronopios, the dilettante hangman? He would go, of course. Anything
was better than sitting here, huddled over the cold keys of his Hermes
portable, on the extroverted California orange crate, eating the Spam
of his fantasies. He reread the poem he was writing, "Stanhopelessly
Balboa-Constricted":

And so no vitaminted Faust
Now walks the harsh Pacific coast:
But more a canapé of doubts,
A slice of Hamlet on wry toast.

Meretricious. But, these days, what wasn't meretricious? *Bethesda,*
he thought, and typed her name. The past looked over his shoulder
as he did so, and wept. Bethesda was lodged like a splinter in the
optic nerve of the past.

So. He covered the typewriter. He snuffed the candle. He stood,
resenting the exertion, and stepped outside into the dark. Barefoot,
he walked up the beach toward the Pike, trying to absorb himself
in the cuneiform print of his toes on the spray-slick sand, trying to
ignore the gulls who cried, as they drummed their wings on the dumb
night air: *Bethesda, Bethesda.*

When he reached John's trailer, he could hear the voice of the
Ossified Man through the window. "The emotional famine which
has begun in Long Beach," John was saying, "will swiftly spread
throughout the land." Stanhope knocked, and entered.

"Howdy," said John. His fingers lay dead in the basket of his lap:
stone periwinkles, broken pencils. On the wall, twitching in the flicker
of the hurricane lamp, snapshot aspects of his former self had been
trapped behind glass, in cheap frames green beneath the flaking gilt:
an unossified John on the highboard, tensed to dive; or broad-
jumping; linen-trousered, blazer-backed, spats-shod among lemon
trees, a Malacca cane on one arm and a girl on the other, grinning.
John had been an athlete and a lover before the disease attacked his
musculature, before the progressive atrophy and the awful petrifaction. He was now a gray rock, sitting under a fez in a tin trailer on
the Pike in Long Beach, where people purchased tickets to touch him.

Stanhope thought: what an extraordinary attraction this fossil has
always exerted over me, over all of us! We squandered so many days
and nights of our lives (John never slept) cursing and boasting and
confessing to him. Perhaps we hoped a part of our selves might be
preserved in his stoniness. Perhaps we half-believed that future
archaeologists might one day disinter him from the crumbled stucco
of Long Beach, and apportion chunks of him to various laboratories
for examination. Would they, in the course of carbon-dating his
ossified tissue, release *our* unstable isotopes? Would they, in the reading of his rings, look down with kindliness upon the light Spring

xylem we had been? Probably not. But we need not be ashamed of our desire for such a tissue-issue. That is the only thing of which we need not be ashamed.

John said: "Stanhope, this is Gongor." Gongor—bald, leaden-eyed, in celery-colored hip-huggers and sheared French rabbit battle jacket—blinked. "Gongor represents the Myth Department of Cucking Stool & Sons, New York," said John. "He has come to see you, Stanhope, about your manuscript."

"You sent them my manuscript?"

"Yes," said John.

"Why?" said Stanhope.

"To be perfectly frank," said John, "I was hoping for a ten per cent cut of the proceeds, as your literary agent."

"But you didn't even like my manuscript."

"I don't like anything," said John. "Still . . . I go on."

Gongor used his hands as guillotines. "We're interested in your manuscript, Cronopios. But there are problems of authenticity. We must, of course, thoroughly investigate anything purporting to explain the origins of Captain Happen."

"Captain Happen?" said Stanhope. "My manuscript is only incidentally concerned with Captain Happen. I am not the least bit interested in Captain Happen, except as an illustration of the Irony Hang-up . . . that all those people should have died giving birth to such a pernicious piece of nonsense."

"Face it, Cronopios," said Gongor. "Captain Happen is the only thing that gives all those other people any meaning whatsoever." The light from the hurricane lamp slashed at his face. "Besides, if you weren't trying to explain Captain Happen, what *did* you hope to achieve with your memoir?"

Stanhope shrugged. "Art is a stomach pump of the emotions."

"Applesauce," said John. "It is Long Beach which is to blame, though all of us, its burnished tots, have to pay the sandy piper. The question then becomes: how can you possibly explain Long Beach?"

How, indeed, thought Stanhope. A flushed mind drains down a thousand caviling replies. Into the replenishing tank flow images of ancient Iowans, strapped to electric cars . . . palm trees like the maimed, heroic thoughts of children . . . sailors pumping each other like slot machines . . . natives at volleyball. And the sea, always the sea: lapping vat of gull droppings, windy horn of moan; abused by rude buoys, mincing sailboats, darkly libidinous atomic submarines . . .

Stanhope asked John: "Do we bake in causality, like an apple in its jacket, doomed to shrink? Does the drama precipitate its objects; or do the objects precipitate their drama?"

John replied: "Only a vulgarian is certain of first principles."

Gongor was exasperated. "Long Beach has nothing to do with it." Unaware of the exchange of significant looks between John and Stanhope, he went on: "I want you to take me around, Cronopios. I want to see for myself the locales of every incident you describe in your manuscript. I want to make sketches and take photographs for our Myth Department. I want to get a *feel* for the past, if you know what I mean."

Stanhope shook his head: "How did Céline put it?" And John replied: " 'Nothing exists, Monsieur Baryton, between the penis and mathematics. It's a vacuum.' "

Gongor, consulting his Accutron, growled: "Look—you take me around, and I pick up the tab for all the time I'm here. That's fair, isn't it?"

"You realize," said Stanhope, "that many of the landmarks have been destroyed. The Ashram has been pulled down and converted into a shopping plaza. Otto's pyramid is gone, replaced by a drive-in church. And Bethesda's houseboat is at the bottom of the Naples canal . . . I sank it myself."

"These things are of no consequence, Cronopios. I just want to walk on all the roads which led, inevitably, to Captain Happen."

Stanhope thought about it. There *were* therapeutic possibilities. "Why . . . not?"

"Then let's start now," said Gongor. "My rental car is waiting."

As they left the trailer, John called after them: "Remember my ten per cent!"

The climb up to Ocean Boulevard was silent. Then Gongor, with his key in the car lock, asked: "Where's the first stop?"

Stations of the double-cross—Stanhope looked down, across the beach, to the vast black marbling of the sea. The question was more complicated than Gongor could possibly know. It was the very question Stanhope had confronted on beginning his memoir. Several devices had suggested themselves: a summoning, for instance, of significant symbols: the surfboard, the laser beam, the mandala, the alpenstock, and the burning octogenarian. Or, possibly, a metaphysical

picaresque, manipulating the chapter-matter according to the flap of
'Attar's lapwing across the Seven Valleys of Mystical Experience,
toward Annihilation of the Self. Or . . . there was always circum-
spection. Sit back, light up a pretzel, and suddenly the memory re-
turns. The taste is that of the Veri-Thin which on Thursday nights in
Long Beach (when his mother went bowling) he used to gnaw alone.
The sight of that deformity had suggested nothing to him before he
sank his teeth intuit. But the smell and taste of pretzels wait, like traffic
tickets in the glove compartment of the *Eigenwelt,* ready to remind
us of the places where we've parked. "Let us go to Cimarosa Street,"
he said. "As Darwin began with monographs on Cirripedia, I will begin with myself."

The rental car leapt like a torpedo into his past.

"Funny," said Gongor, at the wheel. "The churches look like air-
ports, and the high schools look like filling stations."

"There is nothing funny about it," said Stanhope. "Long Beach is
a kind of strip-mining of the soul."

"This is where it all began." He was already tipsy on the vapors of
insecticide, the mingled aromas of mown grass and pepperwood sap,
of barbecue sauce and Bab-o. "At least here, nothing has changed."
Not the fuchsia bushes flaming, nor the eight-foot chainlink anti-Fido
fence leaking electrical discharge. And, as always, the birdbath, the
Osiris knocker, the steelwool welcome mat and the orange door all,
on spying Stanhope, contrived to mock him.

The house gasped, then lapsed into disapproval on their entry.
Silent the puce-colored carpet and the bamboo drapes; silent the
candelabra of Ganassa tusk and the orgone box on top of the stereo
console; silent, too, the bust of Emma Goldman and the pile of
moldering *Monthly Reviews.*

"I might have admired the hard pride of the inanimate objects in
my mother's house," said Stanhope pensively. "But early on, she
embraced and annihilated their privacy. Even in grammer school,
Gongor, I feared this house, as an extension of my mother's centrip-
etal nervous system. How was I to gather *being* from objects opaque
in their servitude?"

Gongor was setting up his Leica, and did not reply.

Stanhope continued: "They (the objects) and she (my mother)
conspired at a stucco sarcophagus, wherein I (dead Greek with
bloody lilac springing from my cleft of chin) would be laid, en-

tombed, among brass trophies of Lions Club Speaking Contests and certificates of Junior Statesmanship."

He opened the plate-glass door and looked out on the patio. There was a smell of cows in the night. "Do you know," he said to the snap-shooting Gongor, "I used to think of this odiferousness as a logarithm . . . the nasty exponent, a power, by which the base (my intention) had been raised to its anti-log (my fear). My fallacies have always been overly pathetic."

Then [1]

*An interior interrogation: Stanhope confesses to his youth
and his shame, his vision and his fatherlessness . . . an account
of the high school graduation . . . the water-polo lettermen
murder the deer . . . arrival of the motorcycle cops . . .
Stanhope's first poem . . . the awful judgment.*

QUESTION: S. Cronopios, you have been charged with Guilt. How
do you plead?

ANSWER: Is there a distinction between guilt and shame?

QUESTION: Can *you* formulate one?

ANSWER: I once told Bethesda that guilt, because it possesses a
particle of moral choice, is a primitive form of knowledge; and that
shame, because it possesses a particle of self-consciousness, is a primitive form of vanity.

Q: Your formulation is itself both guilty and shameful.

A: Rats.

Q: Describe the circumstances of your birth.

A: I was born in Long Beach, in a tract home, under the broken
wall and burning Spanish tile. Fatherless child. Sly spy in babyfat, my
virtues eels of stratagem, coiling and striking for my mother's hand.
Weak-eyed graceless unter-tyke, without friends, without tennis
sneakers. Under the steel patio umbrella, cheating at solitaire, as
solitaire had cheated me. Self-clutching hydramatic griefchik.

Q: When did you first start feeling guilty?

A: When I was ten, my mother gave me a pair of pigeons to tend
to, and a tin box in which to tame them. "Tumblers," she said. They
died of some aberrant mange.

Q: Go on.

A: When I was twelve, she made me take a paper route. "To understand the cash nexus," she explained. Ten new starts and you won
a weekend tobogganing in the Sierras; twenty-five new starts, a month
on the Jungleboat at Disneyland. But when families canceled their

subscriptions because they were moving to Pasadena and switching to Hearst, I was ashamed to report their defection to my route boss. So on weekday afternoons I dragged my consignment of useless headlines home and burned them in the back-yard incinerator, causing smog. On Sundays I tried to sell the extras to women on their way to church, or to men hosing down Buicks. And once a month my collections fell short of the kickback owed the route boss, and I had to steal the discrepancy from my mother's purse, as I stole stale cigarettes from her orgone box, as I stole esteem from her indifference. Is suffering a form of self-importance?

Q: Yes. When you were thirteen . . . ?

A: My mother instructed me in karate and pistol practice. At karate, I was impossible, preferring the embrace. At pistol practice, I deliberately affected incompetence, for the weapon raised sexual problems I was as yet unprepared to resolve. (Besides, I now knew why she had wanted the pigeons.) In disgust, my mother gave up on me, and used my allowance for a subscription to the Congressional Record. I was obliged each afternoon, in lieu of pistols and paper route, to underline the lies in Congressman Hosmer's speeches.

Q: Was there a bank at which to deposit your guilt, that it might gather interest? Did *you* go to church?

A: When I was fourteen. Mainly to annoy my mother, who opposed all organized religion. But I quit, for I was ashamed to be seen —on my bicycle, swaying to the rack—by the tenderloined dentists' daughters disembarking from their limousines at eleven o'clock. I was ashamed of my thoughts: the intimacies I lavished on the defenseless dentists' daughters as they perched primly in their pews, their pewter-colored hair brushed to a dull glow made halo-ly in the light through the plastic stained windows; their eyes glaucous with expectation; their flesh an enticing fragrance of pine soap and maple syrup. The vicar's face shone flaming off the snake-shields of their naked knees. I wanted to bury my head in their miracle fabrics. Arbiter Aidos later told me that contrition, like art, is a sublimated form of rage. Is that true?

Q: No. What about your secondary education?

A: When I was fifteen, I was auctioned off to the nearest high school: Aztec architecture, free-form fishpond, camphor trees and peppermint-striated rubbish cans. "Why don't you want to relate to people?" my counselor asked me. She asked it of a young man in yellow corduroy trousers and maroon sport shirt—the school colors

—string tie, suede shoes, green poncho and oil-slicked pomade. It should have been obvious to her that such a specimen did desperately want to relate . . . but *how?*

Q: Did you try?

A: That dong-tormented spring I traipsed the perimeter of the Bay Shore beach, in search of a male role. Ogled the sun-bunnies at lissome antic-play. Wondered: did my father's mind play sprinkler-like over these same sandy meadows of delight? Had he dared proffer his small snack-self to these same blonde and breasty cannibals? And had Mother been the ripe round fruit of his perambulation? I knew nothing of my father, although I imagined him a sperm-spurned Yeats, gonne maud enough one night to bite the knobby knee of lust, which in Long Beach is deciduous, like the trees. But it was more difficult to conceive of a time when Mother might have found the leisure to get bitten, between bowling tournaments and *I. F. Stone's Weekly*.

Q: What else?

A: I embarked on educational night maneuvers: slipping through my bedroom window, into the ivy, along the chainlink fence to the nylon clothesline from which I hung and dropped, a claw on wires, down to the dicondra. Creeping thence to the barbecue rotisserie, I blackened my face with briquets and bolted. To pad swiftly, silently down the darkened block . . . to listen at kitchen windows to the clang of spoons on pans and skulls . . . to peer through the wind-wings of parked automobiles at grappling bodies, skewered girls. And with dawn a hemorrhage on the hump of Signal Hill, I returned to my window, my room, my narrow bunk and loose-mouthed barbicans, to smudge the white pillowcase with charcoal off my cheeks, and await my mother's surly breakfast summons: "Feed your face." Upon delivery of that summons, the long-necked sunlight thrust itself through my window and like a bloody giraffe disdainfully regarded me: *You whose very being makes me weary like a cradle . . .*

Q: Did you ever specifically ask your mother for help?

A: Often, but she never gave it. Once, at breakfast, in the glazed dinette, over fish eggs and *xnipek* and pineapple juice the color and consistency of semen, she was reading Albert Maltz. On her face (escutcheon of wars, betrayals, intentions) had been gouged out hard lines, moon-rills in a moon-sea of inexhaustible dust. "Mother," I said, "would you buy me a basketball?" "For why?" she screamed. "For regularity? For sociological Ex-Lax? Never, until all the diamonds in South Africa turn to dung!"

Q: Why a basketball? What was the significance of a basketball?

A: Sport was hope. It might mean *Press-Telegram* clippings, scholarships to San Francisco. Chocolate-colored skyscrapers rose from the potato-cellar of my childhood, cities like clusters of Drambuie bottles. Dark, turnip-towered corridors, chasms of azure, through which the tides of me coursed, rivers of garlic and sapphires and mud, toward sewer mouths and concrete sewer bellies, solariums of waste . . . There I would execute my flawless ghostly jump shots. There I would lay up my vengeance. So . . . so our sores are greedy mouths; so our wounds devour us.

Q: What happened during your junior year of high school?

A: My counselor recommended I join the World Friendship Society, then engaged in collecting old toothbrushes to be sent to Pakistan as part of an oral contraceptive program. But I contracted instead with Arrow Truex, captain of the water-polo team, to write all his English compositions for him. In exchange for this syntactical servitude, Arrow manipulated my election to the high school Key Club.

Q: Why did you want to join the Key Club? To what did membership entitle you?

A: A lapel pin. Permission to attend the monthly Kiwanis luncheons at the country club, where all the burghers wore booster badges to remind themselves of who they were supposed to be. And . . . I was assigned the usual Ming girl.

Q: Mimsy Lubricious. A disaster. Why? What happened?

A: Mimsy was a lollipopular seventeen, made for and by the tongues of boys. Her purr-ball hung a lisp on me; I feebly grounded out too short. That bush of hooks and nails, that saucer of tar at the eye of the crumpled cotton flower in the back seat of my mother's gray sedan . . . sad-making. Mimsy was too enthralled at the shards of the pubescent chrysalis about her to make either promises or love. She said, "Naughty," meaning *nought-ye.* My mother's carburetor wept tears of grease on her father's driveway. She said, "I know what you want," meaning that while she didn't exactly know what *she* wanted, it certainly wasn't to deny the race of men—the Trojans and trackstars—her ultimate vanquishment, by giving everything away to a boy with a slick pomade and hands like stricken starfish. No trolls in Mimsy's garden.

Q: She jilted you?

A: I lost her to a college freshman who worked nights at RKO

Keith. He took her up to the balcony and showed her his flashlight. She fell to a movie-house usher. My Key Club colleagues were incensed. At a drumhead session of the Credentials Committee I was, for having disgraced them, summarily suspended, banned from all beach parties . . .

Q: And so, with that suspension, you lost the only community you had ever known?

A: Well, I wanted to be a member of the Key Club because it entitled me to a Ming girl. Without the girl, why go to beach parties? *That* suspension didn't bother me as much as the other one—the suspension of my *life* between the desire and the spasm. I remember standing in the shower stall for hours, wishing it were an elevator, wishing that a faucet-twist would drop me through an unseen shaft down to the floor of the sea. It was—really!—more like shame than guilt.

Q: Surely elevator shaft is a Freudian image?

A: Listen, I tried all that out. As I told Bethesda later on, I thought I could blame it all on my fatherlessness. How was I to acquire a male role if there wasn't a father around for me to murder? But that's a cop-out. Whether one actually murders one's father is of no importance; guilt is an expression of one's ambivalence. I was, then, still a child on my Oedipal-cycle, but where was I headed? How was I to invent a father in an age when God was dead? After the death of God, hadn't Christ anyway been turned into Hamlet? I *could* identify with Hamlet; but in the vast distorting mirror which is Long Beach, I more resembled Caliban. I suppose this explains my subsequent susceptibility to Onalred's revolutionary blandishments.

Q: But that was the year, too, when you had your vision, wasn't it?

A: Yes. I had gone by bus on a Scholarship Society field trip to see "Blue Boy" at the Huntington Hartford Museum. Stumbling by chance upon the cactus garden, I discovered there a phallic prickliness that seemed to symbolize the urgency of my self-doubt. I missed the return trip, and spent the night devoutly macerating there.

Q: Describe the vision.

A: There seemed in the rugged determination of the cacti something more than a mere will to survive the unfriendly intentions of the Southern California desert. There seemed a profound and moving *repudiation* of the desert's essential horizontality. Imagine the cactus lonely at night, rooted in the desert, too stubby to touch the stars. Might not Man be described as a thinking cactus? Didn't Man, by the verticality of his questions, estrange himself from nature, the desert, the elemental trampoline from which he sprang? But Man must come down; like the cactus, he has roots. He must return to the mindless horizontal roll, the desert-nature indifferent to his questions, his estrangement. He must return to the ultimate linoleum of a meaningless death.

Q: Which led you to ask . . . ?

A: Didn't Man hate and envy that horizontal indifference to which he was still attached? Weren't his skyscrapers really concrete cacti, representations of the verticality of his questions? And wasn't there about those representations a threatening phallic assertion? Why? I *knew:* Man, hating nature, wants to *rape* it! Brutal revenge, violent rejoining, bloody redemption, an end to questions, an end to *guilt!*

Q: The redemptive rape . . .

A: Too right. Hamlet, after the long agony of the cactus night, chooses to repeat this most original of sins. And from that bed of nature-rape there will arise a metempsychosed soul, capable of creating an *aesthetic state* (Schiller) and a *non-repressive civilization* (Marcuse). What was the risk? An end to guilt is the end of the *self.* I was prepared to risk the measly prerogative of *my* self. The problem then became, alas, the essential flatitudinarianism of Long Beach—the Squashed Metropolis!

Q: So you went into your senior year with a serviceable vision. Yet something happened at the end of that year—mocking your vision and making you a poet?

A: They had to let me speak at high school graduation because of my grade-point average. The gray cortege of scapulars and tassel-caps seethed down the football field toward their diplomas. Behind the podium stood the principal, a pile of parchment at his knee, arc light making goggles of his eyes. My moment came. I saw it all, knew it as the disembodied eye on the ceiling of a dream knows the violation taking place below, and bears helpless witness. Umber thousands muttered in the stands. And I knew precisely what it was I wished to say to them: that these seniors advancing through the crepuscular light constituted a Primal Horde; that this night of circumstantial pomp symbolized a rite of ceremonial parricide; that they conspired to slay the surrogate daddy who lived (on) (as) (its) principal. Redemption! I opened my mouth; there arose a dirigible of prose. It sought soar; it leaked gas; it proved aerodynamically unsound. And they shot it down! They fashioned their cardboard commencement programs into paper planes and strafed me where I stood, while I tried to explain. Shame, you see . . . nothing but shame.

Q: Surely you should have known better than to—

A: Of course. I should have realized. As I told Bethesda, perhaps I did realize, but quixotically ignored myself. Perhaps that fungus of disappointment which had grown all through my youth over every dream of heroism, every gesture toward embrace—the pigeons, the paper route, the karate, the Key Club—should have prepared me. For there is obviously an Emersonian Oversolecism. Get caught with your participles dangling—indecent exposure of your naked need to communicate—and Long Beach will use those dangling participles to hang you up.

Q: What did you do?

A: With a cardboard commencement program stuck in my ear, I fled. I fled my failure to communicate, the hooting of my mother, the lamentations from the outraged grandstands (like stranded whales heaving eupeptic falsettos). I stripped myself of scapular and threw away my tassel-cap. I sought sanctuary under the camphor trees, next to the free-form fishpond. I solicited solace from a pint of fortified pulque pilfered from my mother's whisky cupboard. I smoked cigarettes as though they were worms. I cannot now recall how long I lay there, obscured by rubbish cans, in my malignant stupor. "Moyst, with one drop of thy blood, my drye soul!" Donne had cried out to Christ. But there was no Christ: only Hamlet, a cactus with qualms, and I was feeling spongy: when voices—hushed, furtive, imprecatory —roused me; low and ingenious oaths laved the air.

Q: Arrow Truex and the band of water-polo lettermen . . .

A: Yes. All attired in their red-breasted jackets with the white leather sleeves and yellow athletic emblems. I possessed such a jacket myself, but was, typically, ashamed to wear it. For I had won my letter not in strife, but by raking up sawdust pits, nailing down starting blocks, assembling rows of wooden hurdles, preparing hectographic memoranda on warming-up exercises, fetching hot dogs and cartons of milk for the stomachs of the gladiators, towels for their necks, band-aids for their blisters. I had been a track manager, a clerk of sweat, and wore my letterman's jacket only at home, in the bathroom, while I pretended to shave. Another abortive attempt at community . . .

Q: Truex and the water-polo lettermen had stolen a deer from the zoo . . . ?

A: Which they dragged after them. Yes. "Strap her down," commanded Arrow. The deer was lashed to the fishpond caryatid from which (oblivious) still sprang a gurgle of green water. Truex brandished an empty bottle of Thunderbird wine. From their jackets the lettermen, chloritic in the moonlight off green water, produced similar bottles. At Arrow's assenting signal they bludgeoned the deer to death with the butt ends of their Thunderbird bottles. "Monstrous freedom!" cried Truex, quoting from an English essay I had ghostwritten for him. "Vertigo of possibility!" Then they stepped out of their loafers and washed their sweat socks in the now crimson waters of the fishpond. I—

Q: A cruel parody of your vision! A crude burlesque of the redemptive—

A: Exactly. The poem—my *first* poem—began immediately in my head:

> But through the water red with doe
> Still shines the all-offending toe.

I stole away from them, and summoned the police . . .

Q: A dress rehearsal for your subsequent, more princely finkdom?

A: Perhaps. Anyway, the police came: ruby eyes in slabs of graphite: pavé-mirrored motorcycle jackets; Kohinoor epaulets; second-skin trousers of mirror-plastic; white vinyl crash helmets in the lowering branches of the camphor trees; polyethylene holsters and shoulder straps. They appraised the situation, and then kicked the lettermen comatose.

Q: And *you* left with the cops . . . ?

A: On a motorcycle, clinging to a bullet-headed policeman named Renaldi Haruspex, blind in the brilliance of pavé-mirrors, down Ocean Boulevard to the station house on the Pike. All night long I listened to the anguished song of John the Ossified Man. And I completed that bloody dawn the first in my series of poems (a *Singspiel* called *Angel's Sloth*) for Renaldi and the L.B. motorcycle cops, the flashing Cinderellas of Death on their silver cybernetic steeds:

> A deer whose eyes were salt licks
> Longed to pour like rain and Morton's.
> I think it is of some importance
> That lettermen, to get their kicks,

Swiped her; and, on Arrow's word,
Clubbed her to death with Thunderbird.

Did they hope to stamp from doe
Cookies of the Tao?
It doesn't matter now.
This is what I know:

The sweat socks of Man are stained with red;
All that was deer to me is dead.

On returning to Cimarosa Street, I buried my letterman's jacket under a yew tree, while my mother barked at the window.

Q: I think that's more than enough. S. Cronopios, you are guilty of Guilt, as charged. You will be released on your own recognizance, since you have so much of it. And you will be detained in Long Beach until such time as a gift of Innocence redeems you. Out, out!

A: You *are* a son-of-a-bitch. You know that means forever.

Now [2]

A roll call of the dead . . . Stanhope and Gongor visit a bowling alley . . . Otto on television: the anguish of the Third Dimension . . . Plans are made for the peripatetic morrow . . . Gongor leaves Stanhope his credit card.

"Would you like me to dig up the letterman's jacket?"

"Certainly not," said Gongor. Gongor was depressed. He had been dragged from Cimarosa Street to the high school to the station house, and back to Cimarosa Street. "I don't really see what all this has to do with Captain Happen," he added. "The sex life of an adolescent is usually unhappy, but seldom of teleological significance."

Stanhope was also depressed. Looking into the past was like looking into a drained swimming pool, remembering a diving party or a water-polo game. The bodies, and the medium through which they moved, were gone. "You miss the point, Gongor. Bethesda is dead. And Arbiter Aidos. And my mother, and Onalred, and Otto, and Dasein. Not to mention Dokhma Koan. I am the reason they are dead. Their fate is my character. Or, to put it the way Malraux did: 'When lepers cease to believe in God, they poison the wells.'"

"Others were equally responsible," said Gongor. He checked his notes. "Pather Parturient. Svam Spade. The aborigine, Gnatpappa. Even Haruspex himself."

"Not *equally* responsible, Gongor. That's why *they* have been able to live with it. Parturient married Sahasrara; they now run a Shearwater cruise boat for harbor tourists. Svam is public-relations director for the Iowa State Picnic; he's introduced the Captain Happenings there. Gnatpappa joined the Peace Corps and went to Spain. Renaldi quit the cops to sell the Great Books program door-to-door. All of them lead busy, useful lives, except *me*. And I . . . I am muscle-bound from the calisthenics of despair."

Gongor looked up and down Cimarosa Street, at the pepperwood trees and the TV antennas, the rubberized lawns and the potted death-plants. Then he pressed a button to raise his window. "I could use a drink."

"There's a bar nearby," said Stanhope. "At the bowling alley on which my mother used to inflict herself, in palmier days."

They went there, and ordered grasshoppers. As bad luck would have it, on the color television set was a videotaped rerun of the documentary *The Many Murderers of Otto Unamuno*. In living color: the garbage of Otto's corpse.

Did it threaten Gongor, as it did Stanhope? Did it threaten the millions of tube-boobies the breadth of the continent? Would the spectacle of Otto's obliteration rile ether dreams in bars and denrooms? Would the spider machines spin out eccentric encephalograms? Would for a moment the tube-boobies know, like Otto, the anguish of the Third Dimension? If so, *only* for a moment. Later, when the tube is dark and the boobies stand barefoot on unwelcome mats before the doors of their refrigerated Hide-a-Beds, they will be incapable of relating the intuition of that anguish to the failure of their self-salesmanship.

Gongor said, "Otto had a good thing going for him. Only he pushed it too far. He was sick."

Stanhope nodded. "How did Nietzsche put it? 'Only by his sickness does man become interesting.'"

Gongor stood. "I'm going back to the Villa Riviera, to transcribe these notes and get some sleep. Why don't I pick you up at Cimarosa Street tomorrow morning?"

"Not at Cimarosa Street," said Stanhope. "I live on the beach now. Just look for the neoprene tent."

"Wizard," said Gongor; and, before leaving, he gave Stanhope his credit card to pay for their grasshoppers. Stanhope read the credit card with his fingers: Braille for the blindly acquisitive. (Otto had once told him: "The plastic credit card has been erroneously accused of stealing all the sex from money. It is more accurate to think of the plastic credit card as transforming money from a metaphor for labor into a movement of information: which is to say, *communion*.") (No wonder Otto was dead.)

Tomorrow they would go to the College, and the College would not have changed. Except for the fact that the only two people who had made it bearable were now gone. The College had purified itself . . .

Then [2]

Why Arbiter Aidos was a right angle . . . description of the College and its inmates . . . Stanhope's introduction to Bethesda . . . second appearance of Renaldi Haruspex . . . first appearance of Svam Spade . . . an account of the Fire Festival, the Hymn to Big Surf, and the holocaust . . . Aidos expires.

"Of some men," observed Arbiter Aidos, "it can be said: they have no sand in their crankcases. I think of David Ogilvy, Cheddi Jagan, Sam Huff, José Ortega y Gasset and John the Ossified Man. Of a few women, too, it might be said that, had they crankcases, there would be no sand in them: Hannah Arendt, Leslie Uggams, Pauline Kael. There is no sand in the crankcases of the surfers."

The surfers thought equally highly of Aidos. According to the surfers, Arbiter Aidos was the only right angle at the College; all the rest were rhomboids.

Why did the surfers consider Aidos a right angle? Certainly not because of his qualities as a teacher. Aidos taught intellectual history ("Selected Pratfalls in the Human Metacomedy"), and intellectual history was full of death and ideas, and the surfers did not believe in death and could not grasp ideas.

Nor did they consider Aidos a right angle just because he drank, although there was in his drinking an extravagant contempt for academic proprieties which must have appealed to them. He drank shamelessly: at faculty meetings, during class, even in the library while collecting notes for his long-deferred chef d'oeuvre, *Science Is Anal Sadism*. Slung over his left shoulder and under his right arm was an old goat's bladder, like a third lung. Connected to it was a tube which looped around his neck and into his mouth. With an ungainly sort of bagpipe pumping, he contrived to squirt a stream of resinated bile at himself. On swallowing it, he would become momentarily merry; his face would turn smooth and pink as a peach; his ears would release a hiss; his soft little knuckleless hands would slice palm-flatly outward in an umpirical *safe!* sign as the wine slid home. But then he would look out the window, through the iron trellis and the lemon tree, over the pasture of mud, to the ruined hacienda of the administration building; and his brow would collapse in a scowl as corrugated as the Spanish tile. "They are counting the number of my turpitudes," he would say, "and then it's adios, Aidos! True. But I still have a tick or two up my sleeve. One day—this week, next week, who cares?—the great yawn which I am perfecting will grow so wide, so deep, that it will swallow me whole. I will turn myself inside out, and disappear from disgrace of the earth."

The surfers, however, did little drinking of their own; they were afraid of flab.

No: what the surfers especially prized in Aidos was his indifference, his sexlessness. They, too, were sexless. Come upon them slumped in a cafeteria booth. Their gold-feathered wrists are webbed in rite. The tide tables are their liturgical text. Their feeble deliberative electricity generates a farce-field ("Ho, ho, rhomboids; money-monks; potato grubs!"), a parasol of Kugelblitz which lights their walnut faces, their helmets of corn-colored hair, their towel shirts and faded denim shorts and brandy-tinted vamp-strapped beach-bunny sandals. A scouring by sun and sea, a surgical nullification, or some new and powerful principle of neutering—"The spirit of plastic at large in the world," said Aidos—has left them genderless. As though they were bred selectively, *for* their insensibility, *to* their hormonic stupor, mutated to tawny appendages of a many-limbed collectivity, with a single cud-like mind chewing away on its singular imperative: to *glide*. Whatever the reason, their bodies were indifferent to every physical transaction save communal sacrifice to Big Surf. And their indifference exempted them, as his did Aidos, from the rampant eroticism of the College.

The educational situation is, of course, essentially erotic. But at the College that erotic essence had been intensified to the toxic point. It seemed (to young Stanhope) as though the architecture itself, the cream-colored adobe and petrified lymph, had been designed to imprison a yearning impossible to fulfill—an unappeasable itch, a dry ache, an objectless longing, a titillated sore. That itch, that ache, that sore, that longing could not be contained by the building materials. So the campus itself conspired at a metastatic shift; sought vessels and hosts among the creatures who haunted its halls like homeless Arabs. Lessing (Gotthold, not Doris) has written: *Es wandelt niemand ungestraft unter Palmen.* Yes, but how and why? Those who strolled under the palms of the College found that the itch had dropped upon them, and was ectogenous. Those who strayed into the hibiscus or the bougainvillaea found weevils of omnivorous ache awaiting them. Those who sat on the bottom-polished sorority benches in the sun-dappled patio were attacked by vapors of vague (but sticky) longing. With its coarse shadow, the campanile tower titillated the burning court. Each swan-swinging of the water sprinklers described with its silvery secretion a caress, to which the parched lawns were unresponsive. Sports cars in the parking lot nuzzled one another's bumpers, and their hooded looks were furtive. The bookstore was a butcher shop: students purchased brown parcels which proved on the unwrapping to contain their own unmentionable body organs, hacked off in the act of *yearn.*

Angst-making. With the exception of Arbiter Aidos—who hovered like a helicopter over this soul-scape of scorpions—the instructors belonged to one or the other of two groups. There was the division of student-haters, who loathed their young conscripts in advance, in order to protect themselves from being loved and then judged (accurately) inadequate. And there was the division of student-lovers, who asked for adoration because they hadn't the temerity to adore themselves.

The student-haters chose for the most part to teach during the day, which seemed safer. They wore flap-pocket smoking jackets and diseased Repp ties and scuffy cordovans and bandicoot grimaces (male); or dark shifts as severe as nuns' habits and biege shoes as sensible as bricks and disdainful expressions as unquickened as cement (female). There was in their scurry from hut to hut an over-the-shoulder anxiety befitting someone who has only just escaped a chain gang or a temptation. They both practiced and preached a kind of tone deafness to the world of beauty and heroism and hope. Ever since writing their master's theses on selecting the psychologically appropriate color scheme for kindergarten furniture in the Alhambra public school system, they had believed that life is an experiment in pure duration, a bottled shriek. They lavished whatever zeal was left in them on the attempt to proselytize this anti-faith, to imitate its terms. Mostly, they succeeded. "Whatever intellectual faculties our students have," said Arbiter Aidos, "in these halls will undergo an atrophy on the installment plan. One longs for a disaster to over-take them in mid-semester, to repossess them for pain, which at least is life." But before the advent of Stanhope Cronopios, there were no disasters in Long Beach; only inadvisabilities.

The student-lovers preferred evening classes, because night applied a patina over their blemishes. The men wore moccasins and mandarin-collared sport shirts and quilt-complected Bermuda shorts: they went hairy-calved to their assignations. The women affected rebozos and Pucci-printed diaper-dresses; bare-armed and barelegged they offered themselves like baskets of eels in the patio moonlight, shimmering expectantly. Wisps of smoke in the form of question marks rose and hooked themselves in the branches of the lemon trees. Everyone behaved as though his license were about to be re-voked. "How," asked Arbiter Aidos, "did Susan Sontag put it? 'All I'm saying is that there are some elements of life—above all, sexual pleasure—about which it isn't necessary to have a position.' " Aidos grinned. "I gave up sex on discovering that, as with a child, you can do anything to a woman so long as you play with her first. True! The sole interesting thing about women is their immunity; and once you've acquired the knack of circumventing *that,* all the rest is push-ups."

The students—ah, the students. Excepting the insouciant mutants (waiting for Big Surf), they were full of an already poignant premoni-tion. They wore sunglasses to keep their eyes from betraying their ambivalence. In the patio, between classes, those glasses were uni-formly beetle-making: or achieved a surreal sense of begoggled Martians, disheartened extraterrestrials groping through a light too bright and a gravity too strong, in search of the only half-remembered spot where they had abandoned their saucer.

They turned blindly toward each other, in mute appeal for help, peering into the plastic shades for glints of recognition: the veal cutlet faces of the boys, trying to grin; the made-down, low-gloss faces of the girls, trying not to pout. But their bodies disobeyed the spirit of appeal; their cardigans and cashmeres, their khaki pants and can-vas shoes availed them not. The girls hugged notebooks to their breasts like shields, as if aware those breasts would never suckle children, had been culturally transformed into advertisements and man-handles. The boys limped off with gawky gait, sensing they had lost manipulative control of that *trick* of boyishness which had always before won them forgiveness for their many sins against intelligence and decency.

And so things stood, or scurried, at Stanhope's time of undergraduation . . . awkward Abelards, uneasy Heloïses . . . hatred and palm trees, moonlight and mud, ache and question marks . . . Arbiter Aidos and the surfers.

Of Aidos, Stanhope wrote:

> You mewl your sex felinely,
> And are supinely spayed,
> Weighed and found not wanting.

"True," said Aidos. "Not wanting and not wanted. The teacher, like the lover, is most effective when he rapes the values without nourishing the emotions. They have no values; their emotions are parasitic. I turn away in disgust, which becomes indifference. Aware of my indifference, they realize they have no hold on me. I am not, you see, susceptible to their necks and knees, and they have no other attributes. They *fear* me!"

"But the surfers don't fear you?"

"No. They even admire me, because . . . I do not lose my ice cubes." He sighed, and pumped his goat's bladder. "They are admirers of you, too, Stanhopeless. I have read to them from *Angel's Sloth*. They were impressed with your definition of 'Bealongchik.' How did you put it? 'While the anagram is feeble, it is of some importance. For the inhabitants of Long Beach do indeed *belong* here; and their *longing* to be somewhere else is contained by the beach.' That makes sense to the surfers, for they are dedicated to escaping what all of you call 'the Void.' In the beginning was the Void . . ."

"I'm surprised they verbalize."

"They don't. But one group—they call themselves the Surfrajets— has an interpreter, a *priestess*. It is she who has asked me to bring you to them this evening."

"Why?"

"The Surfrajets are sponsoring a Fire Festival near Newport the night of March 21—"

"Equinoxious," said Stanhope.

"Shut up," said Aidos. "A Fire Festival—to propitiate the Shade of Big Surf, and plea for high tides during the coming summer. They feel a want of . . . ritual. They intend a ceremony. They want *you* to write a poem for them . . . a Ballad of Big Surf!"

"Who *is* Big Surf?"

"A sort of parody of Ormazd," said Aidos. "They go in for a bastardized Zoroastrianism. Ablutions, chastisements, chastity—you know the applesauce."

A true child of Long Beach, Stanhope asked: "What's in it for me?"

"An A in my course," said Aidos.

And so it was that Stanhope accompanied Arbiter Aidos that evening to the patio and the circle of somnolent surfers. They sat Indian-style around the recently erected Art Department stabile, "The Spirit of Long Beach"—an iron pretzel. (Of the stabile, Aidos had observed: "It is ridiculous, but is it art?") The iron pretzel triangulated the moonlight on the fang-yellow walls of the administration hacienda. The dark faces of the Surfrajets were as blood drops in that triangulation. One gummed an aluminum harmonica; another peered down the barrel of a jeweled flute, sighting birds to shoot; a third litanized: "Dee Why . . . Bondi . . . Makola . . . *the Banzai Pipeline!*" The rest kept silent counsel, cloaked as with a gauze of ether.

Until at last a figure rose from the circle and advanced, ablegate from the Court of Big Surf . . . *and she was not bronze.* She was bark-white and sapling-armed, the soft fern stalk of her femininity unbaked by sun, ungrubbed by hungry bowmen: a still and perfect theorem-bloom. Ivory bracelets, fishskin dancing tights, a blouse of pearl, and eyes the green of cool sea caves, hair the black of Egyptian marble. "Gorblimey," said Stanhope.

"That's the priestess," said Aidos as she approached them. "Her name is Bethesda. Her stepuncle owns a prosperous string of naval bases."

Stanhope accepted the hand she offered, a Japanese paper napkin. "You're so white!"

"Perhaps," she replied with a faint smile, "it's because I'm dying piecemeal, of emotional anemia."

"But don't you ride the waves with the rest of them?"

"Then who would there be to summon the sea?"

He kissed her hand. Might he apply this purifying poultice to the wounds which remained of Mimsy Lubricious? Maybe!

(Much later, he would write:

> That evening, mistakenly
> Attempting to unzip
> The stitches of a scar,
> I spilled my beings.

(But then she was dead.)

"But why," asked Stanhope, "should *you* bother to summon the sea for *them?*" Surely this was no neuter whom he saw before him, her napkined saplings in his hands . . .

"Years ago," she said, "I was worried about the existence of the objective world. Was it real? Was it *void?* Did it persist while I stupidly slept? Or was everything a mannered motion in the mist of my mythy mind?"

"Discrepancy Deutsch," said Stanhope. "The solipsistic hang-up."

She nodded. "And one afternoon, plunged in the abyss of duality, I was walking along the beach. And I saw Seventeen." She indicated one of the Surfrajets. (Stanhope was subsequently to learn that Bethesda had renamed them after prime numbers, believing they were non-composite positive integers, and indivisibly unique. So they were called Three, Five, Seven, Eleven, Thirteen, Seventeen, Nineteen . . .) "He had such a fantastic repose as he sat there polishing his surfboard, such a mindless serenity, that I was offended. I slapped him. 'How can you be so placid,' I cried, 'when all the important questions are still unanswered? How do you even know that surfboard's *real?*'

"He looked up at me and smiled pityingly. 'Of course I know the surfboard's real,' he said. *'I made it myself, with my own two hands.'* " Her cool green eyes challenged Stanhope. "Do you understand?"

Stanhope was stunned by the implications. "You mean . . ."

"Yes," she said. "The craftsman *knows* the world is real, for he has created a new object out of its materials. And because he can hold that new object that he has created, in his hands, he also knows that *he* is real. Only Germans who never use their hands except to kill things could doubt the existence of objective reality."

"Then," said Stanhope, "if my slim volume of verse called *Angel's Sloth* is real . . ."

"Then so is your Hermes portable typewriter!" concluded Bethesda triumphantly.

He looked at her in wonder. "What is it you wish of me?"

"For you to write the Ballad of Big Surf."

"I will do anything you ask."

She cupped her hands over his ears and pecked him on the nose. Then she turned to the circle of Surfrajets and said: "It will be done." They nodded, then made a variety of vague mutterings and gestures in the moonlight. Bethesda turned back to Stanhope. "They have reminded me of another problem. Do you suppose that, using your connections with the Long Beach motorcycle cops, you could get Renaldi Haruspex to let us hold our Fire Festival without the usual harassment?"

"Of course," said Stanhope.

She made her eyes wafers. He accepted them, consumed them, communed with her. Her regard like a gulf stream bathed him. He presented the clean pebble of himself to her, white as the pearl of her blouse, in exchange for the wafers. She took his token, smiling, and returned to the fricasseed surfers, the iron pretzel, the jeweled flute.

Stanhope cried softly: "How did Goethe put it? *'Nun bin ich endlich geboren!'*"

Arbiter Aidos eyed him curiously. "Well," he said, "my wit and worth are cobwebs brushed aside, in your full glare of glee."

But Stanhope abandoned Aidos in a stampede for the parking lot; for Cimarosa Street; for the telephone and a message to Renaldi; for his bedroom and his Hermes portable typewriter and the poem he had to write.

He completed that poem a week before the Fire Festival, and used Aidos as a mailbox to post it to Bethesda. He did not want to see her again until after she had read it.

The afternoon of March 21 he drove Arbiter Aidos down Pacific Coast Highway at the tail end of a car-caravan of surfers. Their bright boards poked out of their convertibles like cannon-noses, like missile-toes.

Waiting for them when they parked in front of the jumbo shrimp shack was Renaldi Haruspex himself. Black-togged and starch-faced on his motorcycle saddle, with a sprig of mesquite tucked behind his ear, Renaldi was spooning scotch-flavored calf's-foot jelly from a cardboard container. His eyes were hard; his aspect that of a B.C. Sumerian sterility symbol. The surfers ignored him as they traipsed by to fill their thermos jugs with juice. Stanhope introduced Aidos.

"Peculiar friends you got," said Haruspex, indicating the surfers.

"Not really," said Aidos. "Just products of the age we live in, like nylon and plywood."

"They look like they were made out of nylon and plywood," said Renaldi.

"Renaldi," said Stanhope, "you remember what I once told you: verticality is a sign of demand; horizontality, of acceptance? Well, these people are at least vertical."

"I remember," said Renaldi. "I didn't understand you then; I still don't, now."

"The invulnerability of the great," said Arbiter Aidos, "resides in their lack of comprehension. We are injured by almost everything we understand." Aidos was one of those people who derive from steady drinking a compulsion to aphorize.

Renaldi caressed his gun, but not threateningly: he was hurt. He had respect for intellectuals, and longed for a marriage of power and percipience. To Stanhope he said, aggrieved: "Tell him I'm not as stupid as I look, will you? I've memorized all one hundred and two of Mortimer Adler's Great Ideas. Tell him at least to be polite."

"Renaldi," said Stanhope, "is the Gideon of the Great Books program. He's left a copy of the Syntopicon in every comfort station along the beach."

Aidos was touched. "Politeness," he said, "is an apology to people for not really liking them. Sorry, Haruspex: it's just that I *like* you."

Renaldi was partially mollified. "Well, I *don't* like this set-up."

"There shouldn't be any trouble," said Stanhope. "They're on their good behavior."

"Yeah," said Renaldi. "That's one of the things I don't like. They'll tire themselves out, behaving so good. Then watch what happens."

"Conspicuous goodness," said Arbiter Aidos, "is a form of vegetarianism."

"Too right," said Renaldi. He now positively approved of the professor. "There's something fanatical about it. One little thing goes wrong, and all hell breaks loose. What's in that goat's bladder you keep pumping away on?"

"Greek resinated wine," said Aidos.

"Yeah?" said Renaldi. "How about squirting a slug of it at me? You can glob yourself some calf's-foot jelly."

Stanhope left them budding buddies, and went into the shrimp shack. Its decor was early seaweed; its proprietor, a truculent gnome trying unsuccessfully to sell french fries to the Surfrajets. As usual, the surfers were stolidly incommunicado, not bothering to explain that greasy foods adversely affected their body oils. Five was sanding and staining arrows for the ceremony; Seven with cruel precision tuned a transistor radio; Thirteen cleaned his ears with a popsicle stick. The others stared out through the plate-glass window at the lowering sun, and the slurred sky, and the tipsy gulls.

And that troglodyte in black domino at the back of the shack, devouring carton after carton of shrimp? If Stanhope had known it was Onalred, there to appraise him, but also on other business (business which the Fire Festival would fortuitously expedite, without anybody knowing it until everything was over) . . . if Stanhope had known, would it all have been different? Probably not.

"Silken girl, bringing sherbet," said Bethesda, and plopped a cup of it in front of Stanhope. He did his best to smile at her, waiting for something more. But she seemed to have nothing to add. He felt his solitary destiny close around him, like a wooden coffin. Was he to be buried alive in her silence? Dirt clods of the passing seconds struck down upon his lid. His head ached from unuttered screams for help.

At last she spoke: "I was greatly moved by your Ballad of Big Surf." She hesitated, troubled: "But there's an ambiguity about it, isn't there? At the end, I mean. Like all metaphysical poetry, I suppose. But it disturbed me. Your sympathy with the surfers is *conditional . . .* am I right?"

Had resurrected Lazarus on arising become risible? In Stanhope's laughter was a Charley hoarseness of relief. "Yes," he said. "So you got that, did you?" He took her Japanese paper napkins. "Bethesda, *they always come back,* don't they? The sea flings them back to the shore on their boards, back to Long Beach, to the cloisters of *Void—*"

The forked lightning of her inclement mind immediately pronged the point; there was rain in her eyes. "I see," she said.

"In grappling with the fact of their inevitable return," said Stanhope, "and the mockery that makes of the escape attempt, I felt obliged to introduce the idea of sacrifice—much as you, in what must have been a similar spasm of disquietude, sought to introduce the idea of ritual. But then, in trying to imagine what meaning any such sacrifice would have to the money-monks of Long Beach, I foundered once more on the reef of the Bealongchik's unyielding indifference. The sacrifice would have *no* effect, don't you see? You should.

The essence of Zoroastrianism is a superfluity of *good* deeds to overbalance the bad. Bethesda, we must do *more*."

She lay her head on its side on the table, between the salt and pepper shakers. *"Kwatz,"* she said. "What is it and why is it, Stanhope? Just living here affects my mind. Is it that subsisting as we do, on a desert, ground-level, single-story, in a world without staircases; moving as we do, always sidewise, like crabs under a crushing sky . . . is it that of necessity we are afflicted with only two-dimensional minds, desert minds? Is there a geographical determinism?"

He sank his hands into her Egyptian marble hair. "I think that's certainly part of it," he said. "If, as Sartre has pointed out, thought has its own geography, then surely geography must have its own thought. And there's no doubt that Long Beach thinks *flat."*

The Surfrajets were rising now, impassive icons dipped in gold, to vacate the shrimp shack and secure their boards and make their way down the sea wall to the sand. The only ones left in the shack were Stanhope, Bethesda and the troglodyte.

"Read the poem the way I wrote it, anyway," said Stanhope. "I don't think it matters, and it may help—at least to dull the pain. Art *is* a kind of aspirin, after all."

She rose with him from the table, a chalice of sob.

At the motorcycle, Arbiter Aidos was declaiming to Renaldi: "Architecture, Haruspex, is the foundation on which all social superstructures are in the final analysis based. The failure of Germany, for instance, to produce a truly indigenous architectural style is the principal source of twentieth-century tragedy. True. The much-bruited tyranny of Greece over Germany (and I myself have often described German thought as a wretched lyric poem, an Ode with a Grecian Yearn) produces, as it were, flaws in the political building blocks of the nation. The subsequent totalitarian orgies were inevitable. By the same token, were Georgian redbrick, Cape Cod stucco, colonial clapboard and California pasteboard simultaneously to crumble, I wouldn't give democracy in this country another ten years. (Indeed, plastic represents precisely this threat.) And were we, Renaldi, to tear down the walls of the Kremlin brick by brick—perhaps under cover of some sort of Point Four urban renewal program—the brutal regime now enslaving millions of Slavs would collapse of its own weight within a fortnight. Let us capture the imagination of a long-suffering world with the slogan: 'The building blocks of politics are building blocks!' "

"Are you going to help dig the trench?" Stanhope asked him.

"Don't be ridiculous," said Aidos. "Renaldi is on duty, and I am drunk."

By the time they reached the beach, a hundred surfers from various clans had assembled; and the trench had already been dug. A deputation of Surfrajets exchanged their shovels for surfboards and, with quivers and bows on their backs, swam out to sea toward the dying sun. Bethesda left to join in the final preparations for the rite. Stanhope, Aidos and Haruspex sat down on a dune to watch.

"If trouble comes," said Aidos, "it will probably originate up there." He pointed to the cocktail lounge on the cliff overhanging their sickle of beach. Attracted by the purposefulness of the preparations below, the customers of Captain Nemo's Gin 'n' Bear It Tonic-Watering Spa had in droves deserted their marimba player to stray out onto the veranda, still clutching the stems of their cocktail glasses. Blue-gilled merchant-pimpish smoothies deducting their funny business with horn-breasted palomino hippie-chicks: twilight gleamed off their Man Tan, and their sneer was radiant.

"Whatever," asked Aidos, "became of the personal sneer? Sneers today come standardized, as though from a machine. Perhaps there is in fact a sneer machine, located in some vast underground men's room below the Time-Life Building in New York, next to the cigarette machine and the candy bar machine and the machine for proving mainland China doesn't exist. Deposit the appropriate short change in the designated slot, pull the protuberant lever and out spits a little cellophaned package of sneer. Redi-Wear! Rip it open, paste it on, examine yourself in the mirror. But why doesn't it seem to fit? It is plastically conformable to the contours of almost every physio-ignominy, and yet—and yet . . . The problem must not reside in the sneer; after all, *it's* been market-tested. The problem must lie in the face. Has something died in the eyes of Americans—the requisite courage to carry off a convincing sneer? Nostalgia-making."

Joining the smoothies and the hippie-chicks at the veranda balustrade were newspaper photographers and, incredibly, a trio of surpliced Sisters of Mercy. Several dinghies had also anchored themselves in the shallows nearby, their bright pennants drooping from an overmuch of gaiety. And: the Radio Free Long Beach fuel barge! Svam Spade was broadcasting the Fire Festival live. On the beach, the surfers had raised their grotesque mahogany totem of Ormazd, and now busied themselves chucking coral chunks, tangerines, plants, cheeseburgers, locks of hair, wedges of pizza, animal jaw-bones and miscellaneous fagots into the trench at the totem's toes. As though in obedience to the whim of Big Surf, a wind rose to roil the clouding green mirror of the sea.

It was growing quite dark. Toward Long Beach, diced light dropped out of the windows of the shore hotels, those huge pocked crypts on earthquake rollers, relics of a departed Brobdingnagian race, now occupied uneasily by conventioneers and other species of dwarfs. On the Pike, blue and red neon nerves began to weave their luridities. Toward Mexico, the highway palm trees were blotted out in pairs by the deepening smudge of night. A curious desuetude descended on the scene. Had a sloop of desire been tacking toward them, it would have veered abruptly, veered in the fear that it had badly mistaken its harbor. For here was the stillness of a death-watch; the sun had altogether failed.

Only the bucket-slopping of the rising waves and the tinkle of the frightened marimba player disturbed the texture of the waiting silence. Svam Spade stood on the deck of the fuel barge, looking through binoculars.

From up the beach came bounding (in high, graceful, slow-motion, gazelle-like leaps and landings) a six-pack of sun-grilled Surfrajet girls, trailing after them the lines to kites. Now the kites growing into the sky behind them burst suddenly into flames, with long fire trails, as though shore batteries had blasted them. The assaulting breakers came in higher, and crashed; withdrew, gathered and then hurled themselves again upon the sand. And in answer to the blaz-ing kites, torches seemed to vault directly from the sea. Were they indeed torches? Were they reflections of the flaming kite-*geist?* They were neither. The tide-borne Surfrajets had mounted their boards at the summons, and ignited the tips of their quiver of ar-rows: and now they came zagging atop the whitening surge, now they came flaming on their polished shields, toward the beach and the hushed and expectant watchers, toward the totem, toward the cocktail lounge. And then at the splitting crest of the wave, as their incandescent bodies hung for a moment before plunging, they loosed their flaming arrows from their golden bows! Arcs of light striated the night sky; burning trajectiles fell upon the totem pyre, upon the altar of fagots, upon the plants and the pizza of the sacrificial trench: Ormazd was on fire!

Look: the silent pyrolaters produced staves of bamboo stalk and thrust them into the burning trench, enkindling their shaggy ends. A torch parade began, a wheel of fire around the flaming totem, the spokes of its long and flickering light grinding over the beach, turning on the sea wall and the cliffs. And then Bethesda was seen to appear in a niche halfway up the sea wall, in a teak-beaked hood of gull-skins, in a shawl of feathers, with a bamboo torch in one hand and a megaphone in the other. "Hearken unto me!" she cried from the illuminated niche in the sea wall; and the marimba ceased at Captain Nemo's. The surfers bent their torches toward her; the night was an ear:

BETHESDA: Flowers of bronze float hot on the tide;
Flowers turn in the churning foam;
Big Surf summons his burning bride
Down to his pearly home.

A sigh swirled up from the listening beach. The hippie-chicks on the veranda swayed.

BETHESDA: From that cavern cool and deep
Where the burning bride will sleep
Whispers Big Surf with the swell,
Clappers Big Surf like a bell:

"Come ride on me and comb the waves;
Follow me to the cool sea caves."

Gulls expire in the fire-shot sky;
Emeralds gleam in the wet-rot eye
Of Big Surf.

Cried the chorus of pyrolaters below: *"Big Surf!"* The smoothies were shaking their heads at the balustrade.

BETHESDA: "Children of bronze ride over me,
Over the bearded god below.
Children glide on my emerald sea
Where the green winds westward blow,
Where the salt tides beachward flow.
Golden-limbed and blind and free:
Children of sun slide over me.
I'm Big Surf."

Lustily: *"Big Surf!"* The Sisters of Mercy gave curiously affirmative nods.

BETHESDA: "No rhomboids we, O god of the sea,"
Sing children of bronze and sun.

Big Surf's arm like a tall green tree
Grows from the spume of the wind-blown sea:

"Children of sun,
For fun, for fun,
Run down the glistening sand to me;
Swing on the boughs of my tall green tree;
Pledge your vows to the silt-cool sea
Of Big Surf."

Wonderingly: *"Big Surf."* Flashbulbs exploded on the overhanging cliff.

BETHESDA: Riding the dream of the wind and the tide,
Away from the split-level cloisters of Void,
The children looked back at the town and cried:
"Rhomboid! Rhomboid!"

But thin-lipped money-monks counting their coins,
Lecherous money-monks scratching their loins,
Heard not the words
Of the golden birds
On the unmown, tree-grown, wind-blown lea,
In the surge and the spray of the shadowy sea
Of Big Surf.

Plaintively: *"Big Surf . . ."* Consternation had overtaken Captain Nemo's customers; they were snapping their plastic swizzle sticks.

BETHESDA: But children, at midnight
When green winds have died,
Naked by moonlight,
Gone with the tide,
Lies the beach
You cannot reach
From your amber-walled cavern under the waves,
From your long pearl bed in the cool green caves
Of Big Surf.

Lugubriously: *"Big Surf . . . ?"* Querulous voices came down from the veranda: "Blasphemy! . . . Sordidness! . . . Paganism!"

BETHESDA: The sea walls are stark;
The drive-ins are dark.
The money-monks sleep on their own green lea
Of crisp negotiable currency.
Are they unhappier than thee?
Do money-monks in cloisters weep
For children cashiered in the shadowy deep?
They, alas,
Are too crass.

The eye of the child in the cave is moister
Than the eye of the monk in his split-level cloister.
Every pearl must have its oyster . . .
Even the pearl of Big Surf.

Cried the distraught pyrolaters: *"Even the pearl of Big Surf!"*
From her niche in the sea wall Bethesda threw her torch like a javelin at the mahogany head of Ormazd: a direct hit, splitting the skull. The surfers as one jumped into the trench, seized the totem, and bore it off burning on their shoulders to the sea. "Even the pearl of Big Surf!" they cried as they reached the water's edge, and heaved their burden into the retreating tide. A fiery fish, it swam away from them.

In a clear silver voice, Bethesda called: "Let us pray for a six-point-five!"

But there were to be no prayers, not even from the Sisters of Mercy. By now, the veranda of Captain Nemo's Gin 'n' Bear It was in uproarious umbrage.

"Barbaric!" screamed the hippie-chicks.

"Mystical!" sneered the smoothies.

"Boring," remarked the news photographers, who were not to be bored for long. For at that moment the hippie-chicks and smoothies began pelting the defenseless Bethesda with green olives and maraschino cherries from their empty cocktail glasses. Then they threw the glasses! "Sorcerer's apprentice!" they cried. "Bitch-witch! *Bohemian!"*

The surfers turned their faces up toward the source of this deluge of garbage and glass. Stunned surprise was promptly and properly succeeded by rage. "Down with the money-monks!" they exclaimed. And from the beach they retrieved their golden bows; to them they fit their smoldering shafts; off them they launched their avenging trajectiles. Once more the air was filled with arrows and the night with flames.

"*Jacquerie! Jacquerie!*" screamed the balcony besieged.

"Great Scott," said Stanhope, rising from his dune. "They've punctured one of the Sisters of Mercy!"

And in fact her surplice was blazing; an arrow protruded from her paunch.

"No!" shouted an anguished Renaldi Haruspex. "Say it isn't so!" He whipped out his revolver from the black polyethylene holster.

On seeing the gun, Arbiter Aidos threw his arms around Renaldi. Enwraptured, they tumbled off the dune and rolled into the shallow sea water. "Violence is unnecessary," Aidos gasped. "How did Saki put it? 'People may say what they like about the decay of Christianity; the religious system that produced green chartreuse can never really die!'"

"You besotted ninnyhammer!" raved Renaldi. "You don't understand—they *aren't* Sisters of Mercy at all! It's a disguise! The one with the feathered barb in his belly is, in reality, Flojo-José y Cabron, the generalissimo who flew the *coup* last month in that spotted banana republic. The other two sisters are his hired thugs. Those miscreants probably think we're Che Guevara!"

Apparently, the Sisters did think something of the sort, for from their surplices they whisked out submachine guns and let fly Mercilessly, spraying the beach with dumdums. The carnage was considerable, although the surfers did better than might have been expected in view of their disadvantaged circumstance. They turned one thug into a flaming porcupine. Stanhope dispatched the other: for Stanhope had wrested Renaldi's revolver from the soggy grapplers; and, as he raised it toward the veranda, his childhood lessons in target practice came back with all the suddenness and overpowering ferocity of his mother's contempt for him. Full, then, of a fierce joy, a seizure of exultation, he let fly: first smashing the submachine gun out of the hands of the Sister; next smashing her (him) off the veranda; and finally emptying the revolver as she fell, her surplice billowing, causing the body to skip and jerk as it absorbed the bullets, before it found its repose on the rocks below.

Stanhope threw away the gun. The beach was littered with bodies bloodstained all over their bronze. Stanhope crawled over them, over the bullet-ridden surfboards and the red pimentos and the twists of lemon peel, over the stems and shards of cocktail glass, past the suspiring pyre, to the foot of the sea wall, where he called up: "Bethesda! Bethesda, are you there?"

Whereupon Bethesda fainted, keeling off the niche in the sea wall, to land on and flatten her gladiator. Whoupon swore—

Renaldi came running to them, his shoes squish-squeaking with salt water. "The bastards shot Aidos," he said.

Stanhope hauled Bethesda up. They staggered across the war-torn beach. Arbiter Aidos knelt in the shallow water, a stupid grin on his face. "They got me in the goat's bladder," he told them. "At first, I thought I was bleeding resinated wine, which, after all, wouldn't have surprised me very much. But then I realized . . ." He gasped. "Stanhope . . . in my office . . . there's a package for you . . . wrapped in brown paper . . ."

"Aidos, for Ormazd's sake, keep your mouth shut—the blood is gushing out!"

At that moment Svam Spade came wading through the water to them, with a portable tape recorder and a microphone. Aidos, the fool, opened his mouth even wider. "The . . . Great . . . Yawn . . ." he gasped. "I haven't perfected it . . . *yet*. I can't quite . . . *swallow . . . myself* . . ." He toppled over onto his back.

Svam Spade crouched beside him and shoved the microphone into his face. "Hey, man," he said, "as a philosophy prof, can't you sum it all up? I mean, this is the Big Jump, Aidos . . . what about a statement from the other side of the, ah, generation gap?"

Aidos, on one elbow, summoned his failing resources for one final attempt to grasp it all: "From among the many sorts of failure," he whispered, "each man . . . unerringly . . . selects the one which will . . . most compromise his self-respect. True!"

And he was gone. Nor was he to be eased in his passing, for the tide came back with the Ormazd totem on its crest and smashed him where he lay, drove him like a spike into the mud.

"Groovy!" said Spade. "Unbelievably groovy!"

"Adios, Aidos," murmured Stanhope. Then he turned on Renaldi. "You knew," he said. "You knew all the time that Flojo-José y Cabron was hiding out in the cocktail lounge!"

"Of course I knew," said Renaldi. "He sought asylum; and he was paying us protection money. There'll be hell to pay for this . . .

Never again, as long as I live, will we permit another Fire Festival."

"Since," said Stanhope, "the local surfing population has been almost totally decimated this evening, there shouldn't be much demand for another ceremony, anyway."

"The Surfrajets?" whispered Bethesda. "Are they . . . are they *all* . . . ?"

"I'm afraid so," said Stanhope. "The Ultimate Wipe-Out."

"Five," said Bethesda, her voice hollow. "And Seven, who slept on his styrene foamie; and Eleven, who never made it to Oahu; and Seventeen, who solved the solipsistic hang-up . . ." She shook her fist at Long Beach: *"Ecrasez l'infâme!"* she screamed.

Stanhope grabbed her by the teak-beaked hood of gullskins. "Come," he said. "We . . . we will pick up the package Arbiter Aidos left for me. And then—I'll take you home." He thought about it. "If you—if any of us—really have a home." To Renaldi, with all the disdain he could muster, he added: "How did Nelson Algren put it? 'Mortimer Adler is the Lawrence Welk of the philosophy trade.'"

"Stereophonically groovy!" sang Svam Spade. "Peabody Place! A Radio Free Long Beach exclusive: DICTATOR PAYING L.B. COPS PROTECTION MONEY SLAIN IN HOLOCAUST OF HOT DOGS!"

"Give me that tape!" shouted Renaldi. He leaped on Svam.

"Hey, man, the fuzz tickles! Renaldi . . . oh, Renaldi, *naughty!*"

Stanhope and Bethesda walked over the bodies across the beach.

Now [3]

Stanhope meditates aloud . . . a page of filler.

Stanhope and Gongor sat in the niche, with their legs dangling down the wall. The beach below them was deserted. Sand drifts had filled the trench of Ormazd. The sea was as calm as a swath of cellophane. "So," said Stanhope, "I lost my first guru."

When Gongor did not reply, he added urgently: "Don't you understand? Aidos' death left me without a teacher, without a father. He had let me down in my time of need. And later, after reading the notebooks of Dokhma Koan, when I became aware of how he had let poor Dokhma down, I knew his flower philosophy to be artificial. And . . . there was Onalred the Ever Ready, waiting." Time's film-footage flowed between his ears, behind his eyes. "The Fire Festival was also significant because it estranged me from Renaldi. Renaldi and Svam Spade began their peculiar relationship, a relationship which piled an unbearable load of guilt on Renaldi. As a result of that guilt, he came to be obsessed by the Ashram. As a result of that obsession, he brought his riot gun with him that eventful Annihilation Night. And *you* know what happened because of that riot gun."

"Captain Happen happened," said Gongor.

"Too right," said Stanhope. He stood. "You're really in for it now. My love affair with Bethesda and Dokhma Koan's death affair with Long Beach are oddly parallel, psychological lines that might meet one day at some Einsteinian elbow, beyond the bend of dimensions. We covered a lot of territory together. So must you. Dokhma Koan saw more of Long Beach than most men, and understood it less . . . until the end. Shall we go?"

Gongor sighed. "I suppose so," he said.

Stanhope looked out across the gelatinous sea. "You know, Gongor, I am trying to accustom myself to the idea of regarding every sexual act as a process in which only one person is involved. When at last we manage to get rid of *him,* there will be nothing left to discuss. Will there?"

Then [3]

At home with Stanhope and Bethesda . . . the notebooks of Dokhma Koan . . . Stanhope and Bethesda retrace Dokhma's footsteps . . . incident at the station house on the Pike . . . Maud Cronopios goes bowling . . . Dokhma discovers the Void . . . advent of Onalred . . . Stanhope is politicized.

Bethesda lived on a houseboat in the Naples canal. Outside, it was broken windows, rotting frames, frayed mooring lines. Inside it was color prints of cannibals with decayed faces, from Picasso's hashish-taking Negro period. To eat, there were pretzels and oranges; to drink, anisette; to smoke, cigars; to read, paperback editions of Raymond Chandler and Ross MacDonald. The burnished spittoon overflowing with dead roses and pearly-white Tiparillo lip pieces; the bench stolen for her from Whaley Park by the Surfrajets; the crankable phonograph fanned about with bleeding sleeves of Hugo Wolf; the sleeping bag, the candles, and the mirror on the ceiling, partially obscured by fish netting . . . were more than merely furniture; they were clutter in the attic of Bethesda's desperation. "I like to lie naked under the mirror, with a candle in one hand and a Tiparillo in the other, wondering if any of the dentists on Neapolitan Lane are watching me through their binoculars." She also possessed a zip gun. "One night one of the dentists came pounding on my door. Either he was maddened by lust, or he'd had a bad trip with his audiac."

The chain-flushed water closet emptied directly into the canal. It was also an escape hatch, through which she could drop for a dip and return unseen. She stuffed her rinds, bones, peels and pits into an old radiator cooling sack, then tied the sack around her neck and hauled it with her on her nude swim each dawn out into Alamitos Bay, where she dumped it. "Early on, when I was twelve and physiologically turbulent, I identified with the automatic garbage disposal unit in my mother's kitchen sink. It seemed the perfect symbol of mature womanhood, of the role I would be obliged to play."

She selected a dead rose from the burnished spittoon, snuffled into it, then clenched it in her teeth. "Well," she said through the rose, "now you've seen it: the vault of my hopelessness. I suppose its squalor is an expression of my desire for . . . my desire for what? Maybe you can tell me? Does it revolt you?"

Stanhope would write:

> Do defunct roses
> Offend your noses?
> Mine, nein.
> To sneeze
> says, "Please
> excuse
> my muse
> for lacking the wit
> to spray her armpit."
> . . . a presumption
> that perfumption
> is a function
> which is unction-
> making;
> mistaking
> soap
> for hope
> of more
> rapport.
> Nope!
> For
> the bathos-tub will run rings around us.

They opened the brown paper package bequeathed Stanhope by Arbiter Aidos. It was a sheaf of papers entitled: *QUEASINESS: The Notebooks of Dokhma Koan.* There was a covering letter from Aidos, which Stanhope read aloud, while the candlelight liquefied their faces . . .

"This, Stanhopeless, is a meager legacy, but it may serve you as a warning. Dokhma Koan was killed by Long Beach because he would not *accept* the City. I fear you are in similar jeopardy. This passion to make psychological sense of the City, to grasp and dissect your symbiotic relationship with it, is basically self-destructive. To seek oneself and to flee oneself are equally vulgar pursuits. Make yourself a flower; all the rest is self-assassination. (I can hear you raising noisy objections. But . . . I no longer have to listen to them.)

"Koan mentions you in his notes. He read *Angel's Sloth*. It frightened and impressed him, as it dismays and depresses me. But the two of you are kindred spiritualists . . . shallow speaking to shallow? He was a naïve, doomed Oriental youth, whom I met wandering around the Iowa State Picnic Grounds with an exhaust pipe under one arm and the other jutted forward, bearing an Edsel grille like a shield. He was rather too far gone at that point, of course, although I hadn't the wit to recognize it.

"Oriental, yes. But I suspect from the style of these notes that he was raised for a while in a French garden of despair, among mechanical cuckoo birds and absurd dyspeptics. (A. J. Ayer has observed that no empirical statements are certain; and that existentialist philosophers 'attach a tragic significance' to this fact. Ayer adds, with that frightening English common-sensicalness: 'It is perverse to see tragedy in what could not conceivably be otherwise.')

"As an Oriental, poor Dokhma was overly susceptible to the phantasms he created out of his confrontation with the West. You are no doubt familiar with the plague theory of cross-cultural fertilization: Western forms of experience—mirrors, motion pictures, electricity, rock 'n' roll, overdeveloped female breasts, Marxism, guilt—are alien bacterial colonies to which the East is peculiarly mune? Robot rapes Lotus . . . or flays her. Well, there are lots of lotuses, like Dokhma, longing to be raped or flayed. And the desire for the whip which they claim they find in the West (and which they tend to attribute to Christian flesh horror, although it might as well be attributed to the poor dietetic habits of the ancient Hebrews) is, I think, largely a projection of their own sick desire, a phantasm arising from their need to be punished for having flirted with our strident Faustianism . . . our anality, if you will. (And even Faust, today, is a phantasm. As you yourself have observed, Faust is dead. He died of a hernia, overexerting himself; and we moderns are derived monotonously from Hamlet. What I tried to tell you then is that Faust and Hamlet are just two different strings on the same hang-up. Well. You, perhaps, are Don Quixote.)

"Alas. Add our sense of guilt to their sense of shame, and you've got a really nasty situation. Koan bared the naked arse of his sensibility, and was flayed. It was, however, largely a self-flagellation, although that does not excuse me for having . . . never mind.

"We shall meet once more at the end of his notebooks. After that, who knows? I shall find a peaceful pasture somewhere beyond Omega; and you . . . what will God do with all the self-assassinated flowers?"

Was Bethesda asleep? Stanhope touched the nape of her neck; his hand tingled; her eyes clicked on like a radio tuner. He marked his place in the notebooks with a cigar. They lay down under the mirror. "You must realize," she whispered, "that I've never done anything like this before. I have always been the quintessential hodad."

"Virginity," said Stanhope, "is a form of nymphomania." And hated himself a little, knowing that the vendors of bodies were more virtuous than the vendors of ideas. Nevertheless, her funk was aphrodisiacal . . .

That dawn he sank with her through the water closet into the Naples canal; swam with her out into Alamitos Bay; dumped for her the radiator cooling sack full of garbage. Gulls in the meridian light wheeled hungrily above their bruised and floating bodies, vectors expressing the tension between greed and fatigue. They dog-paddled back to the houseboat, and had oranges and pretzels and Dokhma Koan for breakfast.

[A]

I came by sky, over the sea lion rookeries of the Santa Cruz straits; over the gray whale migratory route past Catalina Island; over the crippled claw of piers guarding the harbor channel, and the red flares of the anchored warships, and the many-nippled breast of Signal Hill . . . to Long Beach Municipal Airport.

"Mr. Koan," said the skycap, reading my ID badge. "And what brings you to Long Beach, International City, Citadel of Sea Power, Nerve Center of Ocean Research and Technology?"

I am perhaps regrettably literal-minded in such confrontations. "Destiny," I told him, and presented him with a *jalthal,* the traditional Sikkimese white-scarf offering.

The skycap, I thought, sagged a little at the knees. I offered to stand him a drink, but he declined. On reclaiming my baggage, I found myself outside, on Lakewood Boulevard, across from a golf course. The pepperwood trees conferred whisperingly with one another. The night was mild and full of feathers. (The mean annual temperature of Long Beach is 63 degrees.) I hailed a cab and gave the driver the address of my hotel.

"Pubugna!" I cried exultantly as we were under way. We turned onto Los Coyotes Diagonal, and the cabby did not respond. "Pubugna," I said, "was the Indian name for Long Beach." Still he did not respond. "Bahía de los Fumos?" I said. Nothing. I explained: "Bahía de los Fumos was the name Cabrillo gave this area when his ship hove to, along the coast, in 1542. It means 'Bay of Smokes.'"

"Holy cow," said the driver, "you mean they *already* had smog?"

I take perhaps too much satisfaction in being informative. "No," I replied. "The Indians on shore were burning grass and brush. Smoke rose in great columns, like pillars of gnats, before Cabrillo's eyes."

"Why?" said the driver.

I found this characteristic Western compulsion to posit a cause for every effect rather touching. "I believe," I said, "that the Indians were conducting one of their periodic rabbit drives."

The cabby lapsed once more into silence. We swung around the treacherous Los Alamitos traffic circle, and headed west, on Pacific Coast Highway, past palmistry houses, motels in the manner of early cubist experiments, service stations at which sports cars were greedily feeding. The cross streets were of a botanical persuasion, with names like Cherry, Gardenia, Rose, Walnut, Orange, Lemon, Myrtle, Olive, Lime and Linden. At Long Beach Boulevard we bore left, to enter a corridor of stately palms, to plunge down it. Now the streets were numerically designated, in diminishing order, as we sought the sea . . . a tunnel, perhaps, to the negative designation, the ultimate mother-cipher?

My first task on reaching my hotel room was to set up the tape recorder and order my newly acquired music tapes according to chronological precedence. Yet I cannot begin my education into Western music tonight. I am too excited to concentrate. The window of my hotel room looks down over the Walk of One Thousand Lights. Through my binoculars I can see across the estuary of the Los Angeles River, to the piers and the supertankers and the giant cranes. According to the promotional bulletin provided guests of the hotel, each gantry crane is capable of hoisting one ton of scrap iron in a single bite. I open a package of Saltines (likewise provided guests of the hotel) and munch one thoughtfully. Long Beach lies before my craning neck, thousands of tons of scrap culture, as it were . . . Have I the requisite lift capacity?

I am thankful for the waiting bed, and the opportunity of a night's sleep during which to sort my first impressions. I have been taught that the Occident orders its ideas and disperses its sensations; that the Orient orders its sensations and disperses its ideas. Perhaps my mission to Long Beach will validate that general proposition. But certainly my own sensations now are in hopeless disarray . . .

Odd, thought Stanhope, after reading the first entry to Bethesda. Long Beach, inhabited by *his* memories, could not move backward very far in history. The names of its great men would fall on the reader's ear (would fall, in fact, on the city manager's ear) like meaningless syllables, would spin in the suddenly empty mind like transfers for a tram-line in whose existence only acid-heads could possibly believe . . . from Pubugna to bowling alleys? No. Manuel

Nieto: first rancho grandiloquette, land-granted this vastness by the King of Spain . . . his descendants squabbling their way to the Mexican war, then selling out cheap to Yankee carpetbaggers . . . William Erwin Willmore, the first of an endless line of Long Beach real estate operators, and about the only one to go broke . . . Charles Windham, the first mayor . . . Who were these mythic figures, these superburghers? Still: Pubugna—the metropolis of sulk!

Bethesda said: "My first vision of the world was plastic. Polypropylene saints, light filtering through their blood, making fireflies of their wounds. Dangling on wire hooks, the hooks hanging from spokes of a musical wheel, the wheel turning according to a spring which was coiled by a key, plinking out as if on a Lilliputian harpsichord the onwardness of Christian soldiers. I looked with anemone eyes upon the saints, upon the key, upon the detachable horn-rimmed glasses of my father and his hairy freckled hand releasing the musical wheel and the march of the martyrs . . . upon the ceiling from which umbilically depended a stillborn lamp: the curled filament of my possibilities.

"I remember cornstarch for my diaper rash. The plastic bathinette. Oil. Mirrors. Extrusions of silver. A rattle: also plastic, also a key, with a tiny bell attached to it by a pink ribbon. I remember being packaged in non-woven cellulose disposable diapers and boilable vinyl-lined waterproof acetate tricot pants. I remember being deposited in a molded plastic bowl to which butterfly decals had been affixed. I shook my key at the horn-rimmed glasses of my father, at the dacron polyester shift of my mother, at the electric sterilizer and the parquet floor tile and the Teflon frying pan and the pre-fab melamine laminate counter tops. My importunate hunger howls were stoppered with a gum rubber nipple; the milk in the Thermoglas bottle was blue. And I sucked . . . as though on a plastic saint, as though his wounds bled blue in my mouth . . .

"My cry, at the eye of the Nite-Lite Bakelite illuminated wall switch; and the silence of the nursery, of the house; and the darkness whose mouth applied itself to me, as though *I* were a blue plastic bottle, the wounded martyr, as though the life were being pumped from me by a bungalowering anti-bellows . . . The smell of my vinyl-covered bed pad . . . my smell . . . the smell of the polyethylene diaper pail . . . my smell . . . the smell of the yellow Serofoam polyurethane pad on the suction-cupped bathtub seat . . . my smell . . . I lay in my carriage, under the fine-mesh elasticized white nylon mosquito netting. My sleeper was orlon acrylic, my bootee feet equipped with skid-resistant plastic soles. Everything was clean, everything was odorless . . . but not me!

"From the beginning, mine was the synthetics hang-up . . . Orlon acrylic! Dacron polyester! Arnel triacetate! Rayon! Neoprene! Vibron! Vyrene! Santeen and spandex! Why wasn't *I* vat-dyed, non-skid, two-plied, rib-knit, snap-shouldered, sanitized, mercerized, Sanforized, shrink-resistant and machine-washable? *Why was I the only thing in the world which smelled?*

"When I was old enough to creep, I crept into the bathroom and stole the cake deodorant from the diaper pail and took it to my crib to sleep with . . . That cake was the only thing I ever slept with until *you.*"

[B]

I have been to Fault Block II, and seen repressurization, and it works!

For many years, Long Beach was sinking into the sea. This "subsidence problem," as it was characterized, became acute in the late 1940s, when several industrial facilities disappeared from sight in the salt flats at the center of the subsidence bowl, and low-lying areas were threatened with inundation. The horizontal movement accompanying such land shrinkage cracked pavements, damaged bridges and buildings and destroyed oil wells. The downtown business district alone sank six feet!

The usual explanation for this phenomenon is that all the pumping-out of oil resulted in pressure declines in the oil reservoirs. I wonder, however, whether the ocean was not perhaps annoyed at the arrogance of Long Beach in annexing its surface; in building on the sea itself these massive man-made peninsulas; in land-fill programs for parking lots which saw immense quantities of dike rock and dredge material dumped into the water until the water was obliged to retreat.—Anyway, in 1953, Long Beach launched a test program with injection wells, to rebuild subsurface pressures by injecting fluids into the oil reservoirs. Initial success led to program expansion, the unitizing system, the pooling of leases and producing formations, the co-operation of city, state, and major oil companies to create an extraordinary network of injection wells working twenty-four hours a day to save Long Beach. Fifty million dollars and a decade later, not only has subsidence been halted; but the water-injection program has succeeded in *increasing* oil recovery. The Department of Oil Properties estimates that ultimate oil recoveries will be *doubled* as a result.

Eastern fatalism would have watched the City sink into the sea, and sigh, perhaps composing a poem about it . . . the Western will!

This evening I began my study of Occidental music. At long last I shall escape the trap of the pentatonic scale; I shall climb out of the interval of a downward 4th . . .

"I am surprised," Stanhope told Bethesda, "that Arbiter Aidos was unable to perfect his great yawn . . . these notebooks are perfect material upon which to practice." But this was mere bravura. Dokhma Koan had humbled him. He, a native Bealongchik, knew so little about the actual workings of the City; knew only that the City was made rich and smug by its share of tidelands oil revenue . . .

Bethesda was more interested in the newly discovered tidelands of her body. "How did Anaïs Nin put it?" she said. " 'I carry white sponges of knowledge on strings of nerves.' "

"Do you know what might be fun?" said Stanhope. "We could follow Dokhma Koan around, on the basis of his notebooks. See everything he saw, from his point of view and ours. Don't you think that would be fun?"

Bethesda looked as though she thought chewing marbles would be more fun than that. But she nodded, and did what he told her to. She always did what he told her to.

[C]

Stigmata of awkwardness. There is no grace in their social functions, in their leisure activities, in their work, their bus-riding and car-parking and food-consuming. I have walked the streets. I have peered into the windows of snack shacks, seen haste and waste. I have stood knee-deep in oleander bushes, looking through the fences into back yards where patties of ground meat are being charred on tripodally supported steel pyx, apparently an altar of female worship, for the male ecclesiarchs stand grouped about the burning bowl in colored aprons scriven with hortatory insignia. They mutter an Anamnesis unintelligible to me, and the women emerge from the house bearing tumblers of a fizzy solution, to accept small portions of the sacrificial offering. This might be moving if they did not stagger in the process. They are always staggering, except . . .

Except, oddly, in the act of purchase. In that, they are graceful. I have seen single-minded women plundering the shelves of supermarkets, piling high their silver carts with boxes of every size and shape, seizing and discarding cans and bottles, squeezing fruit, examining the relative bloodiness of packages of flesh. I have seen them transferring these provisions from their carts into the posterior sections of station wagons in the parking lots, among concrete tubs of doomed flowers . . . I have seen them, too, riding like priestesses up the escalators in the department stores, fingering miracle fabrics with a sacerdotal air. There is a numbing grace in the acquisitive process . . .

I see now that Western music is a rich language created wholly by art, consisting of sounds which exist wholly outside of nature. The evolution of the harmonic scale is fantastic and inspiring. I must admit, however, that Church plain songs tend to put me to sleep. It is a question of educating the ear, no doubt.

Bethesda said: "The cathedral of me: the hobnails of your boots ringing on my stone. The mirror of me: your solar flare. The tablet of me: your ball-point pen."

The Bay tilted like a bowl, spilling the night into her houseboat. They treaded water in the night.

[D]

On Ocean Boulevard this morning I saw the following composition: a dime telescope bolted to a parapet over the sea wall. A woman of indeterminate age, with limned hair tucked under a gleaming tin hat (like a tambourine, shivering in the sunlight). She is clad in a diaphanous soutane—perhaps the transparent saran wrapping I have seen advertised—and the light passing through the soutane defines the contours of her body, the contours of a potato. She inserts her dime in the activating mechanism of the telescope and trains it. On what? On the gray warships displacing breakwater at the extremity of the channel? No. She trains it on the diamond-sprinkled sand; more specifically, on a trio of young men who are admiring each other's musculature as they bounce about a beach ball. They are marble-limbed subdeities in a topless temple of the sun. They wear only an abbreviated fundoshi-type combination cummerbund and diaper. The woman deposits dime after dime into the activating mechanism of the telescope, as though it were a slot machine of the fantasy life, as though an inexhaustible supply of dimes and patience would surely win her . . . what? A displacement, perhaps, not of the breakwater but of a fundoshi! (Depressing; I had expected in the West to find a system of values based on man's predilections. But happiness, apparently, is not a value in either culture.)

I watched her until I received the distinct impression that someone else was watching *me*. I turned. A canary yellow Sting Ray automobile was parked not twenty meters away, its sun-shot head lamps aimed in my direction. It was, however, unoccupied; doubtless it belonged to one of the young men frisking on the beach. As no one else was in sight, I must have been mistaken in my impression of surveillance.

Only on Thursday nights, when Maud Cronopios went bowling, did Stanhope and Bethesda stop dogging Dokhma's trail. On Thursday nights he took her to Cimarosa Street. It was a very different setting from the houseboat; and they resolved—in taking advantage of it to indulge their fantasies—mutually to reject the systematized vulgarity of all conventions. They could roll about on the puce-colored carpet; they could couple under the glassy gaze of Erich Fromm; they could descend together in the shower stall down the elevator shaft of shame. They shaved each other with Maud's Lady Sunbeam electric leg razor; and admired their bald bodies, the child-making of their scour, the surgical preparation to be followed by bouts of what seemed more a violent scrummage after a mythological Rugby ball, all elbows and cleats, than just sex. Then they would lie with their tongues in each other's mouths and their hands on each other's occiputs, sea fruit and seaweed in a long and silent surcease of suffering, an almost passionless watery communion.

"I always thought," said Stanhope, "that it required a tremendous ignorance to approach a woman, as to approach God. I always thought I knew too much for such proximities to be possible. And so there was in each flirtation a quality of compulsively forcing myself on the desired object, like an impertinence. How gloriously wrong I was!"

They were watched in their explorations and their ingenuities by the dachshund, Caryl Chessman, who was no doubt disapproving of their ambition to weave integuments, but was fortunately unable to report his disapproval to his mistress . . . Maud.

[E]

In low concrete and steel "clear-span" transit sheds, forklift operators bear their burdens of sorghum and pelletized alfalfa, dispirited
ants with immense cookie crumbs . . . mile-long freight trains arrive
from the Great Plains, bringing wheat to Long Beach. Each boxcar
at a terminal siding is upended by hydraulic unloaders, and its contents spilled onto traverse conveyer belts which rush the grain to
bins and tanks and silos, where it will await a ship to carry it to
Asia (my Asia!): enough wheat on board one ship for four million
loaves of bread . . . I stood on a pontoon bridge and looked at
the Van Camp sea food cannery complex . . . I observed fuel barges
in the harbor, their transfusing lines writhing like serpents . . . I
got lost in the violent vegetation of the luau grounds at the Reef
Restaurant . . .

With Monteverdi's help, I am reinventing the dominant 7th . . .
the powerful discords of his madrigals unsettle me . . .

From the harbor, Stanhope and Bethesda walked to, and then
along, the beach. There was a rare rainfall, which they welcomed.
Through its gridwork, they watched lumps of protozoic almost-life
shifting and slithering toward messy reckonings. Since of those reckonings the stone John sang, Stanhope introduced her to him. She
admired his fez; and John cried, for there would be no more
Bethesdas in his life.

Or: they lay on the banks of the Bouton River, weeping for all
the State Collegians unannealed by love. "Tinkertoy!" he called
her. "Erector set!" she said.

Or: they went to Disneyland, and rode doubled-up, Siamese
Fangios, in a single Richfield mini-car. Whatever he suggested, she
complied. Except . . .

Except when he proposed visiting the station house on the Pike.
Of the motorcycle cops she said: "I hate them." She could not forget the wipe-out at the Fire Festival.

But Stanhope insisted, perhaps to test his power over her, but also because it was hard enough to find a community in Long Beach. Having found one at the station house, he was reluctant to let go of it, even though he, too, had not forgiven Renaldi.

They chanced on the station house the night of the roundup: the night the flying squads fuzzywuzzied all the inverts out of all the comfort stations along the beach, and dragged them to the station house to be booked. There the inverts were stripped and obliged to parade naked before the desk sergeant. Hard-ons were billyclubbed. Gray rings of stale desire eddied and flexed in the rotunda; were, in fact, exhaled by the rotunda. The procession of carp-colored thighs, sunken chests, stained fingers, scarified groins . . . the twelve-toned keening . . . the very resignation of the inverts—all testified to the circular ludicrousness of aberrant desire; of all desire, perhaps.

Imagine, then, Stanhope's surprise to find Renaldi in one of the cells, playing philopena with Svam Spade. Svam wore a cage-shaped silk organdy tent jacket, lace appliqués, tapered red velvet pants, white suede shoes with spring-action tongues; and made cool, flowering moves, growing and weaving. Renaldi was furious at being discovered. "Up, you," he shouted at Svam. "Out into the rotunda with the others." Svam was stripped.

"Charge?" said the desk sergeant.

"I found him in the comfort station at Marina Basin No. 5," said Renaldi. "I smashed the dime lock on his toilet stall. He said, 'Sugar, daddy?' and had a flushed look."

"Disposing of the evidence," said the desk sergeant.

"Yes," said Renaldi.

"Renaldi," said Svam, "when are you going to admit that you're one of us? Those pavé mirrors, Renaldi." Renaldi slapped him across his flower eyes with a gun barrel. "Oh, Renaldi," said Svam, "there's something so brave and stupid about your self-denial."

"A *blague* on all you louses!" screamed Renaldi.

The bruise spread on Svam's face, a blue flowering death mark, around the flower eyes, the put-on dragon-snapping astro-orbs. "Congratulate me, Renaldi: I feel pain!"

"He has been desecrating my Syntopicons," said Renaldi.

"Noted," said the desk sergeant.

"You are one of us, Renaldi," said Svam. "You are even looking more and more like us. The contact habit. I bet you already lost your taste for Scotch-flavored calf's-foot jelly. Admit it, Renaldi. A void-white color beneath the black leather, the pavé mirrors. A pure

white wind of yen for yang. A pomegranate blob, full of the seeds
of desire, to eat and be eaten. The death slime is on your fingers,
Renaldi. The Great Puddle sucks on all of us. In it, we are electrical
tadpoles: negative, Renaldi; negating, Renaldi. Admit it!"

They were coming at him with billyclubs when Stanhope and
Bethesda left. And he swayed as they came, cool crater-blossom,
dust-flower of the with-it moon . . .

"What are they doing to him!" cried the girl: Sahasrara Cannibis,
Svam's colleague at Radio Free Long Beach. "They'll kill him."

"No," said Stanhope. What could a stunner such as Sahasrara
see in such as Spade?

"I've called Otto," said Sahasrara. "Bail is on the way. But they'll
kill him!"

Bethesda reached out to comfort Sahasrara. "Don't touch me!
You're not of the Body! Don't touch me!" She lay down in front of
the entrance to the station house. "Fuzz!" she cried. "They have
made their motorcycle saddles a substitute for sex organs! They ride
them as though they were riding their own bodies, their own corpses,
on wheels, forever raping themselves! That's why they hate *us!* Fuzz
does it to himself!"

Stanhope would have liked to remain for a while with Sahasrara,
discussing the matter, but Bethesda pulled him away. She was horrified. He tried to explain: "Perhaps, Bethesda, we are working in
Long Beach toward an abolition of sexual differentiation. Cf. the
surfers. Cf. the Ashramblers, like Svam. Or the fuzz. If so, I'm interested. Or, conversely, we may be inventing new sexes. All the more
interesting. Can you imagine a future in which three polymorphs sit
around morosely, wishing they had a fourth for sex?"

Bethesda giggled tentatively. Stanhope pointed down at the beach,
at the garbage coming in on the tide. Grunion-hunters were exhibit-
ing themselves. Several wore goggles and black diving (divining?)
suits . . . bubble-headed gropers through the Long Beach night,
Stanhope's night: phantom janitors of the beach, with their sacks
and nets and knives, their flipper-footed web tread on wet sand.
"The Pubugnuts are active tonight," he said.

"Please," replied Bethesda, "let's go back to the houseboat. You
. . . you can flamenco my guitar."

[F]

The public library. I have come to secure a history of Long Beach. The librarian inexplicably suspects me. She looks up in irritation when I state my request, as though I were verminous and not fit to invade her waxy and carbolic precinct. (Actually, I am perhaps overly fond of the modern shower stall in my hotel room, and suds myself vigorously at least twice a day.) Books, says her face, are to be ordered and dusted, catalogued and coded: not defiled by human touch, not plundered by fact-famished Saracens. Her passion for skippering a fastidious ship has no room in its narrowness for readers. Indeed, the books seem somehow to have been transformed into appendages of her dry and papery chasteness. To select one under her glittering eye is to venture an unwonted intimacy upon her. I content myself with this afternoon's *Press-Telegram*.

I am comforted by the reading room, by the tufted old frogs who gather here to waste the drowsy afternoon, who curl themselves around the weak shafts of sunlight which fall through the peeling blinds. They are reading the obituaries. I am moved by this dignified preparation for death. I rise, and walk down the aisle between the long brown tables and the green-shaded lamps. I touch and stroke their old tufted heads, with feeling, with gentleness. They look up, wonderingly, and salute me with their spotted hands, in a vague, affecting manner. I do not know the meaning of this salute: the thumb, pinkie, index and ring fingers are hooked loosely in a fist; the middle finger is extended full length, upright, alone. Is it perhaps a fraternal signal, like the secret Rosicrucian handclasp? No matter. It conveys a sense of solidarity which is heartening. We are as fellow outcasts discovering one another; refuse washed up on this atoll by the sea. Of such gestures is a new and profound camaraderie born.

Churches: stucco hippopotami eating Arbor Road: stained plastic. The West has turned the art of Byzantium into a window; the East turned it into a carpet. To see out; to step on . . . there is much to reflect on in that discrepancy.

The world's largest fruit terminal: three and one half million bananas here *at this very moment* . . . the great gypsum hubcaps and the electromagnetic hoists . . . the spangled hatbox of the Long Beach Arena, wherein Seventh-day Adventists are presently adventing . . . pig iron and prunes, urea and shrimp, bauxite and shoes, rutile sand and safflower seed, tallow, melons, cocoanut oil, wine, and frozen California citrus concentrate . . .

They are installing new street lamps on Long Beach Boulevard: modern marbelite standards, with overhanging mercury vapor luminaires. Odd: like gallows.

"I sometimes think," said Bethesda, "that through the mailbox of me you are posting messages to Death."

Well, wasn't that love's franking privilege? Tiparillo eye in the dark radio around them; the light, an electric orange. She amplifies his static. Yet: he was dangerously attracted to her inventions of his character, even when one version contradicted another. Perhaps objective reality (that *trick!*) was a maze of distorting mirrors (Long Beach!), gilded lies, in which we caught aspects of our deformed selves, from which we could not escape . . . even by smashing the mirror, for each mirror was a window leading into a room of mirrors, and each wall of *that* room was another window leading into . . . Bethesda's inventions might serve him as a covering action, might confuse and preoccupy the thirsty mirrors: the attitudinal structures and response-styles of the *Other*. Here he could leave a glove; there, a shoe or tie; farther on, a crumpled shirt, a fugitive gesture, a clever dissimulation, a prophylactic thimble-symbol. Were he quick enough and sufficiently daring, he might flee the mirror maze entirely: quick, silver . . . prismer escapes! But, to what was prismer escaping? Pane-fulness.

Later: "Murderous music," said Bethesda, looking up through the fish net. "I was an unused electrical outlet, waiting in the dying room of a mortgaged house . . . for my plug. Now I have lit your eyes, my world." His metaphortune-hunting was apparently contagious.

[G]

I have been out. I saw: drive-in restaurants; metallic pigs in a trough of cheese and cola, snuffling among greasy tissue papers and spotted cartons. Or were they spaceships, full of aliens uneasily eyeing one another through the peepholes of their protective armor plate, engaged in a complex bartering transaction for which the cartons and the tissue papers were a form of symbolic currency? It must be noted that the automobiles seemed rather more at ease than their occupants.

The night air: a pulpy subacidic sweetness (essence of oranges) mingled with the fumes of lighter fluid (for steel pyx, ground-meat patties). The night rhythm: a paradigmatic (oil piston) pumping action . . . suggestive. I have made myself sensitive to rhythm. I must approach the (apparent) chaos of Long Beach as I would approach the (apparent) chaos of the universe: not with rational constructions, for Long Beach, like the universe, thrusts upon me images too transitory to define the order *which must be* . . . but with an open ear to the tone poem, to the ebb and flow of harmonies, to the contrapuntal play of the singing spheres. Then, what *is* the rhythm of Long Beach? A frightening mechanical repetition? Or an absolute equilibrium which is . . . nothingness?

I also saw: curbstones at the intersections fading flush into the street, permitting the electric cars of the old people to ride bumpless block to block, to slide easily (all the while purring) into . . . yes.

What else? A dark semi-slum, the exposed throat of the City. On its porches, black, fattening ex-Polytechnic High School athletes, their small feats pads of butter disappearing in the porridge of their flesh and years. Behind them, blues of joblessness haunt the darkened rooms of their dingy bungalows; their minds are broken TV sets . . . We permanently interrupt this program . . .

The Salt Terminal at Pier A! The Black Warrior Lagoon! Mountains of salt, cliffs, chasms; warm snow patterned as though great machetes had knifed down through it, trying to slice it to ribbons. But each knife slice has caused a slow silt-fall on either side of the stroke. Ridges, vertebrae, are formed. The trucks and caterpillar tractors lie at the foot of this severe white mountain, unclean things, attempting to propitiate its inviolable purity. I walk up the mountain of salt; I sink to my knees in it; I gaze out over Basin Six at the Koppel Tower and the concrete silos, the tubes of grain like organ pipes; I think . . . *what is the matter?* For something *is* the matter; all my peregrinations call up desolate vibrations. And, on slogging down the sheer salt face to the prostrate caterpillars, I am once again tormented by an impression that *they* are watching me. But it is midnight; no one is about. And . . . why have I written *they?*

Making love on a mountain of industrial salt renders the animal considerably more *triste* post coitum; worse than sand in the crankcase. Still, Stanhope and Bethesda, determined to transcend the travails of Dokhma Koan, burrowed and rolled, naked as worms.

After which, as though to tongue a psychic sore, they attached themselves to a party of graduating high school seniors, wilted from the all-night dance. They sat in couples at iron tables around a motel swimming pool, eating french fries for breakfast. The girls, their hair fallen pinlessly lank and their faces no longer capable of sustaining an ointmented joy, were now appealingly young: in yards and yards of marquisette gown, enormous bubble-light paillettes, *trompe d'oeil* underdresses and crepe bodices, as though bedding for a French courtesan's gigantic four-poster had been dropped over them, with holes for their unadorned arms and heads. The young men were passable, too, having weathered the storm of preparations, having secured and relinquished bouquets, having stickied their fingers on french fries and their mouths on lipstick: now wearily removing gold stickpins from pink collars, loosening spotted ties at parched throats, grinning, even the knife-lines of their sharpie suits and their Italian shoes relaxing.

Leis were tossed into the motel swimming pool. And after the leis, the girls themselves jumped in, plunged through leis, floated in the pool, their dresses around their necks. The growing glow of Eastern light bestowed a grace upon their silent floating, as of bomb-blossoms, slow flowers on the pool of time. Without urgency . . .

"On one level," Arbiter Aidos had insisted, "you *must* accept Long Beach. Human society is based on an irreducible element of forbearance."

$\left[H\right]$

On Seventh Street: an automobile spare parts and accessories store. I look into the plate-glass window; it is like looking into an autopsy. Cut-rate steel viscera: cylinder bores, plugs, disc brake assemblies, oil pumps, windshield wiper motors, embossed key fobs, rubber floor mats, English driving gloves, racing goggles, bell helmets, asbestos dragster masks . . . I wonder if the automobiles have *human* spare parts shops; whether *they* stare lamp-eyed at human accessory organs?

I have graduated from the monodic lament to the exploitation of the violin . . . I am investigating that consummate contrapuntist, Purcell . . .

Bethesda's face in love was slurred, as though he were looking at her through the heavy bottom of a Coke bottle. At times it seemed their love was a stagnant pool of the will, on which their bodies paddled, like canoes, without obsessions or secret feedings on patterns and conclusions. Then, the question was: could there exist between man and woman such a pond of repose, without premonitory mosquitoes?

At other times, it seemed that love was a sore contract granting mortgages on themselves to each other, trapping them in an endless series of foreclosures, evictions misnomerized as intimacies. Then, the question was: Escrow *l'infâme?* "The trick of love," Aidos had said, "is to be able to leap from revulsion to desire in a single bound. I am too old to be a broad jumper." Where would it end . . . this binge of the flesh?

Such were Stanhope's lice-like thoughts on leaving the houseboat to return to Cimarosa Street, to the white-faced house with the fuchsia mustache; to the little tract of lawn stiff with early morning frost (like crystallized electricity); to the orange door opening on its hinges like a pair of shears; to his bunk, and that handball game between analysis and reproach that finally bounced him into sleep:

A hunter poaches
On my reproaches . . .
He me clouts
With *my* doubts,
And routs the gamy beast of me
To Ineffectuality . . .

And, on waking, he would be hung over with chagrin.

[I]

A gang of boys rifling a mailbox. They stare dull-eyed at me as I
pass. Their eyes are olives from which the pupils have been pitted.
I am, admittedly, frightened. It is as though their leather jackets
were black mirrors in which I glimpsed the face of my own death.
I attempt the fraternal salute I have learned from the old people in
the library. It does not achieve the effect of solidarity I had hoped.
Their hostility, in fact, increases; they chase me. I should have
escaped them handily enough, via an alleyway, but at the least
auspicious moment a pink Jaguar, with wire wheels, rolled of its
own volition into my flight path, blocking the alley. The Jaguar was
driverless, but the effect of its intrusion could scarcely have been
more disastrous for my cause had one of the leather-jacketed pur-
suers been at its steering wheel. I was cornered; I tried to scramble
over the Jaguar; I was seized from behind and brutally mauled. I
was left in the alleyway with not only my senses dispersed, but (so
it felt) with my body organs dispersed as well. Obviously, there are
in Long Beach antithetical subcultures, competing fraternal orders,
inimical tribes and cults. The boys in the leather jackets are enemies
of the old people in the public library.

   Bruised and bandaged, I have been trying to sleep. But I have
left the window open, hoping to smell the sea, and my room is filled
with Wurlitzer music from the "Pike" . . . with the chain-sawing
grind of the motorcyclists, those paratroopers of death . . . and the
shredded steel laughter of falling bodies on the roller coaster
as it loops out over the sea . . . and the periodic mournfulness,
the wounded frog-god moan of the foghorns . . . and the bellicose
honking of angry automobiles—a bad night. Yet the stillness at dawn
is more terrifying. I feel the motels and the automobiles are afraid
of dawn. The sea gobbles the light. I look down, and see heavy-
set men in black uniforms moving bins of garbage to a gray truck
whose digestive tract has been exteriorized, and spins and lolls,
swallowing whatever is offered it, gobbling like the sea.

Overhead, the Sky-Knight helicopter patrols, great whirring, many-eyed black clocks, were herding sex deviates into police nets— while, in their homes, on foam rubber, dreaming wetly, were the remittance men and the procurers who had built the City.

The sibyl's eye of neon over the filling station . . . those smothered concussions of the sea. "The dentists are prowling again tonight," Bethesda said. "They drill me with their eyes. 'Open wide,' they say."

Stanhope mused: "Poor Man: our retch exceeds our gasp."

She gnawed on his ear. "Like all anti-heroes, you tend to be your own fat man."

He thought: anything pressed too far becomes a virtue, even love. And virtue is not anti-heroic.

$$\left[\text{J} \right]$$

I believe that the nature of a man's (or a culture's) sensibility is most nakedly revealed in his (its) concept of pleasure. To investigate the pleasure domes of Long Beach—the miniature golf courses, the movie houses, the cocktail lounges, the pizza parlors and Hawaiian restaurants, the shooting galleries and thrill rides of the "Pike"—is to discover a hysterical nullity. These entrepreneurial expressions of pleasure-pang, these service stations of the libido, as it were, specialize in Lethe rites. They are as small chapels of mactation, wherein are enshrined instruments for murdering time; wherein is practiced a systematic diversionism, by means of which the supplicants dull their sense of . . . of *what?*

Perhaps I fall into an error of approach. The error of substituting critical judgment (so Western!) for the willing acceptance which leads to true understanding. (That Eastern acquiescence which breeds generation after generation of starving children, filthy mendicants, erotic bric-a-brac . . . Stop! Contempt for one's own culture is contempt for oneself.) Still, there is error in the comparative approach. It leads to arid satisfaction (or disappointment); it leads away from joy (or . . . horror). The trouble, I suppose, is that I am young enough to modify my preconceptions, yet too old to derive much pleasure from having to do so.

I had preconceived a Byzantine expression of death and the desert, a wild, cancerous excess, a riot of architectural and emotional selves, from which the piers and the peninsulas would be extended in a quest for order. (Western guilt?) I find, instead, a primitive and imprisoning (Ts'in period) geometry, angles which mold and contain the inhabitants, square their thinking rigidly, obsessively. (Eastern shame?) Quincuncial culture!

I had preconceived occasional images of harmonious suffering, cast on the walls of municipal buildings or raised brazenly in public parks; tokens of an artistically realized dissatisfaction. (Again, that ordered form which chaotic feeling craves. I had been led to expect this in the West, which is reputed to act in haste, mourn at leisure, its aestheticism essentially lugubrious.) I had preconceived Greek movement, in contradistinction to the cowering immobility of so much Asiatic art. I find concrete badgers in Scherer Park. I find adobe and plaster. I find a too plastic hybrid of styles and components, which is forever struggling to contain its incompatibles, to keep itself from shattering apart: not movement, but fearful paralysis . . . that unbearable abstract tension which is, perhaps, democracy. I find gross proletarian murals like the seventy-four-foot ceramic banality sprawled across the front of the Port of Long Beach administration building, depicting everything in its eclectic expropriation from the hide industry to the fur seal trade, from the *Golden Hind* to a contemporary banana freighter. For all that I came here to study the exercise of Western will, I cannot believe that what I have seen is not cruelly accidental, gratuitously ugly; that, in comparison with the art of Long Beach, my silk scrolls, my porcelain, my animal figures, my ritual urns and polychrome glass fishes (for all their lack of power, for all their lack of anguish) are incredibly more *willful . . .*

I had preconceived a cult of flesh-worship, a city of tall, tawny, ferocious women. (Perhaps all young men of the Orient seek in the West the meaning, the revelation of Woman; seek, in other words, to be devoured.) I find that Long Beach is either indifferent to or afraid of flesh, except on the beach where a sexless license to exhibit oneself is in effect. I find marvelous, empty packages. Or packages containing flesh which has been pulverized, reconstituted, rectangulated, like the meat cutlets to be found in frozen slabs at the supermarkets.

Enough of this! It is not the fault of Long Beach, after all, that I should have expected something different, needed something different. That I should have hoped to escape the diminutive quaintness of so much Oriental architecture, of too many Oriental women. That I should have hoped to find in the West a "frozen music" of interrogation, flinging questions at God, at Man, at the very materials out of which it has been fashioned. But to have found something *less* than quaintness—a complacency without significations, a complaint without passion—is wounding. And the women . . . well, that is a real bother. I could find one on the "Pike"—but I am deathly afraid of flower-willow sickness.

Stanhope and Bethesda smoked the aftermathematic silence like a rank cheroot. Then she said: "You are very far away, aren't you? And wherever you are, you are lonely. Do you know that that loneliness is the very cleverest of caresses? When you use it on me, I shuck myself of my inhibitions, as though to crowd your vacancy with the close and strident company of all my naked willingnesses . . ."

He refused the poignancy of such a remark, a flower of death.

[K]

The troll-like menace of the aluminum and fiber glass automobile bodies . . . the twisted shapes of exhausted metals . . . *is there an egress from the traffic circles?*

I have purchased an electric toothbrush, out of an obscure desire, I suppose, to signify my willingness to meet the technological state halfway. I bear this, like a torch or thurible, upon my midnight wanderings. The same romantic comedy appears to be playing in both the theaters and the cemeteries: as though both love and death were a graduation to a rumpus room in the sky, stocked with plaster mockeries of anguished works of art, on which the alumni hang their polka-dotted bow ties and their concertina bras, their baseball caps and their support hosiery; on which they momentarily set their cans of beer or their tubes of contraceptive ointment, while grasping ping-pong paddles and/or each other's sex.

On the tape machine: the opportunistic eclecticism of Handel . . .

The space-time discontinuum: a great lapse appears to have occurred in Long Beach . . .

Strange: drawing back my sheets, I discover a black spark plug among the bedclothes, like a scorpion. How did it get here?

Stanhope wondered: is happiness nothing more than a highly developed capacity for self-delusion? There was growing over him an uneasiness, a grub of dissatisfaction on the cheese of his joy. It seemed as though the credit which Bethesda extended to him only enabled him to multiply his disappointments. (What are you doing about Long Beach?) Through the dark subterranean shafts of his pleasure plunged an express of irritation (things to do . . . things to do). At which platform, on what night, would it pause? And of what cruelties and vengeances would it deliver itself? Could Bethesda see that motorized iron warrior-worm in his eyes? Feel its rumbling in his loin-walls?

All men are natural traitors. Offer them love, and, because they possess the power to betray that love, they *will* betray it. Who can resist the exercise of a capacity, however destructive, he believes himself to own? The possibility of Stanhope's betrayal hung over their chiropractic like a little pure-toned silver bell, ready to ring out its dulcet redefinitions, its tiny doom; ready to summon the demon, halt the train, release the dark host to hack hatchet-handedly at the ties which bind, the lies which blind.

He could not know, of course, that there was an Onalred in his immediate future. But we are all, are we not, blindfolded buffaloes turning the water wheel of time, by our dark brute labor effecting a trickle of events? We are.

[L]

There is a poet of Long Beach! His name is Cronopios. A book of his, *Angel's Sloth,* is a terrifying vision of motorcycle cops as horsemen of the apocalypse, of . . . but more of this later. I should first explain how I happened to acquire this book.

I visited a bowling emporium: forty lanes, automatic pin-setters, switch panels to summon waitresses, semaphoric devices for throwing line scores on screens depending from the ceiling, varicolored ebonite bowling balls, slimline plastic contour chairs in multiple pastel hues, compressed air blowers to cool the sweaty palms, and peanut machines to stoke the raging stomachs.

From a vacant-faced poonghie presiding over the desk, I rented a pair of special shoes and crept out to a contour chair to await my turn. When, after an hour, my number had not been announced, I went into the bar. There I found five middle-aged ladies festively imbibing. They wore identical green Shantung jackets with eagles and serpents on their backs (an Aztec totem, I believe); identical bulging purple stretch pants; identical bone-colored suede leather shoes. Although each head of hair had been tinted a different shade, all exhibited the same general consistency—that of curled electrical wire. Beside them in their booth were five identical black vinyl satchels with Burgundy gussets and spring frames; tucked under the handlegrips of the satchels were identical pairs of beige half gloves, with padded palms and nylon elastic backs.

Not without some trepidation, I essayed the fraternal salute of the old people once again. This time, I was more fortunate. They laughed, and slapped one another playfully. I was invited to purchase a round of Manhattans for them. I did so.

"What are you celebrating?" I asked.

One of them replied: "We have just learned that bowling has surpassed fishing as America's most popular participant sport."

I congratulated them. (This interesting game is of antiquarian vintage, probably derived from a Polynesian ritual known as Ula Maika, in which stones were hurled at standing objects from a distance of sixty feet—a distance which has remained constant to this day, at least in Long Beach . . . But I digress.)

One of the women looked furtively about, then said: "Do you know, I found a *poem* about *Maud*." This was evidently of humorous significance; the others besieged her. "It's in that book of dirty verse her son wrote," explained the woman. "The bartender showed it to me." Whereupon she produced *Angel's Sloth,* a slim volume with azure binding. The poem was entitled *"Nostalgie de la Boue."* (Which means, "Nostalgia for the Gutter.") It was explained to me that the gutter is a bad place to put the ball while bowling, for it scores no points. Turkeys, strikes and spares were also explained. On learning of the obligatory configuration of the pins, *I* explained to *them* what Cronopios must have meant by "Pythagorean pyramids.") She read the poem aloud:

> No sanctuary in a bowling lane.
> The huge balls roll, the white pins burst in pain
> Like birds among bullets; feathery rain.
> Their explosion is scooped
> Electrically.
> Her split is recouped.
> Dejectedly, the *other*
> Looks on while my mother
> Turkeys twice, strikes out, and sneers;
> Gobbles triumph, buys a round of beers.
> And I, like the pins, regroup sensations which have scattered
> (As though their coalition really mattered!)
> Into Pythagorean pyramids.
> My ball skids . . .
> Even did I care,
> I would not dare
> To spare
> My Mother.

My excitement might be imagined. "Scattered sensations," indeed! And the unmistakable echoes of the French symbolist, Rimbaud: the mother fixation, the love-hate ambiguity, the recollection of that short, Gorgonian exclamation: *"I is an other."* Perhaps most importantly, a capturing of the repetitive violence of entertainment in Long Beach.

On another page, a second poem confirmed Rimbaud's influence. It was called "A Refusal to DeFrost Too Many Symbolists":

> Please, don't disarrange your senses.
> Neighborly poets make good fences.

An astonishingly succinct juxtaposition of cultural response-styles, and a significant linguistical intuition, too: for language is a kind of pawnshop, isn't it? An outlet for "hot" metaphors, stolen meanings, cheapened images, guilt, sin and rationalization?

I promptly emptied my pockets of paper and coin to purchase the book of poems from the woman, and rushed out of the bowling emporium. There, confronting me, was a row of gleaming automobiles. Odd, their hostile names: Mustang, Cobra, Spitfire, Barracuda . . .

Back in the hotel, I found between my bedsheets a broken fan belt and an ignition scope. What does this mean?

"Look," said Maud Cronopios, "I need the wheels. You and that little portable donut of yours can wait for me at Vaseline Ali's until the tournament is over. Got it? Then drive me back to Cimarosa Street. You can use the layoff, kiddo: with all that exercise, you'll get muscle-bound in your manhood. So wait in the bar—affirmative?"

"Affirmative, Mother." He stuck his thumbs in the eyes of the bust of Emma Goldman.

[M]

I could swear I was followed back to my hotel by a Tempest. Or was it a Fury? Perhaps the visit to St. Teresa's Little Ashram of Ecumenical Oṁ has disordered my imagination. (Otto Unamuno is a dangerous man! And that drone: I have come to believe that if one drops the last six centuries of Western harmony from the history of music, all that is left is noise!)

It has been a day of revelation, a day spent, after my visit to the Ashram, in my hotel room, listening to music and reading *Angel's Sloth*. What can I say about Bach? The architecture of the universe. After him, a certain messiness enters the picture. I was impatient, and hurried through the sonata form, perhaps unfairly; through the raciness of Mozart and the apocalyptic visions of Beethoven; the phantasmagoric tantrums of Berlioz; Wagner, munching the pulp of slain gods; terse, masterful Brahms; clumsy, brooding Bruckner; the chillingly objective neoclassicism of Stravinsky opposed to the intense, direct expression of the atonalists: austere Schoenberg, romantic Berg, aphoristic Webern. I should have tarried among the atonalists, for they were trying to tell me something and I could almost apprehend it, but—but in the early evening I came upon a poem in *Angel's Sloth* (the revelation I have noted) and I could not stand to contemplate it while atonally accompanied. I fled fearfully back to Bach. "The Void Made Flesh":

> The beach is melting wax. I stand
> On the burning strand, my hand
> A small-craft warning. The breath
> Of the sea is as nothing to me.
> My pregnancy is death.
> I am hot with it. The spit
> Of the salt spray sizzles
> On the grizzled griddle of my chin.
> My skin's distended with the growing death.
> My breath in short pants like a child

After wild running seeks a lap.
Mishappenstantially I'm lapless.
The *Void* balloons. Its hollow babe
Will swallow me on my disgorging of it.
I cannot love it: this blossoming extinction
That was spawned by my-and-Time's mismarriage;
For which exists no method of miscarriage.
I stand on burning sand, the dark night's bride:
Months gone toward Motherhood . . . toward Matricide.

And there it is: the Void. I sensed it from the beginning, but Cronopios' poem has made it manifest. The Void: it explains everything. In his introduction to *Angel's Sloth,* Cronopios describes Long Beach as "the cloaca of the Western world . . . a tub from which the plug has been pulled; and we are, all of us, going down the drain."

Yes! The inhabitant of Long Beach (he calls them "Bealongchiks") must sense at the very beginning of his life that somewhere a vast expenditure has occurred, a huge squandering, an immense dissipation. He must be born with the knowledge of that loss, with the certainty that the vacuum created by that primal excess is sucking at *him;* that, for whatever reason, Long Beach is an ever widening hole in the objective world, through which all constructions and flesh and fiddle-faddle will be drawn, will be flushed.

This, then, accounts for the face. The "Bealongchik" comes in many shapes and sizes, in several sexes; but he has only one face. It is a face set against an invisible strain, a tug toward nullity. All his will is in his face: *resist.*

It accounts, too, for the anti-style. There is about his locomotion a tender-soled gait, the overprecision of the souse, as he proceeds on his disappointed rounds. There is about his garb an extravagant tastelessness, as though he had been caught naked at night in a burning department store and hurriedly flung on himself whatever cloths and colors came immediately to hand. There is about his gestures a casual depravity, as though he were unaware of what his twitching limbs described. Why should he waste his time worrying about the affectations of an outer life? To what account would his pride be put, a low-slung wolfhoundishness, a leanness or filigree of mannerism, an assumed fragility, a cultivated torpedo-toughness? He would have no use for these futile gongorisms. He would be concentrating on the Void. He carries that Void around with him, like a disease of the cells or a packet of traveler's checks; or, as Cronopios so tellingly put it, an "anti-pregnancy." The odor of it—of decay? of plastic? of carbolic? of nicotine or oranges or lighter fluid or cow dung? No *matter!*—is always in his nostrils. He knows that the hole in his soul can never be cobbled over.

Perhaps, in fact, hair curlers might stick in the craw which follows the maw of the hole that is sucking him (her) to Void. Perhaps the garishness of Capri pants, the hooked intricacies of foundation garments, the misshapenness of parasols and pocketbooks, the spikes of golf club or croquet mallet, might make him hard to swallow, even for a Void. Perhaps the Void would vomit him back.

At *last* I am beginning to understand. I must get in touch with Cronopios. In the meantime, I can live with this revelation only with the help of Bach, only with the totally invertible polyphony of his *Die Kunst der Fuge*. The pure logic of the fugue at least a little lightens the burden of this awful intuition with which I now must coexist . . .

In my bed tonight, a babbit bearing and a tachometer . . .

Some Buddhist once maximounced: every effect becomes a cause. Propter hoc is ergo a function of post hoc. Onalred was post-hocular; he might as well have been the author of all the ante-hocs, so carefully had the past prepared for his advent at Vaseline Ali's Horn of Malt the night that Maud Cronopios chose not to show up.

Stanhope was complaining to Bethesda: "English poetry falls naturally into iambic or anapaestic patterns. Russian poetry seems predominantly trochaic or dactylic. How am I to escape the iambic hang-up?"

And Onalred was upon them, his black domino an umbrella. "The class relations of a culture," he observed offhandedly, "determine its deepest communal fantasies. America is the hang-up, young man. And you must not *escape* it, but *change* it." His sudden ugliness was splendid; and while there was, to be sure, a menacing air about the Slavonic Vodyanoi quality of his conspiratorial charm, it promised *meaning*.

"But," objected Stanhope, looking up into that map of warts, those blazing eyes, "aren't the intentions of the poet and the, ah, revolutionary . . . diametrically opposed? The poet seeks wisdom, which is the movement from event to knowledge. The revolutionary seeks action, which is the movement from knowledge to event."

"*Ploh,*" said Onalred, sitting down and ordering, significantly, a bloody mary. "A poet requires more than wisdom to inform his limericks. He requires *inspiration.* And what is inspiration but the creative union of the conscious with the unconscious? And what is Marxism but the conscious expression of the unconscious historical process? And what is *Revolution* but the inspired frenzy of History, that tumultuous moment when the masses by sheer elemental pressure explode through the sociopsychic routine and give victorious expression to the deepest needs of historical development? When the instinctual joins forces with the higher historicophilosophical abstractions in the service of the Revolution—there is a role for a poet to play! Paradise regained!" He doffed his blue beret, and shoveled a bowl of pretzel nuggets into his mouth.

"But," said Stanhope, "aren't roles merely attitudes, and acts merely postures?"

"Outside a Revolutionary context, yes-indeedie." Onalred swept cinders off the black domino. "Call me Onalred," he said. Then, bubbling his bloody mary, he went on: "Our vocabularistic fetishes may obscure the search for common understanding. I turn on the language of the Dialectic; you turn off your transistorized receiving apparatus. Suppose I spice up my point with a few psychoanalytical phrases. They are very popular in the West these days." He grinned, tomato-toothy. "If your culture is an expression of the 'reality principle,' are you prepared to grant an *immutability* to that reality principle? Is it not based on what Freud called 'the eternal primordial struggle for existence,' the fact of scarcity, *Lebensnot?* We must delay our gratification because it isn't possible for our species to survive unless we *work*—therefore we sublimate and repress?"

Pause. Then: "I say *applesauce!*" And he broke in half the wooden bowl which he had emptied of its pretzel nuggets. "Most of the so-called 'reality principle' is a sociohistorical phenomenon. Scarcity is not natural or eternal! It has been organized and thrust upon men by their ruling classes! A social production based on individual consumption instead of profit; a planned instead of a market economy; collective instead of private property—social engineering of this sort would greatly modify the 'reality principle,' would it not? It certainly would. And add to such social engineering the technological tools today available to us—add, in the particularly egregious instance of Long Beach, those rich tidelands oil deposits —and you should be able to spring man from the big house of his dehumanizing repressions. Am I right?" He held the pieces of the broken bowl as though they were breasts. "I am right."

"But we *have* already sprung him, to a certain extent," said Stanhope. "Look at the increased time for leisure activities in Long Beach. Life is one long game of miniature golf!" Bethesda nodded.

"Leisure activities!" snorted Onalred. He spun a jagged piece of bowl until it pointed like a dagger at Bethesda. "You mean leisure *passivities!* The ruling classes came to power on the basis of administering the distribution of human labor. The social utilization of the organism as an instrument of labor required that organism's desexualization. If technology indeed released the organism into a leisure capable of *re*-sexualizing it, then the ruling classes would have lost their *raison d'être*. Never! Cast a cold eye about you, young man: examine your concept of 'fun.' 'Fun' in Long Beach, in all advanced capitalistic societies, is hardly to be distinguished from *toil*. It is strident and regimented; it is without a sense of privacy, and without an experience of silence. It is formless, in that it achieves nothing but repetition and dullness; it is crude, in that it takes as its symbols the most casual brutality. There is no self-shaping of privacy; there is, in fact, no privacy whatsoever. And *that* is *precisely* the intention of the ruling classes: to institutionalize the conception and experience of 'fun' in a manner which perpetuates the ultimate objectification of man that was begun by the organization of labor. Am I right?"

Stanhope turned to Bethesda: "Is he right?"

She said: "Do *you* think he's right?"

He said: "*I* think he may be right."

She said: "Then right he might be." Would she have saved her own life by making another reply? Do any of us, objectively speaking, save our lives?

"Mr. Onalred," began Stanhope, his excitement growing—

"Call me Onal," he replied, ordering a round of bloody marys.

"Onal, what about the private life of pot: the mindblower's experience of himself?"

"Exploitation of the peasants of Turkey and Mexico," said Onalred. "Besides, it makes a regressive sort of testimony to the possibilities of freedom within the established order. A false witness! By providing such escape valves, the established order releases steam which might otherwise build up into a threatening and destructive force. By administering over these compensations—and do you imagine there would *be* a narcotic supply if the organization of elitists weren't playing footsie with organized crime?—the ruling classes actually strengthen themselves. Business as usual! It profiteth some people very much when other people loseth their own souls!"

"Then," said Stanhope, "a *real* revolutionary might covertly encourage the constituted authorities to *repress* such activities as go on, say, at the Ashram—"

"Ah," said Onalred, stirring his drink with his thumb, "you are a small dialectical diamond in the rough. Yes! We will spit on and polish you. Correct: close off all these various small valves of compensation, in order to assure the ultimate explosion of the social machinery!" And he plunged his fist into the glass, exploding a blood-red flower of tomato juice and glass all over the table top. In the flower he drew question marks. Ali-Whoops looked up from the bar and scowled.

Stanhope found the very duplicity of it all intriguing. "But," he said, unwilling to nurture a Mongoloid hope, "this is just idle talk. Suppose we agreed. What can we *do?*"

And Onalred raised a tomatoey hand, a red star-claw shifting the angle and drift of their lives and loves. He licked its blunt-tipped points, and said: "Well, son, I'm glad you asked me that question."

How often meaning molts before our very eyes, and still we mistake the naked bird: call "squab" what is surely cuckoo. A cuckoo, of course, is another kind of pigeon.

[N]

I am learning to fear. My fingers when I touch my face in the shaving mirror are worms. This evening I saw one woman totally blotted out. She had been standing before me. My attention was momentarily diverted by the passage of the helicopter overhead. Alas, hers must have been diverted, too. For when I looked at her again, her face was gone. A hole had replaced it; disappearing into the hole as I watched were her legs, her body trunk, her tote bag and her ebonite bowling ball. I rushed forward, crying: "Wait!" Too late. I thrust my arms into the hole; they were grasped! With an effort that left me gasping afterward, I wrenched myself free. Nothing was left of the woman. She had been canceled . . . No doubt *my* face is the One Face now.

In his introduction to *Angel's Sloth,* Cronopios says curiously: "Perhaps the Bealongchiks are misers of suffering; perhaps they hoard their disappointments, stuff them into mattresses, tea cozies, plaster-cracks—hoping to collect enough one day to achieve genuine despair. But are they not attacked by the miser's gross fantasies? (All misers are refugees from themselves, like hipsters.) Someone is going to steal their suffering—by an act of mercy, of tenderness or kindness. Someone will foist upon them a redemption they do not desire, are unwilling to accept. And so they affect their brutal indifference, in order to protect themselves and their accumulated minor desperations. It is a very bad business, indeed, if a God indebted to us for our suffering welches on the deal by dealing us out of an afterlife. But, if we haven't had a before- or during-life, what might we reasonably expect of the hereafter: something equally monotonous, an endless Te-Dium? Long Beach, the capital of Lassitude!"

I confess myself dismayed by this persiflage. It would seem a prime example of the well-known second-rateness of the minds of America's greatest artists—Twain, Dreiser, Fitzgerald, Hemingway, Faulkner, Salinger, Pearl Buck—those gifted vulgarians who so greatly tax the charity and patience of the hard-working literary critics.

Cronopios doesn't understand his own poems! What has "lassitude" to do with the furtive lack of meanings he has disinterred, for instance, in such unpromising materializations as the comfort stations at Marina Basins 1–5; or the hot water boiler in the Public Safety Building; or the bituminous seal-coating on the airport runway pavements; or the Poly Hi Hutch Canteen; or the vitrified clay pipe lateral sewers under the U. S. Naval Hospital?

Then there is this poem, which, I am ashamed to say, seals me off even from the consolations of Bach. It is called "My Church Gives a Very Bad Trade-in":

> We bleed tired blood, and so make bald
> The Good Years of our Youth,
> Which ruthless Time with glassy Tooth
> Impales. Fails our rayon of resolve,
> And the Fiat of our will is stalled.
> Imperatives of "Do!" devolve
> On false cords and ply-lies we bought
> For seven Mary-Dolors; sought
> By counting rubber beads.
> Needs . . . chains.

I shan't soon recover from that poem. Its vision of the deus as machina is convincing. It introduces a note of tricky complication. Have I made it clear that it is the automobiles which have been watching me? Today I was followed in relays (as I went about checking the locales of Cronopios' poems)—by a Bronco and a Hurricane. There is no question about this. Nor any question that it was the Sting Ray which watched me while I was watching the woman who was watching the three marble-limbed godlets cavorting on the beach. Nor any question that the Jaguar deliberately intervened to my disadvantage that afternoon I was trying to escape through the alley. Nor any question that beneath my window now, at this very moment, are a Minx and a Spider . . .

Why? Are the automobiles agents of the Void, an intricate network of unobtrusive spies, able to cruise anywhere unremarked, able at all times to shift the burden of surveillance to another, more strategically positioned make or model? Perhaps, moving at will among the Bealongchiks, their automobiles—their Darts, Sharks, Cyclones—conspire at that human cancellation on which the Void insists. Unknown to driver, to passenger, the auto bears them closer and closer to a Samarra of blotting-out, the drainhole of nullity.

Then I am obliged to reinterpret the industrial expressions of Long Beach which so thrilled me with their willfulness early on. If the autos are in the employ of the Void, might not the cranes, the small-boat hoist at Pierpoint Landing, the forklifts and the freight trains be so, too? Of course. When I plowed down the mountain of salt, I was being watched by . . . the caterpillars.

In my bed, a rocker arm, a torsion bar, and a bottle of turtle wax . . .

But I would not be able to sleep anyway. For another problem occurs to me: are the machines the agents of the Void; or has the Void been generated by the machines, to revenge themselves on their Western masters? I must think this out. But thinking is difficult, under the constant bombardment of these revelations, intuitions, suspicions. I wonder if something is the matter with my tubular shocks?

The net of Onal's argument, like a spider's web, had many different attachment points; but, also like a spider's net, its radial threads invariably intersected its lateral threads at equal angles, cornering Stanhope; and the center of the web, the center of Onalred's gravity, was always the impulse to action.

Having first proposed the Dialectic as a sort of sauna bath for Stanhope after long intellectual debauch, Onalred proceeded over a succession of smoke-filled evenings in the Horn of Malt to flesh in his theoretical propositions with revolutionary romance . . . and the effect was Cineramic.

"Indochina," said Onalred, and while he munched cheese puffs, Stanhope dreamed. Stanhope with Onalred disembarked from a purple-sailed pirate junk off the Tonkin coast . . . tramped with boi-dois in palm-fiber helmets across the Meo highlands, through rain forests lit by bamboo torches . . . lay with congais in the brothels of Hanoi . . . threw stones through the windows of the Bank of Indochina and mowed down the rubber trees and coffee bushes of the plantations of Terres Rouges . . . "Cantonese spice and roast pig's bladder," said Onalred, licking his lips. And Stanhope shivered to reverberations of the fate-shaped Asiatic tocsin, the death gong and the wooden rattle.

Or, munching on wedges of mushroom-studded pizza and washing it down with *crème de cacao,* Onalred loquated of Algeria—of blue-throated doves in the palm trees; jackals among burning stones; sheep on spits and sap-gorged flies; refuse-eating cats and *tchic-tchic* players. And suddenly Stanhope was hacking his way through cork forests, sand dunes, kif addicts, slug-like Mozabite merchants and French paratroopers. "Red mullet!" cried Onalred. "Fried squid! Spiced couscous and black Mitidja grapes!" And Stanhope lobbed schneiderite bombs over iron grilles around milk bars and tobacco stalls; slit the esophagi of sentries; sniffed brine, pine, virgin oil and soiled flowers; whistled through reed pipes; watched like a lizard. *Istiqlal!*

"Long Beach, objectively speaking, is also occupied, am I right? A more subtle—a psychic and spiritual—exploitation, to be sure. But the oil *is* here. Substitute the tidelands for the Sahara; neighborhood restrictions and Japanese gardeners for empire; anesthesia for terror; somnambulism for death; the 'omnivorous quotidian' for History . . ." And you had Long Beach. If you desperately wanted it, as Stanhope did. Onalred ate chicken wings, crunching the bones. "How," he asked, "did Chekhov put it? 'When a man is born, he can choose one of three roads. There are no others. If he takes the road to the right, the wolves will eat him up. If he takes the road to the left, he will eat up the wolves. If he takes the road straight ahead, he'll eat himself up.' There really isn't any choice, is there? You must go left, young man!" And he made his gnaw a grin. "In fact, objectively speaking, you already have. *I* was assigned to liquidate Flojo-José y Cabron. *You* took care of it for me, unwittingly, at the Fire Festival. Am I right?"

Bethesda like a rabbit nibbled Stanhope's sleeve. Stanhope grinned at Onalred: so far, of course, he had slit only the esophagi of phantoms . . . and they bled nothing but ideas. Onalred's face was the photo of a bombed city. "Six chili-burgers!" he cried.

[O]

I went to the Iowa State Picnic in order to escape the surveillance of the automobiles. Yet it was depressing to walk among the old people, to listen to the hardening of their arteries. (Perhaps Death isn't interested in those who are seriously diseased, those who are very old. Perhaps Death is only interested in the young, the strong: the challenges. The querulousness of the aged and infirm might arise from exactly that recognition: they feel neglected by the Dark Prince. He takes them for granted, as an emperor takes for granted an old consort. But one day the consort poisons the emperor.) The signlessness over Recreation Park was oppressive, and weighed down on me as though the sky were vinyl, lowering, crushing me. It had no smell, no taste; perhaps I err even in describing it as heavy. I crush myself under it. I should not have abandoned Cronopios . . . or Bach.

Yet it was at the Picnic that I met a professor of history from the College: Arbiter Aidos. No doubt he took me for a clown, as with my Edsel grille and my exhaust pipe I must have cut a comic figure. And it was of course foolish of me to expect my masquerade to deceive the Void. We labor under the illusion that the clown possesses a peculiar exemption; yet beneath the mascara and the lipstick and the wig, inside the gunboat shoes and the balloon pants, the human being is only diminished. Paying off the Void on an installment plan, with bacon strips of his dignity.

Still, over a Thermos of Metaxa, Aidos seemed to sense the quality of my disquietude. We watched palsied old couples dance a quadrille, while ringed about by pigeons with a disapproving and officious air. Aidos said: "The Harvard psychologist Skinner taught pigeons to dance the quadrille by rewarding them with pellets of corn. I wonder if the pigeons are now trying to teach the old people; and, if so, what sort of reward they're offering? Estrogen, perhaps?"

When I did not respond to this preposterous jocularity, he went on undaunted. "I imagine you are now in a desperate state, unable to figure us out. You came West in search of the source of Greek vitality and genius. That source resides in the intimation that all things must be measured by the duration and intensity of a *single human life*. It died with Faust, almost two millennia later, which is a pretty long run for an intuition. Since then, Dokhma, few men have had the temerity to measure with the dipsticks of themselves the oil level of the Absolute."

In my agitation at this technological metaphor, I began fingering my electric toothbursh. Aidos took it from me. "Our toys," he said, examining it, "are the seed pods of our monsters; previews of devouring destiny. Why am I filled with horror at the sight of a transistor radio or a hula hoop? Because I am a historian. True! I know that Dutch opticians invented the telescope to give their children something to play with—then Galileo borrowed it to look at the stars, and unleashed on humankind a bloodsucking intuition into our own puniness under the Universal Eye. I know that Pascal invented the theory of probability because the childish Chevalier de Mere asked him to supply a foolproof system of winning at dice— and now it is embraced by our insurance companies, reducing us to statistical integers, robbing us of our sense of the uniqueness of our own death."

I said: "Is the hula hoop, then, a symbol of the Void?"

Aidos said: "Perhaps. The transistor radio, now . . . it destroys the silence in which our thoughts and love should grow; increases our dehumanization. Rilke has called music a breathing of statues, space grown from our hearts. The transistor radio with *its* music has turned *us* into statues—and space, empty space, grows *in* our hearts."

I said: "The Void."

He said: "Toys are a form of anti-art."

I said: "And machines? And automobiles?"

He said: "Of course. I am struck by your use of the term 'Void.' Have you visited St. Teresa's Little Ashram of Ecumenical Oṁ? *Their* Void appears to be a kind of pony express depot en route to mystical union."

I said: "All is not what it seems at the Ashram. I hold no brief for Eastern mysticism, but it *is* essentially quiescent. The self-flagellant Western saints may have been action-oriented, but the Eastern mystics weren't. To pretend, like Svam Spade, to be imitating the

East, and then to push your mystical product like a flashy little ponce—"

Aidos interrupted: "Yes. Svam Spade is the Lawrence Welk of the mysticism trade. The Ashramblers (as Stanhope Cronopios calls them) *are* unseemly in their zeal to convert." He mused. "Let us admit, Dokhma, that Long Beach (and the world!) is a dull, cruel, disappointing, death-making place. Having made that admission, how shall we respond?

"We can undertake to change the world, through *action*. I suspect action of endemic futility. The world we live in is a consequence of the fact that we must all eventually die in it too. Many consider death a sort of personal insult; their feelings of inadequacy arise from their inability to avenge that insult. Their actions, from rage and self-pity, tend mostly to be premature death-givings to others.

"Or we can have recourse to another, nicer world: unseen, private, imagined, invented. Like childhood, glue-sniffing, New Criticism, transistor radios and religion. They console, and I approve—*providing* the inhabitants of such worlds are satisfied, like children, to live there alone or in the company of like-minded tyke types. But the Ashramblers insist on vulgarizing their beliefs by trying to make other people believe them too. They are hang-uppity; and authoritarian in their hang-uppityness. The consequent spectacle, like all vulgarity, is embarrassing."

I said: "Surely religion has a social purpose."

He said: "It shouldn't. The pleasure we take in a metaphysical system is the same as the pleasure we take in a work of art—aesthetic gratification. A matter of taste."

I said: "So we have (1) pointless action; or (2) self-delusion which is either (a) harmless, or (b) vulgar. Is there no third alternative?"

He said: "The alternative of the flowers. To bloom wherever you happen to be, in your own special way. The flowers do their own thing."

I said: "I suppose you think that attitude rather Eastern. The well-known orchidaceous approach to life and art: the human being as a tulip! But I came West precisely to seek an escape from that acquiescence, which, while it may not be vulgar, is certainly obscene. For it invites either squalor or fascism. Flowers won't grow in the squalor; fascism will trample the flowers."

He said: "Fascists are impotent Fausts, trampling the flowers in petulance. But, Dokhma, flowers do spring out of squalor. Out of compost heaps! Flowers in their flow to form can crack pavements, parking lots, cellblocks, even freeways! Even Long Beach!"

I snatched back my electric toothbrush and stood. "They will come tramping by, and they will snip off your head and wear you as a boutonniere."

"Wait!" cried Aidos. But I had started to run, scattering the old people as they quadrilled. "Come back!" he shouted.

"No!" I replied, looking back over my shoulder. "I did not come thousands of miles merely to be lectured on the emptiness of energy and love!"

On reaching the perimeter of the park grounds, of course, I found a Falcon and a Wildcat waiting for me.

Love spirals toward objects of affection like a honeysuckle vine, twines round them and too often finds them not objects after all, but shimmering evanescences, mythic constructions out of the sweet dream of the vine for the perfect trellis. Twined round a sunbeam, Bethesda would still believe 'til twilight; then night falls. Twined round a weed, how could she have anticipated the inexorable mower of Fate?

She tried, once: "Didn't Arbiter Aidos describe Onalred's particular sort of *Weltansichtliness* as 'the New Calvinism'—substituting the professional revolutionary for the elect; historical determinism for predestination; machina for deus?"

But Stanhope had lived too long a life without action. The linguists speak of the k's in kill, talk, tick and teak as "allophones of the k-phoneme." Stanhope saw himself—in the light of Onalred's arguments—as a gramophone of the O-phenom (eno-illogical), its needle riding his flesh, grinding out endlessly the senseless lament, the dumb repetition, the ear-rending scream of sameness. He grasped her hands: "Corn chip," he said, "don't you see? In the jumbo shrimp shack, before the Fire Festival, I told you we must do *more.* Atrophy is a consequence of disuse; disuse is a consequence of sloth; sloth derives from over-guilt; over-guilt, from sin; sin, from consciousness; consciousness from fractured animal awareness. The cycle will *always* end in sloth unless we *act!* Perhaps the death of the self is the beginning of true human community! Don't you see?"

Whatever she saw, she didn't like it. Her face was as bone-white as the Tiparillo lip piece around which it was formed. "How did Eddington put it?" she said. " 'Man is one of the most terrifying results of a lack of antiseptic precautions on the part of the cosmos.' " She cursed her flesh because it was not history.

[P]

Having found the pure logic of the fugue inappropriate to my atonal terror, I tried Stockhausen. After Stockhausen, the RCA Synthesizer was the next inevitable step.

It is not that have I never been frightened before. Since leaving the East, reality has constantly terrified me. But always before, in the manner of a poet, I have teased and experimented with my terror, treated it as the English naturalist Darwin treated his insectivorous sundew flower: fed it with urine and cork, stone and snake poison, tissue from the visceral cavity of a toad. What shall I feed it now? The bronze bushing and the cam lobe I found in my bed? No longer have I the desire to contact Cronopios. Is this the lassitude of which he speaks? Perhaps I underestimated his sagacity. Perhaps, after grappling with the Void, you at last resign yourself to its inevitable triumph . . . No! *Not* Eastern fatalism! It can't be —is the One Face then the blankness of a yawn?

Something is growing on me, I can't doubt it any more. Like moss, only metallic. Pimples, fly bites, have hard aluminum or stainless steel heads, like rivets.

The RCA Synthesizer and Lassitude get on well together. Lassitude was waiting for me when I came in the door. He fell full length on top of me. Odd: we conspired at maintaining that position, a marriage-bedding of the inert. No: not odd at all. I summoned the resolve to push against his chest. The flab of him rolled off me, and he lay there, panting. I got to my feet and called room service.

A tapping on the door. I admit a bell-capped old man. He is bent like a question mark or a bicycle frame. I say: "Will you take this intruder away with you?"

"What intruder?" asks the old man.

I should have known, but my differential appears to be slipping. "Never mind. Bring me something to drink. Bring me—" What? I can't decide. "Bring a miscellaneous selection of beverages," I tell him. He goes.

Lassitude rouses himself to a crouching position. He is a sulking, shiftless, scornful, hairy-thighed brute. He stretches himself. There is a flickering in his eyes. Perhaps an obscene idea has just occurred to him, a needle-nick. Or: is the flicker in *my* eyes? The shock of recognition?

On the tape machine: noise ground out by sound-wave generators, transferred as electromagnetic impulses directly to the mylar: noise manipulated and juxtaposed according to an unfathomable perverseness. Six centuries in the harmonic vein have been . . . in vain.

The old man reappears. I pay him in a poor humor, and begin trying the various bottles. Into the whirl-chamber, down the crankshaft. It has no effect.

Lassitude stares at the window, toward the street with Spanish names. He evinces no desire to decipher those names, no impulse toward increased consciousness. Between the names and the brute is a pane of glass: the window, the will. Transparent. But Lassitude, with the miasma of ineffectuality he exudes, foggifies that glass. Impossible opacity. And tears in his eyes. From the fog, or the fluorescent lighting?

I go into the bathroom to analyze my urine. The miscellany of liquors has in no way improved my viscosity index.

Back from the bathroom: Lassitude has not moved. He dozes, fattens. It would require a team of bullocks to pull him from his post. To the elevator; to the basement; then, with the aid of the bell-cap, he might be trundled on a cart to the garbage bin, dumped in, presented to the men in black uniforms, the can of him hoisted up and heaved into the steel jaws of the jowly gray truck, digested. It is not worth the effort . . .

I try to write, but it is difficult to—transmit messages . . . perhaps something is the matter with the linkages in my transmission system . . . synchro-messy . . . can't shift . . . Lassitude offers me his fog bowl. Brute! Vegetable! Rotter!

I call down once more to room service. "I want something else to drink. Something special . . . something containing—" What? "—an anti-foam agent. Yes. And a corrosion inhibiter! And a detergent disperser! And a pour-point depressant! And . . . and . . ." But I have lost interest.

RCA is a comfort to me . . . more than noise and less than music . . . devoid of compassion, bereft of beauty . . . all manipulation . . . tracking down trills and tremolos between different tone colors . . . transforming pitch, color, dynamic and rhythmic patterns . . . achieving complexities and subtleties of structural form and interrelationship which exceed the capacity of my ear and my intelligence to detect . . .

I am pleased. It is in fact the music of boredom. A glorious ennui is born, an exemplary indifference. Abolition of instruments, cancellation of performers. The limits it proposes are the limits of human perception, and it exceeds those limits . . . I indulge the disorderliness of my self-pity . . . It is not my fault that the liquor leaves rust deposits in my carburetor, that my plugs are sparkless, that my box ratios are out of line . . .

Lassitude mutters: *"Aufgeschoben ist nicht aufgehoben,"* and smiles, coyly, twisting . . . twisting a white Sikkimese scarf . . . the tape loop achieves a limitless repetition of patterns . . . computer punch tape fed into the Synthesizer . . . the final, cerebral achievement of a noise which is *anti-music* . . .

The boredom is beyond me now: I will not reach it, cannot grasp and strangle it. It is soundless, yet screaming. It makes itself superfluous, derives that superfluity from its intuition into the superfluousness of everything outside it. Logic . . . I want *not to be.* That is all I want, the last negation. At the bottom of my listless flounderings, I find the same lack of desire, repeating, turning against itself . . . in my exhaust valves is a negative rotation . . .

Lassitude rises, slavering . . .

I think of the mathematicians scarring the computer punch tape, feeding it into the Synthesizer . . . the Synthesizer mixing, modifying, destroying remorselessly . . . The mathematicians are saved, saved by the elegance and efficiency of their self-abolition . . . That I too might be saved, had I the elegance, the efficiency . . . night falls, dodecaphonically multiplied . . . I must drain my crankcase . . . Lassitude opens his ape-arms to embrace me . . .

No!

So ended the notebooks of Dokhma Koan. There was an afterward by Aidos: "Dokhma apparently escaped from the hotel room, for his body was discovered in the wildlife sanctuary of El Dorado Park. According to the official police statement, released by Renaldi Haruspex to the *Press-Telegram,* Dokhma died from drinking two quarts of friction proofing. His notebooks were sent to me because I was the only one who knew him. Of course, I didn't.

"Perhaps each age, each culture, generates precisely that disease which it most richly deserves. Plague in the Middle Ages; syphilis in the Renaissance; gout in the baroque period; cancer in the twentieth century. In Long Beach, now, it seems to be a peculiar atrophy, an irretrievable petrifaction, as exemplified by John the Ossified Man and, in his own unfortunate way, by poor Dokhma: pimple = rivet. We do not die; we congeal.

"Perhaps, Stanhopeless, you are judging me. Perhaps you are saying to yourself: He was not a flower. He was not even a mushroom. He was a toadstool. Perhaps that is true.

"But . . . well. So, what *else* is true?"

What else is true, Arbiter, is that you failed me. You failed me (1) by dying at the very time I needed a father; (2) by leaving me a testament as self-revealing as it was impotent: "From among the many sorts of failure, each man unerringly selects the one which will most compromise his self-respect"; and (3) by proving that dreary testament, bequeathing to me *Queasiness,* a monograph on failure, on impotence, on compromise.

I have had to seek another father, Aidos. And I have found him.

So Stanhope told Bethesda. And, alas, her possibilities of reply were few. For, with all the surfers dead, Stanhope was her only hold on the world; and acquiescence was her only hold on Stanhope. He had broken the hermetic seal on her reticence; pierced the protective wall of her hodaddom. She was like a mollusk whose shell is crushed. She accepted his decision, and waited, naked and sacrificial, for him in the houseboat after his meetings with Onalred. There was in her waiting a quality of dumb beastliness that was rather affecting: as though the body of her emotions were a camel being butchered, maintaining a silent, unprotesting, calm dignity through its suffering, its methodical dismemberment. And in her eyes were enigmatic camel thoughts: shame? pain? forgiveness? pity? pique?

She did ask one question, which he would never forget: "How did Allen Ginsberg put it? 'Who killed the pork chops?' "

Questions, of course, are remarks.

Now [4]

Stanhope recalls: the truth about Dokhma Koan . . .
his plan for Long Beach . . . Onalred's two mistakes . . .
Dasein, reading a literary quarterly.

Stanhope and Gongor stood knee-deep in industrial salt, staring out across the channel at the Koppel Tower, which made a nasty gesture at the sky. To protect his eyes against the salt glare, Gongor had donned sunglasses, and so his face was unreadable. "But," he said, "Dokhma Koan was a Chinese agent, wasn't he?"

"Yes," said Stanhope. "Traveling with a forged Sikkimese passport, posing as a cultural exchange student."

"Then," said Gongor, "*Queasiness* was just an elaborate cover?"

"Much more than that. Dokhma knew he would be in danger, that he might never leave Long Beach alive. *Queasiness* was a code. Dasein Camembert explained it to me in a general way. Apparently, the names of the automobiles referred to various Clausewitty tactical concepts. Of course, Dokhma's exploration of Long Beach was in the nature of a military scouting expedition; that's why he concentrated on the harbor area and the oil reservoirs. And he didn't actually listen to those music tapes; he recorded on them strategies appropriate to situations he had seen. The music tapes were coordinated with the locales."

"Onalred knew this?"

"Onalred found out about it only after he had killed Dokhma." There was bitterness in Stanhope's voice. "I gave Onalred the manuscript of *Queasiness,* because I thought it would amuse him. Later, when I asked for it back, he claimed he had lost it. Of course, he had destroyed it. He made two mistakes, though. The first was in underestimating Dokhma. Dokhma had mailed off a carbon copy of *Queasiness* to a New York literary quarterly, which published it in its Spring Existentialism Anniversary Issue. All Peking had to do was buy a copy of the quarterly.

"Onalred's second mistake was in not reading the notebooks carefully enough. If he had read them more carefully, he would have realized that the Aztec women bowlers were an information conduit for Dokhma. Realizing that, he might have asked himself the questions which could have saved *his* life. Dasein made the same mistake. Otherwise, we might never have been in the Ashram on Annihilation Night."

"How did Dasein get ahold of the manuscript, if Onalred destroyed it?"

"After I described the notebook, she bought a copy of the literary quarterly. The irony, of course, is that the quarterly was subsidized by the C.I.A."

Gongor was thoughtful. "Why would Onalred, an old pro, so underestimate another old pro?"

"Well," said Stanhope, "Onalred was tired. He had seen a lot and done a lot, and if there was one thing for which he had total contempt, it was romance—notwithstanding the snow job he did on me with his anecdotes of Indochina and Algeria. He knew the Chinese were terribly romantic about revolution; and so, because he was contemptuous of them, he underestimated them. Knowing Dokhma's plan for Long Beach, he found it impossible to take Dokhma seriously."

"What *was* Dokhma's plan for Long Beach?"

"It was to sabotage the fluids injection program. To pump air into the oil reservoirs until the City itself was floating on the sea. Then to tow the City one night out into international waters, throw a cordon of junks around it, and set up a puppet government. Then they would offer to exchange Long Beach for Quemoy and Matsu. If we refused, they would burn down the City, and set all the oil deposits aflame. Onalred, of course, was interested only in old-fashioned espionage. This was the kind of harebrained scheme that gave spies a bad name."

"He did, however, take Dokhma seriously enough to kill him."

"No. Those Onalred took seriously, he spied on. Killing was just domesticity for Onalred, a way of straightening up the spiritual house."

"And you worked for such a man?"

"He was my second guru, Gongor. And he handled me very effectively. He piled so much guilt on me that my spying on Otto seemed, for a while, clean by comparison. Of course, while he didn't underestimate *my* romantic tendencies, he did underestimate the mischief such tendencies were capable of creating. How did Trotsky put it? 'One can foresee a revolution or a war, but it is impossible to foresee the consequences of an autumn shooting trip for wild ducks.' "

Gongor brushed salt granules from his sheared French rabbit battle jacket. "You know, it's taking us a hell of a long time to get to Captain Happen."

"Yes," said Stanhope, still bitter. "A whole history of pain and death, to achieve one lousy psuedo-event. Are you ready to visit what remains of Gerontion Gardens?"

"Yeah," said Gongor. "Just let me take a couple more photographs."

Stanhope lit a cheroot . . . a fuse attached to the bomb of the past.

Then [4]

Stanhope chooses to act . . . the protest march of the angry octogenarians . . . Onalred reflects on the loneliness of terror . . . Bethesda in the bedroom, alack!

Pirogues tossed by the froth-mouthed sea; salt smells, and fish, and flowers, and garbage . . . sun-raped bodies sprawled on the beach as though a bomb had dropped among them, as though they were Susan Sontag waiting naked to be ravished by a work of art . . . little blind blue dogs lying in the shadow of the flood wall . . . the amniotic eyes of Onalred as he bit into a sambousik . . . Bethesda hipshot in aluminum halter and Jacaranda panties . . . Stanhope with last-laughter in his heart . . .

"I think," said Onalred, "that we are making the most effective use of you right now. Your anti-Salazar speeches at the University-by-the-Sea have excited considerable comment."

"But it's not nearly enough!" cried Stanhope. He thought of the reptilian old men basking in the sun at the Spit 'n' Argue Club. (He had never been able to reconcile himself to the change of name: to try by verbal fiat to transform that *Verfremdungseffekt* into a seminar for adult education seemed monstrous. And almost as absurd as calling the Pike "the Walk of One Thousand Lights.") He thought of the leathery faces of the old men; of the vigorous stropping those leather faces gave his words; of those who intercepted him afterward, pressing worn coins into his hands, trying to buy with those coins his belief that they had once been Wobblies. "It's just words!" he complained.

"But words are your racket," said Onalred. "You are an artist. The artist tries to *account* for suffering; the revolutionary tries to *diminish* it. I might add that to the revolutionary, the very serenity of art is a kind of insult. But we know it is useful. It helps to prepare a context in which we can operate more effectively."

"I want to operate, too; I am *sick* of words." He quoted from Mayakovsky's last poem:

> " 'But I
> mastered myself,
> and crushed underfoot
> the throat of my very own songs.' "

"A poem," said Onalred, "which Mayakovsky never finished, because he committed suicide. The ultimate *petit bourgeois* banality."

"Then let me finish that poem for him, with my *life!* I can, really I can! Didn't I write the poems for the protest march tonight? Please take me with you. I have at least the right to see how everything goes."

Onalred fingered his throat to soothe the flaming ascot there. His blue beret eyed the sky. "You understand that if you accompany me tonight, you are irrevocably committed. Objectively speaking, *tonight will last forever.*"

But *forever* is meaningless to the young, and a state of *being* to the Bealongchik, and Stanhope was both. Besides, wasn't violent action what he wanted? Wasn't the making of history a raping of nature? "I understand," he said.

Onalred tossed the remains of his sambousik to the circling gulls. "All right," he said. "You can come with me."

"Wizard!" said Stanhope.

"What about *me?*" said Bethesda.

"No," said Onalred. "You can wait for him on Cimarosa Street."

"But that's not *fair!*" cried Bethesda.

Onalred turned on her. "Your particular species of *sexuelle Hörigkeit* is not only dangerous, but unseemly. Your commitment is to *him; his* commitment must be to the historical process."

Bethesda burst into tears. "Mung bean," she said through them, "are you *sure?*"

Stanhope chucked her fondly under the chin. "How did Ingeborg Bachmann put it? *'Our Godhead, History, has tilled a tomb for us/ From which there is no resurrection.'* "

"Too right," said Onalred, and permitted himself to laugh at the gulls.

The gulls cried: *Bethesda, Bethesda.* The concrete Niobes on the flood wall wept into the sea. Onalred led them up the shelf-ridden haunches of the Niobes, to Ocean Boulevard, and the potted palm trees, and his Chrysler Imperial, and History . . .

That infamous night—

The pepperwood trees like Pekingese crouched in spiteful shagginess. The Chrysler Imperial nosed its way noiselessly among them, through the dark, toward the stone pillars and the sentry box and the source of the grinding music. "Silver Threads Among the Gold." Even at that distance, the din of the music was fearful; within the camp proper, it must have outraged the most resolute ossicles. Perhaps (thought Stanhope) the senior citizens were, already, mercifully, deaf.

Scriven in neon, impaled on the spear tips of the iron portcullis like a pulsing nerve, was the welcoming legend:

GERONTION GARDENS

They all shall wax old as a garment; the moth shall eat them up
(ISAIAH)

A guard jacked himself out of the sentry box and double-timed it over to the Imperial, waving a lantern. His uniform was black; his boots, belt, shoulder straps and steel-spiked casquetel were white. Laughing-gas grenades were hooked from the belt, and tucked into it was a nasty-looking kurbash of hippopotamus hide. He flashed the lantern over Onalred. "So it's you again. What's your racket, Mac?"

Onalred gave his unconvincing imitation of a smile. "This young man is thinking of stashing his mother away for the duration."

"The duration of what?"

"The duration of his mother, of course. I told him about your facilities, and he wanted to inspect them for himself."

The guard examined Stanhope. Stanhope examined the guard. There was on the guard's face that stamp of disinterested cruelty characteristic of drill instructors in orthopedic gyms. "Can you afford the fare?" he asked. "No free rides for the old fig-eaters here."

"Where my mother is concerned," said Stanhope, "I'm prepared to make any sacrifice."

"Yeah," said the guard, "beginning with your mother. Ha, ho, ha! Get it? I mean, she's your first sacrifice, right? Okey-dokey; no sense of humor. Well." He motioned with the lantern. "Pile out. You gotta be searched before I let you on the campgrounds. You can't smuggle in anything they might use to kill themselves."

Onalred limped from the Imperial, leaning on his cane. Stanhope came round the front to help him. The guard's frisk was perfunctory; he neglected the cane. They proceeded to the sentry box to fill out phony visitor registration cards.

"Actually," said the guard, "we don't get many visitors. Most of the traffic is the hearse, rolling in and out. Ho, ha, ho!"

The box was furnished in Spartan style: cot, card table, contour chair, console controlling arc lights and P.A. system, a *Gayboy* calendar, a copy of *The New York Review of Books* and a bottle of slivovitz. Clearly the man was a pro; but so was Onalred.

The guard handed Stanhope a selection of leaflets extolling the virtues of Gerontion Gardens' Stowaway Plan. In the first of these, air-reconnaissance photos disclosed the rectangular fortifications. Besides the entrance at one end, there were sentry boxes at each of the four corners. Within the fortifications was an oval ring of acacias. Within that ring of trees was the camp proper. At one end stood the Dry Salvages Recreation Hall; at the other, a parking lot for electric cars and wheelchairs. Between them ran a mall of elephant-colored sand, interrupted once by the whirlpool bath, and a second time by the mushroom garden. On one side of the mall was a shuffleboard court; on the other side, a croquet court. Running parallel to the courts were the bungalows, each painted a different primary color, each topped with terra-cotta tile.

A second leaflet moved inside the bungalows for a glimpse of the reed furniture, the grass rugs, the carafes of mineral water, the narrow bunks and modern plumbing. There were, in addition, photographs of the Dry Salvages pleasure dome: a pool table, a color TV set, a non-calorific cola machine and a chapel.

The third leaflet discussed the vigorous weekday schedule and the various weekend options. During the week, the day was divided into periods, like secondary school: clam juice, finger painting, shuffleboard, group therapy, mush, Esperanto, croquet, nap, whirlpool bath, veal cutlets, checkers, Bingo, television, jello, bed. On weekends, the senior citizens were allowed to play pool, eat figs, receive family, attend slide presentations and race their electric cars around the campgrounds.

Stanhope thought: We are children asleep in our own lives until the shadow of Death awakens us. Sad-making.

The guard pointed to an aerial photo of the parking lot and the electric cars. "We gotta lock up their batteries in the chapel at night. Otherwise, they go joy riding."

Onalred was examining the bottle of slivovitz. Now he clubbed the guard with it. Stanhope bound him with his belt and gagged him with his own kurbash. Onalred checked his Accutron: "Ten minutes to ten. At ten, they change the record, and play 'Auld Lang Syne.' All the senior citizens are supposed to be in bed by then. But not to-night! We've got ten minutes, Stanhope, to lock the other sentries into their boxes and open the gate."

Thanks to the repetitious roar of "Silver Threads" and two tubes of miracle epoxy, they were able to complete their mission in only eight minutes; they retreated then to the circle of acacias. Onalred squatted with his cane between his legs. Little lamps in the bungalow windows spread rings of light on the elephant-colored mall. In the acacias was a stitching sound: birds worriedly knitting sleeves for the naked branches of the trees. There suddenly emerged an old man with a face of yellow leaves. "Greetings, Leer," said Onalred. "All systems go?"

"Affirmative," said Leer.

Onalred unscrewed the tip of his cane. Activating a spring mechanism, he ejected half a dozen batteries. Leer caught them in the sling he had made of his Navaho shawl. Then, cradling the shawl, he stood for a moment in a ring of weak light, his transparent fingers fiddling with the yellow leaves of face. "Death to the glue factory," he whispered; then vanished.

"Silver Threads" unraveled themselves for the last time. "Auld Lang Syne" began. Onalred said: "Watch the doors of Dry Salvages. They've been hiding in there since jello."

"But," protested Stanhope, "the newspaper photographers haven't arrived. And the TV crews. You can't begin without the media. Didn't you tell them ten o'clock?"

"Shut up," said Onalred. "They don't matter." The long-since rinsing of "Auld Lang Syne" coughed off itself. Gerontion Gardens smoked a creepy-reekie silence.

Then into that silence crept a low tap-tapping; a deepening tom-tombo.

"Gubgubi drum," said Onalred. From a high blue window in a corner sentry box the head of a guard appeared, his casquetel spike a reproachful glinty eye. Asked the public address system: "Who's the chucklehead on the bongos? Turn it off!"

But the tom-tombo tapped on; and was joined presently by a plaintive reed instrument, a quaver of half-articulated loss, darting, dying, dopplering in the air of the night. In retaliation, the sentry put on Shirley Temple singing "The Good Ship Lollipop."

Momentarily, the cubed cuteness of Temple drowned gubgubi and reed. But no sooner had she slurped her sign-off ("God bless you, pleasant dreams, nightie-night") than the glum drum plumbed its hollow depths again. The acacias caught its mournful throb and pitched it whole into the night; dark raindrops of it plopped on terra-cotta tile. Then, with a sighing tattoo, it died.

"But the media," whispered Stanhope. "They'll make us do it all over again!"

"Be quiet," replied Onalred. Suddenly: the doors of Dry Salvages burst their hinges; the hall was ablaze with light. From one of the bungalows rose a hideous cackle. From another, steely lamentation. From the rest, that same smoky silence which had enticed the drum-beat moments before. And from Dry Salvages, a rattling voice, the sound of wire in a rusty scabbard, but carrying the length of the campgrounds and curling back upon itself: *"Dull heads in windy spaces . . . dry brains in a dry season . . ."*

P.A. SYSTEM:
"Cut the crap out there, you worm-meat! Who locked the doors?"

BUNGALOWS:
"Ho, ha, ho!"

From Dry Salvages, out of the hearth of light, emerged a procession of bent and ancient fogies, fire in their eyes, fire in their hands: in each pair of phthisic hands, a candle on a dish; over each pair of shoulders, a Navaho shawl; on each pair of feet, white tennis sneakers which were dazzling on the elephant-colored sand. A dotard-strut! A protest promenade of angry octogenarians! Louder the gubgubi; more piercing, the slit-throated reed. They paraded through the doors; they descended the porch steps in ceremonial pace; they marched down the mall toward the bungalows, their tapers flaring.

P.A. SYSTEM:
"Shame! Shame on you!"

But the procession persisted. At the prospect of the whirlpool bath, their file mitotically divided. By fanning about the turbulent waters of that pool, they multiplied their thumb-sized flames in its reflecting surface. Now a circle of dancing light turned within their advancing ring of flame. The overhanging sockets of the octogenarian eyes gulped at that broken flame: each senior citizen made himself a headless trunk, made his missing head a lamp. It was (thought Stanhope) like judgment day at the junk yard, a supreme court of abandoned automobiles.

BUNGALOWS (a keening):
  Virility: senility;
  Pubescence: putrescence.

At first, the rising whisper was confused with the stitching of the birds. But at length the chorus of marching octogenarians gathered fusty force, voiced itself above the deepening drum throb, sought and achieved coherence. Its singsong rendition of Stanhope's words was sinister; its trope and strophe cracked tragic in the fire-shot night:

VOICES OF THE PROCESSION:
  Cry how shall we cry
  Eyes dry can't cry.

BUNGALOWS:
  The canvas is rotten.
  The rigging's weak.
  The seams need calking.
  The strakes leak.

VOICES OF THE PROCESSION:
  Sequestered, we festered:
  Champions of Bingo, Out-Scouts of the Iowa Migrations,
    Pioneers of the Interior Moon,
      too soon marooned
    In the Order of Worms: Third Class
    (We are crabby; flesh is grass)
    And the Order of Sighing Scythes.
  Hear our cries!

BUNGALOWS:
  Usury . . . lust . . . power . . .
  Frenzy . . . folly . . . fear . . .

P.A. SYSTEM:
  Shame on you! Go to bed!

BUNGALOWS:
  Envy and sloth, avarice and lechery;
  Gluttony, jealousy, pride and treachery . . .

P.A. SYSTEM:
  Unless this undignified performance ceases immediately, Latin will be
  substituted for Esperanto in the afternoon language classes. A dead
  language for dirty old men. *Shame!*

VOICES OF THE PROCESSION:
  We have formed a committee
  To see that the jello is pretty;
  To ensure that no one rigs
  The apportionment of figs . . .

P.A. SYSTEM:
  Checkers is canceled for a week.

VOICES OF THE PROCESSION:
  To okay
  Croquet
  Matches. The catch is
  That this
    Committee keeps dying.
    (Here the sighing
    Of the scythe.
    Worm, writhe.
    Still alive
      for another morning cup of clam juice?)
  Don't count dry heads. What's the use?
  In our committee forum
  We can't maintain a quorum.

P.A. SYSTEM:
  Shame! Unspeakable shame!

VOICES OF THE PROCESSION:
  Impermanent Secretary, record this protest note:
  In the Democracy of Death, no one has a vote!

P.A. SYSTEM:
  Death? You said *that* word! *Irrevocable shame!*

BUNGALOWS:
  We hear voices
  But not choices:
  Evasions and accretions of evasions
  (Threatening to cut down on our rations!)
  Squanderings, black-geese honking islands of our squanderings
  (And black pirate flags we planted on our wanderings . . .)
  Pianos, live pianos plinking out our *please*
  (Lie-pianos—mouths full of false keys).

P.A. SYSTEM:
  Shuffleboard is hereby suspended for an indefinite probationary period.

BUNGALOWS (with the reed rising, the drum deepening):
  Do you see? Dare you risk?
  Colored halls, a golden disk.
  Subtle glass, powdery gold
  (Snakes have shields: not the old),
  Tigers, goats,
  Castles, moats,
  Doves with grenadine eyes.
  (A juridical flamingo flies
  By broken chimneys . . .
  Half-peeled hulls . . .
  And mulls the rusted iron
  On the Judah lion . . .)
  It is true: we're the zoo!

P.A. SYSTEM:
  No more finger painting! No more veal cutlets!

BUNGALOWS (the drums are almost deafening):
  Angels with wings of infinite rue
  Scatter brass particles of dew:
  Nether-weather . . .
  Now . . . forever . . .
  Bubbles in petroleum,
  Boils in linoleum;
  Wainscoting rips,
  Postnasal drips,
  Conceit and flabbiness,
  Deceit and shabbiness,
  Haste . . .
  Waste . . .   P.A. SYSTEM:
                                                   Shame!

BUNGALOWS:
Waste and . . .

P.A. SYSTEM:
Shame on . . .

BUNGALOWS:
. . . Void . . .

P.A. SYSTEM:
Shame on you!

BUNGALOWS:
Waste and Void . . .
Waste and Void . . .
WASTE AND VOID!

From each of the high blue windows in each of the sentry boxes in each of the four corners of the rectangular fortifications, guards chucked laughing-gas grenades. A desperate hilarity ensued. Several senior citizens giggled themselves to death.

Out of the acacias into the procession rushed yellow-leaved Leer, his bungalow mattress wrapped around a shuffleboard cue stick and bound with tennis sneaker laces. Snatching a taper from a guffaw-choked octogenarian, Leer ignited his five-foot torch. Swinging the torch on high, he cried: "Death to the Glue Factory!"

At that chilling signal five old men charged out of the mushroom garden with cue sticks and mattresses. Leer lit them into torches from his own; and the newcomers echoed his cry: "Death to the Glue Factory!" The protest parade was in violent disarray. Half its number lay on the mall, chortling. The others jostled one another, stuck their candles into each other's eyes. Three fell into the whirlpool bath; their lapsed dishes floated candle-up in the rippling currents of the water; the birds flapped nervously over the ludicrous mingling of laughter and lament. Leer deployed his men to the corners of the campgrounds and the helpless sentry boxes.

"Quick!" said Onalred. "To the gate! To the Chrysler Imperial."

"But won't the bungalows catch fire?" asked Stanhope.

Leer ran down the mall and threw his burning mattress-torch into the hall of Dry Salvages. "Death . . . *Death to the Glue Factory!*"

"The bungalows will burn," said Onalred, "and the sentry boxes, and the mushrooms, and the croquet court, and the chapel!"

"But—" Onalred seized Stanhope's elbow and slung him forward toward the gate. Stanhope staggered. Onalred whipped his buckling legs with the empty cane to urge him on. A flak of flame now blossomed from each bungalow and burst through each slab of terra-cotta tile. Grass rugs, reed furniture: quick combustion. From the crown of each acacia spat a sudden eructation, a spurt of flame, as though Bunsen burners gassed the sky. Now: rings and cataracts of fire, roaring through the bungalows, the sentry boxes, the Recreation Hall. A telescopic knot of flame foamed into the night, whirling, gasping . . . the cola machine exploded . . . the laughter ceased, and the screams of the burning began . . .

Among those screams, however—amid that great sucking, that voracious whoosh—a peculiar gathering whir, as of the wings of gigantic insects—

And out of the brilliant raging night plunged six electric cars . . . They purred through the iron gate and out into the pepperwood trees, demented jockeys riding them, phthisic hands at their helms.

"Close the gate!" shouted Onalred.

"But the rest of them—" said Stanhope.

"Close the gate, you dunderhead!" Between them they swung the iron gate shut; Onalred bolted it. They ran to the Chrysler Imperial. "Six batteries," Onalred explained. "I only provided batteries for my agents. The other electric cars are useless."

"But *why?*" cried Stanhope. Gold-feathered, fire-fangled birds leapt at and bloodied the moon. All was conflagration.

"With any luck at all," said Onalred, "the thing will spread to the Veterans Administration Hospital. *Shame,* don't you see? The rest of them might as well be dead. Only *my* men were willing to *act.* Objectively speaking, the rest are more *useful* dead. Their fiery demise is the objective fulfillment of the subjective desires of the community—don't you see? Because the community secretly wished for just such a death, its realization will confuse and embarrass the guilty. The community will hate itself a little bit more, and refuse all the more hysterically to acknowledge that self-hatred. If *only* the hospital gets it, too! *That* would be a dividend!"

"But I didn't realize—"

"Of course not. Because you've got the brain of an armadillo. This should teach you the *true* role of the revolutionary activist: not a poet, not an agitator, not even a warrior—but a *sacrificial priest!*" And Onalred kissed his thumbs.

Off they drove. And what was Onalred thinking, as he glanced into the rearview mirror at Stanhope slumped in the back seat: at the frightened face and the shadows of the torch-trees on that face? Had Onalred discovered in himself a post facto longing for brotherhood? Hadn't he learned over the years to be chary of that longing? Death always empties the giver of death, momentarily, like an act of love; and solitude walks in to occupy the vacant room; and, with solitude, a kind of gluttony: for affection and lichee nuts; for compassion and piroshki; for forgiveness and baba au rhum; for human generosity and jumbo shrimp. Murderers have the right to be gluttons. But Onalred probably knew, too, that that temporary slough of longing was a spawning ground of indiscretions; and that he must renounce it, all of it, except, perhaps, the jumbo shrimp. At the very most, a man like Onalred might accept disinterested understanding, were it offered. And, of course, disinterested understanding was precisely what he would never, could never, receive from Stanhope. Did he, at that moment, experience this bleak realization; and is that why he then spoke in anger . . . as it were, defensively? It would be a comfort to think so, but all this is just speculation. Onalred said: "Learn this lesson, and learn it well. For those I kill, I feel contempt. But I feel slightly *less* contempt for them than I do for those *who have never killed*. The great—the *only*—brotherhood is the brotherhood of killers."

Stanhope had succumbed to eructations of his own, all over the vinyl covers in the back seat of the Imperial. Onalred, pulling up in front of the house on Cimarosa Street, turned to grasp the young man's trembling shoulder. (Again, it is tempting to speculate—if it is true that we can only know others through the modifications we work on them, might there have been *that* motive in Onalred's implication of the poet in that night's nastiness? We shall never know.) "Get out. Your mother will give you an alibi."

Stanhope reeled up the walk to the orange door. Maud Cronopios opened it. "You've been sick," she said.

Thinking of the torch-trees, Stanhope answered: "I have a fever."

"Fevers," said Maud Cronopios, "are internal contradictions. Bethesda's waiting for you in the bedroom, no doubt palpitating with dread."

What right had *Mother* to be so contemptuous of him? He stiff-armed her aside, and ran down the hall to his room. Bethesda was caressing his Lions Club Speaking Contest trophy. "Oreo cookie!" she cried. "O, chocolate kiss!"

"Tootsie Roll," gasped Stanhope, "he . . . *he doesn't understand.* Murder . . . isn't murder merely the highest form of masturbation?

Isn't it the ultimate sublimation of self-hatred into self-lust? He doesn't even begin to understand!"

She led him to the bed. He fell, then rolled over. "He doesn't understand. I am not self-possessed—*I am self-relinquishing.*" The torches were still in his eyes, the crackling of dry heads in his ears. He shook himself, and sought desperately for saving signs somewhere in the bedroom. As usual, the bedroom failed him. No puce gloves, no green boots, no ashplant. The gloves he might cut from his mother's carpet . . . were he serious, had he scissors. He plucked buttercups from the bedquilt, full of pang. The secrets of his childhood—the tattered pack of Tarot cards, Hayek's *Road to Serfdom,* the purloined rosary (the scrotum-tightening See?)—seemed to rise from their cupboards and drawers, ghosts of the drowned, smugly to observe that they had warned him, they had told him so, the fault was his alone.

"It's too late, isn't it?" said Bethesda.

He wanted to sink his teeth into her neck: yes, *wisdom* teeth, serious incisors, scissors of hard thought, fangs of his culpability. He wanted to bedabble with blood her Jacaranda panties. But of course he couldn't. The guilt hang-up . . . He began to sob, watering the buttercups.

"Maybe it's always been too late," said Bethesda. "How did La Bruyère put it? 'We are born too late.'" She flung away her aluminum halter; it smashed the table lamp; darkness fell, and splinters of glass.

The glue factory wasn't dead, after all.

Now [5]

Stanhope tells Gongor the truth about himself . . . A visit to Pather Parturient . . . Parturient agrees to help Gongor . . . mutual remembering.

Gerontion Gardens had been surreal-estated, put in traction, subdivided, with cubes and plots, and was now a housing project called Wise Acres. Which displeased Gongor, since it made nonsense of his snapshots. He quoted: " 'The revolutionary activist as sacrificial priest. . .' But you told me Onalred was anti-romantic."

"He was," said Stanhope. "He was just setting me up for Otto. He knew I would never be a bomb-thrower or an assassin, except, of course, inadvertently. But after Gerontion Gardens, I was willing to infiltrate Otto's empire without a qualm. I would not be obliged to kill anybody—just steal certain important files. Onalred expected I would do an especially good job, to prove myself still capable of contributing something to the Cause, despite the fact that I was a coward. Poor Onalred! He just didn't realize the truth about me."

"What *is* the truth about you?" asked Gongor, not really caring.

"I am a mainliner on abstractions." Stanhope gazed out over the plane geometry of Wise Acres and sighed. "I think we should look up Parturient now," he said at last. "He can fill you in on Otto better than I can. After all, he tried to kill Otto. Perhaps he did kill him. That's one more thing we'll never know."

"Where do we find Parturient?"

"At the harbor."

Hair a tarnished silver cup hammered down around the ears; glittering eyes as green as the shields on a housefly's back; caterpillar-writhing of the scraggly brows; syringe-stitching of the avenous fingers; hint of ironic weariness in the cold-blasted desert of a face (the face of a desolate lunar sea, a moonscape of memory and therefore of death); fissure of cynical smile in the crust—Pather Parturient said: "Howdy."

"How is it," asked Stanhope, "that you don't have a tan?"

"Hard work and dedication," said Parturient. "Principles. Long-sleeved shirts and my captain's cap." He motioned them to sit down aft in the Shearwater cruise boat.

"Business good?" said Stanhope.

"Very," said Parturient. "Sahasrara's down below. She's my secret weapon. I give her a man's shirt to put on each morning, then wash her down with a salt-water shower and chain her to the rail. The tourists trample over me to get aboard. They see very little of the harbor on our cruise; but they see quite a lot of the finest female body in Long Beach. It's a good life, Cronopios."

"Have the police been bothering you? I mean, since they let off Gnatpappa?"

"No," said Parturient. "They're probably still trying to figure it out. But if the case *is* reopened . . . well, Sahasrara and I just won't come back from one of our tours. Baja California would be nice."

Stanhope explained Gongor's purpose. When he had finished, Parturient was agreeable: "Sure, I'll tell you what I know. Those TV people irritated me. They came down to interview me for the documentary, and did nothing but shoot thousands of feet of Sahasrara in her wet shirt. Where do you want me to begin?"

"Well," said Stanhope, "we're trying to keep it pretty much in chronological order. Why not start with the afternoon I had my job interview with Otto? You might also describe the Pyramid for Gongor, since he's never seen it, and now it's gone."

"Good-o," said Pather Parturient, and lit up his Afghan hookah pipe.

Then [5]

Description of the Pyramid . . . introduction to Otto and the Tyranny of the Eye . . . Gnatpappa brings kvass . . . Stanhope is offered a job . . . Stanhope and Parturient leave for Vaseline Ali's.

Media, Rare & Well-done occupied a pyramid at the corner of Clark and Willow Streets, on the site of an abandoned Nike missile base, in Long Beach. The pyramidal form was purposeful. It followed triangular lines of dynamic force. It shouted its tactile kinetic energy. It was an umbrella of Einsteinian curves, repudiating the enclosed-space concept of the cube—that sweatbox of diagonally anchored walls, that self-regarding obsessive abstraction of space properties from manifest tensions.

Before each shimmering fact of the Pyramid was . . . well, an *Object,* relentlessly modulating space in an attempt to translate the world within the Pyramid to the world outside. One such happening seemed a representation in barbed wire of an odd group of disconsolate polymorphs, uncertain how to copulate. Another, a slab of tile unimpeachably exempt from the contingent and the accidental, had been wrenched from context (a bus station lavatory) and stood with its graffiti brazen, above a plot of poppies. Before the third facet sprawled a calamitous gravure, as of the weighty defecations of expiring mastodons, the color of cuttlefish sepia.

Inside the Pyramid, its ribs and buttresses and battlements, its naked frames and fretwork, exhibited themselves wantonly. That, too, was deliberate. The Pyramid analyzed and explained itself, clarified its form, recapitulated its own thought processes.

On an ordinary working day at Media, Rare & Well-done, trapped in the distorting prisms of polyester brick, sunbeams twisted and writhed: light *through,* not *on* (like an illuminated medieval manuscript or a television image). Light was an active principle. Those plasticities through which it filtered (merging and permeating) were transfigured by it; inasmuch as they partook of light, they were defined, and insofar as they had been defined, they were apprehensible. There is considerably more, you see, to resin derivatives than dreamt of by Norman Mailer's urea. Plastics are the tears of God: instant Gothic.

On an ordinary working day, trapped in their windowless singing booths, the account executives of Media, Rare & Well-done also twist and writhe. Cf. Pather Parturient.

"The hand," said Otto Unamuno, "cannot perceive configuration, can it, without the help of the eye? But it *can* perceive number. Tactility could be said to be the basis of mathematics." His hand in lateral undulations slid across the cool tiles of the table top: now a mouth, sucking on the sheen; now a clutch of quivering antenna-wires, listening; now a wheel of centipedes, creeping over Cronopios' knuckles, nosing at the veins in his wrist. "Perhaps *touch* is the very *life* of *things* in the *mind*."

Well, the old three-wheeled bore was off and rolling again. Pather tried to catch Gnatpappa's eye, but the aborigine, in the corner, was absorbed in reading Milman Parry's pioneering treatise on the oral character of Yugoslav epic poetry. Pather said: "Many things in life may cause the mind to be touched, but aren't those qualities unknown which may be touched but not figured, pro or con? Mightn't we say that *things* have the *life* which *mind* temporarily borrows by touching them? The difference is between the Rilkean *Dinge* and the galvanometric hang-up. Or, putting it another way—"

"Shut up," said Otto. Otto was the Teutonic dwarf incarnate: flower of parricide, snipped and shaped from a grub on the rotting corpse of the giant Ymir. Eyes plucked out and hung on the Yggdrasill ash tree. Skull gleaming through the parchment-colored skin. Icy gem-knots of neck musculature blue, remorseless. Veins, too, steel-blue, steel-cool with the flow of Hvergelmirian fountain water.

Cronopios was staring with a puzzled frown at the wall behind Otto, on which swirled feverish abstractions, breathing jelly masses, riotous bacilli. Pather enlightened him: "You are looking at the art work of a computer, Mr. Cronopios."

Otto smiled at nothing. "Does it surprise you? It shouldn't. What is abstract art but human thought processes as they might be rendered in computer designs?"

"What," said Pather, grinning at Cronopios, "are human thought processes but computer designs as they might be rendered by abstract artists?"

Otto's mouth worked woundedly. "Jaspers has written," he said, "that the ultimate in thinking, as in communication, is silence. It is a homily grit you would do well to chew some on, Parturient. The tongue tends to wag the man."

And you, thought Pather, are all tongue; no man.

"I should like," said Otto, "to caution you at the outset, Mr. Cronopios. Our experience with poets has been generally unhappy. Their arrogance is stupefying. They consider themselves machines for dispensing autonomous art; witch doctors of the *spiritus mundi;* sole transmitters of a mysterious system of correspondences that only become apparent in *their* poems. They arrive at the Pyramid in a holy snit. The American public has been rudely indifferent to their transmissions, systems, autonomies. They are bitter. They hope through our powerful offices to revenge themselves on the public, to use their rejected talents to manipulate the very audience which has judged them spiceless. They are determined to sell garbage to an audience they imagine as passive and brutish. The worse the product, the greater their delight in promoting it.

"Passive and brutish that audience may be, Mr. Cronopios—*at present*. But *our* intention is to abolish that passivity, that neutral reception and mindless consumption of words, dreams, fantasies and foodstuffs. Our intention is to substitute an almost medieval corporate experience of participation and commitment, based on the electrical collective awareness our new media are creating." Otto sighed, as though disheartened by the mountainous size of the explanation he must scale, its sheer and slippery faces. Pather sighed too, having to listen to it again. "True, Mr. Cronopios, we are hired by the great industrial combines to huckster their pap and games. We are not, however, the least bit interested in the 'explicit content' or the 'private message' they pay us to push. We *are* interested in the media *themselves*—those so-called 'vehicles' which are invisibly busy, subliminally reshaping social and psychological and production processes even as we talk; which are profoundly altering the whole time-space experience of Western man, even as spoiled poets squeeze symbols from their snits. I am usually obliged to sack the spoiled poets, and they scuttle back to the pedagogic trough to lecture college girls on 'the commercialization of the libido.' They have completely missed the point."

Otto's black plastic shades seemed to be looking for the point on the ceiling. "What, then, is the point? To grasp it, we must return to the beginnings of Western civilization. We must examine the history of man's development of tools, the extensions of his sensory apparatus, the outerings of his body organs. The wheel, for example, is an imitation of the feet in the circular motion of running; the house is an outering of the skin; the weapon is an outering of the hand—"

"The latrine," said Pather, "is an outering of the digestive tract."

Otto's hands trembled, then embraced, and were deposited in his lap, where they lay like little furless pets. "But we cannot always foresee and control the consequences of our extensions, Mr. Cronopios. Obviously, a wheel, a weapon, a house have immense and varied consequences, requiring changes of scale and pace in our lives, adjustments of social and psychological patterns to accommodate new objective facts, new relationships; requiring, as well, alterations of sense ratios. If we can define a *medium* as something which *moves information,* then we must understand the extensions of man as media, mustn't we? We must. For each extension is a system of its own, moving psychological information, opening up some possibilities, closing down others."

Pather said: "As Marshall McLuhan has so trenchantly observed, without the light bulb could there be night baseball?"

Otto hissed: "A closed mouth gathers no feet, Parturient!" He subsided once more in his wheelchair: "But where there is extension, Mr. Cronopios, there is *danger.* The danger of exaggeration, of distortion. I give you the obvious distortion of Los Angeles, a city constructed not to accommodate Man, but an extension of Man: the automobile. This is the point: we in the West have lived through several thousand years of a distortion more horrifying even than Los Angeles. I refer to . . . the Tyranny of the Eye!"

Pather employed a rubber band to sling paper clips at Gnatpappa. Gnatpappa, without looking up from Milman Parry, gave Pather the finger. Cronopios was absorbed—another fall guy.

"What is it which we at Media, Rare & Well-done believe?" asked Otto. "We believe that Western man from a primitive synesthetic grace (or Wholeness) fell into Syntax. What do we mean by Wholeness? We mean a haptic harmony of the senses, a balanced interplay of all the senses in the community (or 'field') that is the *mind.* What do we mean by the 'fall into Syntax'? We mean that *language,* the closest approximation of the harmony and balanced interplay of the community of senses, was twisted and distorted into the phonetic alphabet. That meaning was abstracted from *sound,* that sound was translated into a *visual* code, that the cold, egotistical, omnivorous and onanistic *Eye* took over! Reality was transferred from the perception—the *object*—to the verbal formula. The verbal formula was happily and exactly repeatable; it seemed *permanent.* Essence, then, became *manageable,* because it was no longer part of the object, but instead a part of the object's *definition.* Through the 'medium' of the phonetic alphabet—the extension and exaggeration of the visual component in the life of the mind—the mechanical principles of abstraction and repetition emerged into explicit form. So for the *biological unity* of the tribal society, we substituted abstract relations—like exchange and co-operation. And so for the African world of *sound*—in which each sound has a direct personal significance for whoever hears it—we substituted a world of visual facts, facts which were indifferent to whoever saw them. Euclidean space, chronological narrative, artistic perspective, Newtonian mechanics, capitalist economics, and a host of other schematic lies trooped in and took over."

Otto's voice grew softer. "But, Mr. Cronopios, there were a couple of hookers . . . adders in the satin bed of Western complacency. Hook-and-adder number one is psychological: dislocation, hypnosis, which is, isn't it, the filling of the field of attention by one sense only? It is. Meaningless signs attached to meaningless sounds; separation of senses, of functions, of operations, of emotional and political states—mind *and* matter, reason *and* feeling, subject *and* object, cause *and* effect, work *and* leisure! Instead of the Whole, and the Role in the Whole of the One and the Many, the Flow of the Roles in the Modes of the Whole, we are individuated, fragmented, schizophrenic, and *Angst*-ridden. *We have sold our Gestalt for a mess of dualities!"*

"Not bad," said Pather. "First new phrase in six lectures."

"Hook-and-adder number two," said Otto, "is philosophical. The very linear order in which we are obliged to use words results in what McLuhan has called 'a syntactical time-order analysis of qualities.' A *lie.* Why a lie? Because qualities aren't arranged in a time-order, are they? They are not. They are simultaneous and interrelated. It is not philosophically permissible to break a unity into its components, its so-called 'distinguishable qualities'—it becomes no more than a scrap pile of abstractions. *Description* is just a grocery list of theoretical ingredients!" Otto gestured, affecting resignation. "Then, of course, there was Gutenberg's sellout to the Eye-Lie. The printing press raised the phonetic alphabet to its highest degree of visual intensity. With the invention of movable type, the few remaining pockets of resistance to the Tyranny of the Eye were wiped out. The Eye extended itself to Omnipresence, and—and the Garden of Haptic Harmony was dead."

Pather pantomimed the stifling of a sob. Cronopios pretended not to notice. Otto leaned forward and suddenly snatched the shades from his face: the enflamed and empty sockets, where his eyes had been, sucked all the air from the room. "But the ballgame wasn't over, Mr. Cronopios! A motley collection of guerrilla warriors began a century ago their sneak attack on the Tyranny of the Eye. We are now engaged in a great War of Liberation to free the vassal senses. The artist since Cézanne has been recovering the powerful tactile achievements of early Etruscan cave painters—by rendering objects not as he *sees* them, but as he *feels* them. The physicist since Maxwell—ah, tell him about the physicists, Parturient. That's the only reason I put up with you."

Pather shrugged. "How did Maxwell put it? 'Light consists in the traverse undulations of the same medium which is the cause of electric and magnetic phenomena.' "

Otto said: "Translate that."

"Light propagates itself in space at a constant velocity. That constant is the same as the constant relating fundamental electric and magnetic units."

"Which means?"

"Light is an electromagnetic wave."

"Good. And Einstein?"

"Einstein presided over the marriage of Maxwell's equation to the fact that the velocity of light is independent of the source which emits that light. Shortly after the wedding, they gave birth to an infinite role—"

Cronopios, astonishingly, interrupted, saying:

> "Then Light is traveling so fast
> That it can never be surpassed!"

"Obvious, but apt," said Otto. Then, to Pather: "What does this mean to *us?*"

"That it's impossible to form absolute judgments of simultaneity at distant points."

"And what happens to every traditional conception of space and time in the confrontation with that impossibility?"

"They cease to be relevant."

"And what happens to the egotism of Perspective, the Self-aggrandizement of the Eye?"

"It is dealt a philosophical deathblow."

Otto (well pleased): "And Bohr?"

"The Bohr war on inscrutable atomicity! Bohr and his excited gases! Alas, there were quanta in Copenhagen. There seemed to be quanta everywhere, even in the physical instruments in Bohr's laboratory."

Otto (excited by this gas): "Which means?"

"That what Oppenheimer has called 'the ineluctable element of chance'—surely there must be a Sanskrit word for it?—entered into atomic physics, because of the very laws of physics. How could you go about studying atomic structure while there was a constant traffic going on between the atoms in your study specimen *and* the atoms in your instruments *and* the atoms in *you?* When you test a situation, you alter the situation. Sad-making."

Otto: "The instruments themselves are suspect. All is relationship; all is flux. It is impossible to be objective. Nothing is permanent. Permanence never existed. Objectivity is dead. There is no unchanging element in nature to offset the element of chance: not a particle which has not been altered and is not now being altered yet again!"

Pather (tossing sirloin to a famished dog): "Physicists were obliged to abandon the concept of individuality . . . in favor of statistically fluctuating mutual interpretations."

Otto: "Yes! Yes! And *that* is how the senses operate in the community of the mind . . . fluctuating mutual interpretations!"

Pather (winking at Cronopios): "And from out of the sea of this speculative physics, a surfer comes riding the electromagnetic wave. Why, it's . . . General Sarnoff!"

Otto (spinning in his wheelchair): "Yes! Yes! Yes! The electronics engineer! The new electrical media *abolish* sequence by introducing the instantaneous! They extend the whole central nervous system to encompass the globe! Via electrical dilation of *all* our senses, we are creating a cosmic membrane, a deChardinian noosphere, a simultaneity of stimulus and response, a collectivity of awareness! Electricity requires *commitment* and *participation,* not indifference and detachment . . . the Whole instead of Explictiness! Unity instead of Individuation! Resonance! Harmony! Flux! Flow!"

Pather: "Advertising and television—"

Otto: "—are turning the world into one vast tribe, a global village, a biologicoelectrical bag! And they are only the first faltering steps in the infancy of Electrical Man! Someday—we shall live to feel it!—an electric simulation of *consciousness* will, by generating a kind of massive extrasensory perception, enable us to *bypass speech itself!*"

Pather: "And Whole Being Sprouts will spring in the Garden of Haptic Harmony."

Otto: "Too right!" He thrust out his hands for Pather to grasp. "Vision is Neutral! Audition is passionate!"

Pather: "The Mind is a Möbius Loop."

Otto: "The Ear is the Organ of the Whole; the Eye is the Organ of Cupidity!"

Pather: "The Ideogram is a Gestalt; the Advertisement is an Ideogram."

Otto: "There is no such thing as Change; there are only Simultaneous Relationships!"

Pather: "Is the medium the message?"

Otto: *"Yes,* the medium is the message."

Together (rising, four-limbed, twenty-fingered, bliss-pricked): "The Medium is the Message! The Medium is the Message! *THE MEDIUM IS THE MESSAGE!*"

Pather helped Otto back into his wheelchair. Otto, panting, gestured: "Gnatpappa—fetch us some kvass." The abo abandoned his methodical paper-rape of Milman Parry, to shuffle disgustedly from the room in woolen shoes. Otto coughed, and gulped.

"So," he said. "So, now, Mr. Cronopios, you . . . you grasp our intuition into the nature of the electrical media. If so, you glimpse our *true* function, which is to encourage and control the coming revolution with those media. The question then arises: what do you think that *you,* as a *poet,* can do for *us?*"

"Well," said Cronopios, and crossed his legs as though to gain a scissor hold on the scruffy neck of thought, "the job of the poet is, isn't it, to restore the, ah, primitive *wholeness* of apprehension? I mean, language wasn't originally concrete. For example, *spiritus* didn't originally mean just 'breath' and then by metaphoric manipulation come to represent the abstract 'principle of life.' There was a single *primitive* meaning in which both the abstract and the concrete were united, were held in the mind *simultaneously*. 'Breath' and 'principle of life' were *one and the same thing,* if you follow me."

"I do not follow you," said Otto. "I was already there. You are decades behind me."

"I mean," said Cronopios, "that poetry seeks symbolic representations in which the concrete and the abstract are *not* dissociated. The poet, ah, *struggles to unify.*"

"A vulgar formulation," said Otto, "but let us for the moment deem it adequate. Your understanding of your function is not altogether inconsistent with our understanding of our purpose. But why did you come *here?* What can you *give* us?"

Cronopios beamed sincerity. "All my poetic life," he said, "I've searched for that paradox-resolving symbol which could accommodate the apparently irreconcilable processes of technology and psychology. Now, I think I've found it. I think *you* will approve."

Otto was silent and interested. Pather mentally congratulated Cronopios: Otto was very seldom silent, and almost never interested in other people.

"Shall I tell you," said Cronopios, lowering his voice, "of my dream, my vision? It is a vision of images, each a lens, each a jewel: each lens, each jewel, each image a mirror in a corridor of mirrors, ruby-facets hung in a dark hall, hung in silence, waiting. I see seep into that corridor a wave of frequency. I see it sweep over the mirrors. I see it summon from the jewels an explosion, a sunburst, a crystal pulse of coherent optical radiation. Electrons jump the energy gap! A positive feedback loop achieves and sustains the oscillation, the pulsing, the self-feeding sunburst of the jewels! I see *light* rescued from the chaos of individually radiating oscillators, uncontrolled emissions: *I see light made coherent!* Surely an achievement worthy of a poet's song!"

"The laser beam," whispered Otto, moved. *"Ein Schauspiel nur."*

"Too right," said Cronopios. "You see: what I have to offer you is *enthusiasm!* The laser beam, with all its contradictions: *light* as a powerful surgical tool, able to peel away the brain as though it were a pomegranate, to expose the naked cell-seeds. *Light* as a *destructive* force, capable of incinerating armies. And, most important, *light as a medium of information!"* He touched fingertips to temples, soothing throb. "I attended Mr. Parturient's lecture at the College, when he discussed the work of your client, Emissions Unlimited. When I could grasp the idea that light could be thickened and modulated, like radio waves; that it could convey a density of data equivalent to all the information moved by all the combined radio and TV channels in America; and that it was capable of communicating that data almost instantaneously—at the *speed* of *light*—then I knew I had to seek you out. For by helping to promote the work of Emissions Unlimited, I would at the same time be exploring the possibilities of my vision. For they are, are they not, testing a *psychological* relativity principle? Closing the curve of our metaphysical speculations? Woofing at the warp of time and mind? Peering into the very bowels of matter? *And they are doing it all with mirrors!*"

Pather couldn't stand it any longer. "One part hoo-hah, three parts glup," he said. "Unfortunately for your conceit, Cronopios, the best sort of amplifying agent for communications purposes is the helium-neon *gas* laser. No mirrors! No rubies! A discharge tube instead of a corridor of jewels! How disappointing; how oppressively excremental! To peer into the bowels of matter, I mean, and get a helium fart in the face!"

Cronopios sat back, looking crushed. "Parturient," says Otto, "believes that pure crudity has the same breathless, ruthless quality of returning to essentials as does pure abstraction. The less able he is to handle abstractions, the more he resorts to crudity." A grisly death's-head smile flowered on his face: he had an idea. To Pather, he said: "Your Emissions Unlimited copy, of late, has been *all* gas and *no* light. Mr. Cronopios, being a poet, might even be able to write. I think I'll hire him. I think I'll assign him to assist you on that account. Yes: I think that's exactly what I'll do."

Gnatpappa reappeared, bearing demitasse cups of kvass. They drank in silence. The kvass, as usual, tasted as though it had been used to clean old paintbrushes. Otto, however, made a show of savoring his: the distillation of his triumph over Pather. Smacking his lips. "Parturient will familiarize you with the Emissions account, Mr. Cronopios. I regret I must leave. I've an appointment at the Ashram. Svam Spade and Sahasrara Cannibis have organized a gang-bhang, and I promised to listen. Gnatpappa?"

The aborigine propelled Otto's wheelchair out of his office. Staring after them, Pather lit a sausage-shaped cheroot. "The Black Body," he remarked.

Cronopios failed to understand. "Gnatpappa, you mean?"

"Not Gnatty; *Otto*. After your masterful exposition on the nature of laser light, I am surprised you don't know the meaning of the term. A 'black body' is a perfect radiator or absorber of energy. Otto has even managed to absorb Sahasrara!" Cronopios looked hurt. "Cheer up," said Pather. "I only attacked you because I knew that would make Otto hire you. I didn't want to see all your homework go to waste." He grinned.

Cronopios avoided the grin. "What was all that about the Ashram?" he asked.

"St. Teresa's Little Ashram of Ecumenical Oṁ. Otto owns it."

"But—what does that collection of pill-eaters and cop-outs have to do with all of *this?*" By the loop of his hand he seemed to be trying to lasso it: alphabets, emissions. So, thought Pather, the poet has opinions!

"Listen, Cronopios: what do we mean when we say 'rational'? We mean that which is uniform, continuous and sequential. But Otto considers uniformity, continuity and sequence artificial constructs of print-culture. So he is attracted to and interested in whatever attacks those constructs—whatever is manifestly *irrational*. It's much easier to *sponsor* irrationalities than to go looking for them. So Otto owns the Ashram, and a left-wing literary quarterly, and a right-wing private army, and a craft union of Fraternal Philologists, Order of Paradigm-Swotting, and an organization of female novelists for the promotion of *coitus reservatus* and our Vietnam policy. And, now, a *poet*."

"What about physicists? What about *you?*"

"Ah, me! Well, I am, am I not, a Child of Light? Otto thickens me, and I become massive in the wallet. Cronopios, are you going to be congenial? I mean, if I were to suggest our adjournment for a quick snort of something more potable than kvass, could you reconcile it with poetry and the laser beam? Do you drink in the afternoon?"

"So long as someone else's massive wallet pays for it; my wallet is a wraith."

"Done," said Pather, and bowed him to the door. They went to Vaseline Ali's; and there—by the rotting silver waters of the Colorado Lagoon, among housewives in hairnets and cub scouts threatening each other's throats with corkscrews—exchanged lies.

Now [6]

*Stanhope and Parturient reconstruct their conversation . . .
the present whereabouts of Svam . . . how Otto made his
money . . . Sahasrara shows herself . . . psychocatalysis as a
tool for literary criticism.*

"I was preoccupied during that conversation," said Stanhope. "For
one thing, I had been greatly impressed by Otto's argument. For
another, it made me uncomfortable to be in Vaseline Ali's, sitting
perhaps in the very booth where Onalred had introduced himself to
me and Bethesda the night my mother never showed up from her
bowling tournament."

"And I," said Parturient, "was preoccupied because I was already weighing alternative solutions to the Otto problem. Do you
know, Cronopios, I think all your blathering about lasers first put
that idea in my head? The whole thing might never have happened."

Stanhope disagreed. "Arbiter Aidos used to say: it is a waste of
time to worry about the future; it will always succeed in creating
an appropriate past."

"Sahasrara!" shouted Parturient. "Bring up some pisco sours and
a bowl of cheese puffs! Let's see. As I recall, I talked about Vaseline
Ali's. About how I preferred it in the afternoon, because at night
the art theater down the street flushed itself every two hours, and
savage children appeared suddenly from its exits, in the alleyway,
with zip guns in their hands. Have you seen those children, Gongor?
A terrible, neon-hard, single-faceted moral insensibility is reflected
in their faces. They're the faces that will stare back at you, in coma-
languor, from tomorrow morning's newspaper, after some outrage.
I told Cronopios I thought it must be an effect of the art movies;
the hoodlets come out thinking of themselves as Italian anti-heroes,
with a lighted cigar for a penis. He did not agree. *He* thought it an
effect of Long Beach, not art movies . . . one more inevitable ex-

pression of the generalized Bealongchik *Dämmerschlaf*—is how I believe he put it."

Sahasrara, in wet shirt, appeared with the pitcher of piscos. Gongor, whose interest had obviously been lagging, began to twitch. Sahasrara's body was of the sort that all men must believe they will someday have the opportunity to possess; otherwise they would curse God and flush themselves down the toilet. Gongor removed his shades.

"Does Sahasrara never see Svam any more?" asked Stanhope.

"Never," replied Parturient. "Of course, Svam was never a man to her; merely a companion, a sort of portable *I Ching,* and therefore perfectly safe. Had Svam been a man, they would never have split over something as meaningless as a philosophical contradiction. I suppose she might like to see him again—a first guru must be almost as unforgettable as a first love—but Svam himself has made such a meeting impossible."

"How so?"

"By becoming public relations director of the Iowa State Picnic. Sahasrara would never go there. There are old people there, and that reminds her that there is an end to youth; that the body decays; that the capacity for pleasure will ultimately diminish. She is, you might say, scared to death of death. Although I supposedly won her because of my acceptance of death." He snapped his fingers to regain the attention of Gongor. "To resume our reconstruction—I tried in that conversation with Cronopios to warn him about Otto. Obliquely, of course. But Otto *was* an evil man. As I told Cronopios, Otto made his fortune with what he called 'Invigorators.' A clever reversal of the old German *Onaniebandagen,* those little armor-metal corsets they used to strap over the genitals of young boys to keep them from masturbating. Otto developed the exact opposite: electrical devices for stimulating the sexual muscles. Fully adjustable, he used to advertise: from slightly pulsating tickles to muscle-jerking throbs. In the privacy of your own home, to the privacy of your own parts, apply the Unamuno Invigorator. See the nerve twitch, the muscle jump, the tissue swell! At first, he marketed only two basic types, the Invigorator Rod and the Invigorator Pad. The rod was mainly for loners. The pad could be used by two people at the same time. Later, he got fancy and diversified his line. A battery-operated jockstrap . . . a plug-in gopher hole . . . a Group Invigorator for cocktail parties and Kiwanis luncheons, like those automatic milking machines you see on modern farms . . . Anyway, he made his pile. And he and Gnatty were whipping up new models right to the very end. I counted on that, you see." He sucked on his sour. "My purpose in telling Cronopios nasty things about Otto was to break the prophetic spell Otto seemed to have cast over him. I didn't know Childe Harold of the Hang-ups too well, then; and hadn't yet realized that he preferred to mortify himself in any old cathedral of beautiful lies, rather than to live in a rude little hut with his very own rude little truths."

"I don't think Otto was really an *evil* man," said Stanhope.

"Then you are in a minority," said Parturient. "Svam Spade thought he was evil. So did Gnatpappa. So, as a matter of fact, did your mother."

"Is misapprehension a valid form of moral judgment?" said Stanhope. "They all misapprehended Otto. Svam thought Otto had sold out to Karl Jaspers. Gnatpappa, no doubt poisoned by the polemics of the Pigstickers of Islam, failed to understand Otto's *real* purpose. And my mother—well, she never understood anybody, not even me." He watched the gulls make scarves in the air. "I don't suppose it matters any more, does it?"

"It doesn't," said Parturient. "Cronopios broke up our conversation shortly thereafter. I was telling him about my psychocatalyst; I had to make my weekly visit to him that afternoon. The psychocatalyst was trying to figure out why I could no longer manipulate mathematical symbols. He was actually a specialist in writers, not physicists. I asked Cronopios what he, as a poet, thought of explaining Dante, Goethe and Shakespeare in terms of castration complex, paranoia and masochistic cyclothymia."

"And I," said Stanhope, "replied that I tried not to think about it at all. Why isn't every masochist or paranoid a Dante or a Shakespeare? The trouble with psychoanalyzing literature is that you've got to say pretty much the same thing about works of mediocrity as you say about works of genius. All artists are sick, like people. Without an intuition into excellence, you are saying nothing about the only interesting problem: why one makes great art out of his sickness, and another makes *Tiny Alice*. Do you agree, Gongor?" But Gongor was watching Sahasrara sun herself, envying the sun.

"Then," said Parturient, "Cronopios stood up and said it might be a good idea if he went back to the Pyramid and familiarized himself with the files of Emissions Unlimited. That annoyed me. I told him to go familiarize himself; and that during the night no doubt brilliant new ideas would occur to him: nocturnal emissions. I told him to come back when he had a little less time to spare."

"Actually," said Stanhope, "I left because, as usual, I was feeling guilty." He thought back to the small crisis of conscience that had come over him in Vaseline Ali's. He had begun to sniffle, and had wondered whether the conditioned air of the bar were to blame; or whether, alternatively, the sinuses of History were dilating. On excusing himself and walking out of the conditioned air, onto the asphalt parking lot, he had felt hopelessly compromised. Around him, dung-colored towers of adobe drooped. At and past him swung pantophagists on skateboards, professional Lagoonies blind under their bleached eyebrows, their prosthetic limbs cleaved seamlessly from bronze lava. Smoke rose behind the adobe, anguillous from Los Angeles. The Lagoonies had trundled on toward the water and the flat-bellied sun-basted beach girls with the nipples like erasers. The afternoon and the asphalt and the sky (which was, after all, only an elephantiasis of asphalt) had oppressed him mightily. And his questions, like the scallop-trails of smog-smoke, curved around an incompletion, embracing vast emptinesses. He had asked himself: *Was war wirklich im All?* And then, feeling a desperate need for Bethesda, had rushed to Cimarosa Street.

"Do I get to tell about my visit to the psychocatalyst?" said Parturient. "After all, if he hadn't failed me (*did* he fail me?) I might not have done what I did. So it's significant, isn't it?"

"I only wonder," said Stanhope, "that if we decide too many things are significant, we won't have dispersed the guilt so completely that only small, invisible particles might be left to attach to anyone. And then everybody will be guilty, which is anti-climactic."

"Oh, come on!" said Parturient. "Gongor's happy sitting there, hurling fantasies of violation at my wife. It's not fair, Cronopios, that you should get to do *all* the remembering, is it?"

"I suppose not," said Stanhope. Perhaps, after all, that was his role: to be a philanthropist of his own past . . .

Then [6]

Parturient learns that he's out of context.

Parturient: climbing out of his baby blue Alfa-Romeo, doffing his Tyrolean hat, snorkeling the air. (There was about the air a smell of kelp and iodine.) Parturient: in moccasins slipping through the topiary hedges to the electrically revolving door of the office building. (There was about the building that indefinable infirmity of the New.) Parturient: shafted by the elevator, charged prickly by the carpet, using Langweil's receptionist as a lightning rod. (There was about the receptionist that curious disarray of face and form, that resigned fanaticism which afflicts the women of Long Beach in their middle years.) Parturient: assured by the receptionist that Langweil would be with him shortly, settling himself on the sofa to peruse a copy of *Omphalos*. (There was in *Omphalos* a monograph by Langweil—"Mary McCarthy and Norman Mailer: The Vulture Fantasy and the Italian Method: An Experiment in Symbiosis.") Parturient: flinging aside *Omphalos,* staring morosely out the window over the Japanese truck farm to the derricky horizon . . .

Thinking: *brains washed while you wait.* Kafka, crippled by the indulgence of his sadomasochistic distortions of aesthetic transformation: the spermatozoon as prototypical bedbug. Van Gogh, painting houses as though they were women and women as though they were gnarled trees: desiring Gauguin. Joyce, a passive homosexual trying to splice Aquinas and Freud. Leonardo: ten years is too long to take painting one picture, even if it is the "Mona Lisa." Darwin: *The Origin of Species* as symbolic parricide. Gulliver—

"Well, if it isn't the Original Mr. Monday Crust," said Langweil. Langweil was boyishly vulpine, with a pearl-buttoned whipcord ranch jacket, khaki jodhpurs, and a smile like something the stomach threw up in revulsion. Pather followed that smile into the inner sanctum. "Let's see your buffer zone," said Langweil.

Pather stripped, and lay down in the phone booth. (Making a connection? It *did* look like a phone booth tipped lengthwise. It was actually a combination Skinner Box and Orgone Energy Accumulator: twenty layers of celotex and sheet iron, bars, pedals, plastic peep-panes, optional sun lamp. All it lacked was an Unamuno Invigorator.) Pather plugged in his own EEG electrodes, tapped the mike to make sure it would record his ruminations, antlered himself with earphones and said to Langweil: "Search and destroy."

Langweil was already shadow-boxing around the office: he fought fifteen rounds a fifty-minute hour. "Light up a pacifier, if you need it."

Pather did so; and a fan began pumping in the booth, to suck away his fumes.

"Well, what's your *Gestimmtheit* this afternoon? Resentment? Repentance? Sympathy?"

"My thing-itself in its thisness went thataway, and won't come back. My intersubjectivity is lonely, and thinking of suing for aliena-tion of effectiveness. Estrangement!"

Langweil chuckled. "And the dream? Last week, as I recall, you were going to run off to Tahiti with a bottle of heavy water."

"I dreamed last night that I was sitting in my living room, and turned on the television set to watch the World Series. But some-thing happened to the picture tube. *You* came on, Langweil, with three ghosts. Do you know what you said?"

Langweil, dancing, feinting, shook his head.

"You said: 'In October 1963, I turned to a deep study of the World Series, feeling the need to reappraise the nature and destiny of Western man. Stealing from Norman O. Brown and Leslie Fiedler the suspicion that all was not nearly so *mirabile dictu* as everybody pretends, I was dismayed by the spectacle on my Zenith. When that struggle of contending and incompatible myths concluded so abruptly in Chavez Ravine, I knew, in Antoine Roquentin's revealing phrase, "Something has happened to me, I can't doubt it any more." Indeed, something has happened to all of us—but what?

" 'I submit that we will not find the answer to that question in the sterile chain of mean-minded causalities which oppress the sports pages of our metropolitan newspapers. It lies deeper, festering in the American unconscious. I propose to prove that, in the words of Lionel Trilling, "We are all ill." I address my remarks to those of you intrepid enough to follow me, with gun and camera as it were, up the anal canal—to find out why, when the Yankees blew four straight, all America cried out with Baudelaire: "Sublime ignominy!"

" 'The truth, the urgent meaning of October 1963, is that sixty million Americans in the spurious safety of their living rooms witnessed nothing less than the Advent of Eros, that Sloucher whose rough hour had come round at last. The victory of Los Angeles over New York was a triumph of Dionysius over Apollo, of hipster (Dodgers) over Puritan (Yankees), of civilian (dour ex-farm boy Alston) over military (pugnacious ex-marine Houk: Anal Re-Tenshun!), of vital self-indulgent nihilistic libido (Hollywood) over Establishmentarian Superego (Las Vegas odds)—the symbolic ravishing of Yin by Yang, of James by Dreiser, of Edith Wharton by Jack Kerouac, of . . . need I go on?' "

"I wish you wouldn't," said Langweil.

" 'Let us fix a blank and pitiless gaze on the Bronx that warm October afternoon. The first game. Picture the teams as they disposed at the top of the first inning. Let us ask ourselves: was it an *accident* that the Yankees sent to the mound as their chevalier a man referred to as *Whitey Ford?* Was it an accident that *Whitey* (or *Ford*) sought to thwart the legitimate aspirations of a line-up of nine men (the number of Supreme Court justices), five of whom (a majority) were *black* (Wills, Gilliam, Roseboro and the Davis boys)? And was it an *accident* that "Whitey" and the "Yankees" were opposed in their campaign of social oppression by . . . *a Brooklyn Jew* (Koufax)?' "

"Were you frightened at an early age by Maxwell Geismar?" asked Langweil.

" 'No! We find in this syzygy of circumstances not accident, but historical design! Not coincidence, but allegory! Not an amusing footnote to von Neumann, but a clash of archetypes in a Play of of the Shadow! Now let us cast our cold mind's eye five days forward into time. It is the bottom of the seventh inning of the fourth and final game, in Dodger Stadium. Once again, that old Boer *Whitey* is on the mound for the Yankees, a "money pitcher," as they say. Whitey wheels, deals . . . "Junior" Gilliam (a revealing terminological degradation of a member of the black races) laces a vicious drive down the third-base line . . . Cletis Boyer (a white Southerner) stabs it on one bounce, whirls, and rifles a perfect throw to first. What happens?' "

"I give up," said Langweil. "What *does* happen?"

" 'Freud has written, "None is too big to be ashamed of being subject to the laws which control the normal and morbid actions"—

not even, alas, Joe Pepitone. Let us zoom in by telescopic lens to Pepitone: Yankee first baseman, Bronx-Italian-American *arriviste,* lower middle-class Everyman. Dare we guess at the vague terrors and unacknowledged expectations playing in this man's mind as he waits with outstretched glove for Boyer's throw? What blind frogs of fantasy stir in the sediment of his subconscious guilt? What antagonistic basilisks of hope and horror raise their snouts? Surely we need not remind ourselves once more of Nelson Algren's "Mammy-freak," a symbol of our time's tortured liberalism. Surely we need not reiterate the dream and the panic night-sweat of the White American, the psychic exploiter. Let us ask ourselves: if *we* stood in Joe Pepitone's cleated baseball shoes, wouldn't *we* be torn between contradictory psychopathological desires and needs—on the one hand, the longing for punishment, castration, the comeuppance of death; on the other hand, the longing for chaste Edenic black-white male love? Can you feel the question flex its fingers in your mind as Gilliam hurls himself toward first? Who did Joe Pepitone want "Junior" Gilliam to be? Forgiveness, or Retribution? Love, or Justice? The Raft, or the Rack? *Nigger Jim*—or *Malcolm X?'* "

"Come back to the resin bag, Huck Honey," said Langweil.

" 'He doesn't know! He is paralyzed! The ball eludes his grasp. Gilliam rushes by . . . achieves second . . . and keeps on going all the way to third. (Repudiation of tokenism: but he is not yet *home.*) That three-base error was more than a simple mistake, or a failure of nerve, or a case of sunspots. It was the confrontation of Hamlet and LeRoi Jones. And while Hamlet was thinking it over, LeRoi Jones scored from third on a fly ball, and Norman Podhoretz mopped up with a thousand years of ghetto-cunning. As Irving Howe has written: *We know that the nightmare is ours."* ' "

Langweil paused in his shadowboxing to smile at the phone booth. "Surely 'Norman Podhoretz' is stylistically mistaken. Koufax in action was more like the Stern Gang."

Pather grimaced. "One of the things I find refreshing about you, Langweil, is that you seem totally immune to my contempt."

"It's merely a form of transference; *and* a projection of your contempt for yourself. You're regressing, Parturient—back to the child's garden of words, back to the point when you opted for the abstractions of physics . . ."

"No doubt as a result of some postnatal nastiness. Let's see: when I was two, I concluded after a searing and voyeuristic experience that procreation was an act of sexual mutilation. Dad was doing it to Mom. When I was ten, I was traumatized by a color print Picasso. The masochistic female matador surrenders her sword to the Papa-Bull—*that* meant Mom might have enjoyed it . . .”

Langweil bobbed, feinted, then landed a left to the solar plexus of his phantom sparring partner. “Be careful when you play with words, Parturient. How did Valéry put it? ‘Every word is a bottomless pit.’ I just wrote a monograph about it for *Omphalos.*”

“Did you know,” said Pather, “that Otto Unamuno bankrolls *Omphalos?*”

“Of course. He also owns this building.”

“Doesn’t that disturb you?”

“Why should it?” Langweil roughed up the phantom in a clinch.

“Well, you know what Otto thinks of Freud. The subconscious is merely a slag heap of discarded audile-tactile sense impressions, impressions the Eye refused to acknowledge. And you know what Otto thinks of Jung. Jung was wasting his time by concentrating solely on the *content* of myths, when only the *form* is important.”

“Parturient, *I* don’t feel threatened by Otto. *You* do.” He stepped back, slapping the phantom at will. “It’s all a question of style. We all of us must have a style of defense against the internal demands of our elemental past and the external dangers—and possibilities!— of *real* forces. *I* am examining the architectural style of *your* defenses. Why *is* it that every time you come here, you end up talking about Otto?”

“I give up. Why *is* it?”

Langweil took a jab, delivered an uppercut. “Put this in your cyclotron and see if it splits. The American physicist today is basically schizophrenic: half Faust, half little boy. Faust wants knowledge; little boy wants to be loved, to be thought *good,* to be forgiven whenever his Faust-half hatches an accidental horror. At a certain stage of the game, little boy Faust decides he can abrogate his contract with Mephisto, because Faust has assured little boy that Mephisto (please read, *evil*) doesn’t actually exist. But evil *does* exist, Parturient. It is the objectification in the outside world of your secret inner terrors. And Otto is apparently functioning as *your* Mephisto.”

“Golly. Last week the problem with the physicist was that he was trapped in the denotative fallacy. He lacked ‘radiance of content,’ didn’t he? Associative powers?”

"True," said Langweil. "That's part of it, but not *all*. Listen, Parturient, none of this is *easy*. A schematic drawing of the psychic and emotional confusion of man is going to look at least as complicated as a diagram of a synthetic carbon derivative." The phantom had a glass jaw; Langweil floored it, then thrust his arms aloft in a victory "V." "In my own way, *I* am trying to abrogate your contract with Mephisto. Try to understand me in terms of your own work—that is, your theoretical work before you found yourself being devoured by the cipher. We are both trying to transform the outward manifestation into a complex of inner stresses, aren't we? You express those stresses in mathematical symbols; I express them in neuroses and psychoses, that's all." A gong bonged. "Up you get," said Langweil. "Two rounds; eight-ounce gloves."

Pather disconnected himself, climbed out, and donned boxing trunks and gloves. "Tell me," he said, "this boxing and blabbering you go in for, isn't it unprofessional? Aren't you supposed to stay inside your disinterested *wu wei:* silent and objective?"

"That's passé. Existential psychocatalysis believes in *action*. How did Henri Michaux put it? 'In the old days I had too much respect for nature. I put myself in front of things and landscapes and let them alone. No more of that, now *I will intervene.*' "

Gong. Langweil came at him, head-faking. Pather crouched, spun and lunged, loosing a Kid Gavilan bolo punch. Langweil deflected it, jabbed with his left and crossed with his right, catching Pather on the ear. Pather danced back. "Come on, stumblebum, mix it up," said Langweil. "Unleash the latent aggressions." Pather chopped him in the eyes, took a body blow, butted Langweil under the chin, then sank his left to its laces in whipcord ranch jacket. "Good," gasped Langweil, doubled over. Pather brought both gloves down on the top of the psychocatalyst's head; Langweil sprawled on the carpet.

"It would be interesting," said Langweil, "to pinpoint the connection *and* the difference between the creative activity of the physicist and the artist." He got to his knees. "The ego begins with sublimation and reaction formation. It grows up to higher integrations of motion." He almost reached his feet—but the kill was sweet and up in Pather; he waited with the calm of an anteater for his prey to show itself. When Langweil reached three-quarter length, Pather *intervened,* whipsawing him. "Hostile," said Langweil, collapsing under the cuffing, and rolled over onto his back. "From unconscious creative thrust to conscious creative mastery," he went on, "via multiple identifications and associative transformations. But, as we said last week, the physicist is basically denotative. Or is he?"

"Zipper your lipper," said Pather, backing off. "Stand up. Take it like a psychocatalyst."

Langweil turned over and propped himself on his elbow. "The two dangers to creative activity are (1) narcissism; and (2) unresolved Oedipal aggressions and their unconscious primitive recoil."

"Applesauce," said Pather. "What's going to become of all you ball-shrinkers and lobotomizers when the molecular-biology boys whip up a little macro-molecular life? They will, you know. And then zap: no more Oedipus. Who'll take the rap?"

Langweil was on all fours. "True man," he said, "has no condition but himself." Then he scowled. "Say, maybe we're getting somewhere. Have *you* a condition, even your*self?* You sought knowledge. You acquired it. But you acquired that knowledge *outside a context of being!* Am I right?" He rocked on all fours, wagging his head. "I am right. You spent all your professional life constructing elegant abstractions. But a price must be paid for that elegance. The price is—"

Gong! "Oh, fudge," said Langweil. "I'm afraid our hour's up."

Not now? Not yet? Infuriated, Pather kicked him in the head. "That's the spirit," said Langweil. "Same ring next week? And, say: you might write up that baseball fantasy for *Omphalos,* you know. You could call it 'The World Series in Living Color.' "

Parturient: outside again. There was now in the air a death scent of cypresses and alkali dust. Fading sunlight gleamed off the tin-sided shacks, the windows of the trailer camp, the doors of the tamale parlor. Pather took the corner on two wheels. In the pedestrian crosswalk, a pair of splayfooted matrons were shoving their strollers, from which infants smirked like half-peeled tangerines. Pather did his best to run them down.

Now [7]

Interlude

"Being," said Parturient, "is an even bigger trap than becoming."

"Being," said Stanhope, "is a lapse of haste."

"Long Beach," said Parturient, "is outside a context of becoming. It's already gone by, hasn't it?"

"Too right," said Stanhope. So Parturient had managed to learn that!

The gulls now circled above the solar-bathing Sahasrara. A mottling of shadows moved across her sacrificial body, tics of desire, ripples over the golden lollipop. Stanhope thought of sapling-white Bethesda . . . Gongor had disappeared, like a lump of margarine, into his hot-dream-stew of lust . . .

Then [7]

Stanhope is perturbed . . . Bethesda tries to comfort him . . .
assignation on the miniature-golf course . . . Onalred loses
his temper . . . Whittaker Chambers jumps out of a peach tree.

It was late in the afternoon of Otto's interview with Stanhope. Up
and down both sides of Cimarosa Street, the bodies of little children
lay inert under iron croquet wickets. The appearance of Bethesda
on sponge-soled espadrilles went unremarked.

Maud Cronopios, wearing *peau de soie* sweat shirt and graffiti-
speckled leotards, opened the orange door and gestured with her
brandy alexander. "He's in his room," she told Bethesda. "No doubt
crepitant with revelation."

Bethesda slid by the hostile woman, through the litter of *National
Guardians,* down the carpeted puce corridor, to Stanhope's bedroom. He was lying on the Albanian rug. "Rutabaga!" "Artichoke!"
"Jujubee!" "Mung bean!" She leaped on top of him and nibbled his
earlobes; he unstrapped her espadrilles and licked her little lotus
feet. Mrs. Cronopios' bowling trophies frowned down from their bu-
reau perch.

"Well," said Bethesda, "did you get the job?"

Stanhope nodded. "I was assigned to help Parturient on the
Emissions account."

"Wizard!" exclaimed Bethesda. "That's even better than we'd
hoped!"

"Yes," said Stanhope, "but . . ." He was agitated.

"Where's the grief?"

"The grief," he said, "is that I rather *liked* Otto. And Parturient.
I think their theories might even help us to figure out Long Beach."

Bethesda straightened up and went to the window overlooking
the bloody spikes of pyracantha shrub. Snoozing in the steamer chair
was Caryl Chessman, the Cronopios dachshund, a half-gnawed praline between his paws. That praline might have been Bethesda's

heart; she was at a loss. She had changed since the Festival of Big Surf, with Stanhope's help; but most of her silences still were really reticences, with no grace in them, and no grasshoppers would ever come to pluck and comb them. At last she said: "How *can* you like them? Aren't they enemies of the oppressed classes?"

"Cauliflower, do you really believe that?"

It was unfair of him to ask her what she believed. He knew she believed what she thought *he* needed to believe. She had sought since the Fire Festival to make herself a portrait of his opinions, a perfect cameo on which his moods were overlaid like glazes. How then was she to cope with his despair? Was it, in fact, despair? Hadn't Stanhope himself once told her that despair was merely a Taj Mahal built around an inadequate sex life? Still, his hesitations had all the maundering impotence of despair. "How does the Yiddish apothegm put it?" she asked. "Shoulders are from God, and burdens, too."

He shook his head. Negating what?

"Spearmint," she said, offering herself like a wounded bird.

"I sometimes think," murmured Stanhope, "that the emotions are a tub of water. Any concentration of life displaces the will." But he looked up at her by the bedroom window. (Her eyes, he thought, are larkspur blue, the color of shelled gull's eggs.) He said: "I'm sorry, Almond Joy. I'll have to thrash it out with Onalred this evening."

She looked down on him, on the Albanian rug. (His ears, she thought, are pinkly, delicately turned, like the thighs of marmosets.) She said: "Stan . . . *hope!*" Then, advancing to him tenderly, she added: "How did Louis Aragon put it? 'To speak the dark dialect of man and woman . . .'"

Through the window came the sound of pistol shots. Maud was target-practicing.

That night . . .

Hanging from a pole above the porte-cochere was a wire cage. In the cage crouched an emaciated priest, carved out of balsam wood. His gills were green; his limbs were blue. One hand had been arrested in a spiderly genuflection; the other gripped a squirt-bottle aspergillum, containing hot liquid butter. Directly under the cage was a popcorn machine. By pressing the big toe on the bleeding left foot of the caged priest, you could automatically butter and bless your corn . . . with his.

Leave it to Long Beach: mocking up a model Venice just to play miniature golf! A sort of Renaissance Knotts Berry Farm, thought Stanhope. The wax monsters, the winged lions, the mechanical cuckoo birds and the motorized toy gondolas chugging up the gutter-sized canals managed uncannily to capture the flavor of their Adriatic prototype. Had the prototype somehow mysteriously contrived to copy the golf course, instead of the other way around? Not impossible, for here—in this masterful mingling of delicacy and grossness, of adulation and debauchery, of barbarous Byzantine mosaic and sickening *pietà,* of mirrors and organs and angels with tuba horns—was a perfect microcosm of greed and prefabricated history. And through this plastic lie lock-stepped the Bealongchiks in dream languor, swinging rubber-handled clubs, over the Bridge of Sighs to the 19th hole.

Stanhope found it persuasive. Doubtless the irreality and impermanence of the Long Beach night heightened that persuasiveness. There was in that night a hallucinatory hint, a premonition: that the desert itself flexed toward a violent reclamation; that freeways and real estate huts, used-car lots and junior high schools, Astro-Gas Phil-ur-Oops and Hamilton-Burger (Drop)-Drive-(Out)-Ins would be sucked like spaghetti strings down into the maw of the earth; that alone on the face of the triumphant desert would remain a refugee tribe of pelvically retracted clitoral-type harridans in polyester pedal pushers, scavenging their way Sierraward in desperate quest of gin and osteopath; and that steadily gaining on that tribe would be giant, moon-maddened, omophagous lizards . . .

Onalred would not have chosen to play miniature golf: surely it was inconsistent with his self-image. Onalred would have attempted to rent badminton rackets and a shuttlecock from the boy chewing morning-glory seeds and the girl with the personality of an exhausted plant. And *they* would be so lapsed in mystic rites of ennui that it would have taken Onalred at least twenty minutes to accomplish the transaction. Still, Stanhope was late.

Stanhope knew that waiting made Onalred uneasy. Not that Onalred wasn't good at waiting. But his waiting here would be conspicuous for its purposefulness; it would call attention to itself: for Onalred was a bad *loiterer.* In loitering there is a quality of vitiation, of listlessness, which he lacked. And listless loitering was, alas, the prevailing mood of Long Beach night life. In the vacant faces of the simpering girls (Chinese pajamas, gaily colored mukluks), in the dribbling grins of their slung-jawed escorts (snakeskin calypso pants, vinyl huaraches) there was no intelligent expectation, no articulate desire, nothing but a twitch: as though the odors of maguey and oleander had started stub ends of old psychic amputations throbbing painfully. They would be suspicious of Onalred's purposefulness. "Dig the chubby sapajou," they would be whispering. "Out of such slack pinguidity, what malign puissance?"

Stanhope made his appearance among the pygmy banana trees next to the dagger-eared statue of Friar Sarpi. "Shalom," he said. "Care for a couple of two-handed innings?"

Onalred acquiesced; tossed; and won the serve. Stanhope chose the end of the court with the breeze in his face. "What have you got for me?" asked Onalred.

"Nothing," said Stanhope.

Onalred chopped at the shuttlecock with a vicious downstroke; it sped across the net and plummeted at Stanhope's feet. "What do you mean, *nothing?*"

"That doesn't count!" shouted Stanhope. "You can't serve overhand in badminton!"

"Jesuitical lickspittle," said Onalred. "I repeat: what do you mean, *nothing?*"

"I mean," said Stanhope, "that I just wasn't designed to be a spy."

Did Onalred think to himself: *on the contrary . . . ?*

"I *liked* Otto," said Stanhope. "I even liked Parturient."

"There are no likes and dislikes," said Onalred. "Nor insults. Nor personalities. There are only *events* and *factors.*" He tried another overhand smash, but Stanhope intercepted it at the short-service line and executed a perfect drop shot. "Trotskyist nose-picker!" cried Onalred. "That was an illegal scoop!"

"Tell it to the Comintern," said Stanhope.

"Listen," said Onalred, "who designed and manufactured the germ-plasm pistol? Who developed the cartridges for it—poison ivy and bubonic plague? Who even now is at work on a portable laser gun to be employed experimentally on Southeast Asians?"

"Emissions Unlimited," said Stanhope. "But—"

"Butting is for goats. Who is the public face of Emissions Unlimited? Who does their congressional lobbying, their promotions, their community relations and their bribery?"

"Media, Rare & Well-done," admitted Stanhope. "But you don't understand. Otto and Parturient believe that the media they use are more than merely vehicles—are, in fact, messages in their own right, subliminal psychological messages. They aren't at all interested in the 'explicit content' or the 'private message' that goes out."

"Physicists like Parturient weren't particularly interested in the 'explicit content' of the Manhattan project, either," said Onalred. "Hiroshima, however, got the message."

"All arguments from analogy are false," said Stanhope. He ran off a string of seven aces before Onalred could recapture the serve. Onalred then smashed his first attempt into the net, and had to try again. On that second try, Stanhope cried: "Foot fault!"

"Counterrevolutionary mad dog!" replied Onalred. He strove to swallow and digest his wrath; his grin was ferocious; he bent at the knees.

Nevertheless, using an unanswerable top spin, Stanhope finished him off with another string of aces. "Vomit-eating crypto-fascist hyena!" screamed Onalred.

Representatives of the outside world chose that moment to intrude. "You've had your turn," said one of them, presumably male, in Marseilles sailor pullover, black acetate tights and alligator lift shoes. "Bug out, sapajou!" His theoretically female companion brayed at this display of wit, her lips a red weal on a very common face; spaniels and terriers seemed to be struggling to extricate themselves from the folds of her foofaraw.

Onalred swung his racket menacingly. "A bayonet thrust to burst the bladder," he growled, "and the monster leaps into the light of day." He stuffed the shuttlecock into the young man's mouth, hammered it down his throat with the racket, and stalked off.

Stanhope ran after him, saying: "Was that wise?" Thinking: he has lost his gift of bluff. Onalred paused to glare at the great bronze duck of a god on the green of Hole #7. Stanhope said: "It seems to me that I got it wrong at the beginning. I mean, means and ends. It seems to me that the world we are trying to make will be at least as much a consequence of the means we use as of the ends we profess. That's what it seems to me."

"Your seems are crooked," said Onalred. "Let's examine your attitude."

"I don't want to examine my attitude," said Stanhope. "I want *out!*"

"*There is no out!*" shouted Onalred. "Do you think I didn't expect this? The dialectic of the situation detaches certain disaffected portions of the middle class from their natural class interests and connections, and attaches them to the interests of the oppressed classes. It is not that they consciously respond to external necessities, but rather that they express certain internal conflicts which reflect contradictions in the world outside. Of course, they are drawn only to the ideational aspects of the Movement, to its emotional superstructure, not to its base in reality." He was furious now. "The dilettantes sign up for Revolutionary action, and then faint dead away at the sight of blood on their toenails after their very first pinkie-dip. They join up for purely personal motives. They want to *risk* something of themselves, to overcome, to return from the scene of the risk deliciously *altered,* to find themselves more *complicated.* I know. And I know also that the longing to make yourself more complicated than you really believe you are is not only vanity; it is a specifically middle-class vanity. And I played your vanity like a xylophone! Have you forgotten the day on the beach when you begged to become a part of the action? Have you forgotten the action you became a part of? Have you forgotten that you are standing in blood all the way up to your deodorized armpits?" He seized Stanhope's arm: "I'm not asking you to barbecue any more octogenarians. I'm merely asking you to find out a few things for me about Emissions Unlimited and their laser gun."

Stanhope was silent. And what scrimshaw song would he whittle on the whale tooth of his silence? "Then," he said at last, "I must make this substitution for Rimbaud:

> "The poet is not a thief of fire,
> But instead a thief for hire."

Onalred shrugged. "He ended up a slave-trader; you, a spy. Where's the grief?"

Everywhere, thought Stanhope. "What's become of Leer and the other escapees?"

"They're hiding out in Lincoln Park," said Onalred. "They call themselves the Iowa Avengers. They sneak out into the park after dark, and deflower little girls with their shuffleboard cue sticks. You must have read about the body of that eight-year-old blonde they found last week beside the drinking fountain—snub nose, ponytail, sunsuit? I believe Haruspex blamed it on sexually demented carclubbers from your old high school."

"Is that what you call revolutionary action?"

"In a way, yes. Obscenity is one form of class warfare. But I let the Iowa Avengers get away with it for another reason: I've taken motion pictures of them in action (that eight-year-old), and so managed to extort myself a perfectly reliable messenger service and a network of undercover operatives. People avert their eyes from the old and decrepit, as they avert their eyes from cripples and amputees. It works rather well. The Avengers are frightened I'll give the film to Haruspex. Little do they know: a print of it has already won second prize at the Cannes Film Festival!" He shook his head, perhaps reflecting on the superfluousness of such a fact. Theirs was hardly a irony-poor diet . . .

The always hungry Onalred plucked a pair of peaches from a tree near the 17th tee. As they sank fangs into them, a voice came down from the tree:

"Beloved children, I am sitting on a branch in a peach tree above the seventeenth tee of a miniature golf course in Long Beach, California. Three feet below me, you are both sucking cyanide from an old peach pit. Carry on: Death is the ultimate hang-up."

Was it in fact an ecstatically unhappy and joyfully wounded Whittaker Chambers who then fell out of the peach tree with a tin plate of pumpkin pie? "You see," he said, "I have not come back from hell with empty hands."

Onalred commandeered a slice. Stanhope said: "I thought you were dead."

Putative-Chambers replied: "A funny thing happened to me on my way to Whittier."

"But," said Stanhope, "how do you keep yourself alive? What do you *do?*"

P.-C. smiled. "I see that you are a young man of great simplicity and a great gentleness and sweetness of character." To Onalred, who had eaten the whole pie, he added: "You are a streak of incongruous cruelty." To Stanhope again: "I run a rug shop in Los Altos. You want a Bokhara, see me."

Advancing in martial tramp from the badminton courts came an enraged battalion of CDC Volunteers, brandishing miniature golf clubs. "Metaphysician!" they Hissed. "Irredentist!"

P.-C. welcomed them with his arms. "Dear children, you come running to me, you snatch at my lapels, you cry, 'Father! Father!

Don't!' In my wretchedness, I was talking too much again. Thank
you, my children. Here, take to my heels. Follow me. The fairway to
the seventeenth green is strewn with peach pits. I know my way
through the Valley of Peach Pits." He turned and galloped away
with surprising speed.

"The metaphysician heels himself," said Onalred.

"Do you suppose," said Stanhope, "he was *really* George Cros-
ley?"

"Hard to say," said Onalred. "I didn't get a chance to look at his
teeth." He gazed up into the peach tree. "Certain disaffected portions of the professional revolutionary class will be infected by the
virus of the rotting bourgeois culture from which they rose on the
impulse to make the Revolution serve their individualistic aspirations
for romantic action and utopian morality—and will betray their revolutionary commitments to wallow in the slime of idealism that was
their origin."

Onalred's face was now an East Berlin. His appeal was affectingly
hopeless: "Only a year ago," he told the peach tree, "my self-control
was complete . . . and, I don't mind saying, a source of relief to
feeble-willed fellow operatives. My gestures, my most casual manipulations, seemed tokens for a sealed train into a glorious future.
But now . . . now I gorge myself on pumpkin pie and shove shuttle-
cocks down young men's throats . . . What has become of my *discipline?* If, in so brief a period of residence, Long Beach has managed
to sap *my* sangfroid, what about Maud?" Again, as after the fire at
Gerontion Gardens, he stooped to kiss his thumbs. Then he whispered: "Among blackamoors and parrots, apes and golden calves,
must *I* be the only clown?"

Stanhope was much moved. He hooked one of Onalred's thumbs
and said softly: "No. You are not the only clown."

Onalred swung to engage the other thumb; they locked. He said:
"I was hoping that . . . you would, you see . . . perhaps substitute
for *him*"—indicating the vacated peach tree—"for, it, well, takes a
lot out of a man to lose a first-class operative, and—the two of us?"
Stanhope nodded. Thumb-in-thumb they waded across a canal,
and deserted mock Venice for the boulevard.

"Then," said Onalred, not looking at him, "you will continue with
your assignment?"

The moment of mutual need had slipped away. Perhaps it had

drowned in the canal. But how else was Stanhope to make himself worthy of it than by saying *yes,* a sad-making yes compounded half of affirmation, half despair? So he spoke, his inwit agenbitten, as the Long Beach night like a hideous Moor embraced them.

Now [8]

Stanhope reads a letter from Renaldi . . . some thoughts on the Ashramblers . . . Otto's plot.

Parturient said: "Surely it wasn't really Whittaker Chambers?"

"No," said Stanhope. "It was Renaldi Haruspex in drag. He was waiting for Svam. A difficult time for Renaldi. I received a long letter from him the other day, describing that time, among others." He produced the letter. "Let me quote from it aloud: 'When I was a little tyke, I bussed at the Villa Riviera for the rich Texans who, in those summers before air conditioning, journeyed to Long Beach and the seashore for their month of sun and sour mash. Many the bathroom floor I mopped, looking up to find the feral eyes of their tall bronze women on me. All limbs were cleavers then. Came the war. John (the now Ossified Man) and I supplied jam-fattened floozies with a taste for brass to officers without any taste at all. I grew up a chalk-eyed witness to such rites of self-indulgence. Self-denial was my style. But at the time that concerns you, there was an unknown x in the algebra of my need. Was Svam Spade nailed at the ankles and wrists to that x, that swastika? I never believed the car-clubbers assaulted that eight-year-old. I was sure it was some kind of Ashram sacrifice—a message to me from Svam through a mutilated agency. In seeking Svam, I was of course seeking myself. And wearily I would mount once more my motorcycle, to plunge into a night that was pregnant with stillborn gerbils . . . roaring past Hoady's through Recreation Park, down the concrete basin of the San Gabriel River, to the jungle-jim at Cecil B. De Mille Grammar School. Hustle, buster, hustle. The tortoise x recedes, slowly but as smug as Lakewood, nourished on Zeno's consolation. For all the horses in the motor of my need, I could not overtake its illimitable, infinite divisions. Stanley, surely *that* should have been one of the 102 Great Ideas?'"

Parturient shook his head. "Poor Renaldi."

"Well," said Stanhope, "what chance has a policeman against such as the Ashramblers? His business was to make sense of events and to assign blame. But they . . . they accumulated experiences and refused to evaluate them. They were adding machines of experiences, without a total bar. They never feel any obligation to analyze debits and credits . . . only to keep punching up their kicks."

Parturient grinned. "You make them sound like artists. Surely art also asserts the autonomous right of the imagination to assume, as a chameleon, whatever form is close at hand and most readily available—without responsibility—refusing all order of temporality or decisions?"

"Applesauce," said Stanhope. "You yourself taught me differently. Theirs was the ultimate cop-out. They refused the prophetic role."

"Ah-ha!" said Parturient. "Surely *that* is the one hundred and third Great Idea?"

Gongor accepted another pisco sour. Parturient said: "So you were still a spy. How long did it last?"

"A week," said Stanhope. "Then, on the same afternoon, you and I visited Radio Free Long Beach . . . and Otto explained his plot."

"Yes," said Parturient. "I remember."

Someday, thought Stanhope, they will package memory, as now they package women: to be thawed, fried and devoured . . . the wrappers-remainders-reminders to burn.

Then [8]

*The fuel barge . . . Sahasrara and the despair of finitude
. . . Svam Spade and the ergo hang-up . . . Parturient lusts
. . . the four grades of realization . . . Stanhope learns
about the dolphins.*

Radio Free Long Beach was a pirate station, operating from studios
in an abandoned fuel barge anchored outside the breakwater line. Its
programs were relayed to a secret transmitter atop St. Teresa's Little
Ashram of Ecumenical Oṁ.

Although periodically raided by coast guard patrol boats and narcotics agents on water skis, the station and its staff had always escaped unscathed, convicted of nothing more serious than bad taste.
The barge *had* been known to venture closer to the City. It had been
sighted several times from Navy Mole, from Rainbow Pier, from
Bluff Park. It was rumored to have appeared just off Vista del
Golfo on one occasion, humming and glowing at midnight; on
another, to have passed under the J. H. Davies Bridge and into the
Marine Basin, full of dark laughter; and on a third, to have sailed up
the channel into the San Gabriel River, hurling scatological insults at
Orange County. Besides which, it had shown up at the Fire Festival
to broadcast live the death of Arbiter Aidos. Still, to Stanhope as
Parturient's scull hove to alongside, it seemed distinctly unseaworthy.

Parturient explained: "Another of Otto's little projects—a private
wavelength for the mindblowers." Otto was not the only one with a
project, however. Parturient had made known his designs on one of
the station's two announcers: Sahasrara Cannibis. And Stanhope—
well, he had his instructions, too.

They hauled themselves up the ladder, saluted the hoses and the
rusting winch. On entering the principal cabin, they were confronted
by a peculiarly expressionless female voice, issuing from a monitor:

"The Despair of Infinitude is due to the lack of Finitude." The
voice belonged to Sahasrara; and her face through the studio window

was as expressionless as her tone; smooth and characterless as a slice of boiled potato. (Stanhope wondered: is it necessary to turn your face off when you turn yourself on?) Her chromium-colored hair was severely and surgically parted down the middle, exposing a pencil-shaped scar of scalp, communicating an impression of upward growth, as though the forehead in its self-extension would extrude a white tubular grub. "The Despair of Finitude is due to the lack of Infinitude." No doubt grub-sprout was destined to disturb that infrequently modulated, hi-fi, grooving-it expression, but with what result? "The Despair of Possibility is due to the lack of Necessity." A split, perhaps, with the face divided and falling like leaves of a folio, open upon her shoulders, to reveal insects and ganglia of roots and worms, sun-blinded strings of twitch. "The Despair of Necessity is due to a lack of Possibility." Her body, however, was not expressionless. It was a body marvelously contemptuous of the feeble restraints and conventions of the Aqua Mist permanently pebbled nylon pajamas striving to contain it: enormous floating breasts, balloonfish which swam to the studio window and flattened themselves against it; hog-shank thighs, polo pony calves, ballerina ankles, and feet like chunks of alabaster.

"From *Anfang* to *Schluss*," whispered Parturient, "what a *Stück!*" Their progress toward the control room was arrested by an angry red light. They peered through the slot at the other voice of Radio Free Long Beach, Svam Spade. His hands were wet flowers on the panel of knobs. He faded, segued, plucked and plugged; then spoke into his own microphone: "This is Radio Free Long Beach, Songbird of the Absurd, coming to you from the giant kelp forests of the Pacific. Out of joints? For a smoking experience positively colloidal in its impact, try Chasms. Chasms are a fine blend of specially selected toxics: essence of turtle turd and poppy, sulfur and old rope. The olfactory ambivalence of a Chasm will leave your nostrils limp and your bowels loose. Remember: *you* don't smoke a Chasm; a Chasm smokes *you*. Available at discriminating candy stores, and on the handball courts of most Long Beach junior high schools."

Chimes as flat as Oklahoma. Then Svam again: "The time at the chime is . . . but Time is an interminable annelid." He lit up a Chasm. "If it is true—and it is—that all our *I*'s are lies; that the *I* is a social construct created by experiential transactions and the attitudes of *others,* then . . ."

Sahasrara: "Then the *I*'s do not have It."

Svam: "What is the meaning of Buddhism?"
Sahasrara: "Three pounds of flax!"
Svam: "Is a dog possessed of the Buddha-spirit?"
Sahasrara: "Wang-wang!"
Svam: "Beware the Other—"
Sahasrara: "For the Other *Attenuates*—"
Together: "Tame the Attenuator! Tease the Hairy Ape!"

Raucous laughter: reminding one of Teamsters muscling in on the jukebox racket, happily engaged in crushing skulls. A gasp: reminding one of being rudely awakened at night in one's warm bunk by the press of a cold battery-driven electric carving knife on one's throbbing throat. Carnival music: over which Edna St. Vincent Millay reads "Childhood Is the Kingdom Where Nobody Dies." Then Sahasrara once more:

"And now, the Radio Free Long Beach Little Theater-in-Arrears is ashamed to present *How the West Was Lost,* a musical adaptation of the jeremiad by Oswald Spengler, originally staged last Annihilation Night at the Ashram by the Intermedia Kinetic Environmental-cases. In this exclusive recording of that never-to-be-repeated performance, Max Lerner plays the part of the White Liberal; Sonny Liston plays the Goth; and Elizabeth Taylor is Democracy. Score by Ravi Shankar and Lawrence Welk; book by John P. Roche; lyrics by Conor Cruise O'Brien and Irving Kristol. The bold choreography of the St. Vitus Jungenbundle Dervishes & Anti-Mime Troupe could not, alas, be captured on mere mylar. *How the West Was Lost!*"

It began with a great rush of running water, growling, gnashing, ripping. Then came a heavy voice with a Southern accent: "How did T. Eugene Connor of Birmingham, Alabama, put it? 'My dawgs don't get a chance to brush their teeth after ev'ry Negra.' " And so on. The red light extinguished itself. Parturient flung open the control room door. "Svam Spade," he proclaimed, "prize pupil of the great Forty Watts himself!"

Svam looked up from the switch panel without a discernible quickening of interest. *"Cor ad cor loquitur,"* he said. He wore a yellow-and-magenta striped Arabian jumpsuit. His face in that drench of color was the cold dry gray of elephant blubber, into which had been hammered eyes that glittered like the blind heads of nails.

"May I," said Parturient, "present Stanhope Cronopios?"

"You may," said Svam, "if he comes accompanied by a receipt, and I can exchange him at the May Company for something more useful." He gave no indication of recalling their encounter at the Fire Festival, nor the night of the invert roundup on the Pike.

Stanhope asked: "What is the purpose of Radio Free Long Beach?"

"To irritate everybody," replied Svam. He opened a program guide and scanned it. "We broadcast all the Kiwanis luncheons live, which is deadly. We cover the shuffleboard tournaments in Lincoln Park. We've hung a mike on John the Ossified Man, and for twelve hours you heard nothing but the sound of his steady flesh-petrifying. We've had programs consisting of recorded toilet-flushing, nipple-sucking, faucet-leaking. Everything that Craig Hosmer inserts into the Congressional Record we read aloud to the overture from *Die Meister-singer*. We used to feature a thrice-daily report on the progress of subsidence, before the fluids-injection program killed it. We'd come on saying: 'In the last eight hours, Long Beach has sunk x inches into the sea. Go, baby, go! Out of sight!' In between regularly scheduled non-programs, we have pornography, recorded at 7.5 and played back at fifteen. Or Zen formulations such as you just heard. Or heavy breathing. Or the uninterrupted ringing of a telephone. Or—"

"Why?" said Stanhope.

"To discomfit all the people who ask *Why*—that's why. We are dedicated to confusing your sense of propriety and logic, exposing you to chaos, shattering your cause-and-effect mechanism, the 'therefore' or ergo hang-up. Our motto: Where Ergo was, let Idiocy be!" He smiled.

Sahasrara emerged from the studio, entered the control room, pivoted her head, registered and dismissed the intruders, then lay the burden of her permanently pebbled breasts on top of the control console and struck up a Chasm. Parturient promptly affected intense interest in the console knobs.

Stanhope said: "Parturient tells me that you once read one of my poems on the air."

"Ah," said Svam, "so you are *that* Stanhope Cronopios. Yes. We had some fun with 'The Void Made Flesh.' I read it myself, on a live remote from the traffic jam at Lakewood Boulevard and Firestone. Of course, Cronopios, you and Radio Free Long Beach are in total opposition. You are afraid of the Void. We search for and embrace it. Oṁ, after all, means Void: the Void of the Real neti-neti Self, without shape or horizon or end . . . the Self which has successfully graduated to the Fourth Grade of Realization."

"What does this toggle do?" asked Parturient.

"It tickles," said Sahasrara.

"Grade One," said Svam, "is the waking awareness of external objects."

"Together," said Parturient, "we might bridge the subject-object cleavage." He twisted a nipple; but Sahasrara was not turned on.

"Grade Two," said Svam, "is dreaming, perceiving within oneself the possibility of an enjoyment devoid of gross objects . . ."

"Would you mind," said Sahasrara, "devoiding yourself of *my* gross objects?"

"Grade Three," said Svam, "is the deep dreamless sleep in which one experiences the unity of knowledge and bliss . . ."

"My Kraft must be Ebbing," said Parturient. "She doesn't even blush."

"Grade Four," said Svam, "is the end of perception and knowing altogether . . . negation of the phenomenal world . . . death . . . Oṁ . . ."

"Blushing," said Sahasrara, "is a mild form of conversion hysteria —an erection of the entire head."

"Obviously," said Svam, "the first step toward Oṁ is to attack and destroy the ergo."

"Obviously," agreed Stanhope. "You can't make an Oṁ without breaking a few ergos."

Svam Spade looked at Stanhope as though he were so much lint in the leviathanic belly button. Then, to considerable and unpleasant effect in the close quarters of the control room, Svam vatasara-dhoutied. "You're wasting your interminable annelid," said Parturient to Stanhope. "He's so cool you'll only burn yourself trying to touch him."

Said Sahasrara: "The original cool is derived from yogi bowel gymnastics."

"The yoni mudra bit," said Svam complacently. "I have coaxed my Kundalini serpent up from the base of my spine to the thousand-petaled lotus of my brain. At each chakra station—the genitalia, the navel, the heart, the throat, the eyebrows—the local lotuses, knowing me, have turned their petals from down to up—"

"Which is known," said Sahasrara, "as the flower becoming *cool.*"

"I've tried yogi bowel gymnastics myself," said Parturient. "I mastered jala-basti, the art of sucking up my bath water through my rectum. It's handy whenever the drains of your tub are clogged. If you happen to take baths, that is."

"*Your* Kundalini serpent," said Sahasrara, "is still hanging in your jockey shorts."

An annoyed Parturient struck back: "Sahasrara, I have some bad news for you and Svam. Otto sent me to tell you that the Shearwater cruise boats have listed Radio Free Long Beach on their new harbor tour. Starting tomorrow, you'll have tourists gaping at your fuel barge every two hours. You have been officially classified in the promotional bulletins as 'quaint.'"

Svam made little fists, and with only partially subdued ferocity managed to mutter: "*Avidya!*" But in an awe-inspiring exertion of the will, he almost immediately regained his self-control. "The blue hills are simply blue hills," he observed. And, as an afterthought: "The white clouds are simply white clouds."

Sahasrara was more upset. "Perhaps," she said, "the System is endowed with an autonomous power of ridiculization of the System." She looked beseechingly at Svam. "You know, I'm feeling a little attenuated."

Svam handed her a sugar cube. "I bet that bastard Otto did this to us deliberately. I told you he was up to something." To Stanhope and Parturient, he said: "Bug out! Tell the dwarf I'll burn us down to the waterline before I let this barge become a tourist attraction!" When they did not immediately move, Sahasrara turned and advanced on them, her breasts avenging prows of warships. They retreated from the control room. Svam and Sahasrara followed them, snapping their fingers.

Stanhope was troubled. With one foot in Parturient's scull, he turned back to Svam and said, "What do you hope to accomplish? Why the gymnastics and the ergo-breaking?"

"Self-realization," said Svam.

"But," said Stanhope, "what comes after this self-realization?" He envisioned a world of Om-burghers, their luncheons less lively than those of the Kiwanis.

"If," said Svam, "one dreams that one shall soon wake up, one does not ask oneself what one will do in waking life."

"But," said Stanhope, "that is precisely what one *must* ask oneself, or continue to dream and never wake up. Questions are the difference between men and asparagus."

"Three pounds of flax!" shouted Svam, and kicked Stanhope into the scull.

"One more question!" shouted Stanhope back at him. "On board this barge, how do you dispose of your waste?"

Svam found this inquiry so bizarre that he stuck his fingers in his ears. Sahasrara, too, was puzzled, but it was she who supplied the reply: "Through those hoses," she said, indicating the python-like lengths of fuel-tubing which lay lax on the deck. "Into the ocean."

"That's why the narcotics guys can never find anything when they raid the place," said Parturient. "It's all been flushed into the sea."

"Ah," said Stanhope, "that explains it, then."

"Explains *what?*" screamed Svam.

"The dolphins, naturally," said Stanhope.

Svam was furious. "Cronopios, are you putting me on?"

Stanhope grinned. "Of course not. Even with alterations, you'd never fit."

"Nobody puts me on, Cronopios! Nobody! Not even Otto!" Sahasrara, sensing her guru's *Gerinnung,* wrapped herself around his knees and wailed.

"You'll have to do the paddling, Cronopios," said Parturient. "I find I'm feeling rather attenuated."

As they drew steadily away from the fuel barge, an anguished Svam-and-Sahasrara sandwich cried on the wind: "Tease the Hairy Ape!"

Now [9]

Another interlude . . .

"I never did understand," said Parturient, "what you meant about the dolphins."

"Onalred used them as messengers," said Stanhope. "Lately, on their passage out into international waters, as they went by the fuel barge, they had been experiencing curious and disruptive sensations. Their sonar apparently went haywire, unreliable, and they didn't know how far they were from the ocean floor. I was instructed to see if the radio station was responsible. Inadvertently, of course, it was— by disposing of its various waste products in the manner it did. Lilly's experiments with dolphins have recently proved what I at the time supposed . . . Dolphins on LSD *do* undergo a psychological crisis; their sonar system is short-circuited; their sense of space relationships gets all screwed up."

Gongor roused himself. "What do you mean, he used dolphins as messengers?"

"Later, Gongor," said Stanhope. "I had to explain it all to Dasein Camembert, which, of course, must be recorded. There's no point in going through it twice."

"And then," said Parturient, "we went back to the Pyramid."

"Yes," said Stanhope. "And I tried on another father figure, although poor Otto never got the chance to fail me."

Then [9]

Stanhope is disappointed by the computer . . . Otto explains the human brain . . . Parturient is disgusted . . . Otto reveals his plot . . . Gnatpappa (?)

> Sarnoff sank into a swoon
> And Logic died.
> McLuhan took the cathode tube
> Out of his snide.

Otto awaited them on their return from the barge to the Pyramid: in the computer room. "It is time for Cronopios to learn precisely what it is we do here," he said.

Parturient was glum, brooding no doubt on his uncoaxed Kundalini serpent. And Stanhope found it difficult to listen. Part of his mind was back on the fuel barge; another part was absorbed in his disappointment with the computer room. For Stanhope had imagined something vastly more romantic, more threatening, than the dinky little police call box version of a computer he now confronted. He had imagined a bank of perpetually spinning disk-reels and impassively registering notational gauges; a battalion of sexless keypunch girls converting their questions into the binary idiot-language of "on" and "off." He had prepared himself for this promised confrontation: He had studied Boolean algebra. He had formed opinions on the relative merits of analogue versus digital; on parallel versus series; on short code versus complete; on memory as flip-flop, electrostatic, magnetostrictive, ferroelectric or acoustic delay effect. He had excited himself with visions of dynamic pulse, storage registers like picture tubes, guns shooting electrons out of their glass locations . . . This glorified typewriter he considered a betrayal of his own imaginative powers. For it was nothing more than a teletype machine, hooked up and plugged into the IBM 7090 ten miles away at Emissions Unlimited. Otto had been apportioned a certain amount of 7090's precious time, and assigned a code designation to identify himself when claiming that time. Gnatpappa simply sat there, dialed the computer, and asked his questions by tapping them out in basic English.

It *was* odd, though, to find Gnatpappa in this temple of low hum, blue walls, gray machines. Cicatrix scars, pubic tassel, computer. Like a knot of swollen black carrots in a bank vault. "Poor Gnatpappa," said Otto, uncannily divining the subterranean flow of Stanhope's thoughts. "A classic example of what can happen when a new medium is introduced into a culture unprepared to absorb it. His aboriginal culture was strictly Stone Age. His grandfather's pride was invested in the stone ax he had so laboriously fashioned. That stone ax was a symbol of his manhood as well as a tool with which to work. The missionaries on arriving in Australia thought to ingratiate themselves with the inhabitants of the Bush by providing free *steel* axes, handing them out to the women. What happened? The males presently realized the superior efficiency of the plentiful steel axes; and so they borrowed from their women. The result was a loss of male dignity and pride—not to mention the disrupting of labor patterns and the decline of an operative idea of craftsmanship. The cultural order of the Bush underwent a disintegration. Gnatpappa is culture-free."

Thinking of Svam Spade and his sugar cubes and Chasms, Stanhope said: "I wonder if the new technology isn't simply an extrapolation of your steel ax incident. Whether the fact that our machines have taken over so many of our aggressive functions—the making of things, of money, of war"—maliciously, glancing at Parturient—"and, in the instance of drugs, the making of women, as well . . . hasn't wounded our own idea of manhood; hasn't robbed us of our aggressive masculine definition."

"Applesauce," said Otto. "You miss the real significance of electrical technology, of computerized automation. With its adaptable, instantaneous and automatic character, it releases us from our specialized functions, our *work* hang-up. We are liberated to become nomads of knowledge!"

And of course Parturient couldn't pass up a challenge. "Beware the Electronic Other, Cronopios. You may find yourself being automated right out of existence. Pre-punch a computer with a rhyming dictionary and it'll write our poems for us. Or spin out a million different versions of the Sermon on the Mount. Or—a different kind of sermon on another kind of mount—a million different versions of 'Howl.' One of the computer versions is sure to be superior to either of the originals."

"Marmalade," said Stanhope. "The computer deals only in permutations. It has no values, no sensibility, no taste, no critical judgment. It would be just like the monkeys on their typewriters, trying to tap out Shakespeare. Even if one of its versions happened accidentally to be superior to the original, it would have no way of knowing *which* one."

"You miss the real significance of the computer as guru," said Parturient. "*It* would decide which poems were superior, along some such aesthetic scheme as that version which most economically conveys the intended sense—"

"Shut up!" cried Otto. "Parturient, you have made a career out of your insufferability!" He made his hands a bowl, and peered sightlessly into them. Then, quietly, he began: "When the first modern electronic computer was built, its builder thought he was modeling it on the human brain. Tough darts, von Neumann! The history of that mistake is instructive. The activity of our central nervous system is, of course, electrical. Our peripheral receptors receive impressions and our peripheral neurons depolarize to send a message to the central nervous system—"

"The local lotus," said Parturient, "turns its petals up . . . is *cool.*"

"—generating a pulse potential that runs down the neuron's axon to a little clutch of roots. On the roots are microscopic pimples. They are valves. Agitated by the pulse, they open, releasing the *synaptic transmitter* into the *synaptic cleft.* Other nerve cells in the vicinity pick up the signal, and if it's strong enough, *they* start depolarizing. Very much like a two-value marker system, isn't it? A digital computer: the neuron is either 'on' or 'off.' But those peripheral neurons also function as *scales,* don't they? They weigh the stimulus, deciding whether to depolarize. And inside the central nervous system, all the other cells are weighing pulse potentials, distinguishing between sequence and simultaneity, co-ordinating valve spouts, discerning the *pattern.* Pattern and scale: like an *analogue* computer, yes? Then tell me *why,* Cronopios, the brain functions at such a *puny* level of arithmetical precision and at such an exalted level of *reliability,* compared to any machine model so far developed?"

"I give up," said Stanhope. "Why?"

"Because the computer accumulates and amplifies its errors! Because a little error at the beginning is compounded into nonsense at the end. The computer can say *and;* it can say *or;* but it can't say *no!*" He paused to knead his knuckles. "The brain, because it operates on some sort of *statistical* message system, can say *no.* There is, in fact, a *hyperpolarizing* activity in the brain, which occasionally tells the neurons to cool it."

"The physics of the superego," said Parturient. "I myself have always suspected that the key to aberrational behavior lies in a leaky sodium pump."

"So, said von Neumann and the boys when they realized their mistake, the computer is *not* a machine model of the brain; still, it's a wonderful toy! They missed the point. Everybody is always missing the point!" He wheeled himself away from them, turned his back, listened for a moment to Gnatpappa typing. *"Why* did they think they were building a machine model of the brain in the first place? The usual Western bias. They thought it was impossible to express really complicated situations without resorting to formulae and numbers, rooted in the *logical* process. (What about music? What about myth?) So they *assumed* that logic was the language of the brain; and so they chose logic and mathematics to be the language of their machine model; and so the computer's task was defined in terms of numerical equalities and inequalities. Then, when someone pointed out the obvious to them—that logic and mathematics, like our spoken and written languages, are just historical and accidental forms of expression—they retired in a snit to play with their toys." He spun round on them again. *"They never stopped thinking mechanically!"* A corrosive smile. "If they had, they would have realized that the computer and the brain *are indeed approximations.* For they are both in the business of processing information; *they are both based on electrical activity.* Electricity does not *flow;* it is not turned *on* and *off.* It is a *condition.* It has *space!"*

Parturient was disgusted. "You are a pusher of cheap mysteries, Otto."

"Bug out, sapajou," said Otto. To Stanhope: "The central nervous system is characterized by *field activity,* Cronopios. It constitutes a single unified field of experience: impressions in the brain are exchanged and translated, enabling us to react to the world as a *whole.* Organic Unity of Interprocess! The very speed-up made possible by the instantaneous nature of electricity tends to eliminate *all* specialism of space and subject. Do you grasp this? The key is *feedback*—in the brain, in the computer. By introducing an information circuit or loop, you end the one-way *flow* or mechanical sequence of reasoning and operation. You end *lineality*. What is automation but the instantaneous synchronization of numerous operations? The end of the assembly line? Instant processing of knowledge by interrelation? What electricity is *now* doing to society, via the new media and the computerized automated plants, is what electricity has *always* done for the brain: creating an *implosion* of impression, experience, production, consumption and learning . . . all bound up in the *same* process! Electricity is *sheer* information, illuminating everything it touches, storing or moving perception and knowledge, making possible easier and quicker recognitions of patterns and contours of changes and developments. And *any* process that almost instantly relates impressions and experiences in a total field is approaching *conscious awareness!* Our computers are specialized right now; when one is built which is not so specialized . . ."

The blue light of the computer room vesica-piscized Otto. "We are now at the stage of abstract manipulation of information to create *wealth.* But there are *other* things we can create—or *destroy*—with abstract manipulation of information."

"What things?" asked Stanhope.

"Socrates," said Parturient, "should have had such a glass-jawed straight man."

Otto said: "We, Cronopios, *are turning all mankind into a computer.* Properly keyed, properly coded, we are creating an electrical machine that, fed the data we determine, will make the calculation we desire. I do not speak of propaganda. The data are not the messages, but the media moving those messages. In the brief time you have been with us, you have already learned the different psychological messages characteristic of the different media forms. You should by now have mastered the rudiments of our thinking. *Hot* media are those which extend a single sense in high definition (which is to say: well filled with data and requiring very little participation or filling in or completion). Such media are radio, movies, photographs and the phonetic alphabet. *Cool* media, on the other hand, require participation and involvement: because much has been left out. The telephone, TV, cartoons, Chinese ideograms. That is the theory —*and we are testing it.*

"McLuhan has written: 'We are certainly within conceivable range of a world automatically controlled to the point where we could say, Six hours less radio in Indonesia next week or there will be a falling off in literary attention. Or, We can program twenty more hours of TV in South Africa next week to cool down the tribal temperatures raised by radio last week.' That, Cronopios, is precisely what we *are* doing! *We are programing emotional climates!* We can keep a given culture stable, or . . . we can keep it *unstable*. And, of course, nobody pays the slightest attention to us. Emissions Unlimited loans us its computer to help us make our calculations. And the rest of the world thinks we're just hucksteríng consumer goods. They miss the point, and I will *stab* them with it!"

He began to laugh. There were steel fingers in his laughter, which scratched the walls, tore at the fixtures and at Parturient. Otto could not see, of course, the sudden look of all-consuming hatred on Gnat-pappa's face. Stanhope saw it, but he had his own identity crisis to worry about.

Now [10]

How Onalred reacted to Otto's plot . . . what Stanhope then decided . . . Parturient agrees to take turns for the next flashback.

"So," said Stanhope, "I had two morsels of information to feed Onalred that night in the lifeguard shack. He ate them along with a two-pound bag of potato chips. (If the potato chips could be thought of as the fried ears of all his victims, their crunch was the release of crackled cries he never heard, of recriminations locked in tonguelessness.) He determined immediately to reroute the dolphins' passage, avoiding the barge. But of Otto's intention to program emotional climates, he was contemptuous: 'Electricity!' he sneered; 'Orgone Energy! Bad Faith! Repressed Libidinal Instincts! The kept cosmeticians of the West are always coming up with a new miracle putty to plaster the Medusa-face. That face is still stone-making. What about the laser gun?' So ended my thrall . . ."

"Why?" asked Parturient. "You stuck with him through the barbecue of octogenarians. Why fink out when he refuses to take Otto seriously? It makes no sense to me."

"Indifference to the fate of senior citizens is one thing," said Stanhope. "Indifference to the enormous possibilities—for both good and evil—of the imaginative life is something else again, and insupportable! Onalred, behaving like a bureaucrat, was diminished in the dazzle of Otto's electrifying vision. Of course, I learned later that he took Otto rather more seriously than such offhandedness had indicated. By that time, however, it was too late. On leaving the lifeguard shack, I sent a night letter to Washington."

Sahasrara had gone below to dry, boil and bake some banana peels for supper's smoke-in. Gongor was therefore restless. "Captain Happen . . ." he began.

"Patience," said Stanhope. "We're getting there. We have come to a very important part of our story: the day that I met Dasein, two murders were committed, and Parturient decided—well. Parturient, shall we take turns? I'll handle me, Dasein and . . . Bethesda—if you'll take care of you, Otto, Gnatpappa and the miscellaneous extras."

"To every ding-a-ling his thing," said Pather Parturient.

Then [10]

*Stanhope loses a mother and gains a friend . . . Otto makes
a connection . . . Bethesda's difficulties are all ironed out . . .
the recline and parsifal of Pather Parturient.*

Stanhope stood aft in the Shearwater cruise boat, sea spray in his
eyes and gloom in his heart. A herd of sheepish clouds trampled
the skyline, rode over the bleached pagodas and the shore hotels.
Night was applying itself to Long Beach like a deodorant pad.

The cruise boat wheeled in the harbor. "East Basin," said the
squawk box, "Pier E," and cast about desperately for objects of
significance to remark. "Home of Howard Hughes' famous *Spruce
Goose,* the huge plywood seaplane constructed here during World
War II. A wingspan of three hundred and twenty feet . . . a length
of two hundred and nineteen feet. Although it has actually been air-
borne only once, the *Spruce Goose* is one of the largest planes in the
world."

A gigantic plywood bird which had been grounded after a single
flight. Was not the *Spruce Goose* a proximate symbol of Long Beach
—of Man himself?

Near Stanhope sat a woman in black vinyl aviator's raincoat,
snapping match spines and singing to herself in Spanish. He thought:
she hugs her loneliness, as a stabbed man hugs the cruelly loving
knife. He thought also: I brandish my betrayal like a kinfe . . . will
anybody hug it?

In the intervals between squawks he could pick out a few phrases
from the song the match-snapping woman sang:

> . . . porque habian premeditado
> venganza tarde o temporano . . .

"The so-called Black Warrior Lagoon," said the squawk box.
"That white mountain is industrial salt, imported from Baja Cali-

fornia." The salt mountain Dokhma Koan climbed only a week before his death . . .

> Fue un dia martes por la tarde
> Este tragedia fatal,
> Que ha conmovido al pais
> y a todo la Capital . . .

"The world's largest fruit terminal," said the squawk box. And beyond, a bed of old automobile bodies and broken railcar axles, awaiting transmogrification.

Stanhope and the black vinyl woman were now joined aft by a pair of teen-agers who promptly sutured themselves and stuck their tongues into each other's eyes. The poem began in Stanhope's head:

> Love is—said Apollinaire—
> Like a lugubrious bear,
> Dancing. Chancing on this circus,
> I bare my love. The jerk is
> Off. Awfulsomeness, my clowning:
> Not a dancing, but a drowning.

Had he mouthed the words? The black vinyl woman rotated her bowl-shaped face toward him for a moment, gaped and turned away again, perhaps in embarrassment at the nakedness of his susceptibility. She stood, walking quickly back into the cabin, with a slap of her hemp-bottomed sandals on the dew-damp deck. He thought: I hate her for leaving me alone. But it was everybody else, really, whom he hated: for not leaving him alone.

The Shearwater docked at Pierpoint Landing; and still Stanhope had not been contacted. He disembarked, glancing nervously about him. From a gummy saloon were blown the stench of fish and the transistorized bathos of Beatle music. Was it the fish which turned his stomach, or cirrhosis of the Liverpool? He hurried by a band of bored young men surrounding the seal pond. Blood foamed at their lips. They waited as if for a coagulation. Blue lamplight flickered in their buckles and their bootstraps. They flexed themselves, bent their bodies like archers' bows, fit arrows of cigarette to them and loosed the flaming eyes at passers-by . . . at Stanhope.

He was being followed. He paused at a vending machine for a stick of licorice, and peered into its mirror at the street behind him.

The woman in the black vinyl raincoat! Stanhope ducked, then darted behind a Sea-Land van and into the parking lot. Reckless zigs, ragged zags: he achieved the protective shadow of a Buick, and squatted, waiting. But he hadn't lost her. He could hear the approach of her hemp-buttomed sandals. Whom did she represent? Which side was *his* side? She drew abreast; he lunged at it. She yielded, falling with him, throwing him off balance. So it had come to this. (No matter how long he practiced, his mother, too, had always been able to throw him.) With an expectation honed to the edge of delicious-ness, he anticipated her tommyhawking elbow to his groin, the sub-sequent coccyx thwack. On his knees, he gazed up admiringly; she bent over him; he licked the crater of her face.

"Nitwit," she said. "I'm here to help you. And I should have thought your precious motorcycle cops would have taught you to defend yourself a little more efficiently." She removed her vinyl raincoat and bound him up in it, then dragged the bundle across the parking lot to Panorama Drive, where a motorbike was waiting. Stanhope was strapped to the handle bars of the motorbike.

"I didn't think they'd send a woman," he said.

"It was in August 1940," she explained, "and it was hot, and the sand gave off geysers of steam and the brick was soft, and there was the man with the beard and the eyes like supernovas, and I loved him, and I was the one who opened the hatch, and out of the hatch rushed blood and the alpenstock, and the alpenstock was in his brain, and the blood drowned the Mexican sun, and the coronas and solar flares of the Mexican sun were blood, and my hemp-bottomed sandals made skull-shapes in his blood: *voici le temps des Assas-sins*. So I dedicated myself to destroying the man with the pipe and the mustache. He's dead now, and was succeeded by the man who bangs his shoe, but they're all the same, aren't they? There is blood on their collective corn. And no bird sings."

And so they rode away from the harbor. Was it the quality of his betrayal which made the City-shapes so full of menacing meaning? Long Beach! Shall we scribble our signatures on your oil derricks? Shall we press our fearful blue palm-prints on your handball courts, your chili bars? Who would believe it? Laminated joyboys in plum-colored calypso pants gunned their Maseratis around liquor stores. State Collegians Against the Military-Industrial Complex straggled up Spring Street toward Douglas Aircraft, to picket the night shift. Iron pterodactylic street lamps stood bug-eyed sentry watch at the gates of shopping centers: cowpaddies of neon and thermoplastic, from which children caged in grocery carts gave off curdling ululations, and women with bandaged heads ate trading stamps, and there seeped from Muzak speakers a spayed and interminably complaining waltz.

Her name was Dasein Camembert. She had been sent, by reason of special experience, from Washington in answer to his night letter. "When he was a child," she said, "they made him remove his badge and his braid and his eagle buttons. Red-billed storks swallowed adders and frogs . . . pigeons above the machine shop . . . peacocks with crowns on their heads, spurs on their legs, mirrors in their tails . . . Do you understand?"

He understood. But what had his mother to do with the *Fourth International*?

They crossed the San Gabriel River and got lost in El Dorado Park. (The body of Dokhma Koan had been found in El Dorado Park.) For half an hour they circled the honor farm, Stanhope's suggestions proving worthless. Not without compassion, Dasein Camembert observed: "Topographic cretinism." At last they came upon a bus, and followed it to Harvey Way. The bus knew a direction, nosing its great domed hulk down darkened streets, streets on whose exposed flanks festered tract homes. And Stanhope knew that in the back yards of those tract homes grandparents would be crouched under striped aluminum canopies, playing strip poker and drinking gin. The City itself was a dishonor farm; and he was mayor.

"Onalred!" muttered Dasein to herself. "Swimmer in the sewers of seven continents!"

"Turn right," said Stanhope, for they had finally arrived at the familiar pink water tank at the mouth of Cimarosa Street; the mailbox hunched like a dwarf, like Otto; the disreputable pepperwood trees.

A silence like a swamp. A rap on the orange door, unanswered. Entry into an obscene hush. "Mother!" cried Stanhopefully, for the objects of the house seemed to have reasserted their implacable *chosisme*. Could it be . . . ?

Dasein crossed the living room to the plate-glass door and sheathed it, disclosing a patio shot by mothlight. There—Shantung peignoir sprawled motionless in deck chair, before the portable TV set, beside the bottle of Algerian rosé—lay Maud Cronopios. "She's bought it, of course," said Dasein. "I am a carrier of death." Coals in the bowl of the barbecue rotisserie gleamed like the eyes of demented Congolese. On the grill steamed a foil-ful of frozen enchilada. Dasein sniffed at the rosé and wagged her head. "What's this contraption around your mother's neck?"

"A pneumatic traction brace," he said. The smell of the patio salt deposits oppressed him. "You strap it onto your shoulders. It presses a padded bar up and under your chin. Then you pump the lung up to a given pressure, expressed in pounds. It stretches the neck, relieving your back of the strain of holding up your head. Mother injured her back in a bowling tournament three weeks ago. Since then, she's pumped herself up to twenty pounds, three times a day, for fifteen-minute periods."

"I see," she said. "Then, while she was booze-bleary, watching TV, *he* slipped onto the patio and pumped her to death, strangled her in pneumatic traction. Clever; nasty." She moved toward the electrified fence. "What's this . . . another casualty?"

Stanhope was staring down into the empurpled and unrecognizable face of his former mother. He turned. "That's Caryl Chessman, our dachshund."

"I'm afraid he's bought it, too," said Dasein.

Tears sprang to Stanhope's eyes, like the salt excretions of the patio concrete beneath his feet. What poisonous curculio could have wished, would have dared . . . He threw himself abjectly on his mother's hardening corpse. The deck chair tipped over, spilling the body on top of him. He couldn't move until Dasein unpiled them.

They hauled the two bodies into the silent house, down the corridor, to Maud Cronopios' boudoir, and deposited them side by side on the Guatemalan bedspread. The luminous color photograph of Erich Fromm beamed down benignly from the wall. The light from the bulb screwed into the jaw of the plasticized buffalo skull summoned a silver flickering of flakes from his mother's hair curlers. Odd . . .

"You know who did this, don't you?" said Dasein.

"Of course not," said Stanhope. "Nor can I imagine why."

"Why? *He,* as usual, is liquidating his accomplices."

"I don't understand. *Who* he?"

"Onalred," she said. She lay down on the bed beside Maud. "In Romania he was known as Viper . . . in Spain, as Mollusk . . . in Czechoslovakia, as Yak . . . in Mexico—" Her voice faltered. "In Mexico . . . there was blood on the boots of the policemen, and blood on the blade of the alpenstock, and his pen was dipped in blood, and his beard was caked in blood, and *I* opened the hatch—"

Stanhope opened the window. The cow dung was active that night. He closed it again, turned and said softly: "Would you like to tell me about it?" For Dasein, like Bethesda, was obviously one of the broken birds. We are all responsible for the broken birds.

She stared silently at her hands. Stanhope left her to retrieve the bottle of Algerian rosé. When he returned, she was in the middle of her monologue: "I remember, sometime after Mexico, a locked room, doors without knobs, the windows vermilion, a fat lady changing linen, her hands in my hair . . . I was screaming, screaming like the horses of Guernica . . . They strapped me into a coffin and wrapped coils around my feet and stuck wires in my brain and they gave me little jolts of electrical juice and I saw flowers bombing my brain, exploding in my skull . . . and I peered into the exploding flowers and the light from the bombs burned out through the sockets of my eyes, flamed out from inside my head, and everything was brilliant in the room, in my head, and I was blind—"

"So is Otto," said Stanhope. She did not hear him.

"—but it was only temporary. When I could see again, there was a man without a nose. How do you suppose he kept his horn-rimmed glasses on his face, without a nose? He took notes on a green-lined pad of yellow paper after reading the meters and the gauges, and the bulb above me was like the bomb in my brain, and he wore brass buttons and took notes, and the needles on the meters were needles under my fingernails, my skin, and he asked: '*Who is Guernica?*' I had to laugh . . . I choked on my laughter, as though it were an alpenstock."

Laughter, thought Stanhope, is the convulsion of one's *amour-propre.* "And then?"

"I escaped. For a bit, I ran guns to Palestine. Do you know Palestine? Guernica's brother? Rock beds of wadi, howling jackals, cockroaches and cactus fruit and sand flies; barbed wire and pup tents; iron mugs and white cheese; onion porridge and radish-scented tea. But the earth was fat and red. And we plucked stones from the brow of the red-brown hills; we spread phosphate and lime on the fat red earth. They had a dream, you see: of terrace-work on the red-brown hills, of olives and figs and pepper and laurel and poppies and cyclamen. Of the roses of Sharon. But it was not my dream. In my white Bermudas, my khaki shirt, my sunglasses and my gum boots, I was without dreams. I danced with them, but there was horror in my horra. I used to sneak out nights, to get gang-banged by Arabs."

"And no bird sang," said Stanhope.

"Too right," replied Dasein.

He thought: perhaps Long Beach is a sort of Palestine. And asked himself: is *everything* sad-making? Then he lifted her head and poured rosé into her mouth. "When did Uncle Sam catch up with you?"

"In Milan, actually," she said. "I was hoping to write my memoirs for Victor Gollancz, and had gone to Italy to recover the energy of my spite. One morning I was lying naked on raffia matting, trout-colored in the dawn, next to a slumbering Etruscan boy named Tarquin. I had picked up Tarquin the night before, outside La Scala after an indifferent performance of *Orfeo*. His idea of cleverness had been to call me 'Eurydice.' I reached across him for my pack of Lucky Strikes. He stirred, mistaking my desire, and began methodically to scrub my erogenous zones. 'No,' I told him, C major to C sharp, 'Eurydice is dead tired.' Do you understand? He didn't. I preferred Monteverdi's organ to the boy's. But Tarquin tumbled me over onto my stomach. I cried out: 'I will not be humped like a camel!' At *that* moment one of Uncle Sam's professional nephews kicked down the door, galloped into the room, and ventilated poor Tarquin with a Mannlicher-Carcano beebee pistol. Gin-colored eyes, Roman haircut, commando fatigue jacket, French shoes . . . he carried me off to the consulate on his motor scooter. 'With so much commercial traffic,' he told me, 'you should be erogenetically re-zoned; you're no longer a residential neighborhood.' At the consulate, they gave me my choice: help them get the man with the pipe and the mustache, or find myself shipped back by diplomatic pouch to the funny farm for a little more shock therapy. The rest . . . the rest is hysterectomy . . ." She began to sob.

Stanhope extinguished the bulb in the buffalo skull. "Dasein," he said, "don't torture yourself: grief is a species of onanism." Then, in the gloom lit only by the luminescent eye of Erich Fromm, he—like Sartrean consciousness—posited and grasped—the object of—her in the same act. *Forgive me, Bethesda,* he thought . . . *but there is a mercy of the flesh.* Her banditti blouse unwound like an adhesive bandage. "I vowed," said Dasein as they sank to the puce-colored carpet, "I vowed I'd snap his spine and nail it to his sickle . . . I took an oath . . . or was it an oaf? There have been so many, Stan. I am a carrier of death, a wastepaper basket of the Revolution's manhood."

So it was that Stanhope betrayed Bethesda as Bethesda was being murdered. How did Pierre Reverdy put it? *Le coeur rend bête.*

Midnight: under the glyph of the grinning monkey god in St. Teresa's Little Ashram of Ecumenical Oṁ, Otto Unamuno swore. "Give it up, Gnatpappa."

The Australian aborigine wordlessly ceased his tinkering with the drive system. Otto sighed. The system had such gorgeous possibilities. A flexible spline, turning inside a rigid circular gear ring, generated an elliptoidal wave shape which could be harmonically transmitted as positive motion through a hermetic seal. The problem in relating the system to genital excitement was to develop a vibratory bell chamber or fluxing plastic bellows-lung that could be fitted directly onto the human body. Transmission of the elliptoidal shape would then presumably activate the attachment's flux or vibratory capacities in a repetitive wave-pumping. There would be something manifestly spiritual about a stimulation induced by harmonic waves. If à Kempis had been accurate in describing suffering as "the terrible initiative caress of God," *this* might be the ultimate ravishment.

Let the Word go out: God flux man.

Gnatpappa's tinkering with the system had so far resulted only in an efficient single-stage speed reduction unit. Useful, of course, mechanically, but not immediately applicable to Otto's quest for the connection between nerve ends and Jaspersian Transcendence. It was late, and Otto weary. He would be obliged to resort once more to conventional devices.

"Hoist me up, Gnatpappa." The abo applied clamps; the wires trickling through pulleys plucked Otto from his wheelchair and swung his crippled body across the ceiling. There he dangled, as though drooling from the grin of the monkey god. "Down, Gnatpappa." He was lowered onto the lace-trimmed, satin-covered bier, and his wadded silk dressing gown removed by the abo. "Now, let me feel you." Gnatpappa lay full length on Otto. Otto's hands drew subtleties from the snakeskin band around the coarsened brow, the flat planes of the face, the tendons in the neck, the dilly bag slung from that neck on a string of human hair, the cicatrix scars on the chest, the frogman totem at the base of the spine, the pubic tassel and the woolen shoes. *"Das kecke Beserl,"* Otto murmured.

He sighed again. "Music, please." The abo rolled off and turned on the stereo speakers. There entered the chamber that first E-flat major of the bass bassoon. Triadified, it was more than music: it was an acoustic insinuation, a notational prurience. From the silver bowl beside the bier, Otto selected a rotten apple and bit into it. He lay naked under the notation, curving himself like a blood-drunk ear. The abo attached the elastomeric coupling to the rotor shaft of the fractional horsepower engine. The coupling was of a convoluted configuration, like a large piece of ribbon candy. The ticklish part of the business was joining its secondary orifice to Otto's organ. Gnatpappa turned the key on the suction cup until Otto groaned. *O felix culpa!*

The sun hero on his bier, ravaged by blind darkness . . . maximization of angular misalignment between engine and organ . . . the wild boar rooting in the primeval beginnings of Man . . . increase of torque to the limits of physical stamina . . . the drum of pulse, the Inner (Receding) Africa . . . introduction of sinusoidal speed variations . . . horn figures, the terzettoing of Rhinemaidens . . . engine hum, coupling tremble. . . *O felix copula!*

Light, and the Eye: spider fibers of the optic nerve, discharging sharpened spikes of impulse . . . the Eye of fanning knives . . . the cool, surgical light, the inimical blue lines of the Omnivorous Eye: the female genitalia . . .

"But it's Three, don't you *see?*" cried Otto, who could not, from his sun bier to the bass bassoon. And he thought in despair: I, Palindrome, reversed myself at the swinging compass point of Time, to a division of insipid violins, and even inside out I'm *toot*. Still . . . he was possessed by the acoustic insinuation, and he knew:

Wotan! Brünnhilde! Siegfried! Three against the Emasculating Eye!

The elastomeric coupling became a universal joint.

Tacked to the floor of the lifeguard shack was a linoleum map of the world. Onalred liked to stride over the egg-shaped hemispheres, to grind his heels on tiny, peninsular pseudo-nations.

But tonight such feets of scourge had been omitted. Why?

Onalred, ordinarily something of a slob, had been ironing his black domino for an hour, with particular attention to the pleats. Why?

He kept his face averted. Why? He refused to remove his beret. Why? And he had summoned Bethesda to the lifeguard shack even though he didn't like her very much. Why?

Bethesda's eyes were full of whys as she watched him from the cot. In her mind was a glowing: fire of slag heap, red coal-eye of wispy smoke-thought, slow will's taffy pull of passing barge . . . the usual fears and desires for Stanhope. But what was in Onalred's mind? Young (he had told them on a confessional occasion) he had sprung a beard, emulating Lenin. It had been accidentally ignited by the spark from a spit of shish kebab, and his fellow operatives had called him the Burning Bush. He seemed now to be chewing on some nettle plucked from the burning bush of the past, as he stared out the window.

The dolphins, however, were not running that night. "What do you see?" she asked.

"Yellow China," he replied harshly, "erupting from the sea. The Rising Yeast." Bethesda knew his warts would be glittering like jewels. "This China is unbreakable."

Wasn't that rather deviationist? She always consulted Stanhope on points of doctrine. "What do you mean?" she asked.

He laughed unpleasantly. "You know what I mean. What's the matter? Can't the schematic frangibility of your self-hatred accommodate itself to an *apertura a la sinistra?*"

That was certainly nasty. And what did he mean, self-hatred? "Stanhope," she said, hoping to jolly him, "has written a poem about China. It goes like this:

> "Shall the Mao-Mao rack us
> Up on their abacus?
> Choo-choo,
> Choo-choo, Chou En-lai:
> Here's mud
> In your blood-
> shot eye!"

Onalred spun to the cot and pressed the steam iron on her brow, smoothing out the seams.

"I don't understand!" she screamed. "Doesn't it scan? Why, you're not—"

Then she was silent. The smell of her scorched flesh filled the lifeguard shack.

"If," said Dr. Langweil, "I should ask you to describe the Garden of Eden, how would you go about it? How do you conceive of it?"

Prone in the connection booth, Pather said: "I'll play your silly game. How *would* I go about it?"

"Humor me," said Langweil.

Pather thought. Then said: "Imagine a drum. A vacuumized, hermetically sealed cylinder. All right. Inside: a tree of dees."

"Dees?"

"Hollow electrodes, creating a magnetic field."

"Ah," said Langweil, "we are talking about a cyclotron."

"Very good," said Pather. "Note that a cyclotron has a good deal of 'radiance of content.' Now. Ions are introduced into this field. They revolve and circulate. They cross and circle the dee tree. After every half circle, the polarity of the electrical field between the dees reverses. The ion particles elongate, accelerate, gather energy. The increased energy expands their circular orbit. They *spiral . . .* widening, widening—from inertia to the speed of light in microseconds. When they reach the outer limits of the dees, they burst through a channel or orifice . . ."

"Well?" said Langweil when Pather paused.

"Can *you* conceive," said Pather, "of a beryllium apple?"

"What do you mean?"

"At the end of that channel, on the other side of that orifice, let's say there's beryllium. The accelerating ion particles spiral around, up, out, *exploding* through the channel. They bombard and shatter the beryllium apple. Got it?"

"Yes. But—"

"Langweil, have you ever seen series photographs of the ion spiral in a cyclotron?"

"No."

"Sad-making. For, you see (or haven't seen) those photographs make the spiral passage *visible;* disclose the track of the accelerating particles as they approach the speed of light. Do you know what that track looks like, in the photographs?"

"Never having seen the photographs, I couldn't be expected to guess—"

"*Serpents,*" said Pather. "It looks like serpents."

Langweil checked the EEG. "Parturient, there's something wrong here. You're dodging me, aren't you? You would have me seize on this and conclude that your hang-up derives from generalized feelings of physicist guilt for having created the atom bomb. Yet look at these revealing graph-dips. What are you covering up? Any one of us can pick up that kind of guilt by reading *The New Yorker;* it goes well with *pâté de foie gras* and Tío Pepe."

"You were the one who asked me to visualize the Garden of Eden."

Langweil shook his head. "You're hiding inside this pretty little metaphor; the cyclotron as Eden. Why? Come *on.* The metaphor trips a little too lightly over your lips; you almost *relish* your guilt, that generalized guilt. Why? Nonsense! We went through the little boy. We went through Faust. Now you would apparently have me believe you began as Parsifal; and somewhere along the way you got yourself transformed into Cain. No! Little Bo-Pepys has lost his *Ahimsa* and don't know where to find it! A *lie,* Parturient." Right, left, uppercut, rabbit punch. "Let's try it again. Begin at the beginning. Constants. That's why I asked about Eden. Where's your *moral* constant, Parturient? Do you even know what it is? How have you betrayed it, as you claim to have betrayed it? Tell me what it is . . . the hook you hang your precious value scale upon? And *where* is it?"

Pather closed his eyes. All gray; symbols floated by, washed-out, shrunken; values and dimensions and relationships, nothing more than spidery arabics. "*h!*" he said, "Planck's operative quantum. *e,* the basic unit of electrical discharge. *c,* the speed of light. Those are the *only* constants."

"Yes. What of it?"

Pather was angry. "Are you dense? Those three letters constitute *the* mathematical formula of empirical reality. Interrelationships, denied by those three letters: the stupid, impossible mosaic! I propose a theory of wave mechanics. What am I doing when I propose it? Grasping is what I'm doing. I'm saying that every movement of particles—atomic nuclei, electrons, light particles, pick 'em—every movement likely corresponds to a specific wavelength, the intensity of which at any point in the system indicates the *probability* that the particle is to be found at just that juncture . . ."

"All right. So you're dealing in probabilities. We all do. Do you find it insupportable? Does it scare you?"

"Oh, it's marvelous! Hunky-dory! An abstract, hot-rod, kiddie car to Nowhere! I don't know the *significance* of *h,* or *e,* or *c.* I don't know the meaning of their mathematical relationship. I don't even know if there *is* a meaning to their mathematical relationship. All I know is that they probably exist—"

"So? So you're not God. So you don't know it all. So you snivel?"

"So I don't like my world! What does *my* world have to say about thought or imagination? I look at *h, e, c* . . . what have they to do with music or pain or silence or beauty or joy or blue or red? Nothing! They have nothing to do with any of those things!"

"Or with the price of eggheads," said Langweil. "What you're really saying is that they have nothing to do with *you,* aren't you?" For the first time, Pather saw him light a cigarette. "They have nothing to do with the prime pork loin of tender sensitivity you slide between your sheets at night. The well-known self-abolition hang-up. Not *your* sin, Parturient; a hand-me-down sin. The sin of Aristotle, Galileo, all the boys who separated the world into that which is measurable—by size and weight—and the rest of it, form, color, smell; and said: forget smell, form, color, buddies, because they're too tough to measure. The sin of the feces-fingerers: the Tyranny of the Quantitative."

"Well?" said Pather, his voice rising. "Isn't that a reasonably respectable hang-up? I mean, there's a precedent, isn't there? That's why I went to work for Otto. I was under the illusion that he was interested in getting rid of the dualities. But no! He's just a little Mussolini of the Media, pushing a particularly nasty form of Skoptsyism."

"Otto, again . . ." said Langweil.

"Yes, Otto! Otto *hates* light. I mean, he *hates* it. Because he's blind! Light! The *only* immutable . . . and he hates it!"

"You're moving away again," said Langweil. "You're avoiding the real issue—"

"I'm not! Don't you see? *He hates light.* Light, which is both waves and particles, both energy and fluid, both mathematics and love! He *hates* it because he can't see it."

"Now you're the one pushing the duality," said Langweil.

"It's the only way out of the duality! If you think of light as the purest manifestation of expression of matter, it makes possible all the color and form of the universe."

"But do *you* think of light that way?"

"Yes!"

"No. You just said, where's music, beauty, red and blue? No. You're scared it's actually the other way around, aren't you? Scared it's all just symbol structure, without substance . . . waves in a gray mathematical sea . . . that it has nothing to do with *your* soul! That's why you *want* to feel guilty about the atom bomb. Guilt at least is personal, isn't it? Your own little masturbatory object!"

Pather was exhausted. "So you turn it all into an archetypical Pascalian crap game: mathematics and mysticism. We all—"

"Shut up," said Langweil. "If there were ions of contempt, you'd accelerate them in microseconds to bombard all the intelligence in the world, rather than admit what's wrong with you. And what's wrong with you, Parturient, is so painfully obvious, so *banal*—"

"Is that the case?" said Pather icily.

"Yes-indeedie!" said Langweil, stubbing out his cigarette and immediately lighting another. "You painted such pretty little abstract pictures with your mathematical symbols, didn't you? You hung them on the wall of a neutral universe, didn't you? And then—and then the umbilical cord, the 'I' connecting you to the universe, got sliced, didn't it? The abstractions abolished their progenitive vulgarity. *And you were lonely!* Parturient, you're having an identity crisis! Just like *everybody* else! Jesus!"

"You think that's funny, do you?"

"Yes. Because *you,* above all others, should know that none of these obnoxious little dualities really exists. Subject and object are now and always have been connected. And they are connected by the very 'I' you think you've misplaced. They are connected, *because knowledge itself is an act.* The 'I' and the universe are connected, because *intellectual* activity has *physical* consequences. If it didn't, all knowledge would be a mirror image of the physical world, wouldn't it? But it isn't; we know it isn't. You yourself have told me that microphysical experiments indicate that every measurement—*every accession of knowledge*—alters the observed object; in some instances, invalidates the measurement itself. Right? Well, that raises some problems, but it solves some, too. Use your brain, man. If an act of pure knowledge has physical consequences, then it is also likely to have moral significance. Well? Isn't it? And isn't it about time, then, that you climbed out of the playpen? Isn't it about time you had your epistemological diapers changed?"

"I'm certainly climbing out of this phone booth, this coffin!" said Pather. "I don't pay fifty bucks an hour to get insulted."

"Then you've come to the wrong place. Existential psychocatalysis employs the insult as one of its principal therapeutic weapons. By all means, climb out. *I'll* climb in. Maybe mental health will only arrive in this country when a new generation of psychocatalysts resolves to insult its patients beyond endurance, beyond defense. The Zen trap into questionlessness! When those patients are told that their real problem is that they are so relentlessly boring!"

Furious, Pather stomped into his trousers, stabbed his way through jacket sleeves.

"O, Ormazd!" cried Langweil from the connection booth. "This crude, interminable card game of phenomenological bridge: *pour-soi* finessing *en-soi*'s king, *en-soi* trumping *pour-soi*'s ace. Look into the heart of *Erlebnis,* my hearties! Espy the wind! Your bowels run amuck. Consciousness, you say, is a great emptiness, a wind blowing toward objects. Too right! *Your* consciousness is indeed a wind—it is hot air! It is a fart! Physicists: the New Brahmins, contracting intentional consciousness into itself: *farce!*"

Pather turned the ultraviolet lamp to its highest power, hoping to turn Langweil into a rasher of bacon. "Come back any time!" shouted Langweil. "Maybe you'll discover the Pre-Personal, eh? The transcendental Consciousness, eh? Don't worry about *me,* Parturient. It only Husserls when I laugh!"

Pather slammed the door. The receptionist looked up, fearful and paralyzed in the lamp of his anger, like an animal at night in the middle of the road as an automobile bears glaring down on it. Pather considered raping the receptionist, among scattering copies of *Omphalos.* How might he broach (breech) the subject (object)? He could say: I want to know you . . . in the biblical sense, of course. Of coarse. Since the act of pure knowledge has physical consequences . . .

He settled for unplugging her electric typewriter, and ran out of the office.

What now? Obviously, it was a time of crisis. And what did Pather Parturient always do in a time of crisis? He went straight to the Colorado Lagoon to pick up a girl. Just as, in an airport waiting room, he would have gone straight to the concession stand to pick up a paperback book: a print pill (a love lozenge) to dull the dislocation (the *Angst* in the pants). Among crotchedty volleyballers in stained sweat pants, he *found* a girl.

Her name was Oona, a red-haired Irish nurse on twenty-four-hour furlough from the Veterans Administration Hospital. No Sahasrara she, but Pather was attracted to her Irish-nursy whiteness, her almost lewd etiolation . . . Hoping to twist that Irishness to his advantage, Pather asked her: "Do you know the poetry of Stanhope Cronopios? 'Loleda and the Swan?'

> "A sudden blow: the great wings beating still
> Above the struggling maid. She wrings its neck
> And flings it down and steps upon its bill,
> And says: 'You dirty bird!'
> > Après le kill,
> She had it stuffed and set it on a shelf . . .
> Poor Agamemnon had to stab himself."

"I don't understand what it means," said Oona.

Did that discourage Pather-in-crisis? Definitely not. Rather it served to heighten the desire of the old skin skiver. For the vulnerability of such an admission was an invitation to abuse. Perhaps, he thought, at the jellied heart of the flaky pastry of her, he might discover the white cool killer diamond with the cutting edge . . .

They left the lagoon together, for the Club Descartes Blanche (Coito Ergo Sum) nearby. "Am I," asked Pather on the rocks, "nothing more than a sex organ for machines . . . a cybernetic fecundator?" He asked it not only of Oona on the next stool, but of all the sailors at the bar; and of the young hunks of roasted mutton in the back room abusing ping-pong balls with rubber-laminated paddles; and of the confetti on the floor and the sand in the beer and the spiders in the eyes of the pompon girls.

"What do you mean?" asked Oona conscientiously, slurping her shoulders.

"I mean: do I exist only to help technological monstrosities propagate themselves?"

Thought, like a stone, muddied the puddle of her brow. Charming: under that disorderly mop of auburn hair, she was both docile and brainless. He thought: oxidation seems to end in rust more often than it does in flames.

And when they battened down the booths and crossed the bar at the Club Descartes Blanche, he succeeded in luring her to his atelier on Bay Shore. It wasn't difficult! He was experienced, and her only alternative was a cheerless return to the Veterans Administration Hospital, with its mean huts and surly paraplegics. But on his porch she hesitated, uneasily pondering a nearby tableau: high school hood-lets relieving their beer-bloated bladders into the muddy canal. (How languid, thought Pather. No: not languid. Cronopios had once ac-curately observed that there was no languor in the fatigue of Long Beach, nothing of the consoling sadness of sated passion; it was, rather, the fatigue which succeeds violent and pointless exercise.) Oona was uncomfortable; and Pather, opening the door, was panic-stricken, for he felt he was already becoming bored. In his behalf he enlisted another Cronopios poem, composed for electric autoharp and disco-tics:

> At three o'clock in the morning,
> You pause before my door.
> At three o'clock in the morning,
> It's always Either/Or.
>
> I remove my silk foulard;
> You let down your Kierke-Guard:
> *Ex - is - tenz!*

She decided to come in. He mixed Don Equis and aquavit. Then, to the accompaniment of a tape of Elisabeth Lutyens' Motet Opus 27, they engaged in some intricate and juvenile toe play on top of the Turkish coffee table. "Is that music?" she asked.

"Sing along with Wittgenstein," he said.

"I mean—"

"Germans. An all-male choir a-cappellamenting selected maxims from *Tractatus Logico-Philosophicus*. Do you like it?"

"Am I supposed to?" Score one for her side. He shucked her of her starch. She cradled her breasts, as though they were rare cool snow-things, offered by a child. They reminded Pather of the feet he had just finished playing with: withered, blue-veined, unnaturally white from sun-proof cotton-sockliness. O Sahasrara . . . Light thickened to Matter!

Even though she wasn't Sahasrara, he went through with the usual transaction. "We are all of us, Oona, vessels of physical possibilities, cups of elemental form-potentials. Sex and the Dance are ritualized expressions of Pure Form trying to achieve its own fulfillment. Ah!" As had been his recently monotonous custom, however, Pather found not liberation into fulfillment but doomed tumble in free fall, illusory escape, pursuit, recapture, inevitable return in maxim-cuffs to Wittgenstein.

Still later, standing before the bathroom mirror, over the white basin, between the black plastic bidet and the strangled stork of a shower stall, he saw the cipher trembling. He bisected it: the bisecting line should have been the ego-*I*. It wasn't. In measuring himself, he had destroyed himself. Was the *I* which he could not encounter in his consciousness made impossible by the syncretinous disunity of his representations? Or was it the *They* which in fact dismembered those representations? Too bad Wittgenstein wasn't around to ask about it. However, since he wasn't, Pather must destroy in order to be able to measure. True? True. He shouted out to Oona: "I'm going to murder a man, Oona. Or, more precisely, I'm going to murder half a man."

She didn't understand *that,* either.

Now [11]

A symbol is explicated . . . Gongor refuses to go to
Marineland . . . Sahasrara removes her shirt.

"Neither do I," said Gongor, smoking his banana peel. "You weren't
contemplating suicide, I trust. And you wouldn't murder your own
psychocatalyst, would you?"

"Of course not," said Parturient. "Killing either one of us would
have been a violation of the doctor-patient professional relationship."

"Nor," said Gongor, "do I understand that jazz about the Eye and
the female genitalia."

Stanhope sighed. Gongor was hopeless. "Various tribes and a
number of mythologies associate the eye with female genitalia," he
explained. "It was natural for Otto to extrapolate that intuition . . .
the Eye became his Emasculator. Against it, he proposed the mystical powers of symbolic sets of male sex organs."

"The Triangle of Pythagoras!" said Parturient.

"The Trinity of Christ," said Stanhope.

"The Triad of Hegelian Dialectic!" said Parturient.

"And, of course, the pretzel," concluded Stanhope. He stood.
"Gongor, if you are ready to move, I think it might be possible to
finish this off tonight."

"Where is there to go?" asked Gongor.

"Marineland. Bay Shore. Cimarosa Street. And the Ashram."

"But we've been to Bay Shore and Cimarosa Street," objected
Gongor. "Marineland is not even in Long Beach. And you told me
the Ashram is now a shopping plaza."

Sahasrara had removed the wet shirt, and was now bathing herself by the moon.

Stanhope was disappointed in Gongor; in a War of Abstractions,
we are all of us foot soldiers. "Very well," he lied. And brooded:
"Marineland, of course, is not in Long Beach. And yet . . . I will
always think of it as my berefting place."

Then [11]

Stanhope tells Dasein about the dolphins . . . Dasein tells Stanhope about Bethesda . . . Stanhope resolves revenge . . . a truly shocking revelation.

Few things (thought Stanhope) are funnier than the truly monstrous. And few things are more monstrous than the need for beauty and romance. (He *knew*.) Watch the women as they watch the dolphins play: the middle-aged in miniskirts, dreaming dully behind eroded faces; the teen-aged under great hives of hair, their eyes like arrowheads; the prepubescent strapped into superfluous bras. Flesh the color of burnt sugar; minds undergoing steady granulation in the humdrumdom of the afternoon; mouths falling greedily (in Almond Joylessness?) on sticks of peanut brittle, or sucking up orangeade with a desperate soul-thirst, engaging little slivers of carton plastic in their bold and regular teeth. The grandstand was a riot of enflamed cloth, a molten motley of bright colors (as though crayons in a coverless tin box had been left out under the sun to dissolve on one another) which seemed to express some deep sullen mystique of abstract vapidity, some non-representational fatigue. The sky was blue enamel, peeled periodically by flaky white gulls. The pool gleamed like a sheet of undulant tin; beneath its surface, plum-dark and palpitant in the roiling waters, roved the dolphins. A torn line of silk froth presaged their cresting: *Tursiops truncatus* rises and tumbles through a burning hoop, fetches a plastic ball, plunges after peanut brittle wrappers and gratuitous carp—pink-eyed, clown-princely, blow-holing its obscure delights. "You mean," said Dasein Camembert, "he uses *dolphins?*"

"Yes," said Stanhope. "I'd check the staff of the oceanarium for any old men past the retirement age." He had seen Leer lurking among the tortoises. "I know they operate a gasoline truck tanked up on salt water, and run it regularly between here and San Pedro." A bus line for purloined (and purposeful) porpoises. "Then the dolphins rendezvous with Soviet trawlers in international waters."

"But how do they communicate?" asked Dasein.

"Hydrophones and underwater loudspeakers," said Stanhope. "They train the dolphins here: electrical stimulation of different parts of the brain. Then they truck them to San Pedro and chuck them into the ocean. The trawlers are equipped to receive and record their signals. Although dolphins *are* capable of vocalizing within the same ranges and parametric sets of variables as humans, and their noise emissions *are* transformable into our acoustic range, Onalred considers it safer to operate at higher frequencies. The dolphin can emit sounds at frequencies up to one hundred kilocycles. I imagine that on the trawlers they slow down the sound track, damp the highs, something like that. I don't know much about the trawler end. I only know about the oceanarium because Onalred drank himself almost insensible one night in the lifeguard shack, on lookout, and bragged."

Dasein's cave-face darkened; her words seemed to fly out of it like bats. "I have some unhappy news for you, Stan. The Coast Guard checked that lifeguard shack this morning, after my report. They found . . . they found Bethesda."

The pause that distresses. A chubby man in cork helmet and knickers threw strips of shark steak into the pool. Putt-putt, went the dolphins; squeak, whistle, bark, grunt, rasp. "What are you trying to tell me?" said Stanhope.

"We must all matriculate someday in the graduate school of death," said Dasein. "In Mexico . . . in Mexico, after they levered the alpenstock out of his skull, the man with the blood-caked beard took twenty-two hours to die . . . and when he was dead, an autopsy disclosed that he had a brain of extraordinary dimensions . . . two pounds, thirteen ounces . . . and that his heart, too, was overly large . . ."

"Cut the crap, Dasein! *What are you trying to tell me?*"

"Bethesda is dead," she said. "She was . . . apparently, Onalred *ironed* her to death. She was . . . she was *pleated*."

The fact was a dagger in his brain; his brain was a blubbery squid, trying to grasp this quirk of dirk. "But *why?* She was no threat to him. It doesn't make any sense!"

"Events," said Dasein, "are merely a sort of notation of our feelings. Please don't blame me, Stan. I *told* you I was a carrier of death."

"*Yimach shmo vizichro!*" shouted Stanhope. He bolted from her to the guardrail circumscribing the pool. He vomited his continental breakfast into the undulant waters. A flattened beak snapped at it and squawked at him. On his knees, peering into the maw of 160 dolphin teeth, Stanhope was suddenly self-conscious. He had longed for a paroxysm of despair; he had achieved a humiliating hiccup. There seemed about his retching an insupportable quality of unctuousness. He stood up, ashamed of himself. From out of the hairy hives of the teen-aged girls buzzed bees of delighted perturbation. An *incident*. . . . a flaw in the marble of monotony.

Dasein took his arm. "Let's go inside," she said. "The gloom will soothe you." They walked into the watery green winds of the aquarium. "Strange," said Dasein: "In death, the face skin sulks while the skull grins. I suppose that's why we need undertakers; with their thumbs in the putty, they protect us from having to cope with that contradiction in our hour of emotional dishabille." They stopped at a huge tank. As though a technicolored turkey molted light, bright feathery aspects floated, turned, shimmered, coalesced. Through the shale of those aspects sank fish like slain champagne bottles, gaping and gasping. Their mouths were lesions.

Stanhope pressed his cheek against the cool glass of the fish tank. There appeared to him out of that green coolness an angel of melancholy, dark-eyed, alabaster-limbed, her wings suggesting inexpressible possibilities of caress. She must operate as a sort of reverse Proserpine; instead of gathering lost loves to her, she was summoned by the sentimentalities of the losers. She lavished herself on the authors of those sentimentalities; permitted the losers whatever intimacies their disorderly imaginations could devise, in order that they might enjoy the full deliciousness of their self-pity. Stanhope wanted to beat off the angel. It was not fair to Bethesda that she should be thus enjoyed, more loved in the losing of her than she had been while still imperfectly around.

What, then, was he learning, pressed to coolness? There seemed something in motion beneath his unhappiness, something mysteriously conferred, a new part of himself, a hard, bright, resolute part, some little silver fish of a thing, a glistening guppy whose scales shot off semaphoric messages, sending up into all this gloom insinuations of relief . . . Why relief? Had he perhaps failed Bethesda in so many unacknowledged ways? (He saw now that, like most loves, theirs had been half mysticism, half cupidity.) And had her death then at a stroke erased a bad debt from that bloody accounting book, the human ledger? How odd that Onalred should serve him so, should be the instrument of his deliverance, through *cruelty*. He saw now that in betraying Onalred to Washington, and in expecting Washington to deal with him, he had confirmed Onalred's judgment of his essential frivolousness. Surely an opponent worthy of Onalred would have gone after him personally, to destroy not only the network but the preconceptions of the stealthy porpoise-master, the Nero of octogenarians. (In some weird way, to go after Onalred seemed suddenly to be the same thing as going after Long Beach . . . as going after dreams and the betrayers of dreams.) Onalred, in severing Stanhope's last ties with the human community, had simultaneously severed his last ties with compunction; had managed (unknowingly?) to estrange the young poet even from the traditional mechanisms of escape, like the dark angel of melancholy.

He turned to Dasein. "*I* will get Onalred," he said. His tone was steely: as though he snapped that sword-edged blade of statement into the safety razor of his will, and was now at last prepared to scrape Fate's throat.

Sensing this, Dasein asked: "Have you signed a pact with Victory?"

"No. I have signed a pact with Death." How else would he ever be able to forget Bethesda, and the gift of her perfect acquiescence . . . her physical and spiritual largesse?

On their way to her motorbike, Dasein said: "Shall I make funeral arrangements? Arlington, perhaps?"

"No," said Stanhope. "There will be no monuments for Bethesda. None, that is, but the death of Onalred. For we monumentalize our dead, Dasein, not to assuage our grief but to make it permanent. Monumentalization is an opportunity to create the perfect loving-object, permitting us to adore a blind facet of our unhappiness, making us feel we are better than we are because we are so richly enamored of the very loss we have sustained."

Climbing onto the motorbike behind her, he tried to gain a grip on those ice-smooth memories, those molten mercury drops of rue. He saw the past for what it was: the gate unhinged, the garden deserted, the marble fountain dry, the statuary rotting, the burning courtyard littered with the bodies of dead birds . . . dead gulls. "Onalred!" he cried, cherishing his hatred of the porpoise-master as man cherishes his grievances with God.

Dasein glanced over her shoulder at him with a troubled look, then pulled into a roadside Sodium Alginate stand. *Isolate of Brown Kelp: Prevents Absorption of Radioactive Strontium in the Intestines.* They bought chocolate-covered bars of it, and sat down to lunch by the Bay.

"Stanhope," said Dasein at last, "there is something you should know before you take on Onalred yourself. I don't know quite how to tell you this. But . . . why do you suppose that, directly on meeting you, I wanted to see your mother?"

"I have no idea," he said.

"I knew your mother," said Dasein. "I had met her before . . . in Mexico."

"So?"

"Let me put it another way." She paused. (What, wondered Stanhope, was so equivocal that she should shyly and shamefully sniff round it, like Mary Worth on the scent of misfortune?) Dasein said: "Why do you think Onalred should have murdered your mother?"

He considered it, bouncing his speculations off the inflatables which bobbed in the Bay. "I believe I asked that question on page one hundred and sixty-two?"

"Yes. I told you she was an accomplice, and that he was liquidating his accomplices. Then we started rolling around on the puce-colored carpet, and never took the matter up again. How, when and where did she become his accomplice? And what was the exact nature of her accomplicity?"

He shook his head.

Dasein said: "I have suggested Mexico. She was there when I was there when Onalred was there. Has it not struck you that you were born, in Long Beach, in May of 1941 . . . *nine months* after the incident of the infamous alpenstock, the murder of the man with the beard and the eyes like supernovas? That is a meaty bone of fact for you to chew on."

"I don't understand," he admitted.

"Stanhope . . . you are the hatched egg of a plot laid in Mexico almost a quarter century ago. Stanhope . . . *Onalred is your father!*"

Air-cushioned hovercraft skipped across the blue plate of the tranquil Bay. Sportyaks and Trojans, Aqua Cats and Avengers, Vikings and Marauders described a dizzy riot, a waltz of colorful, burning insects. Skiff, schooner, catamaran and yawl all were caught in the ripplings of this revelation; all sought a configuration capable of containing it . . .

Stanhope said at last, carefully, as though the verbal terrain were mined: "So much the better for me; so much the worse for him!" Then his fatherlessness had been phony. It distressed him to learn that in choosing a father figure, he had inadvertently picked his own father. But, then, actually, he hadn't done the picking, had he? And now, now at last, there was a perfect liberation to be achieved! A father to be killed! And social, patriotic and personal reasons for killing him—as well as the psychological imperative! Onalred! His father? Who could or would have guessed it?

"I'm afraid there's more," said Dasein.

More? His father had killed his mother, hadn't he? And his lover, hadn't he? Not to mention his dachshund. What more could there possibly be?

"You were," said Dasein, her face averted, "an extraordinary *experiment* . . . a wedding, as it were, of Mendel and Lysenko. For— Stanhope, prepare yourself!—Maud Cronopios was both more than and less than your mother. She was also . . . your aunt."

"My aunt?"

"Yes. And Onalred is also your uncle."

"But . . ."

"They were brother and sister," said Dasein. "Incest," she added succinctly, "the game the whole family can play."

Well. He asked the hovercraft about it; they exhaled bad breath and the Bay grimaced. He asked the Sportyaks; the Sportyaks had nothing to say. He asked the inflatables; they hissed and sank.

"Their hope, you see," said Dasein, "was to create—to procreate— a perfect agent, a *revolutionary sweet pea,* combining acquired and inherited characteristics. Of course, Lysenko has since been discredited. Had he not been, you would be a living discredit to him."

What could he say? He must say *something,* if only to pile the words into a hat rack on which to hang the Homburg of his nausea. "Well," he said, throwing away his bar of sodium alginate, "well, it seems to me perfectly disgusting."

Now [12]

Third interlude . . .

"But that means," cried Gongor, "that you . . . that you—"

"That I," said Stanhope, "am, in a manner of speaking, Captain Happen's half brother. And cousin. As a matter of fact, I'm his closest living relative." *relatives, surely.*

Gongor mopped his brow with his rabbit battle jacket sleeve. Parturient was spreading mayonnaise on Sahasrara. They listened for a while to the small mouths of the sea sucking on the sides of the ship. Then Gongor said: "I wonder if I might have some more dried banana skin?"

And Stanhope said: "There are, of course, certain relevant details to be cleared up before we reach our climax. Just a few days after these rather sobering disclosures, I sustained what might be called a jar to (or *of*) my pre- (or post-) conceptions . . ."

"Lettuce get on with it," muttered Parturient to the mayonnaised Sahasrara.

Gongor gulped.

Then [12]

*Why Stanhope still believed Onalred to be in Long Beach. . .
Ali-Whoops provides a clue . . . a visit to the College
confirms an awful suspicion . . . Stanhope re-evaluates the
situation.*

From the mud-colored cork tips of her puffed-to-death cigarettes,
Dasein fashioned butt-chains, rhomboids, swastikas on the table top
of the corner booth in Vaseline Ali's Horn of Malt. On ravaging an
empty pack and crumpling it, she slumped: lit up and sucked on a
joint of anxiety. "The airport, the harbor, the bus terminals have all
been staked out," she said. "And the Mexican border." (That border
over which Onalred in the guise of a wetback, with fringed serape
and white-walled huaraches, had slipped months ago to hitch his
way with migrant pickers north, following the grail of the Orange.)
"But we can't patrol every freeway ramp in Long Beach, can we?"
Of course not. Nor could they post sentries at the traffic intersections
along the broad boulevards, those paved extensions of a Will-to-
Squalor which flowed anonymously across the indistinguishable sub-
divisions of Los Angeles County. Should he elect to venture deeper
into the interior, Onalred would escape them: men with fewer resources, less cause, no practice, and one tenth his ingenuity had succeeded in disappearing forever into Paramount or Compton.

But Onalred was still in Long Beach. Of this, Stanhope was convinced. For one thing, men like Onalred must manufacture a logic to
inform their own drama—precisely because they are *not* romantics.
After the daggers, after the strut, after the piano wire, as the curtain
moves menacingly toward its descent, there must be a moment for
counting corpses; a moment for the slit throats of the chorus to articulate a purgative. Had not Onalred—on locking the octogenarians
inside their garden as the bungalows burned down, as the ignited
birds leapt from their flare-trees, as the charred bodies on the
elephant-colored mall writhed and chortled and cried—had not Onal-

red *kissed his thumbs?* He had. And what meaning did that peculiarly
Spanish after-genuflection gesture have? It meant that Onalred (his
father!) believed in Fate. To be sure, it was a man-made, self-made
Fate—a sort of dorsal-diuretic dialectic—but still Fate! Surely such
thumb-kissing signified a sense of one's self-drawn circle of possibility; conceded limits and definitions and imperatives; proffered a ritual
token to the dark and bloody-mouthed gods of History. A pregnant
superstition! If we are not permitted to arrange for the circumstances
of our own death, then what a meretricious concept is the Will! Stanhope believed that as long as *he* lived, Long Beach must remain for
Onalred unfinished business, unfinished *art*. To flee, leaving behind
him his botched revolutionary sweet pea (that pea deposited a quarter century ago in Time's Burbank to gather its disinterestedness),
would have obliged Onalred to admit the awesome, imponderable
power of the anti-principle of Chaos. He would never again be able
to kiss his thumbs.

When, however, he proposed this to Dasein Camembert, she was
doubtful. "In my experience," she said, "life is a series of messy abor-
tions. And those who linger on, clinging and pleading for logic, for
fulfillment, for purgation—like the endless on-one-elbow aria of a dying opera star, or the hortatory renewal notices for a magazine subscription which has lapsed—those who insist on some final definition,
some summing up of the meaning of failure and death, are either
fools or virgins. Onalred is neither."

No: but he was Stanhope's father, the third eye in Stanhope's
brow, through which he must look coldly at the puny shade of his
hero-potential cast on the wall of the world. And Stanhope was convinced he would find him, in Long Beach, under volleyball netting,
perhaps, at Alamitos Bay, in black domino and blue beret, sketch-
ing sickles in the sand, with a gull on each shoulder (Bethesda!),
their wings like ears eavesdropping on the soft surf-wistful and spray-
whispery espionage of the sea. He would find him: and on hard regard remark his face (my face!), with the same-sized sockets, skull
and brow, the oblique angle of the jaw, the nosebone like a fork, the
large overworked mouth, the blunt-tipped fingers and the whorly-
haired belly and the feet (my feet!) like small blue bags of broken
stones and berries. He would find him: the man who had shaped his
shame in the blind and blood-soaked Mexican darkness, the *camera
obscurantist* peeled finally of his shadow-rind, the black orange of
his long absence, on which his son had been obliged to feed all these

hungry years in Long Beach—the face of his father, his uncle, his enemy.

To convince Dasein that the search in Long Beach must be continued, Stanhope lied. Onalred, he told her, had on several occasions sworn never to quit the Metropolis of Sulk before burning down the Oil Storage Terminal on Channel 2 of the Inner Harbor. "He has a dream of twenty-one million gallons of petroleum exploding at midnight; of flaming warships, tankers, tugs; of a forest fire of masts, mirrored in the sky; of the death by fire of the navy yard, the claw of piers, and the *Spruce Goose*." Onalred, of course, would have scoffed at such a project; but Dasein, like Dokhma Koan, was a romantic, and it was her imagination which burned . . . So the search went on: from the green-gilled priest in his cage at the miniature golf course to the weed-grown shuffleboard courts of Lincoln Park; from Dewey Correctional High School to the supermarkets of Bixby Knolls; from Shoemaker Bridge to Coyote Creek; from Edison Company to Sunnyside Mausoleum . . . without results.

Until—until, on turning as usual in the late afternoon to Vaseline Ali's, Dasein confessed: "My motorbike and my resolve both need a grease job."

It was as though her despair were a prayer overheard by the Great Impractical Joker. No sooner had they seated themselves and ordered bloody marys than Ali-Whoops himself appeared in their booth and said: "Say, Stanhopeless, I saw your mother last night."

"You lie!" cried Stanhope.

Putty-faced, peanut-eyed, broom-handed Ali was offended. "I do not either! Mildred! Mildred, haul your polyunsaturated fat-ass over here!"

Mildred looked up balefully through binoculars of shot glass. "I'm busy," she said.

"The only time you're busy is when the fleet's in," said Ali-Whoops. "Listen, didn't we see Maud last night, in the bowling alley around one in the morning?"

"Too right," said Mildred. "And she cut me dead, the slummock."

"She herself is already dead!" said Stanhope. "How could she cut you?"

"Then they must have embalmed her with joy juice," said Mildred, "because she's still grinding the old thighs. She wore some sort of ridiculous costume: black domino and blue beret; and at first I didn't make her. But then I noticed that reverse spin she was putting on the ball. I said to Ali, I said: that's far out. Just like old Maud's wrist action. And when she picked up a spare on a seven-to-ten split, I *knew.* 'Maud, you old rhinoceros!' I cried. 'What's happening, baby?' She turned her back on me and stalked out. Right, Ali? Didn't even finish the line. But it was the slummock, all right. Nobody else in Long Beach can pick up that seven-to-ten split."

"But what can this mean?" asked Dasein.

"Trouble," said Stanhope, rising. "To the motorbike! We must visit the College."

Maud Cronopios had bequeathed her body to the biology lab at the College. On arriving there, they found the lab empty and the body already dismembered, its organs distributed among jars on various shelves. With the help of lab reports, Stanhope and Dasein managed to sort out the "Cronopios Jars" from those containing frog, cat, rat and tupaia parts. They ranged the jars in order on a counter and examined them.

Clearly, something was very wrong.

Dasein picked up the telltale jar and held it to the light. "I've heard," she said, "that when a beaver gets scared by hunters, he bites off his own testicles and leaves them on the riverbank to fool the hounds. Onalred might have planted—"

"Be *serious,* Dasein," said Stanhope. "Look, do you . . . do you *recognize* this?"

"Well," she said, "it's been over twenty years, of course. And in its present state of unreadiness, I . . ." But she nodded. "Yes. It belongs to Onalred."

"Are you certain?"

"I told you, Stan: I was a wastepaper basket of the Revolution's manhood. *Yes.*"

Stanhope brooded aloud: "Being brother and sister, they no doubt resembled one another. Onalred in beret and domino was always somewhat camouflaged. And the body we found in the patio, my mother's peignoir and pin-curlers, remember? The purple face, after strangulation in pneumatic traction. I never thought to strip the body . . . I just assumed . . . This means—"

"That your mother killed your father, instead of the other way around."

He resented her for the brutal simplicity of her formulation. But facts were facts. "So," he said slowly, "this explains the apparently senseless accessory murder of Caryl Chessman. She couldn't take him with her, obviously; he'd give her away. And she couldn't leave him, because he would look for her."

Dasein was downcast. With tears in her eyes, she turned to Stanhope: "This means that I shall never be able to avenge the alpenstock." Then she added: "It rather drains most of the zest from the engine of my will."

Stanhope poured each of them a beaker of lab alcohol. He had his own qualms. "I have very little use for my mother," he said, "but anyone who killed my father can't be *all* bad." Outside, in the mud, begoggled Martians groped toward the administration hacienda; the palms were shaggy exclamation marks. Inside, unable to locate an ash tray, Dasein opened and employed the jar of Onalred's sex. Stanhope said: "Why do you suppose Maud has remained in Long Beach? She hates the place."

"What difference does it make? We know she's here. She was seen last night."

Yes; in a bowling alley. That distinctive wrist action. All trivia are death-infected—as though to repay us for our wastefulness. Of course, the working responsibility for Stanhope still belonged to his mother. It was possible in the ash of that reflection to spy a weak-eyed coal of hope . . . to blow on and fan it. For Stanhope had need of *some* purifying action; and he would have to make do with his mother as target. Could he? "Dasein, if Maud killed Onalred, then Onalred couldn't have killed Bethesda, since Bethesda was ironed to death hours after we discovered the corpse in the patio, a corpse now proved to have been Onalred's. This would seem to indicate that my mother killed Bethesda."

"So it would," agreed Dasein.

"Then," said Stanhope, "then . . ." It was possible to hate again. To Dasein he said: "It should be good enough for you that my mother is the sister of the man who murdered the man with the beard and the eyes like supernovas; and that she still works for the man who bangs his shoe; and that she has, incidentally, murdered an innocent bystander: Bethesda. It is enough for me that she has been, or failed to be, my mother; and has murdered the only person I ever loved, besides myself. Our duty is clear. I would recommend removing all your agents from their stakeouts and stationing them in bowling alleys."

"And you?" said Dasein. "What will you do?"

"I shall go home to Cimarosa Street," he said. "Home, to wait for Mother."

Dasein touched his cheek. "Are we all of us, then, born and destined to die under the sign of the alpenstock?"

"It certainly looks that way," said Stanhope. He would pluck that sign from the sky; he would grind it under his heel, crush it as though it were (as in fact it was) an aunt.

Now [13]

Fourth interlude . . .

Parturient was licking the mayonnaise off Sahasrara. He looked up, a white ring around his mouth. "My turn? Very well. Imagine, Gongor, that we are back at the Media, Rare & Well-done Pyramid. I was trying to decide on an appropriate technique . . ."

Gongor gestured toward Sahasrara. "I wonder . . . if you don't want those leftovers . . . I would . . ."

"You want maybe a knuckle sandwich, Gongor?"

Stanhope said: "You know, Parturient, I sometimes wonder how many people have choked on the tongue in your cheek?"

Then [13]

Pather lases a plot while Otto jaspers . . .

Wafer-thin slices of percussive shading; sonorities stretched and snapped; saxophone shrieking . . . "The Step-Grammar of advertising," said Otto, "is akin to the sliding phonics of jazz: improvisatory, verb-oriented, attacking the noun and its middle-class solidity, its 'squareness' in the Whitmanesque sense of the four-sided Jehovah 'chanting the Square deific.' We wound the self-sufficiency of the noun by activating suffixes, like *-ize*."

They were listening to Dregs Fahid and his Hyper-Jazzbos & Errors. Or, rather, Svam Spade listened; Otto blathered; Gnatpappa tweetered and woofed; and Pather was in a fever of speculation. How to do it? He might d-c excite parallel plasma tubes with hot cathode emissions. Two gas lasers, then? With lasing action established between both plasma tubes? Maybe. Fold the beam 180 degrees . . .

Poor Dregs was on the far side of the stereo console; on the near side his paid hypes were needling him: all rats scamper over Wedgewood, and whine as a backdown: the mating call of repressed barometers. He kept on trying to call them to attention with his sax. They went tinkle-tinkle, we don't reed you. Dregs gasped. "He's finding something," said Otto. Svam nodded. "Finding it," went on Otto, "but unable to tell us what he's found." Svam shook his head. "The sound," said Otto, "is the sound of the terror of discovery. Or the discovery of terror. The instrument is unable, inadequate, to express the Transcendence which Dregs has achieved. He and it will disappear into that Transcendence."

Well, not quite: Dregs went on bleating, while the barometric beat dropped down for a count of prime numbers. External prism assembly, thought Pather. Optical filtering to maintain lasing in the desired mode. Easy enough to rig. The prisms would fold the beam, focused between concave end mirrors . . . "A case might be made," said Otto, "for describing the Jaspersian Transcendence as a metaphysical equivalent of McLuhan's synesthesia." By whom? Not by Svam, who looked warily hostile. By Dregs Fahid? Dregs was very unhappy with the barometers. "Both," persisted Otto, "are jazzy attacks on the error residing in 'trying to secure as a content for knowledge what is true only as a limit for consciousness and a demand of the self' . . ." Svam stuck his fingers in his ears. Dregs muffled his sax with his underpants. The hypes went on needling, licking ice cubes. But, thought Pather, something's lacking: an appropriateness. Concave end mirrors appealed to *him:* but Otto wouldn't be able to see them; and would therefore be spared raptures of agony, folded like the beam into that split second of trapped realization . . . Gnatpappa damped the highs.

"What we are attacking," said Otto, "is, is it not, the empirical, exclusive, *Dasein-*self; not the Transcendent Inwardness, the authentically aware *historical* self, the *Existenz.*" Dregs was attacking his combo; he had been jazz-napped by the terror mob out there in space-warp, and the needles weren't about to pay his ransom-wampum. Dregs stared into death. "The electromagnetic revolution could then be said to be conspiring specifically at a realization of Jaspers' 'The Encompassing.' With the electric dilation of all our senses, of our central nervous system, we are permitted to glimpse 'the Transcendence lurking in the opacity of the here and now.' What do you think, Parturient?"

I think I live inside a soft-boiled Dali-clock that saxophones each sour hour, a clock gone giddy from mad repetition. Then he thought: *sound,* of course! Do it with sound . . .

"How did Jaspers put?" asked Otto. Dregs didn't know; Svam didn't want to know; Gnatpappa didn't care. " 'If truth is bound up with communication, truth itself can only *become* . . . in its depths, it is not dogmatic but communicative. Out of the consciousness of a becoming truth, first springs the possibility of a racial openness of the will to communicate in actuality—a will, however, that can never fulfill itself except in a historical moment which, precisely as such, becomes incommunicable.' "

"What," asked Pather, "is the light bulb but just such historical moment, indefinitely prolonged?" Dregs Fahid's racial will-openness seemed lesion-like; blood gurgled from the sax. Now: bombard a . . . what? A sapphire crystal? Yes. A giant pulse of ruby laser light, bombarding a sapphire crystal, producing hypersonic vibrations. Hypersonic sound!

"Yes, metaphorically speaking, the light bulb," said Otto. "Jaspers was talking about language, of course. And he might just as well have been talking about Dregs Fahid. But with an electric dilation of our senses—the abolition of time by the introduction of the instantaneous and the all-encompassing, we might—"

Hypersonic sound would appeal to Otto. He would at least be interested in discovering whether it could mount an assault on his senses as intensely satisfying as a sex machine. Sound waves instead of the harmonic waves he was working on now . . .

"I wonder," said Otto, "whether I might introduce this idea into the Ashram ceremony tomorrow night."

. . . Borrow one of the Emissions Unlimited laser guns. How long would it take to rig? Hypersonic vibrations of 60 billion cycles per second would certainly amplify the sound waves so intensely that the crystal would crack. Could do it in thirty billionths of a second. Much too short a time! Slow it down; stretch it. A swing circuit, from 10 billion cycles to 20, back to 10, up to 30 . . . Gnatpappa was staring at Pather, grinning. Why? The opacity of the here and now. "Gnatty, we must get together some night over a jug of Mogen David and re-create each other's consciousnesses. What do you say, sweetheart?"

"Screw you, Mr. Charlie," said Gnatpappa.

A racial openness of ill will. "But Gnatty, we must love one another or dye!"

Dregs dreamed a pathological sabertooth, impaled himself upon it; the barometers kept falling. No rain in sight. The needles had them in stitches. Dregs had bled it all already, bled it all. All God's chitlins . . . Svam Spade trembled. Otto whirled in his wheelchair, his face turned up as though his mind were smashing through the roof, as though his blind eyes nailed stars to the wall of the sky; and his hands were birds with sprigs of peace-promise in their beaks, sent up as offerings; and his head, an old earth, pocked, cratered, of running sores and vast dry seas and mineral veins exposed and twitching like nerves: up, up, as though to pierce finally the glass bubble, the silver flower-bell of the universe itself, and let in the wind, and let in the Dregs . . .

"*Das Umgriefende!*" he cried.

Gnatpappa rose, a black sword; then suddenly sheathed himself; and only the eyes were alive in a tower of non-committal tar, a telephone pole of ebony later-babyness.

Now [14]

*Stanhope recalls waiting for his mother, forming his reproaches
. . . advent of the Other . . . a telephone call from Dasein
. . . a letter from Renaldi.*

"I was at home," said Stanhope, "or that which I mocked, as it
mocked me, by calling *home*. Feeling sorry for myself. Wondering,
who was I? Mourner of a pleated priestess; discard pile of surrogate
daddies; doggerealtor of death's weed-stabbed parcels, swampy plots;
portmanteau of pawned ideologies; mainliner on abstractions; lover
—incredibly, defiantly—of my inimical and discontented self. Yet was
I more than these? I considered the history of my cowardice almost
breathtaking in its majestic effects: silver-hooved and fire-maned,
snorting a dischordant music. Surely no ordinary coward . . ."

Sahasrara now wore saran wrapping, and dozed against Parturient.
Gongor, too, was dreamy. The lighted ends of their banana-skin cigarettes made a square in the air.

"And what did I see through the plate-glass window overlooking
the patio? Obscurities, children of my condition of longing. Was I
capable of a generalization? To wit: the alternately stimulating and
obtunding influence of absolutist magnetism. My mood? My aspect?
The content of my thought? I lay then on the puce-colored carpet in
the middle of a night torn by helicopters and motorbikes; and I
gnawed on a pretzel found marvelously preserved amid the wool of
filth in the vacuum cleaner bag upon emptying that bag in the afternoon; and I watched the curtain move like a sail in the wind over the
dicondra; and I thought:

"Mother! You, who denied me tennis sneakers, basketball, identity, Bethesda . . . even my own father, my last hope of redemption.
You, who womanized me to the extent that I could find a partial
manhood only in Art, in the deliberate exploitation of my womaniza-
tion (that petrified posture of self-defense) . . . I could only forge
my small triumphs out of the initial defeat, the crushing solitude of

my lack of role. You, whose flawless contempt for me was the marble mausoleum of my self-esteem . . . what do you expect from me now?"

He let the mood deepen. Gongor nodded.

"So I sat at Cimarosa Street, and watched the smoke from my Tiparillo rise and wreathe the grinning plaster skull of Emma Goldman; and knew only that I was twenty-three years old, and I had never really expected to be twenty-three years old, and it seemed a horribly futile thing to be, having so casually become it, no longer capable now of becoming it but doomed in the brief irretrievable being of it. Then I wondered: was I, in fact, the Cronopios I had always assumed myself to be, or, instead, at this crucial juncture, the awful *Other* (call him Onalred)? Obviously, the Other and I existed in an inimical-mimical relationship. The Other was always gaining on and expropriating my causes and concerns; or cunningly short-cutting his way ahead of me, setting traps and braying at my discomfiture. I had lately wondered, too, as I approached the house on Cimarosa Street, to which of us copies of *Partisan Review* were posted quarterly; from which of us Salvador de Madariaga solicited monies for Spanish Loyalist refugees; of which of us time and taxes were flattered and extorted. Perhaps it was immaterial, and certainly lack of it. But of this I found myself convinced: the Other had written my poems. They were his revenge on me for our unhappy bondage. I had liked Rimbaud and Women. But the Other had caricatured Women and Rimbaud, and so co-opted them. (Who among us has the courage to believe in and take seriously an idea or a person after it—she—has been caricatured?) I had fled in something close to panic from poetry to various revolutions (sexual, social, economic, electromagnetic); but the Other had caricatured those, too. So I was forever in retreat; forever with the brush of my shame from the bucket of my funk painting blue new walls of recently discovered Winter Palaces of the heart. My function was to suffer and to brood; the Other's, to mimic my suffering and my brooding. It seemed to me that he had all the advantages, and I had all the anguish. But then why did he hate me so? Spinoza, I suppose, was wrong: the stone wants to be a tiger and the tiger wants to be a stone. The Other must get tired of being my vicarious veins; I was certainly weary of the constant and debilitating struggle to resist the machinery of his impiousness. But I thought I *knew* why the Other hated me . . . it was because I was still *sincere!*"

They were not listening. And Stanhope, alas, knew too well who it was that had written that last paragraph. Not me, he thought; no, not me.

He stood up and began to pace the deck. "I thought then of something Arbiter Aidos had once told me. 'If nothing else,' he said, 'let us be grateful for our evanescence. How did Chief Crowfoot of the Blackfoots put it? "What is life? It is the flash of a firefly in the night. It is a breath of a buffalo in the wintertime. It is as the little shadow that runs across the grass and loses itself in the sunset."' And, through the medium of my mind, I sent this message to Aidos: Chief Crowfoot can go shove an oil derrick up his wigwam."

Gongor's head was a gleaming hubcap; his eyes were closed. Stanhope whirled and shouted: "Then the telephone rang!" Gongor's eyes blinked open. "Distempered child! Plastic papoose perpetually rediscovering the *Angst* of a nippleless night cry. Me! Me! Now! Now! Hate! Hate! Flinging its little spears of petulance . . . screaming its loss of babyhood . . . white-nailed, pink-fingered little fists of insistence, drumming the taut hide of our cylindrical repose . . . I answered the phone. I told it: the number you have just dialed has been temporarily disconnected for the past twenty-three years. This is a recording. At the sound of silence, speak. Your message will be automatically erased.

"It was, naturally, Dasein. She said: 'Your mother was spotted last night in a bowling alley on Ximeno Avenue. *She guttered twice,* then walked out in her rented shoes without paying for the line. She was tailed to St. Teresa's Little Ashram of Ecumenical Oṁ. Yes! She went in, and hasn't been seen since! We have the place surrounded. Hurry!'"

"Well," said Stanhope, "I had to go, didn't I? But it seemed to me as I went that I had split too many infinities; and, as a consequence, flunked life." He cupped his ears. "Dropout-making." Then from his jacket he brought out Renaldi Haruspex's letter once more. "Gongor, you may be unhappy with the form I have chosen for our climax . . . it seemed at the time the only possible one. But at least Renaldi can give you an outside picture. He writes: 'So that night I was standing there behind the little iron-barred window of the station house, looking out at the Pike, watching the varnished faces, the fun-lovers trundling by with reefers in their ears: and for what? For target practice? Nothing like holding a riot gun to make you feel depressed. The phone was ringing. But not for me. Lew Archer used to be my hero, but Lew Archer quit the force, walked out into the begonias one afternoon, a free lance. Who was left to me? I have always needed a friend. You used to be my friend, Stanhope. We used to discuss the Great Ideas. But you didn't like me any more. That left . . . Svam Spade? I both hated and loved Svam Spade. I was tired. Tired of being a cop in a country that hates cops. Tired of *losing*. Tired of the *telephone!* Long Beach was lost. All the Archers, all the heroes were dead. The desert was littered with their bodies, slain heroes who bled plastic, and out of the plastic this new Long Beach was being built, as though the desert were a mirror of its own sterility. Do you understand? Architactless apartment houses, like airport hangars; drive-ins rococ-coughing in the night, no longer my night; drained swimming pools; sand-blasted beach huts; pillboxes with wall-to-wall carpeting; bamboo; grass matting; rattan; rum on the flagstone; hugger-mugger in the lanai . . . I saw it all, down the sights of my riot gun. I watched . . . like the old people whom the money-hooks fished out of their bungalows and dragged in-town; the old people sitting in the decaying hotel lobbies, dying while the rubber plants around them live on and on; the hunchbacked, turtle-like old people, with the newspapers over their knees and the red geraniums withering in their brains. Answer the telephone, you idiot: I told myself. And then I did as I was told. "Station house. Pike. Haruspex." It was *you*, Stanhope. And I thought . . . well, I thought we were to become friends again. I thought you wanted to talk to *me*. But you would have talked to any cop, wouldn't you? Because there had been a murder, and it was very complicated, and I must listen carefully . . . The riot gun I brought along with me, Stanhope, was my organ of despair . . .' "

Stanhope let the breeze take Renaldi's letter from his hands and sweep it off toward Catalina. "I think now," he said, "we are ready." Parturient and Sahasrara stood, for they had roles to play in the drama too.

Parturient said: "How did Novalis put it? 'Union joined not only for life but for death is a marriage that gives us a companion for the night. Love is sweetest in death; for the living death is a bridal night, a sweet mysterious secret.' "

And Sahasrara said: "How did Samuel Beckett put it? 'Gurgles of outflow.' "

And Stanhope said: "For your delectation, Gongor . . . another version of *How the West Was Lost,* a frug, as it were, of the *fantoccini* . . ."

"You mean . . . ?" said Gongor.

"Now," said Stanhope.

Then [14]

At last, the Ashram . . . Parturient guides Stanhope and Dasein . . . the audience is dismissed . . . the Heavyweight Championship . . . Stanhope chases his mother, Parturient chases Sahasrara . . . Otto is impatient . . . Dasein is abused . . . Otto is erased . . . Renaldi is telephoned . . . Dasein is suborned . . . Maud is resourceful . . . the helicopter descends . . . CAPTAIN HAPPEN HAPPENS!

The theater is horse-shod, or half-assed. Members of its audience—steadfast in their dedicated agnosticism about reality itself—munch bars of sodium alginate, doodle propositions on their scorecards, pinky-polish their pearl studs; sprawl, squirm, scowl, sputter at each other as though they were, as indeed they are, walkie-talkies. The stage is a massive representation of the Ashram, gleaming, unispherical: a huge synthetic Orange. Although it is intended to communicate an impression of brass solidity, that would naturally interfere with the view of the audience, and so instead it has been spun of fine wire mesh. Besides, transparence *is* the most liberating value in art today, permitting us to experience the luminousness of the thing in itself.

On each Blue Shift of the Hexagons, the Orange will revolve, dissimulation being a laborious business of gears. Behind the Orange is an ersatz sky, rather nasal-misty, sniffling. It will darken, as do the designs of the agonists.

A tongue of ramp hangs out of the Ashram and into the laps of the disgruntled. (For them, life is a metaphysical supplement to the sweatiness of art; and the theater exists to objectify their lack of will.) Stanhope and Dasein enter left, by way of the men's room, to the accompaniment of the overture from *The Love for Three Oranges;* and must hack their way through the disgruntled. They make it to the ramp; Prokofiev does not. On the ramp, in their path, lies a serene-rapt young man stoppering his maw of yawn with both fists. They blunder over him in their haste.

YOUNG MAN: I *am* sorry. I was . . . I was finding consolation in contemplating the thought of Schopenhauer's finding consolation in contemplating the Upanishads.

STANHOPE: May the Secret of the Golden Flower fall into your beeswax.

They embrace briefly. The young man slumps to the ramp once more. (The audience is moved, and heard to mutter: "Autonomous . . . exemplary . . . a man-handling of the ineffable . . .") Stanhope and Dasein penetrate the Ashram, which accordingly illumines itself. We are faced with and participate in a vestibule. Our eyes, like those of Stanhope and Dasein, are immediately hooked on the circular energy pattern of the great glass mandala suspended in the vestibule. Surrounding the mandala, feeding on its zircon glitter, are green lions, black crows, red dragons, eagles and vultures and ravens and doves. A psychedelic cabinet meeting on Vietnam. From the speaker system issues the unsyncopated saw of raga-time. On vinyl screens are successively projected selected shorts: of Nagasaki's slow death-blossoming; of big-bottomed female defecations into the jeweled camera-eye at the bottom of a plastic toilet bowl; of Renaldi Haruspex picking his nose.

Mirrors in the shape of scimitars encincture Stanhope and Dasein. Out of this mirrored multiplicity of images a distorted figure hesitantly ventures, then pauses, apparently unwilling to step as yet into the action. This prolonged uncertainty discomfits the audience. An auditor cries out: "Chance is a repertoire of moralities." It is the right thing to say, for the figure (Pather Parturient) completes the presentation of himself, and speaks.

PARTURIENT: Nobblies to the right. Acid-heads to the left. Sadhus, Zen-percenters, astralnauts and metanoids straight ahead. Are either of you Christian saints? Christian saints are presently in short supply, and must quadruble-up with the alchemists, the cracked neo-Platonists, and other assorted non-alignear groove-boobies. (He examines Stanhope.) I'm afraid we have no accommodations for poets. Poets are always dropping out at the Halfway House of Illumination. They want to come back with something. Distressingly anal of them. Agents of flip-out, Svam Spade says.

STANHOPE (shocked): *You,* Parturient? But *why?*

On the vinyl screens: a flowering of flattid bugs; first films of liberated Nazi charnel houses; newspaper front pages reporting the suicide of mild-mannered, jobless George Reeves . . .

PARTURIENT (grinning): Annihilation Night! Once a month, the middle of each month, Ides of I-Loss . . . Ecumenical Assault on Hang-Uppityness. What, Cronopios, were Pythagoras, Kepler, Einstein and Planck, if not mystics? Besides, Sahasrara Cannibis has converted to Nobble; and is rumored to be running around in diapers.

DASEIN: Have you seen someone in black domino and blue beret?

PARTURIENT: At least five such someones.

DASEIN: What do you mean?

PARTURIENT: Ah, look at *me*. (He displays himself: skullcap, chasuble, buskins.) Six mindblowers have I seen this evening and mistaken them for mirrors of myself. Our fantasies are mass-produced, like gumdrops . . .

STANHOPE (interrupting): Parturient, this is *important*. We're looking for my mother, and she may be dangerous!

PARTURIENT: Aren't they all? Mothers, I mean. Criminally dangerous? But not here, surely, Cronopios. No mothers in St. Teresa's Little Ashram of Ecumenical Oṁ. We are all of us seed-hoarders here. Mother, by extension, implies child. And children . . . well, children are not only excrement; they are also *responsibilities*.

DASEIN (prowling about): What's the floor plan of this asylum? How many rooms?

PARTURIENT: No floors. Countless rooms. I don't know the plan. Our Ashram consists of an indefinite and perhaps infinite number of hexagonal galleries, with vast hot air shafts in between. There are many forked paths in the Garden of Haptic Harmony! Spiral staircases of varying ascensions . . . and the mirrors! So many mirrors that you forget not only *where* you were, but *who,* as well. It is a sphere, madame, whose exact center is any one of its hexagons, and whose circumference, now that you're in, is inaccessible.

As he completes this sentence, the light in the vestibule dies, extinguishing mandala, lions, vinyl screens, mirrors, raga-time. There is a whir, as of the action of magnetic axes. Stage black. The Phipps Family sings "Just Before the Battle, Mother." Sound of a match. The three faces—now behind mesh—are grouped around a candle.

PARTURIENT: How did Novalis put it? (He strikes a finger like a match, spikes his lips with it.) "The greatest magician would be the one who would cast over himself a spell so complete that he would take his own phantasmagorias as autonomous appearances." *Man* is that magician. (Looking at Dasein with the perfunctory leer, he appends:) The question is, have I dreamed you, or have you dreamed me?

DASEIN (unaffected): You must be something I ate.

They traipse. Their feet make hollow tin-can sounds. A passage-way is indicated. Parturient's candle brings to life marble facets which depict in series the Sufi lapwing's flapodyssey over the Seven Valleys of Mystical Experience: Quest, Love, Enlightenment, Detachment, Unity, Amazement, Annihilation of the Self. Kabuki musicians beat on hand drums, sing *Tsuchigumo* . . . The Dance of the Spider.

PARTURIENT: Octopoidal pilgrims, the better to lacerate ourselves, compeers: a Sivaree! (The pilgrims inch in contractile snakings from Desolation through Earthly Paradise to the Enigma of Being; from the Cloud of Unknowing to Final Union, Utter-Merge, the theo-pathic stateliness of fish-in-the-seething self-obliteration. The final facet suggests a bottomless basket of woven tentacles, molecular skulls. There is a hole, a funnel-tunnel, at whose profound nadirical eye a metronome prismatically vamps slat upon slat of hard blue light . . .) Light behind, but filtering through a thicket of instants . . . a mirror-bush of impressions rather more felt than seen, but so altering that *tactile* images on one's acknowledgment of them shift and are irretrievably lost: the body as a kaleidoscope of nerve im-pulses . . . (Minamoto slays the spider.) The trick of it is so to sit-uate yourself that on the Great Blue Shift of the Hexagons, you pass through the right facet into the appropriate Suite. (Magnetic whir, and . . . the three of them disappear. From the basket of tentacles flit flies of light, bats which have been wing-tip-equipped with flam-ing luminaires. Shadows move on the wall: an impression of a forest of barber poles. Then bats and barber poles are alike blotted out. There creep into the black silence a twitter and a moan, striving to resolve themselves into a chamber concerto by Charles Wuorinin. We hear without seeing Parturient . . . as a large figure is defined stage right.) The Illumination Suite: three cells (or chambers), and of course no bath. First cell: the Chamber of Apprehension of the Hulking Absolute, for those who, going steady with God, will be mar-ried on their graduation from the Self . . .

STANHOPE: It . . . it looks like a *blue* Sonny Liston.

It does, indeed. He is reading *Esquire*. The audience is restive. One of its members hurls a bar of sodium alginate at Sonny Liston. Liston goes down for a ten count. Darkening . . . and the stage is frozen black once more. Jimmie Williams and Red Ellis sing "A

Rose from Mother's Wreath." Light-thaw. We see Marguerita Oswald pregnant with a space-time capsule.

PARTURIENT: Second cell, Chamber of Becoming-Went-Whither. (To Marguerita:) Sit down; take a load off your fetus. (To Stanhope and Dasein:) Reception of the phenomenal world—the maya-maze—is clarified by a deliberate short-circuiting of the sensory apparatus: body-bodhi. We are experimenting with cruelty as a short-circuiting device.

The capsule grows, swallowing Marguerita. Filters play. The Vienna Male Choir sings *S'gibt Kein Schöner Leben.* Stage center: two brown potatoes, the size of footballs.

PARTURIENT: Third cell, Chamber of Intuitional Energy, a community Wing-*Dinge,* during which one transforms oneself by Electric Kool-Aid into a sort of Japanese transistor of the Oversoul, capable of amplifying and demodulating signals from the Resplendent Transcendent.

The potatoes communicate through their grubs.

FIRST POTATO: What's happening?

SECOND POTATO: I am. (They begin to glow.)

PARTURIENT: According to our Excrementalist Visionaries, this is the Atomic Pile: either that to which the atoms add up; or that—Anti-Matter—which the atoms—Adams—dispose of, drop, pass on in waste—

DASEIN: *We* are wasting time—(The audience disgrunts affirmatively.)

PARTURIENT: Time is precisely what we *should* be wasting: the curved Einsteinian bile-duct! Now, behind *this* facet . . . (A weedy, Sargassomer aspect, full of glistening fish shapes and long vegetablic scarves, like guitar chords. The Stanley Brothers and the Clinch Mountain Boys sing "Come All You Tenderhearted.") The Introversion Suite. The decor is nautical, for in such voyages toward liberation, we are all of us Flying Dutchmen, self-cleansers: and our souls are sailboats lost on the windless sea of Somnolence. Beware, though, buccos: of Creeping Quietism, soul-scurvy, sluggardization. Your sail must seek out the cinnamon-scented breath of Am, De-Odor of Sanctity, Noetic Waft of That Which Is. Here one's yawl is swallowed by one's yawn; and the All-Am awes one overwhelmingly. One surrenders . . . and Multiplicity is resolved into Unity. To become a stew is to cease to stew. Do you follow me?

They have to; they are lost. Unplopping of a plug. The weedy sea with a gurgle is drained through a hole in its floor. Pump sounds: the blackness is sucked from the Suite. We see first an orchid-anused Our Lady of the Flowers, on a half-baked shell. About him appear Simone de Beauvoir and Madame Ngo Dinh Nhu. They produce cushions, seat themselves Indian-style, tuck napkins into their décolletage and raspingly sharpen steak knives.

PARTURIENT: The Ecstatic Suite, wherein—rapturous trance!—the flushed tank of the empty mind is filled with the fizzy Idea of God: End of Becoming, Beginning of Being. I-Hood, Space and Time flee before the ravaging blue hounds of Pure Apprehension—

Madame Nhu wrenches the orchid out of the anus; it is transformed into a rose.

OUR LADY: I am Rose of Lima, the Bean of Peruvian Being.

PARTURIENT: The diamond-eyed All-Seeing Source, All-Issuing Origin, All-Smelling Father Nose Beast, which is heavily upon you like—why, like a Mother! The trembling fingers of the starved soul extend and curl, to pluck the Sempiternal Rose. Although of course it is the Sempiternal Rose, turned Venus Flytrap, that plucks *you* . . . and chews . . .

OUR LADY (singing):

> The verb "to be"
> Terrifies me
> Conceptually.
> To object to objects
> Is ideal;
> To steal
> Being from Seeing
> Is freeing
> Ego . . . Oh? No?
> Come, then: we shall blow our knows
> In the Sempiternal Rose.

SIMONE DE BEAUVOIR (plunging her steak knife into Our Lady): The contradictions that put the flesh in opposition to the spirit, the instant to time, the swoon of immanence to the challenge of transcendence, the absolute of pleasure to the nothingness of forgetting, can only be resolved by writing very long books about them. In the typewriter will always be materialized the tension, anguish, joy, frustration and triumph of gossipience . . .

Half the audience is outraged; the other half is laughing hysterically.

PARTURIENT (turning to the audience): So . . . a fugitive sensibility, desperate to make the obscene. Are these the wrong trees to plant on your imaginary landscape?

AUDIENCE: How much do you expect us to take? Banality is one thing: perhaps you can use the Banal theatrically. But boredom is nothing-else again.

PARTURIENT: There's no such thing as boredom; it's only another name for frustration.

AUDIENCE: Clever, but deceitful. You're trying to make our boredom a moral issue.

PARTURIENT: No. Not a moral issue. Nor an aesthetic issue. An *ontological* issue! (He turns his back on the audience.) Now let us recede.

Simone de Beauvoir and Madame Nhu between them cart off the bleeding body of Our Lady. Rain begins to fall. With clinks. It's raining coins. We are in a bank vault. Archie Campbell sings "Trouble in the Amen Corner."

PARTURIENT: Dark Night of the Soul Suite. Sometimes called Long Beach. Chambers of Impotence, Blankness and Solitude. The illuminated pilgrim's transcendental powers are as yet awkward, adolescent, pimply. He is fatigued by so many intense and progressive affirmations. He backslides, suffering from a consciousness of imperfection, an obsession with sinfulness. Coy God, only glimpsed, tauntingly retreats: a complicated mutual strip tease of acquired attributes is in process.

The rain of coins is succeeded by a snowfall of plastic credit cards. Mummies on the floor of the bank vault stir, writhe.

PARTURIENT: The pilgrim experiences negation, inhibition of the will, a sense of total deprivation, hopeless lassitude. Sunya-sin! Omnivorousness! Nullity and Void-Pluperfect! In his despair, the languishing pilgrim contemplates desperate remedies: to commit suicide; or, more drastically, to go to graduate school in business administration. He needs help, and the Ashram stands ready to provide it. For the sadhus, there's a hot-line hookup direct to the Dial-a-Guru switchboard—

VOICE OF THE GURUS: Abnegate.

PARTURIENT: For the acid-heads, there are turn-off pills.

VOICE OF TIMOTHY LEARY: A box of sugar cubes, a jug of thorazine, and I-Thou beside me, grooving the Wilderness . . .

PARTURIENT: For the saints, the recorded Voice Who Spoke to St. Catherine—

VWSTSC: Dig up the root of self-love with the knife of self-hatred.

The snowfall of plastic stops. Night. Walter Huston sings, "Lost Out Here in the Stars." Mandalas manifest themselves; dolphins plunge through them. More bats and barber poles. Then a wind. The clank of iron dollar-signs marching out the door. Deeper night.

PARTURIENT: I'm afraid I can't show you the Annihilation Suite. It is being saved for dramatic effect later on. Besides, I am an inappropriate M.C. *My* hang-up is that I unwittingly annihilated myself years ago—which, of course, doesn't count . . .

AUDIENCE: Suspect interiority! Show us the Annihilation Suite!

PARTURIENT (ignoring them): If, however, we speak of the soul as an iron bar flowing with white heat, becoming like to fire itself yet remaining iron, then melting into another quality altogether—we do make, I am reliably assured, a metaphorical approach to this experience of Annihilation, this sense of the ultimate mutability of Us in an Immutable which derives its immutability from its matterlessness. That's the key: it doesn't matter not because it can't, but because it isn't!

Sister Rosetta Tharpe sings "Shine for Ormazd."

PARTURIENT: There are other suggestions. As Ruysbroeck put it: "To eat and be eaten! That is Union! Since His Desire is without measure, to be devoured by Him does not greatly amaze me." Or, as doughty little St. Teresa herself put it: "Such great graces leave the soul avid of total possession of that Divine Bridegroom who has conferred them."

STANHOPE: Too many suites are spoiling my appetite. Is there much more?

PARTURIENT: There are all the game rooms. For instance: the Chapel of Confrontation . . . (A puppet show: Julian of Norwich, clutched at the throat by the paws of the black-freckled fiend . . . St. Teresa, hurling a bottle of holy water at the brimstone-stinking Satan perched atop her breviary . . . St. Ignatius Loyola, with bloody hands plinking the spinet keys of the triple plectrum . . .) That's my personal favorite—Luther and Lucifer trying to fart each other to death.

STANHOPE (to Dasein): Gas warfare according to the Danzig convention.

Banyan trees, drums, cups of milk curd, golden nose rings . . .

PARTURIENT: The Indian Reservation. All the din, stink, profanity and unruly uproar of an Oriental temple-shrine or a stag smoker. I was happy up there for a month, practicing vajroli mudra, until they caught on to the fact that I was deliberately screwing it up.

A Gymnasium . . .

PARTURIENT: For the Germanically inclined. German mystics were always very virile, of course, and viewed the Dark Night of the Soul as a sort of exercise in character building, toward matriculation—as one of them put it—"in the upper school of true resignation, suffering love." The question they are now trying to answer: Will parallel bars meet?

A sandbox of gelatin, in which bodies thrash . . .

PARTURIENT: Just one event on tonight's card in the Total Theater of the Inter-Media Kinetic Environmental-cases . . . chillum pipes and sitars, flagellation and Marvel comic books, Noh-go plays and stroboscopic therapy . . . continuous showings of old Vincent Price movies . . . basket weaving with live worms . . . even *confession.*

Cribs, a bathinette, Brahms . . .

PARTURIENT: The Norman O. Brown Memorial Nursery, for the Nobblies. The polymorphous perverts get together to play with stuffed animals, teething rings, and themselves.

Moans of the damned, on suede couches, refugees from Egon Schiele . . .

PARTURIENT: The Clinic. Treatment for bad-trippers, freak-outs, Catholics, Jungians, Shylox, mothers, scotch-drinkers, constipate de foie grasshoppers, and so forth.

Night once more. Unrelieved, unforgiving. No bird sings.

PARTURIENT: We're not permitted an advance peek at Otto's Grotto, which is being prepared for this evening's ceremony. But you, Cronopios, might imagine what will go on there.

STANHOPE: Then again, I might not.

PARTURIENT: Well, if we admit his central proposition—that Light is Sin—then, ah, Rite makes Blight. A marriage of Jaspers and Skoptsy. Later on, you'll see what I mean. Or, rather, you will fail to see, and so *know* what I mean.

AUDIENCE: You are making terror *cute.*

PARTURIENT: Yes. The Noel Coward of the Theater of Cruelty.

AUDIENCE: We are not amused.

PARTURIENT: Bug out, sapajous.

STANHOPE: Parturient, is there no conflict among various sects of Ashramblers? I'd imagine at least a few of these approaches would be mutually incompatible.

PARTURIENT: No. Oh, some yogis push works; some, meditation; some, knowledge. Some think the maya is merely social; others, that it extends to include-out the whole material objective world. They differ on the therapeutic utility of wu weisiness. The question of miracles is bothersome. Yogis claim to shrink, expand, levitate, teleport, to immunize themselves against outside influences and suppress all bodily desires and needs. The acid-heads don't buy that; they've been traumatized by unfortunate incidents on Pacific Coast Highway. There they've been, busy turning on, when along comes the maya in the form of a Mack truck or a Greyhound bus, and they are unable to escape it by shrinking, expanding, levitating, immunizing. So they conclude that miracles belong to inner not outer space. Too, yogis and saints are always wanting to manufacture stigmata: boils, blisters, leprous nodules, catatonic states—physical mortification being good for the soul. Whereas Nobblies and acid-heads rather love their physical bodies, and hate blemishes, even self-inflicted. Then Nobblies and acid-heads disagree on sex (although they all oppose children). Acid-heads are genitally organized; Nobblies consider the whole idea perfectly odious.

They have reached a desolate plateau. On the horizon appears a rabble of revolting viaducts, advancing on Klee-feet. Joh Reedy and the Stone Mountain Trio sing "Oh, Death."

PARTURIENT: Actually, the yogis, saints and sadhus have nothing to say about the real operations of the Ashram; they've been imported principally to teach their methodological technique to the acid-heads and Nobblies. What a technique! Eastern thought, historically resisting crystallization into concepts; its categories fluid; its grammar shifty; its logic immune from contradiction because it consists wholly of paradoxical statements; its symbolic and literal meanings hopelessly homogenized—extremely attractive to all Ashramblers, for they believe, with Otto, that Aristotle's table of categories was a sort of Trojan zebra, foisting the unconscious dualisms of Greek grammar upon the unsuspecting cosmos. (He sighs.) But saints and sadhus cart along with them a lot of excess baggage: fasting, meditation, good works, self-discipline. No thanks! Nobblies and acid-heads are perfect children of the middle class, used to getting what they want quickly and easily. Why shouldn't truth, salvation, satori be as effortlessly acquired as a new bicycle, a sports car, a college education? Their attitude is that Beatitude should be arrived at as painlessly as possible. They can *afford* to *buy* their grace!

The audience stirs uneasily, eager to interrupt. Parturient executes a *hold* gesture.

PARTURIENT: So we have powdered Grace (just add saliva) and an ecumenical contempt for the empirical scientific method. A strong combination! On one hand, easy access to the Absolute; on the other, a methodological technique which frees you from the inconvenience of questioning, testing the quality of your marvels. The empirical scientific method, after all, is hard work—like the disciplined creating of art. Dump it! Any test inhibits the very ego-loss prerequisite for occasioning whatever marvel is in question. *Nice:* because it quite establishes your personal visions beyond judgment. Makes them self-ratifying, incontrovertible. What these people all share is that self-validating belief in the Intuitional and Irrational . . . a belief in Revealed Truth which is not susceptible to rational proofs. You and I are the anachronisms, Cronopios, clinging to such outmoded concepts as rationality, work, order, duty, vocation, maturity. The Dionysiac Pack is upon us, and their cry is: if thinking must be done, let our machines do it for us, as once our servants did our living for us. We are content to *feel*. And anything momentarily interfering with our feeling *good* is a hang-up. Even the idea that we should *do* something to *deserve* feeling good, to be proud of ourselves for an achievement, is a hang-up. Guilt hurts: abolish guilt! Then, having abolished guilt, dispense with responsibility and duty—duty being only yin-deep anyway. And having dispensed with all *that,* we are no longer obliged to *work*. Work is self-deception . . . feces-manipulation. Ashramblers *see through all that*.

AUDIENCE (irritated beyond silence): How did Antonioni put it? Let us dispense with "the superannuated casuistry of positives and negatives."

STANHOPE (to the audience): Then what is left?

PARTURIENT: *Play. Love*. Let us love one another and play with one another: a play without point or purpose since, no matter how solemn, its intention is to submerge itself in process, to avoid *results*. And a love which is generalized and transitory: non-monogamous because monogamy would require *adjustments;* and without children because children are results and responsibilities, meaning guilt feelings and work. Appealing, isn't it? At last, a way to have Fun without being Father. No longer to be tormented by those questions which urge us on toward testing and assessing our experience; toward validating our tentative notions about the organization of the universe; toward trying to alter and control our environment and ourselves. The big thing in this is to escape language, that first instrument of questions and controls; for language *seeks* definition, a communicable agreed-upon-ness, which, because it will always be only approximate, will also always be insupportably tension-making and fatiguing. Words are guilty of association with rational comment and abstract idea. So hypothesis, prediction, analysis and evaluation—all the messy apparatus of communicable truths—are tossed out the Ashram window . . . if the Ashram had windows. To be beautiful, passive, stroked, loved, endlessly and repetitiously, is the new Ideal.

STANHOPE: The New Pornography!

The audience hisses.

STANHOPE (to the audience): No, I see it, feel the force of it! A giving up and away of the terrible adventure; a sighful sinking into the primordial ooze of questionlessness.

AUDIENCE: But in *Angel's Sloth* you articulated a longing for an end to questions.

STANHOPE: Not at such a price! There was an element of assertion, of insistence, in my desire—the *quest* in *ques*tion—an aspect of conquest; a hope of honor: to end the questions by answering all of them. Not this cult of the cunning vegetable! What is the cerebral cortex *for,* this most complex evolutionary achievement, this question-asker?

PARTURIENT: Oh, well, the cerebral cortex is the sad-making mechanism: the instrument of repression, the perpetuator of tension. They are against tension. They blame tension on the nasty old reality principle, or genital organization. Genital organization estranges the organism from the full play of its instincts. It is not "free," as an animal operating wholly within its instincts is free, tuned in, complete. They long for a return to the unexcited quiescence of the instinctual life . . . the pre-state of integral sloth.

STANHOPE: Have they never seen a bitch in heat? Is that what they call "unexcited quiescence"? Without dignity, even without pleasure? Are they so unaware of the *tyranny* of instinct, the pathos arising from slavery to one's uncontrollable impulses? The whole *point* of genital organization is to give Man a means by which to control his sex life, to look at it objectively, even to laugh at it . . . and *escape* that tyranny.

PARTURIENT: Their view is more conspiratorial. The organization of sexuality into genitality is a psychological response of the organism to the inimical reality principle, a reflection and concentration on specific objects to avoid punishment; whereas the body desires pleasures in *all* its orifices and zones. Then genital organization was itself socially organized into monogamic institutions, the better to repress. All sublimation is repression; all repression is tension-making; all tension is bad. Therefore language, science, art, culture—all based on sublimation—are all bad too.

STANHOPE: Surely not all sublimation is repression. Agreed: there is a socially organized "surplus repression" which desexualizes and objectifies Man as an instrument of labor. But there's also that *non*-repressive sublimation—a cherished ability!—which makes possible the transformation of our blind animal necessity-for-fulfillment-of-want into *desired* gratification. Which makes possible an intensified and more complicated pleasure. It seems to me that the very fact that Man's *reasoning* has explored and exposed the nature of repression indicates that reason is not solely repressive and not always destructive. Perhaps the cerebral cortex is nature's attempt to understand itself by transcending itself, transcending the instinctual. *Some* form of sublimation is necessary to free ourselves from the tyranny of impulse, if only because there is a scarcity of *time!*

PARTURIENT: They like their impulses. They want to indulge them. Sublimation defers gratification of impulses. And there isn't a gratification they are willing to defer.

STANHOPE: What has self-indulgence to do with the desire for integral sloth?

PARTURIENT: Madness is the Ex-Lax of the Libido; express the repress!

STANHOPE: They would then sacrifice the more complicated pleasure available to more complicated organisms. They would, incidentally, make all social order impossible!

PARTURIENT: Anarchy is the Kleenex of the Anal; you blow my mind! Social order *is* repression; culture is evil. When the Enlightenment tired of trying to *understand* the world Marx came along saying *change* it. The New Weariness says it isn't worth understanding because it's all a joke (or an imposition); and it isn't worth changing because the joke is meaningless (and any substitute order will just be another form of imposition). So junk sublimation; ignore the world. Avoid a lot of hard work, pain, delay. A couple of years from now, Leslie Fiedler will put it this way: "Let the experiment be over; let the focused consciousness blur into the cosmic night; let the hallucinatory monsters bred of fragmented consciousness prowl that night again; let the perilously sustained absurdity of the 'soul' be abandoned; yet let the demons who once trafficked in souls thrive anew." Yes! The Demon-Tribe of Soul-Traffickers, of which *Otto* is Big Chief Green Light!

STANHOPE (turning to the audience in appeal): But, so long as there is life, there will be questions; and so long as there are questions, there will be tension. Then this lust for an all-encompassing gratification, for submergence in the instinctual, for annihilation of one's inconvenient and vulnerable *self;* this hunger for absolute equilibrium can end only . . . (He stops, thoughtful, appalled) . . . only in *madness* or . . . Yes. The ultimate equilibrium, the final integral sloth, is . . . *Death. That's* what they are practicing, isn't it? The object of their embrace? Theirs is a love affair with Death!

AUDIENCE (rising): That is quite too much.

PARTURIENT (grinning at them): Well, the footing is pretty tricky along the forked paths in the Garden of Haptic Harmony. Have we stubbed Artaud?

AUDIENCE: Stylistic devices are techniques of avoidance!

PARTURIENT: You object to our implementation of indeterminacy as an artistic principle?

AUDIENCE: On the contrary. We object to your contemptuous attitude toward madness as an authentic metaphor for passion.

PARTURIENT: You are pledged, then, to the flip-out as a proof of grace?

AUDIENCE: We are pledged to an applied Hegelianism, which seeks its Self in its Other. The "other" is experienced as a harsh purification of the "self."

PARTURIENT: Yes. While the libertinseled "self" goes on busily colonizing and exploiting all the bizarre domains of experience. You wish to combine the thrill of vicarious experience with the satisfaction of a predestinarian sense of (spiritual) grace and (social) futility. You aspire to a Peeping-Thomism on somebody else's subconscious. But if we conceive of the theater as an exercise in interpersonal abuse, there is no reason why we shouldn't abuse *you* as much as you are accustomed to abusing us, is there?

AUDIENCE: More casuistry. You seem incapable of grasping the one imperative: theatrical ideas must be sensory stimulants, not intellectual depressants.

PARTURIENT (to Stanhope): This audience suffers from delusions of adequacy.

AUDIENCE: Attention must be paid to such an audience. Attention must be paid!

PARTURIENT: I think it is time we reviewed the audience. Cronopios?

STANHOPE: I think you cannot play *Oedipus* to an audience of Peter Pans.

PARTURIENT: Miss Camembert?

DASEIN: Perhaps bad temper creates a cramp in the muscles of receptivity.

STANHOPE: There is nothing the matter with this audience that an overdose of Seconal wouldn't cure.

DASEIN: I disagree. There is something more drastically the matter with this audience . . . something criminal.

PARTURIENT: Yes?

DASEIN: They are not sincere.

PARTURIENT: They are not sincere!

STANHOPE, PARTURIENT and DASEIN (together): *They are not sincere!*

PARTURIENT: We have arrived at a consensus. This audience, lacking both sincerity and redeeming social value, should be closed down before the second act. (To Stanhope . . .) I should mention that the second act is pretty sexy. (To the audience . . .) Go home!

AUDIENCE: You can't do this!

PARTURIENT: I don't see why not. The notion of an unemployed audience is hardly a new one. The theater has been working toward it for years. Now, at last, we have summoned the resolve to pan *you*. Get out! Ushers, take them out!

Ushers appear, wearing pea jackets, black leather gloves, motorcycle boots and Edith Piaf death masks; they drag members of the audience from their seats.

AUDIENCE (weeping in rage): But . . . but . . . (They realize rage is unavailing, and put on, like sackcloth, a penitential air . . .) Couldn't you . . . at least . . . we mean, it's only fair, after the money we spent and the time it took us to paste on our standardized sneers, really, might we be permitted a sneak-peek at the Annihilation Suite? *Please?*

PARTURIENT: No more than you deserve. (Claps his hands.) Let there be light.

A facet swings open on its oiled hinges. A chamber is lit. The walls are yellow. And the only furniture is . . . a gigantic pink egg.

AUDIENCE (stunned): But . . . but what is it?

PARTURIENT: Four hundred and fifty-one pounds of Silly-Putty.

AUDIENCE (bitterly): May you eat too many Heisenbergers, and die of Uncertainty Poisoning. (They try passively resisting the ushers; the ushers swoop them up in their arms and carry them out of the theater.)

PARTURIENT: And so the fugitive sensibility has been caught at last. We shall be able to move forward with much more vigor now. Are you ready for the second act?

A Blue Shift of the Hexagons is upon them, a sliding, a rending, a whir: the plateau tips, spilling them into a corridor: the corridor slopes, balloons, extrudes them into . . .

The Second Act. Another hexagon, large, gloomy. Upon its facets: various insignia sprouts and playful luminosities (a grinning money god, a triangle enclosing lingam and crescent moon, a Veil of Maya, and a huge yellow Bindu-Dot). In its center: two twin blocks of polyurethane, internally lit a liverish green. Semicircling the anterior prospect of these blocks: submarine couches, awaiting recumbents. Parturient, Stanhope and Dasein recumb.

About the blocks there mills a motley crew. An altercation is in lack of progress. Participating are: (1) five black men, island-eyed in impenetrable oil-pond faces, wearing togas and tarbushes: the flower of a militant sect known locally as the Pigstickers of Islam; (2) a rice-white, bare-chested, gangleshanky young man with too much pubic hair covering his face and not enough dhoti covering the rest of him; (3) Svam Spade, hipper-than-thou in Guadalajara bullfighting togs, high heels, and a cravat of knitted pussy willows; and (4) Sahasrara Cannibis. What a sight is Sahasrara! Too bad the audience has been dismissed. She is tonight attired as a Nobbly, wearing nothing but disposable diapers and, hung on a thong from her neck, a leather pouch containing the standard canister of baby powder. Her mountainous strawberry sundae frontage explodes on the hexagon, challenges it unblinkingly: and it is this shameless display of natural resources which has caused the altercation.

DHOTI-BOY (pirouetting in rage; leaking fulminations from all his body faults): It is simply impermissible, Sahasrara. You *know* it will give an unfair advantage to Gnatpappa. I am sensible of your intention, which, I take it, is to mock the very localized sexual response such an extravagant exhibitionism can provoke. The fact remains—you *will* provoke it in Gnatpappa!

SAHASRARA (heaving her moons of flesh): So. *Our* faith must be armored over to protect *you* from the boomerangs of your own smutty-mindedness.

DHOTI-BOY: Applesauce! I'm not asking that *all* the Nobbly girls cover up their dugs. Gnatpappa won't be able to see *them*. But *you* are a part of the ceremony. You know Synecdoche will be totally unaffected by the spectacle of you; he's immune. But Gnatpappa—

One of the Pigstickers of Islam seizes Sahasrara's left breast, squeezes it, then disdainfully flicks away the pretzel-nugget nipple with the nail of his middle finger.

PIGSTICKER (rolling out his baritones in a wheelbarrow): I see; your assumption is that the sight of this pair of gross white glandular inflatables will of course incite the black animal to a frenzy of lust. Look, Aunt Charlie, you can have all your Little White Sisters of the Mushroom, minced or fluted, creamed, stuffed, stewed, sautéed. We have already partaken of the mysteries reputed to be festering there, and found them savorless.

DHOTI-BOY: You don't understand! This is the heavyweight championship of genital organization. *No* outside influences should intrude . . . obtrude . . . protrude . . .

SVAM SPADE: We seem to have reached an adjournment of minds. (He strokes his pussy willows.) If Synecdoche Wessel doesn't like the setup, truck him back to Monterey. But leave behind that bag of bhang . . . the Ashram doesn't pay for no-shows.

DHOTI-BOY (beside himself, and no more attractive as twins): So, you think you're setting up another of those infamous "Long Beach decisions." Let her wave around her milk factories! Synecdoche will still prevail! And I hope the rest of you get diaper rash!

SVAM (about as perturbable as moss): Ashram rules—ten seconds to lift-up at five pounds; fifteen at ten; twenty-five at twenty; half a minute to hoist at twenty-five pounds. Are we ready?

A gong. The Nobblies creep barefootishly into the hexagon, holding hands, and lie down on the submarine couches. They look back at the door through which they came, and . . . it's Otto! In his wheelchair, with his skull lit queerly from within, like the polyurethane blocks. By a radar unknown to ordinary men, he stations himself so as equilaterally to triangulate his wheelchair and the blocks. He switches off the electric motor, and nods.

Svam mimics that nod. Another gong. And the Veil of Maya parts to admit Gnatpappa. Gnatpappa is naked in his black marbling of muscle, sweatbandless, dilly-bagless, pubic tasselless, his scars an advertisement of his barbaric resolve. He bounds onto the block nearest the Veil of Maya, opens a topside hatch, and descends a step-ladder within. There he stands, thigh-deep in polyurethane, facing Otto and the Nobblies.

A third gong: the lips of the great yellow Bindu-Dot grin, split, emit—the *Champion.* Synecdoche Wessel is fat; but to say it and leave it like that is an inadequacy akin to observing that Lyndon Johnson is vain. Synecdoche is that quintessential proto-Bloat from which all proximate synonyms and similes for "Fat" are etymologically derived. Here, at last, is the Flabbonic Source, the swollentropic principle to which all paunch is but a feeble and imperfect prayer. Before such Myth-made-Fleshy, all men who have ever dreamt of tissue excess must propitiate themselves abjectly, must in their groveling petition him: O, Lard, Lard, Thou Dost Exceedeth Me, and Thou Art Most Gross.

Still, Synecdoche has a champion's grace, a style as extravagant as the ton of him. On being hauled up onto his block by Svam and Dhoti-Boy, he makes benign gestures with his blubbery hands; coyly detaches his string-bead loincloth; drops it to the floor and achieves an excruciating little shimmy. Then he sighs, lowering his bulk into the block. This accomplished, with imperial reserve he signals his preparedness and smiles.

SVAM: The Heavyweight Championship of Genital Organization! The weights, please, Sahasrara. (Sister Rosetta Tharpe sings "Blow You, the Trumpet of Zion.")

Sahasrara claps her hands; and into the hexagon slip bald-headed girls in vinyl envelopes, bearing little velvet cushions on which silver weights, like Christmas-tree ornaments, repose. These cushions the bald-headed girls deposit before Sahasrara, their scalped noggins and her breasts for a moment mingling in a surreal-spherule explosion, as of proliferating white basketballs in a high-scoring dream.

Sahasrara looks up at the contestants. Gnatpappa is grim. Although the owner of the obviously more pleasing and classical physique, and equipped with the larger organ, he inspires very little confidence: his very economy of sinew seems too thrifty. Synecdoche Wessel, his four-inch spigot almost lost in the dirigible of his immense pink presence, is a lullaby of unconcern.

SVAM: Two pounds!

Sahasrara plucks up the silver weights from the velvet cushions and holds them aloft. Synecdoche and Gnatpappa shake their heads, both waiving the puny practice weight.

SVAM: Five pounds!

Sahasrara selects and secures the appropriate ornaments, then approaches the contestants with them. Employing an elastic slipknot, she attaches the five-pound weight to Gnatpappa's depending organ. Whether as a result of competitive zeal or as unwilling witness to the eyefulness of Sahasrara's dishabille, he immediately erects, drawing the weight up the wall of polyurethane. On moving now to Synecdoche's post, Sahasrara seems less impressive. Her balloon fish, which have appeared heretofore as enormous, might swim forever in the fathomless sea of Wessel's flesh, and expire before finding its kelp-covered bottom. She attaches the weight. A chime begins sounding off the seconds. Gnatpappa maintains his vigilance. Synecdoche casually achieves lift-up. The same weight, yes; the same derricking which Gnatpappa has earlier and more quickly accomplished. Yet there is a readily apparent difference: the difference between a flower's flow to blossom form, and a powder cap's thrombotic burst and abrupt, death-giving expenditure. The Nobblies sigh.

PARTURIENT (whispering to Stanhope): Synecdoche began his training in the blush of pubescence and the shame of tumescence, as an adolescent frightened he would waste his essence by anarchic discharge. He gave up sex entirely, in order to preserve and protect the vital fluid, the precious and perishable bindu-nectar, the soma-rasa whose manufacture—to distill a single drop of it—requires forty drops of blood and forty biochemically busy days. He studied the Eastern mystics and outdid them. Perhaps now he is a tank of the stuff. In the event of a nuclear holocaust, he might become a national resource, a one-man reservoir capable of artificially inseminating a whole new population.

SVAM: Ten pounds!

It must be admitted that Sahasrara performs her official functions

in an exemplary fashion, handling the organs of the contestants like
so much sausage. She attaches the ten-pound weights. The chimes
begin to sound again. Again, and as dreamily, Synecdoche by the
count of five has with the pulley and winch of his will hauled up the
weight. It takes Gnatpappa several seconds longer to accomplish the
same feat. There seems *too much* dedication in Gnatpappa's body,
too much struggle toward discipline. He is not loose, but dry. He
lacks the powerful purity, the bottomless composure, the flaccid
dreaminess of the Champion. This is the well-known Floyd Pattern:
for Gnatpappa, the weight exists to be overcome; and there is something both admirable and dispiriting about his triumph over each obstacle, as though his effort simply redoubled the intransigence of the
succeeding obstacle, depleting his own powers of overcomeuppance
in order to effect that redoubling. But for Synecdoche, the obstacle—
the weight—is abolished; or incorporated. It becomes a part of him,
as though he were a female principle so all-encompassing that he
could receive the entire material world, and maintain his Buddha-
like equanimity.

Svam: Fifteen pounds!

Sahasrara adds the five-pound weight to the ten-pound weight already attached. Gnatpappa attempts to concentrate his will in his
groin. Slowly, as the sweat streams down his body, as his lips peel
back from his teeth, as his tongue sticks out—and, in a parody of the
lower erection, stiffens and points at the monkey god—slowly, he
manages to raise the weight. And Synecdoche? His hands folded over
the immense valise of his flab, the vast cargo-hold of the freighter of
him—he, too, lifts the fifteen pounds: as though smartly saluting at a
bugle note or the appearance of a superior officer.

Svam: Twenty pounds!

And now—oh, horrible hype!—Synecdoche shakes his head. He
waives the twenty-pound weight! Gnatpappa is obviously distressed.
The Nobblies whisper; exchange awed giggles; squirm on their submarine couches.

Otto: What's going on? (It is explained to him. Mysteriously, he
smiles.)

Stanhope (to Parturient): I don't understand. If the Nobblies
are so down on genital organization, what possible pleasure can they
get from such a competition?

Parturient: For the girls, the whole thing is ludicrously funny,
and comforting. To see that vainglorious organ, that object of idiotic

envy, used as such a hoist, for such a pointless end, puts it in its place. For the boys, that organ, that blind agent of a demi-urge, has always embarrassed and betrayed them. This brute labor mocks its pretensions, compromises its independence, repays it for the responsibilities it has thrust on them. The contest is their revenge on an unwanted manhood.

Gnatpappa is of course obliged to waive the twenty-pound weight too. Pride rides our shoulders, a malignant dwarf with a glass whip . . . an Otto.

SVAM: Twenty-five pounds!

Sahasrara makes ready the respective members. And now, via that invisible yet crackling electricity by which shame and glee and hate are instantaneously communicated to all the guests at a disastrous dinner party; to all the conscripts caught in a malfunctioning elevator . . . the onlookers are aware that the moment has come. The decisive chord seems already to have been struck, plucked on an unappealable tuning fork; and, while the tremulous vibrations of that ringing stroke have not yet in their undulating reached the inner ear of the observers, have not yet shattered the crystal of their suspense, they *know* it is upon them . . . in the air and altering it: the shoe, the bomb, will drop.

NOBBLIES: Nobble, nobble.

Otto is intent. Even Parturient stops his sniggering and for a moment concentrates more on the contest than on Sahasrara. It seems that Synecdoche has but to flex himself: his member rises, an anti-aircraft gun, and swivels, training itself on the eye of the monkey god. For an instant, hanging over them like the clapper of the bell of the soon-to-be-shattered crystal suspense, Synecdoche's triumphant derrick terrifies the Nobblies. This demon-apparition casts its long shadow over their blameless faces. Will it spit at them? Fire-seed? Sperm-flak? How many children, how many obligations, how many complications might it carelessly, wantonly discharge upon them, shoot into their naked reluctance . . . ? Nervously they draw close, lick each other's elbows and insteps, hiss and quaver.

But Synecdoche is content to hoist the weight. His face—the face of a corrupted cherub, drowning in a tub of flesh—is vacant of desire; vacant even of curiosity: which vacancy is perhaps the final intimidating assurance of a champion . . .

PARTURIENT: How did Madame Guyon put it? "The resigned soul as God's weathercock."

And Gnatpappa: Oh, shame! He strains, but knows (they know,

we know) that the fork has already pitched its decision into the hexa-gon. He is doomed to lose.

OTTO: Is it up? Is it up?

Gnatpappa glares at Otto, hatred radiating from his glistening black face, the face itself a lamp of hatred, a death-giving lamp which drains off that energy required by the groin. So, indulging his enmity, Gnatpappa abets his own disaster. He ignominiously discharges.

NOBBLIES (putting their hands over their eyes): Revolting.

A thread of semen-drops trickles down the green side of the polyurethane block. Gnatpappa is limp: and the weight hangs there unhoisted: and at last the heaviness of its hanging tows his body onto the shore of pain: and he screams.

PARTURIENT: Where did all that beauty go?

Through the great yellow Bindu-Dot rush the Pigstickers of Islam, furious. They slice the elastic slipknot, releasing Gnatpappa from his agony.

SVAM: Winner and still Heavyweight Champion of Genital Organi-zation, Synecdoche Wessel!

The Pigstickers shake their fists. One inserts his thumbs in Svam's nostrils.

PIGSTICKER: You *plotted* this, you eunuchs! You brought Gnat-pappa here only to humiliate him! You thought, in your practiced self-deception, to perpetuate the sexual bondage of the black man, to exorcise your fear and hatred of our *instinctual wholeness!*

PARTURIENT (clapping a comradely hand on the Pigsticker's shoul-der): Now, mind you, this is just a letter from the vicinity of my in-feriority complex, *but* . . . couldn't it be that Otto is responsible? *He* infected Gnatty with that contagious Western sense of guilt, didn't he? And mightn't that sense of guilt have occasioned, sponsored, in-sisted—

The Pigsticker catches Parturient in the throat with a cleaver of hard-edged hand. Parturient falls, gasping, on Sahasrara, and lies there, his head between her breasts.

Svam Spade, in search of an ear, his nose bleeding, finds Stanhope; remembers for a moment their earlier encounters—at the Fire Festi-val, on the fuel barge, in the Pyramid—then chooses to forget them, because all the other ears are occupied.

SVAM: In a way, it *was* our fault Gnatpappa lost. Although we had the best of intentions. We wanted Synecdoche to lose: we hate cham-pions, of course. But the trouble was that our hatred, while palpable, was impotent: that impotence which arises out of one's fear of a champion. To project such hatred, such desperate hope of failure, on a champion is in effect *to betray the challenger*. Because such desperation is compromised by its concomitant conviction of hopelessness. The challenger can't help but smell that wish-fear-hopelessness. The telepathic logic of the unconscious which *we* permitted to invade the precincts of this competition *psychically* upset and weakened Gnatpappa. So we did betray him, by the very violence of our need of his triumph. For such a desperate need is in fact its own antithesis, isn't it? Its violent expression arises from the fury of our failed selves; and is, therefore, a projection. A projection, alas, which unconsciously cries out for the ultimate rape *by* the champion, that violation which is a *confirmation* of our inability to resist that rape. We offered Gnatpappa as the sister of our shame (ours is a family of shame), to be the object of that deflowering *we* secretly desired . . .

Parturient presses Sahasrara's great breasts over his eyes and ears, as though to make himself an anti-hero sandwich.

PARTURIENT: I wonder. The masculinity of Black Power might actually rescue us from the cop-out of the Nobblies and the acid-heads. *That* might be our only hope: that the black man—whose many disguises our bourgeois young have for so long been busy imitating, ignorant of the fact that those disguises and postures are impostures and self-caricatures—that the black man should turn on the imitators of his parody of himself, turn on the female impersonators who have used him as their launching pad out of the hermetically sealed sweatbox of the ranch house which is the middle class . . . that that black man should turn on them with the full force of his outraged and categorically denied dignity as a *man;* and be, as a result of the violence *he* authors, the miraculous rescue-instrument, the unwitting savior of *our* lost manhood . . . wouldn't that be a kick in the three pounds of flax! For we would be using the black man yet again: the rack upon which we are stretched to a grace we are incapable of winning by and for ourselves. Ha, ho, ha!

He kisses Sahasrara's breasts. She feeds him a knuckle sandwich. He spins, trying to disassemble the pinned corners of her diaper. She belly-bumps him off her, rises and sprints toward the Veil of Maya. He uprights himself and rushes after her, crying—

PARTURIENT: Stop, Sahasrara! How did St. Augustine put it? "A natural craving cannot be in vain."

Parturient might have found easier prey had he remained, for the

Nobblies are now changing each other's diapers. The close air of the hexagon is full of the silt-drift of baby powder from their leather pouches. Stanhope himself is tempted . . .

DASEIN (elbowing Stanhope): Look, Stanhope, look. See the blue beret. See the blue beret run away from us. Run, blue beret, run. Oh, let us run after the blue beret!

STANHOPE: Mother!

He vaults after the figure in black domino, through the Bindu-Dot, up a spiral staircase, into a corridor of betel nuts which cry upon their crushing: crack-alack . . .

Now: the ugly scene which he has only just fled is mercifully extinguished. We see Stanhope *inside* a metronome, confronted, enwombed, by a thousand mirror-facets, variously distorting their communal image of black domino and blue beret. A thousand mothers taunt him, beating their black bat-wings against the hairiness of the whole situation.

STANHOPE: I see you! I know now that I have always seen you . . . for exactly what you were and are. I see my whole life full of you, like a septic tank!

MIRROR-MOTHERS (derisively): Ho, ha, ho!

STANHOPE: I see you, standing before the orange door on Cimarosa Street—in your giraffe-stenciled calf-coat and your poor-boy tunic, your hopsack tights and your Wellington boots. Behind you, the stucco ripples and the fuchsia bushes bend and wave like frilly flabby flaky ballerinas. I see you step from the porch. I see your eyes like drops of hot-melt adhesive. I see your hand rising like some elephantiasical needle on the speedometer of Death. I see you blast with beebees from the denuded child's-bone branches of the infant tree those sparrows whose twittering had disturbed your concentration on the early poems of Pablo Neruda. And I see myself sneak from the garage, wherein I had fearfully sequestered myself against the advent of your sinister intent; and I collect the bloodstained feathers of the slain sparrows; and those feathers stiffen on my palm, needles too on the enormous gauge of your inexorable willfulness . . . I see you, assassin not only of the sparrows, but of my hopes and dreams as well . . .

MIRROR-MOTHERS: Tell it to Congressman Hosmer! Tell it to John the Ossified Man!

A sickle of shadow slashes at Stanhope's tentative advance. He releases the safety catch on the Smith & Wesson revolver which

Dasein has supplied him. Where *is* Dasein? (As a matter of fact, Dasein has been temporarily abducted by the Pigstickers of Islam, who are—more to her pleasure than to theirs—methodically, according to the alphabetical order of their X's, attempting through her prone agency to scrub their spanners spic of Gnatpappa's infectious humiliation.) But abruptly, to the dramatic relief of all concerned, the magnetic axes choose once more to assert themselves; and the Blue Hexagons turn shifty on Stanhope again; and with a shudder he is hurled into another aspect of the irreality . . .

While Stanhope is seeking his mother, Parturient is seeking Sahasrara Cannibis. We join Pather under the Sephiroth Tree of the Kabbalah, among—inexplicably—smiling disciples of Krishna the Repairer (garage mechanic of the Metaphysical Volkswagen Bus).

PATHER: Is there a lingam franca?

They chew pan. They juggle tambourines. They gesture with arms around which are coiled silver reptiles. They sing.

KRISHNAUTS (singing):

> In the beginning was the Verb:
> The root I-Am medicinal herb
> To ease the ache of our I-sores.
> So let us now be verbivores.
> Abolish "to have" . . .
> Embrace "to be" . . .
> Come be trans-
> Itive with me.

PATHER: How sad for you that the East has opted for the reality principle.

KRISHNAUTS: As sparks issued from the same fire are destined to return to it; as the dewdrop trembling on the lotus slips into the shining sea . . . so Atma is alone-ness; so Atma is all-oneness.

But there is Sahasrara, flitting among Gupta sculptures!

PATHER: Sahasrara, come back! Come back, Sahasrara! Wait for me! How did St. Mecthild of Magdeburg-Hackborn put it? "Come, my bride, and enjoy my Godhead . . ."

SAHASRARA (disappearing into the woodwork): Anaclitic hang-up on the loose!

The Sage Sons of the Purple Pioneers sing "Goodbye, Old Paint."

Sticks of incense in bronze trays; bruised apples, rotting pears in silver bowls; forked tongues of orange flame from candles in pots overlaid by filigree of an obscene elaboration; midnight blue velvet carpeting; burial urns; and Otto, suspended in the center of his Grotto, turning at the ends of his cables, an angel in wadded silk dressing gown.

It is a homage-mass in honor of the proximity senses. (Parturient has accused Otto of neglecting the coprophilia. How, Parturient has asked, will electricity or plastic simulate taste and smell? It may be that Parturient has a point.)

Racked along the wall like umbrellas for Zulus are the Pigstickers of Islam. They wear chalk-white Marilyn Monroe death masks. Sitting on top of an urn, ill at ease despite his new costume (Queen Victoria), is Svam Spade. *He* wears a Booker T. Washington death mask. On the rug of midnight velvet blue, beneath the angel-Otto, lies a Gnatpappa naked and sobbing in defeat. Red Sovine sings "Little Rosa."

OTTO: Of course, I hate them too. You understand that. The female impersonators: virgins, vamps, whores, teases—they are not manly roles, are they, Gnatpappa? They are not. (Musing to himself, since there is no audience to which he might otherwise muse . . .) Who would *want* to impersonate a female? Woman the Temptress . . . small, hawk-faced females rubbing butter and honey on the stone columnular lingam. (To Gnatpappa, and Svam, and the Pigstickers . . .) Why does every new generation long for *Götterdämmerung?* Because it longs for the destruction by violence of everything it has not made itself. This generation is more fortunate than most, in two respects. First, it has the atom bomb to play with in its fantasies. And second, it is unencumbered by any desire to make anything for and by itself, except the scene. So it is free to pursue its tryst with Terror. (Svam seems about to protest; but his Queen is not high enough to win the trick.) Why tryst with Terror? Because Terror fondles your unmentionables. Terror promises you an easy, passive redefinition, a change, an ultimate rending and rendering, a fulfillment. From the vessel of Dread we chug-a-lug our draught of Apocalypse-longing. Everything will be utterly changed; and the responsibility will not be ours, nor the guilt, nor the failure. It has been taken out of our hands. The machinery is in gear, turning, turning—and when it stops, something definitive will have occurred. Something awful, yes; but also

something absolving, because it will constitute a proof of our help-
lessness.

Violins. With the projector-pencil Otto paints pictures in the gloom,
writes words of light on the night around him, hieroglyphs which begin to fade even as they are completed, shapes and exclamations dying
immediately on their achievement of form.

OTTO: But we know, don't we, Gnatpappa, that it is only in the
minds of clerks that a desperation which is *unmanageable* occurs, in
the minds of Snopeses and Svams. (Svam is offended, is about to protest; but Otto ignores his gestures, and he subsides. How often, it is
worth wondering, was the one-track mind of Queen Victoria dis-
raelied?) With their coiled images of lust; their rage at the inequita-
ble distribution of money; their egocentricity; their taste for the
power to humiliate and brutalize—we know that, don't we?

Gnatpappa does not reply. Svam relieves frustrations by snapping
his fingers in time to the *Tristan* now offered over the intercom, a
Tristan which seems to have been made palpable by the blue velvet
rug and the bruised apples and the burial urns . . . erotic, mystical,
in praise and adoration of sleep, the paradise of rest, the holy silence
of passivity.

OTTO (to himself, sadly): Like Germany, I am an admixture of
the demonic and the bourgeois. (To Gnatpappa) I understand how
you feel. What I am offering you is a consolation perhaps best
realized in the nineteenth century. With its lavishness, its grandiosity,
its magnificence of scale, its Homeric leitmotivs, the "splendid long-
windedness" of its Wagners and Tolstoys. With, too, its organization
of effects, its cult of detail, its manipulations of meanings and symbolic
senses. For that century too was possessed of a scientific self-
sufficiency. And it too was redeemed by its pessimism, its musical
bond with night and Death. *Night* is the consolation I am offering
you, Gnatpappa. And you promised, if you lost the contest . . . remember.

The lovers' cry of transport: *Selbst dann bin ich die Welt.*

SVAM (can it be derisively?): Wang-wang.

OTTO: Kant claimed Time to be an immutable form of human perception. Kierkegaard put it differently. "Time," said Kierkegaard,
"does not really exist without unrest; it does not exist for dumb animals who are absolutely without anxiety." (Musing again . . .) How
did Kierkegaard *know?* To the blind, all things are sudden.

On his head Otto lowers the crown with the sapphire-crystal. The sapphire-crystal stares across the Grotto, beyond Gnatpappa, to and at the felt-covered altar on which twin tubes in silver brackets sit. Two black ruby-eyed sleeves which, in their turn, are trained on the sapphire-crystal. Their intestinal reflectors, their resonant cavities, are not visible. Their electrons are not yet excited.

OTTO: Unrest is discontent. Discontent is our permanent condition. Time is therefore Guilt. Art and Money are crystallized Time, crystallized Guilt. History is a Dialectic of Neurosis. And where is Parturient? I *require* Parturient to help me fulfill the promise of Apollinaire.

SVAM (dutifully repeating that promise): "And the roses of electricity still open/In the garden of my memory . . ."

Pather opens a hatch, peers in, sees not Sahasrara: only the gurus, hunched over their switchboards, whispering into their mouthpieces—

GURUS: Abnegate . . . abnegate . . .

Pather bolts the hatch. The corridor is strewn with Nobblies.

NOBBLIES: Is *he* of the Body? Obviously not. He is not of Love's Body. How did Robert Desnos put it? "The scholars of light never invented anything but not very thick darkness." Mathematics is the crucial discipline in converting human love to a suprasensual life. Science is morbid. A non-morbid science would strive for union with nature, not mastery over it: erotic exuberance, not compulsive manipulation.

PATHER: Why? (He is genuinely interested in knowing; he despises nature.)

NOBBLIES: The concept of matter is an unconscious projection of man's anal disturbance into his picture of the world, making of the universe one vast alembic of cosmic sublimation.

PATHER (disappointed): Grape juice. Thinking, analyzing, inventing, are not just anomalous acts; they are the normal respiration of intelligence. The ego—like the child—is naturally a scientist, observing and testing reality, trying to form an accurate picture of it, trying to adjust the organism so as to protect it from the dangers—and win for it the rewards—of reality. Also, like the child, the ego is just plain curious.

NOBBLIES: The will to power is an extroversion of the death instinct.

PATHER: The will to powerlessness is an introversion of the castration complex.

NOBBLIES: Separation anxiety. The aggressive fantasy of wanting to become the father of one's self.

PATHER: Self-castration. Kill father by killing the possibility of fatherhood.

NOBBLIES: Oral, anal and genital organizations are functional distortions. Beware the aphimixis of erotisms.

PATHER: You lack the courage of Freud's pessimism. (He walks over their bodies toward the end of the corridor.) You have co-opted Freud for Disneyland.

NOBBLIES: How did T'chen put it a thousand years ago? "Ceaselessly spinning in its silk, the stupid silkworm."

PATHER (looking back): Pornography used to be the vanguard of the polymorphous perverse. Today that vanguard is advertising. Tomorrow it will be Communist China.

Reinhard Linz and the London Philharmonic Orchestra play march music from *The Magic Flute.*

OTTO: We can't begin without Parturient.

Gnatpappa rises to his knees, stares at the sapphire-crystal. The Pigstickers are dancing to *Tristan,* stepping on and grinding under insects with their toes and heels.

OTTO: The Pollution of Light into Lust and Desire: Light is the Medium of Sin.

SVAM: Auto-plastic versus allo-plastic.

Gnatpappa turns to the black tubes, the ruby-eyed sleeves of light.

OTTO: The Blind Seers: Homer, Milton, Joyce, Ray Charles! Gnatpappa, you promised!

Once more, the apparition, among bamboo stalks . . .

STANHOPE: I see you, Mother. I see you crouching behind the portable TV set, with your periscope up, turning, peering, prying, spying, over the fence into the neighboring plots of dicondra, at neighboring pudges in flowering sport shirts, at neighboring rites round other rotisseries: your mouth curled down at its corners and your knees knocking. And I hear you repeat, over and over again—invocation or exorcision?—"Troglodytes . . . troglodytes . . . troglodytes . . ." As the moon rises and the smog deepens and the blimps flashing their red exhortations float by overhead, footballs heaved from shore to shore in some continental contest, scoring points in some charade to whose secret point we could neither of us penetrate . . . I see you, hear you, while I stand with my mallet in my hand, measuring cold-eyed the distance, croquet hoop to croquet hoop. "Troglodyte . . . troglodyte . . ." But you were not talking to me. You never *talked* to me, Mother.

MAUD (wearing an ebony Patrice Lumumba death mask): Self-pity was the only discipline you were ever able to master.

STANHOPE: Perhaps. I understand that. But I understand more than that, Mother. I understand that when you crouched with the peri-scope, prying and spying, you *longed* to be one of the flowering pudges in the neighboring plot; you *longed* to consume your slab of charred cutlet and your quota of daiquiris, to receive your besotted caress, endure your squeeze and stab, sleep off your stupor and at dawn embrace the cipher of the new day's dreariness. Like *them.* Long Beach included you out, didn't it, Mother?

MAUD: That's a lie!

Reinhard Linz and the London Philharmonic play march music from Verdi's *Aida.*

STANHOPE: No, Mother. The truth, for once. How else explain your aberrant desire for bowling, than as a longing to belong? But you would never belong, as I could never belong. Long Beach included both of us out. But we might have made do, Mother, if only there had been love in that house on Cimarosa Street, if only there had been a pact of the lonely *against* Long Beach! But no. No love, as there were no clocks. Only bleeding Diego Rivera posters. Only fat stapled pack-ages of the Congressional Record, piling, towering, yellowing, crum-bling in the bedroom closet. Only a dart board adorned with a glossy pic of a glossy-cheeked Lewis Strauss. Only target practice and Shostakovich; the smell of Chinese tobacco and the baleful regard of peasant figurines; borscht in the washbasin and blood in the bathtub and—later, later—curled blackened slivers of microfilm in *our* barbecue rotisserie . . . a poor substitute for cutlets, as target practice was a poor substitute for love. There *should* have been love, Mother . . . there should have been—

MAUD: Banana oil. (And she disappears once more.)

PATHER (on entering Otto's Grotto): Don't touch that switch.

Gnatpappa backs away from the black tubes. The Pigstickers turn their Marilyn Monroe death masks on Parturient. Svam Spade blows and pops himself out of his hoop skirt as though he were a wad of bubble gum; uses an urn as stool.

PATHER: I can only control it by duration. The light oscillates in the resonant cavity at four hundred and seventy-three million cycles per second, using up all the excited electrons. That energy which is released through the partially transparent end-mirror can deviate from its fundamental frequency only a few thousand cycles per second. (To Otto) Do you understand?

OTTO: It is not required that I understand. Only that I feel.

PATHER: You'll feel, all right. The ruby-laser light bombards the sapphire-crystal, creating hypersonic vibrations. Those vibrations will penetrate all the way to your anteromedial hypothalamus. Sound waves will excite the sex center of your brain.

OTTO: Wizard.

PARTURIENT: I will keep increasing the duration of the beam until you signal us—by sighs or otherwise—that you've reached maximum satisfaction. We'll lock the laser source at that point, to repeat at periodic intervals a beam of the desired duration.

GNATPAPPA: What's the other tube for?

PATHER: Just a spare. In case this one konks out on us, we can switch to the other; and the ceremony will go on without an interruption. (He opens a box.) As a safety precaution, everyone but Otto must wear these. (He removes a dozen pairs of protective goggles.) Being blind, Otto won't need them.

OTTO: Parturient, are you wearing a death mask?

PATHER: Is that necessary?

OTTO: I think it makes for ever so much more fun. Svam, get him one.

Svam fishes a Benny "Kid" Paret death mask out of a burial urn and brings it to Pather. Pather hangs it on his ears. Then they all don protective goggles.

OTTO: You realize, Gnatpappa, that after me, it's your turn. Without goggles, Gnatpappa. To be blinded by monochromatic light, by spatially coherent optical radiation . . . that is an appropriate purgation . . . that is a satisfying salvation from the sinfulness of polluted light, the lurid desire . . . After me, Gnatpappa—*shame ends!*

PATHER: Kill the candles.

Svam does so. And as he does so, another figure slips into the Grotto, wearing a Patrice Lumumba death mask.

PATHER (to himself): Black domino? Blue beret? Cronopios' peripatetic mother?

On the intercom: the finale of *Die Meistersinger* . . .

OTTO: Spirit is historical by representing itself in retrospect as a transparent totality. *Existenz* is historical as eternity in time, as the absolute historicity of its concrete empirical existence in a spiritual opacity which is never removed.

PATHER (muttering to himself): Opacity Unlimited, coming right up.

Only the incense sticks now hold out against the Grotto's famished darkness.

OTTO (irritated): Svam? Speak up, Svam!

SVAM (without enthusiasm): Spirit in its immediacy is the Potential Idea, whose . . . whose universality unfolds itself into full clarity.

OTTO: *Existenz* in its immediacy is its historicity in relation to Transcendence, which is to say: the irremovable immediacy of its faith.

SVAM (swinging his bustle like a bowling ball): Faith is Being.

OTTO (gratified): Too right.

PATHER: Bombards away . . .

A finger of light—half a millimeter in diameter—leaps from the ruby-eye to Otto's sapphired brow. Pather has only an instant to observe the intrusion and rush of the figure in black domino.

PATHER (wonderingly): A mother's about to smother me.

Then he is attacked from the rear: by Pigstickers, Gnatpappa, even Svam! As he falls to the midnight blue velvet rug, he manages to shout:

PATHER: How did Rilke put it? "Then God rushed forward from His ambush."

And just before his horrible scream, Otto is heard (as if in reply) to cry:

OTTO: *Jeder Engel ist schrecklich!*

PATHER (as total darkness and many bodies fall): A quote from the very same poet! By the great nose horn of the Titanotheriidae, the old bastard is going out in style!

INTERCOM (singing chorus):

> Though Holy Roman Empire sink to dust
> There still survives our sacred German art . . .
>
> Yesod, that's my maybe;
> Astral light's not wavy:
> Yesod . . . sentience's going naoow!

The acid-heads are playing Mental Monopoly and exchanging libidinal cathexes in the Dark Night of the Soul Suite.

FIRST A-H: I always end up with Maslow Gardens. Self-actualization turns me off.

SECOND A-H (who has just landed on Jung Manor, which the third acid-head has previously developed with two pads and a psychedelicatessen): All right. I own all four Allports. I'll trade two functional autonomies for a rent exemption.

THIRD A-H (reading an invisible card): Go directly to Individuation. Do not pass Creative Self-Hood. Do not collect unemployable insurance.

STANHOPE: Have you seen someone in black domino and blue beret?

ACID-HEADS: A quest! A quest! (They don yellow Lao Tzu death masks.) Who are you?

Who, indeed? An embarrassing question!

STANHOPE (deciding out loud): A poet.

ACID-HEADS (severely): Language, because it tries to identify and mediate reality, is an Apollonian hang-up: the manipulation of symbolic excrement out of fascination with the fact of one's own death. The unconscious becomes conscious by means of mechanisms of transference, which are memory residues of external perceptions. Condensations of unconscious meanings . . . displacements of accents . . . the substitute-gratification hang-up . . .

STANHOPE (impatiently): You may go right on pissing your autisms all over my architecture. It will continue to stand. How did the French poet put it, on repudiating the hashish-eaters? "I imagine to myself a man—a Brahman, shall I say, a poet or a Christian philosopher—who has scaled the arduous Olympus of the spirit. The God Apollo—master of all knowledge, he of Francavilla, Albrecht Dürer, Goltzius, whomsoever you please: has not every man who merits it his own Apollo?—is enticing from his bow its most vibrant chords. Below this man, at the foot of the mountain, amidst the briars and mud, the human herd, the pack of Helots, is grimacing from false delight and howling in the pangs of its poison. And the poet sadly thinks: These unfortunates, who have neither fasted nor prayed, who have refused redemption by toil, are demanding of black magic the means of raising themselves all of a sudden to superhuman existence. The magic makes dupes of them, shedding upon them a false happiness and a false light. Whereas we, the poets and philosophers, have redeemed our souls by unremitting toil and contemplation. By the constant exercises of our wills and the enduring nobility of our devotion, we have created for our use a garden of true beauty . . . we have performed the only miracle for which God has given us leave."

ACID-HEADS: Which French poet?

STANHOPE (grinning): Charles Baudelaire! Who also observed: "He who has recourse to poison in order to think will soon be unable to think *without* poison."

The acid-heads, offended by his co-opting of the poet of evil, confer. Feeble cries issue from the Chamber of Blankness to their left. And, accompanying those cries, a litany whose steadfast dreariness is familiar to Stanhope—

VOICE: Twelve days and twelve nights in the prison train . . . wasteland and solitude . . . the fox had laid its stealthy tracks to the very train itself . . . fifty-three degrees below zero . . . Odessa . . . the harbor surrounded by troops . . . an icebreaker to plow their way for them through the frozen Black Sea, by night, in a gale . . . What an irony that the black ship of exile should have borne the name of *Ilyich!* Hilarity-making.

STANHOPE (rushing forward): Dasein! Dasein! How's by you?

DASEIN (looking up, wearing a Tibor Dery death mask): What makes others wither, elevates and inspires and fortifies me. How then can I lament destiny?

STANHOPE: You look as though you wouldn't lament a stiff drink.

DASEIN (nodding): Vodka is just as much a political factor as the word.

The acid-heads, knowing alcohol to be Establishmentarian, flap and cluck. Dasein's despair, however, is miniature compared to that unleashed upon the Ashram at this moment: a despair so huge it requires a giant of a scream to contain it; a scream so agonized it seems archetypical: as though it were a repetition of that haunted cry, that dismal recognition, which the forebears of the foolish sphenodon, the opossum, the *Mus musculus* and the lemur all made on their intuiting the evolutionary scheme: the scream that was torn from them upon their learning that they had achieved a forward step in the cruel and painful enterprise which is man-unkind. Is there pain in the Ashram worthy of uttering such a scream? If so, where?

A Sufi facet is displaced, and a distraught Sahasrara staggers in upon them.

ACID-HEADS: Well, well, if it isn't the Community Chest.

SAHASRARA: Help!

FIRST A-H (to the others): You know, this nobble-nobble religious-poetic hang-up of childhood as lost innocence turns me off even quicker than Maslow Gardens.

SAHASRARA: Something awful has happened to Otto. He's . . . he's *dead*.

ACID-HEADS (respectfully): The Ultimate Bad Trip.

STANHOPE: Where?

SAHASRARA: The Grotto.

STANHOPE: Take us there.

He drags Dasein after her. Sahasrara of course has been initiated into the secret of the shifty hexagons. She manages by applying palm prints on the walls to manipulate their altering relationships. So they reach the Grotto swiftly. And, on arriving, wish they hadn't. Charles Trenet sings "La Merde."

What a mess. There hangs Otto, in a sort of ski lift; and he is totally headless. As though a species of centrifugal force had exploded and shattered his skull, scraps of brain and splinters of bone have been flung all over the room. In various states of injury and disrepair, wearing various ridiculous death masks, Svam Spade, Parturient, Gnatpappa and miscellaneous Pigstickers are coughing and vomiting. And . . . why, it's Mother! A wayward piece of Otto's skull must have slapped her senseless. She is only now groggily returning to consciousness, hauling herself up by the lip of a burial urn.

STANHOPE (waving his Smith & Wesson revolver around): Arggh.

PARTURIENT (bleeding, furious): Boobs! Dolts! Ninnyhammers! Cabbageheads! I was *already* going to use *both* tubes! I was going to alternate beam bombardments. I was going to steadily shorten the interval between beams as I lengthened the duration of each beam. In two minutes, the beams would have hit him simultaneously—at a combined force of sixty billion cycles! The hypersonic sound vibrations would have cracked the crystal. But you, you quarter-wits, you managed to extend to him a swift mercy he did not deserve, and at the same time redecorate the Grotto with the garbage of his brain!

STANHOPE: What *happened?*

PARTURIENT: They jumped me. *All* of them. The clodpated mooncalves were so goddamned anxious to annihilate Otto that all they could think about was trampling over each other to get their paws on the auxiliary laser. They wanted to turn it on. *But it was already on.* It was cycled with the first laser. Whoever got to it first, and flicked the switch, shut *off both* lasers! Then the next one turned them on again; and the one after that turned them off again; and the one after *that* . . . I doubt if the Great Immutable Ham-What-Am Itselflessness knows what happened! The circuitry must have gone haywire. They hit Otto with beams of unequal duration and unequal force. Instead of cracking the crystal and neatly splitting his skull, they smashed the crystal and tore his head right off! The beams bounced back from the mirrors on the ceiling and went after all of us! Don't you see what this means?

STANHOPE: Aside from turning Otto's Grotto into an abattoir, no.

PARTURIENT: It means . . . Look, with all the bodies climbing over one another, with all the paws on the switches—we don't even know which one of us killed him! We don't know which ones inadvertently switched both lasers *off,* and which ones switched them *on* again. Confound it! All the *purity* is gone! The meaning! *I* wanted to kill him. *Me.* It was *my* idea. And it would have been perfect . . . it would have been *beautiful.* Now . . . now, *nobody knows who did it.* These interlopers have turned a work of art into a stupid obscene cartoon. Death-giving was my means of destroying the mirror image, my ticket to dignity . . . and they've cheated me out of it! (He throws up his hands.) Oh, *fudge!*

STANHOPE: But why? Why would anyone . . . why did *all* of you want to kill Otto?

Electrified baboons could not have created a babble as demented and as unintelligible. Stanhope fires a warning shot above their loose-mouthed heads. They look at one another, from behind their death masks. Finally, Parturient gets the ball rolling.

PARTURIENT: I killed Otto because he hated Light. Because these Annihilation Night rites of ritual blinding were a blasphemous offense against the purity and possibility of Light. Otto's Instant Oedipalsy!

GNATPAPPA (with the Pigstickers nodding); *I* killed Otto because he was using hot and cold media to manipulate the emotional climates of the developing black nations of Africa and Asia. The same old jazz of the white man as psychic exploiter!

SVAM (his Queen Victoria hoop skirt hanging around his neck, his Booker T. Washington death mask askew, grinning): *I* killed Otto for rather more complicated—and, I think, rather more profound—reasons. Like: Jaspers turns me off. I mean, the Jasp delivers a lot of static about the absolutization of limited empirical things in the world, the known and investigable . . . and, all right, I dig. I'm also for preserving thought from the empty understanding and endless formulation of speech which no longer comprehends . . . preserving and holding thought free for Transcendence. But when the Jasp goes on to say that thought in its priority must actually be achieved in the clarity of the unlimited—yet always determinate—*knowledge* of *knowledge* . . . when he says that thought must always *reason* in order to perceive that which is more than reason—well, man, I smell cop-out. Like, we know it attenuates. Reason, I mean. The feel's the anti-thing. For two moons I suspected Otto of selling out to the rationalists. Like, he was recording all our pseudo-events. Why? He was a phony, that's why. One of the Manipulators!

Maud Cronopios leaps suddenly for one of the black ruby-eyed laser tubes.

PARTURIENT: It's split. Try to use it and you'll totally erase yourself.

Maud drops the tube.

STANHOPE: And you, Mother? Were you in on this little gang-bang of death?

MAUD: I was. Why do you think I stayed in Long Beach? But I'll tell you one thing: it's positively the last time I'll ever work with amateurs. *I* killed Otto because he was a German agent. When you told Onalred about his programing of emotional climates, we knew he had to be working for someone. The two big tribal-based cultures in the West are Russia and Germany. We *knew* it wasn't Russia, so it had to be Germany. It fits: Germany's very audile-tactile; integrated; in tune with the drum of pulse. Cf. Hitler's use of radio. So Otto had to be exterminated. There's some indication he was bank-rolled by a renascent Nazi movement in Bavaria . . .

STANHOPE: Mother, I must add to the long list of your crimes the unforgivable one of stupidity. First, Otto's money came from the sale of his sex machines, his Invigorators. Second, his programing of emotional climates was purely experimental. You are as incapable of understanding the motives of science as you are those of art.

PARTURIENT: The same applies to Gnatpappa. The only reason Otto used the underdeveloped countries as test specimens was because unrest and discontent in that part of the world wouldn't surprise anybody. Black men had nothing to do with it. He was perfecting his technique before going after bigger game—such as Jacques Barzun and Morningside Heights. That leaves only me and Svam with *decent* motives. And Svam's problem is that he's too feeble-minded to understand Jaspers. Until they invent a Jaspers Pill he can wash down with *ayuhuasca,* he'll always be too feeble-minded to understand Jaspers.

SVAM: I resent that. If what you say about his experimenting is true, then what I suspected about his sellout to the Manipulators is also true. Science is anal sadism!

During the confessions, Sahasrara has sunk to her knees, with her arms over her breasts—regarding Parturient with wonder. Now she turns to Svam with a scowl.

SAHASRARA: But Svam, even assuming you're capable of under-standing the Jasp, don't you see your hang-up? You don't like Jaspers *because* Jaspers likes reason; you don't like Otto *because* Otto likes Jaspers; *therefore* Otto is a cop-out; *therefore* Otto must be killed. *Because* and *therefore,* Svam—by attempting to manipulate reality, you have hopelessly compromised your hippiness! You're just as ergo-istic as all the rhomboids you've put down!

PARTURIENT: So . . . only *I* remain.

STANHOPE (with disapproval): Parturient, you killed Otto because of his religious beliefs, and that's contrary to the democratic ideal.

SVAM (struggling to recover from Sahasrara's wounding attack): Democracy, according to Lawrence, is energetic negation. So he negated—

MAUD (sneering): The emotional basis of democracy, according to Tocqueville, is *envy.*

STANHOPE: Shut up, all of you! (He turns to Sahasrara.) We've got to call the police. Where's the nearest telephone?

SAHASRARA (who is back to looking at Parturient with wonder): The Dial-a-Guru switchboard. But the police can't get in here now. The ramp is closed, and there aren't any other entrances or exits.

STANHOPE (irritated): Then when *can* the police get in?

SAHASRARA: At midnight, I suppose. Like the baseball stadia of the future, the Ashram features a retractable dome. It opens at the stroke of twelve on Annihilation Night, to allow all the free spirits to fly up into the embrace of the Absolute.

STANHOPE (thinking out loud): Then the cops could come in by Sky-Knight helicopter when the dome retracts. Dasein, where's your Luger?

DASEIN (examining herself helplessly): I don't know. I must have dropped it while the Pigstickers were . . . were purging themselves of their shame.

STANHOPE: Take my Smith & Wesson. Keep them covered. I'll call the cops.

SAHASRARA (rising): Parturient, I'm *sorry*. I didn't understand. Now I do. You made a pact with death, didn't you? You were willing to accept the consequences of that pact, weren't you? Subjectively speaking, you stopped fighting *against* death. And we know that the war *against* death throws mankind out of the actuality of life; results in denial—repression—of life. The war against death traps us in a preoccupation with the past and the future. But by seeking instead of fleeing death, you made possible the re-creation of the present tense, which is the tense of life . . . which tense is tensionless. Parturient, I relinquish myself to you!

Sahasrara runs across the midnight blue velvet carpet to bound on Parturient.

Stanhope backs out of the Grotto. In the corridor, he applies palms to various sections of Sufi-facet, without success. Acid-heads approach him from the other end of the corridor, their game of Mental Monopoly having ended on the purchase by one of Watts Mews and his construction of a replica Ashram: he has sold the rest of them their liberation.

STANHOPE: How do you work the walls? I've got to get to the gurus.

ACID-HEADS: Got to get? The rules of communication are not necessarily the rules of the universe.

STANHOPE (carefully): It is necessary that I reach the gurus.

ACID-HEADS: There *are* no necessities.

STANHOPE (seizing one of them by his ears and kneeling on his Lao Tzu death mask): There may be no necessities, but there *are* several *nasty* probabilities. I suggest that if you'd prefer to avoid the probability of my pushing your Lao Tzu death mask all the way through your head, you will work the walls for me.

ACID-HEAD: Since you put it that way. (He fingers the marble pilgrims.) But *hurry* is a hang-up, man. Time is crystallized guilt.

A facet swings open. Stanhope steps in, then turns.

STANHOPE: I will defer the gratification of my hurry-hunger long enough to paraphrase the way Jorge Luis Borges put it: Denying temporal succession, denying the self, denying the astronomical universe, are *apparent desperations* and *secret consolations*. Our destiny, as contrasted with the hell of Swedenborg and the hell of Tibetan mythology and the hell of the UCLA mental ward, is not frightful by being unreal; it is frightful because it is irreversible and iron-clad.

Time is the substance I am made of. Time is the river which sweeps me along, but I am the river; it is the tiger which destroys me, but I am the tiger; it is a fire which consumes me, but I am the fire. Long Beach, unfortunately, is real; I, unfortunately, am Stanhope. *Every morning when you wake up, the empirical world is still outside!*

ACID-HEADS: You are not Stanhope, nor Faust, Hamlet, Don Quixote, Parsifal. You are Tarzan!

STANHOPE: You depress me.

ACID-HEADS: You are your own thorazine.

STANHOPE: I see a great empty failure of nerve . . . a fear of the responsibility of *trying* to act meaningfully. I see pumped into that failure of nerve, that flab of the will, any old anti-rationalist gas around: dope, electricity, libidinal impulses, varieties of strained mystagogical applesauce. I see the resulting blimp released as a revelation; and, in its shadow, the Dionysiac Pack. Feel! Maybe *your* self-validating visions will prove luckier for you and for the rest of us than all those other revealed truths which seemed inevitably to find their sexological expression in de Sade and their political expression in Hitler. But I doubt it. For once the Pack has exhausted itself, the same old problems still remain. And the revels of the Pack have delayed any work on the problems, for we shall have to clean up after you once again. I once told Svam that questions are the difference between men and asparagus. The children of the blimp are asparagus.

He leaves them, and is confronted by a guru wearing an Ernest Hemingway death mask.

GURU: Abnegate.

STANHOPE: Abdicate.

GURU: Why?

STANHOPE (kicking the guru out of his swivel chair): Three pounds of flax!

As lucklessness would have it, Renaldi answers the telephone at the station house.

RENALDI: What *is* it with you, Stanhope? Are you the Finger of Death? All right, all right. I might drop in around midnight!

Back to the Grotto. And in the Grotto an almost indefinable change has taken place in Stanhope's absence, a restructuring of social interrelationships he is hard put to identify precisely. One manifestation is that Dasein and Maud have discarded their death masks; Sahasrara is wearing Tibor Dery now, and Parturient wears Patrice Lumumba. Another manifestation is the joyous coupling of Sahasrara and Parturient, who roll around on the blue velvet rug wearing nothing *but* those death masks. A third manifestation is that Maud smiles, and Dasein points the Smith & Wesson *not* at Maud, but at *Stanhope.*

MAUD (whispering to Dasein, with the air of clinching a case she has been pleading): *La politique ne connaît ni ressentiment personnel ni l'esprit de vengeance. La politique ne connaît que l'efficacité.*

STANHOPE: Carve it on your nose. Dasein, what's going on?

DASEIN: Your mother has . . . has put things in a slightly different light.

STANHOPE: And that light is flattering?

DASEIN: Well . . . yes. (Her hands tremble; the snout of the Smith & Wesson describes an arc.) She explained . . . she told me, made me see that . . . (She cannot go on.)

MAUD: What I've done is to update the Permanent Revolution for her.

STANHOPE: The Permanent Revolution?

DASEIN: *The Permanent Revolution!* You see, Stan, she . . . she doesn't work any more for the men who bang their shoes . . .

STANHOPE: She doesn't, does she? Then who does she work for? Sam Yorty?

DASEIN: She . . . she works for the man who writes little poems.

MAUD: And the man who writes little poems believes in the Permanent Revolution, as the man with the beard and the eyes like supernovas believed in it: that Permanent Revolution which was betrayed by the man with the pipe and the mustache, and is being now betrayed by the men who bang their shoes and worry about consumer goods.

STANHOPE: She's lying as usual, Dasein. Onalred loathed the man who writes little poems. Maybe he loathed him *because* he wrote little poems, but nevertheless—

DASEIN: That's the whole point, Stanhope! We were so upset to find that Onalred was dead and not your mother—his sister—that we never bothered to ask ourselves *why* she killed her brother—your father—

STANHOPE: You're telling me she killed him to objectify the Sino-Soviet split?

DASEIN: Not exactly—

MAUD: The old Stalinist party hack—

STANHOPE: Don't you dare talk about my father that way!

MAUD: I'll talk about your father—my brother and husband—in any way I please. For men like Onalred, all women have always been media, not people. Unspoken messages between tribal groups; units of economic, biological and symbolic significance, exchanged in a way that keeps the general structure—the male hierarchy—dynamic, coherent, functioning, tyrannous. Well, he got *my* message, he did!

STANHOPE: But surely there is equality between the sexes in the Soviet Union! I mean, all those female tractor-drivers . . .

MAUD: So I thought, too. But Onalred, by what he did to me, proved different.

STANHOPE (thoughtfully): I see. You refer, of course, to the blood-crime, of which I am the issue and the perambulatory recrimination. Yet surely that has nothing to do with politics, Mother. That was a question of personal honor. As I see it, Onalred would understand his sister's virginity to be the repository of her brother's honor, especially in a classless society. But this is difficult: because that virginity, that honor, is then precious precisely in terms of its perishability. It must be lost in order to have existed. So he lost it for you. And you could not forgive him for having used you in the process of his self-definition. You *were* always short in the compassion department, Mother.

MAUD: The Yoknapatawpha Ranger rides again! Sweet pea, you're hopeless. I'm not talking about *sex*. We got together in Mexico because I was the only one he could trust and he was the only one I could trust. After all the blood we had known together, incest was like a bath: for in cherishing each other, we cherished ourselves; and we were the only ones still capable of granting each other an absolution, being the only ones equally guilty of such monstrous crimes. Do you understand that? But then *he* dumped *me* in Long Beach, and left me there for *twenty-three years*. There is *no* absolution for that crime . . . except death. I only wish his death agony could have lasted for twenty-three years!

STANHOPE (turning to Dasein): She has removed the manhole lid. You are looking into the sewer of her mind. How can you—

DASEIN: It doesn't matter. Revolution *is* revolution because it reduces every contradiction to the single set of alternatives: life or death. Do it unto others before they do it unto you. Can you imagine what my life has been? To have pawned myself to Lenin; on his death, to have been redeemed by Trotsky; on *his* death, to have been handed over to Henry James via Philip Rahv; and from Henry James via Lionel Trilling to J. Edgar Hoover . . . Stanhope, to be *pure* again, to be purified in the fire of the eyes and the blood of the brain of the man with the beard, to carry on his work in the employ of the man who writes little poems . . . *This is my chance!*

STANHOPE: He's such a lousy poet. More importantly, Dasein, I would remind you of young Bronstein's words: Marxism is "more epigrams, quotations and venom than content."

Dasein wavers, but Maud seizes the Smith & Wesson revolver.

MAUD: Elbowroom, cried Dan'l Boone! Out of the way, sweet pea!

STANHOPE: Wait! One more question: Then, if, to spite my father, you have all this time been working for the man who writes little poems, did you know Dokhma Koan?

MAUD: Of course. He was not only my contact, but my opium supply. It's a measure of Onalred's deterioration over the years that he didn't make the connection, even after reading *Queasiness*. Who else but me could have set up those bowling teams as cells?

She flanks Stanhope, dragging Dasein after her. Dasein loses a hemp-bottomed sandal. Stanhope stoops to scoop it up as they exit. Tucking the sandal into his pocket, he tries to formulate the exact terms of his disappointment . . . when an astonishing thing occurs. In the violence of their coupling, Sahasrara and Parturient inadvertently effect a Shift of the Hexagons. The facets come rolling, the ceiling splits, bodies are tossed against the walls like dice, and Stanhope—

The Soviet Army Chorus sings "Meadowlands."

—Stanhope finds himself, miraculously, staring down into the blue nadirical eye of the metronome at the bottom of the Annihilation funnel-tunnel. And there, its pearl-handle likewise blue in the nadirical light, is Dasein's discarded Luger, the very gun she dropped while the Pigstickers were employing her as an Exercycle to shed their flab of shame!

Stanhope seizes the Luger. Now what? He is in the well of Annihilation. By pressing his knees against the anterior wall and his buttocks against the posterior wall, he finds that he can with a sort of reverse shimmy force his way up the well. Halfway up, he looks up, to see that the zenithian hatch opens on the 451 pounds of Silly-Putty. That won't do. But within reach is the grating of a ventilator outlet. Stanhope is happily inspired. Yanking the ventilator grate from its brackets, he crawls into the hot-air shaft which feeds in its sinuous passage every suite and chamber of the Ashram. Belly-flopping himself forward, he can with impunity peer through every ventilator grate into every room, on the lookout for the decamping duo. Some of the sights he sees are perfectly appalling, but they have nothing to do with this narrative.

The Sveshnikov Chorus sings "Down the Volga."

And, in the marvelously reconstituted vestibule, under the great glass mandala, Stanhope finds them! Irony of ironies, what should be projected on the vinyl screens around them than Onalred's very own candid-incamera film of the Iowa Avengers, deflowering with cue sticks that snub-nosed eight-year-old in Lincoln Park!

STANHOPE (kissing his thumbs): Freeze! I've got both Dasein's pearl-handled Luger *and* the decided upper hand.

He is, in addition, cheered by an unsuspected tactical advantage: not only is he protected from their fire, being inside the hot-air shaft, but his voice caroms wildly off the sides and shallows of the shaft, seeming to issue onto the vestibule from any and all of a dozen gratings. Maud searches the ceiling. Dragons and vultures, ravens and lions look back at her. The mirrors multiply her image and her confusion. (As well as Stanhope's sense of incipient fulfillment, for this implosion of hovering mother figures, this silver-sourced orgy of *das Ewigweibliche,* rather plushly sets the stage for an operatic purge.)

MAUD: First of all, he's probably lying. Secondly, he never could shoot straight.

Stanhope replies by blasting off her blue beret.

STANHOPE: Long ago I lied to you about my prowess at target-shooting. But there can be no more dissimulation between us. Obviously, I have not lied about the Luger.

He has sacrificed one of his advantages by proving the others to her. She now knows behind which grate he lurks. She directs her voice to that grate.

MAUD: You wouldn't shoot your own mother.

STANHOPE: Can you come up with a single reason why I shouldn't?

MAUD: Well . . . why do you think I ironed Bethesda to death?

STANHOPE: That's something I've been meaning to ask you.

MAUD: Sweet pea, she stood between us. You held her, whether you knew it consciously or not, as a hostage against *me.* I hoped that . . . that, after disposing of Onalred, that we . . . that the *two* of us together might—

STANHOPE: Sail down the Yalu River on a Sportyak, into the glorious yellow Oriental sunset? Mother, you slay me! You're too much! I mean, my father tried incest with you, and look where it got him. Pneumatic traction! The *two* of us—not a chance! And when you confiscated all those other hostages I tried to hold against you— and my youth was a history of confiscation, of expropriation!—when you took away my Book of Mormon and my introductory copy of *Human Events* and my Playmate calendar . . . when you burned in the back-yard rotisserie my library edition of Sidney Hook's *The Hero in History*—did the two of us get together *then,* Mother? Did you make advances *then* into the territory of my loneliness and my need? No! So now I say to you: applesauce!

Whereupon Maud, withdrawing a collateral of cunning she has banked during years of revolutionary terrorism, during years of TV Western-watching, spins Dasein about to face Stanhope's grate; steps behind her; and, applying a strangle hold with one arm and aiming the Smith & Wesson with the other, speaks—

MAUD: There has always been a worm of sentimentality in the gut of your will. You might gun me down; but you could never bring your- self to perforate Miss Camembert!

DASEIN: Bad faith, Maud! Bad faith!

MAUD: Tell it to Isaac Deutscher.

STANHOPE: This desperate *espiegkerie* avails you naught, Mother. Contrive as you can, you're trapped. There's no exit. The witching hour will soon strike. The dome of the Ashram will retract, and Renaldi Haruspex will descend on the scene by helicopter. You have explored the finite, Mother; and the Infinite wouldn't have you with bells on.

MAUD (undaunted): He'll arrive by helicopter, all right. And he'll land right in the middle of the vestibule. And he'll be confronted by a thousand mirror images of us. And while he's trying to figure out which of them is we, and where those we may actually be, *I* will dis- pose of him—your kept cop!—and steal his helicopter.

A fiendish plan, but one admirably flexible.

STANHOPE (affecting discouragement): Oh, fudge.

Maud laughs. But Stanhope is not without a plan. Of course he is incapable of killing Dasein. (He kisses her hemp-bottomed sandal.) Those with whom we have lain lay claims by their physical largesse upon a generosity of remembrance we would mock only at our deadly peril; the gods don't like ingrates. Never having lain with his mother, however, and not being able, despite his best efforts along that line, to secure for his conscious mind an admission of that popular subcon- scious desire, he owes *her* no such generosity. In fact, to shoot her might satisfactorily slay not only Mother, but any such lurking psychological imperative as well—in a single expenditure of lust and loss. Well, then, what's to be done? He *is* more than a little bored by Dasein's clandestine affair with bathos, her repetition-compulsion to be violated. *He* cannot kill her, but it would not especially grieve him if someone else took care of it. Someone else like Renaldi.

He waits. He waits until midnight. And a gong of such ear-piercing punctuation and punctuality that the rinds of the Ashram Orange seem cymbals whose gigantic clash occasions their shocked peeling . . . a screaming shuck of metal sections . . . the opening of a vast brass flower to accept the weight of the Nasal-Misty night sky . . .

There is Renaldi's Sky-Knight helicopter, hovering. There is Mother, with a strangle hold on Dasein. There are the mirrors and the mandala. *And Stanhope intervenes.*

He fires at the *helicopter!*

It works. No sooner does Renaldi realize he is among hostiles than he opens up with the riot gun, raining bullets on the vestibule. The effect is spectacular. Not necessarily because the dragons, vultures, ravens and lions are ventilated like the grate behind which Stanhope waits, and burn in their tumble from their perches; nor necessarily because the vinyl screens are torn and flap like battle flags in the windy vestibule; nor even necessarily because the mirrors shatter, heaving great glittering swords inward, downward—although all of this is sensorily stimulating.

But, most significantly, Renaldi's rain of bullets slashes the supporting superstructure of the great glass mandala. It shudders at this invasion of the malignant maya. It begins to swing and rip. Maud is about to drag Dasein from under it, when—

When who should appear but Synecdoche Wessel, bearing his bag of bhang on his back. Maud just isn't up to coping with this apparition. Concluding that Synecdoche is an enemy, she shoots him. It is her last mistake. Synecdoche is surprised. He looks down at the holes in his lard, at the body oils spurting out. He is about as affected by the bullets as a dinosaur would be by split-peas spit-shot. But the loss of fluids distresses him mightily. He fixes on Maud and the smoking Smith & Wesson, and he moves forward! Maud empties the gun into him . . . he advances . . . she throws the gun at him . . . it glances off his brow . . . he drops his bag of bhang and lifts his bloated arms . . . Maud and Dasein cower . . . Synecdoche pours his vat of flab upon them, and they fall in the torrent of his flesh.

And there it lies—with Synecdoche sprawled full length over the stunned bodies of Maud and Dasein, trying with his thumbs to plug the leaks in his hide—as the mandala comes down. It lands directly on top of the three of them, and they are instantly dispatched. The helicopter still hovers, as though appalled by its lead logic, and . . . yes, *awed* by the beauty of what that logic has achieved. For the sunken mandala is fanned about by glittering swords of shattered mirror— *and a huge star has been formed*. A star that traps and refracts the swan-swinging of the blades of helicopter-light; a star that sends spiraling upward into the night a circular energy pattern whose deep-throated vortex threatens to suck both Renaldi and the moon right out of the Long Beach sky . . .

STANHOPE (to himself): It is the perfect revenge of the mandala on those who—as perfectly—exemplify the opting of the East for the reality principle.

And from out of the Sufi-facets of Quest, Love, Enlightenment, Detachment, Unity, Amazement and Annihilation of the Self creep the astonished Ashramblers, their death masks in their hands, to regard with an awe as excessive as Stanhope's this Star of Death; and to watch with a paralyzed wonder the reluctant descent of the helicopter onto the mandala and the mirror-swords.

SVAM SPADE (knowing that his moment has come): A happening with historicity! *God has blown his mind!*

Like Otto, Svam has style. He tosses his Booker T. Washington death mask onto the mandala-star. The others, equally moved by the manifestation, and Svam's gesture, follow suit. Death masks of Edith Piaf and Ernest Hemingway, Marilyn Monroe and Patrice Lumumba, Tibor Dery and Lao Tzu and Benny "Kid" Paret are lobbed, are free-thrown, onto the mandala and become a mound of skulls.

The Ashramblers join hands and sing:

> Star of Plunder, Star of Blight,
> Star whose glass has slashed the night:
> Downward sinking,
> Upward blinking,
> Might we cite Thee in a rite?

ACID-HEADS:

> From the marriage of the mandala it's easy to infer:
> There are no gratifications we need bother to defer.

And Parturient turns to Sahasrara, singing:

> I pledge to paw what all you own:
> Each orifice and every zone.

Stanhope climbs out of the hot-air shaft with the pearl-handled Luger in his belt and the hemp-bottomed sandal in his hand. He looks down.

STANHOPE (bitterly): How did Swinburne put it? "The beast Faith lives on its own dung."

Then yet another extraordinary thing happens. As Stanhope climbs down the wall, the Long Beach moon breaks through the Nasal Mist, and throws a gigantic Stanhope-Shadow on the vestibular wall. The Shadow climbs as he descends. Distorted by the vapors of the burning vinyl screens, fragmented by the swords of mirror, spun up and sucked upon by the whirling blades of helicopter-light, the Shadow becomes a huge silver-plated Fish-Man, mottling the faces of the watchers, turning, groping, incandescent . . . then, as suddenly as its appearance, with an upward movement as of mirror-wings, it leaps at the moon and plucks it out like Otto's eye! *Gone.*

SVAM: It's . . . it's . . . would you believe? . . . It's—*CAPTAIN HAPPEN!*

They will believe, for so it is to be mythologized: the wedding of the virginal Synecdoche and his tank of Bindu-nectar to the mandala and the mirror-swords, creating a superhipster, a dauntless defender of shantih-town against the attenuations of the Rhomboids . . .

ASHRAMBLERS: The Ultimate Anti-Word, made Shadow . . . *Captain Happen!*

Darnell Miller sings "Mommy, Will My Doggie Understand?"

On his escape from the Ashram, Stanhope sought the salt-scouring sea; strove, among grunion-hunters, to wrestle and pin the purport of events. Was the hemp-bottomed sandal he had seized in Otto's Grotto a talisman, a divining rod? Was it his mission to tromp the strand, detecting and destroying jelly-chain caches of Onalred eggs? To find microfilm in bowling balls? He hoped not: it was inconsistent with his self-image. (Later he would smile on these parochial concerns, admitting the adverse judgment they made on his powers of prophecy —to have been so preoccupied with himself at the very hour of the birth of Captain Happen!) Morosely, he made mud pies and watched the tide drown them. He thought the hotels moved toward him on their oiled anti-earthquake rollers. He imagined the sirens screaming in the night were all Bethesda, summoning him to an accounting he would never be prepared to give. He was depressed.

And it was on the beach that Renaldi found him, at dawn, with the hemp-bottomed sandal clenched in his teeth. "We booked the Aussie abo for Otto's murder," Renaldi said.

"Gnatpappa? Why him?" asked Stanhope. "The others are equally guilty."

Renaldi was annoyed. "Listen," he said, "Long Beach is the thirty-second largest city in the United States. Do you think it's easy, being Number Thirty-two?"

Stanhope turned a ravaged face on him. "One of the many things I don't need right now is a sensitive cop!"

Renaldi hoisted an arm to chop him down; then, gazing at himself in the pavé-mirrors of his motorcycle sleeve, he relented. "All right," he said. "I agree. The others are equally guilty. But it's complicated. We figure the aborigine will get free legal help from the ACLU, the NAACP Legal Fund, the New York *Times* and either Melvin Belli or Edward Bennett Williams or Louis Nizer or F. Lee Bailey. They may have to take it all the way up to Earl Warren, but Gnatpappa should get off in the end. The other murderers would have more difficulty bankrolling a succession of pleas."

Stanhope frowned across the water. Was this endless self-victimization actually a purposeful reduction and canceling toward a pure, elusive integer? Did they seek through their shucking to achieve a simple essence which, tragically, *did not exist?* Renaldi placed a hand on his shoulder and left it there. Stanhope looked at the hand. Renaldi said: "When do you suppose it will end? This senseless *samsara,* I mean?" Stanhope didn't know.

They watched dawn fry its egg. "The sun, after all," observed Renaldi, "is but a morning star." Stanhope turned; Renaldi searched his face.

They embraced: the lack of pity of a policeman, the self-pity of a poet . . . knowing that Long Beach was watching, wanting that witness to the desperation of their need for a consolation as drastic as the binge of death which had brought them together among spawning grunions, and hunters of grunions, and spawning grunion-hunters.

And—*mirabile dictu!*—the gulls burst into a chorale. And do you know what the gulls were singing? They were singing Schiller's *An die Freude,* with background accompaniment by Ludwig van Beethoven.

Now and Forever

An anti-climax . . . the truth about Gongor.

Gongor rubbed his hands. "I think I've got everything I need," he said.

"Sit down, Gongor," said Stanhope. "Have you never heard of a dying fall?"

Parturient yawned. "Must we really go through a dying fall?"

"We must," said Stanhope. What was life but a dying fall?

"Then," said Parturient, "tell me: why *did* your mother iron Bethesda to death? The answer she gave you in the vestibule of the Ashram was certainly a lie."

"What does it matter?" asked Gongor.

"If *it* doesn't matter," said Stanhope reprovingly, "then neither does anything else." He thought about Bethesda. "I suppose," he said, "that Mother saw in Bethesda that same blind sexual willingness to wait for twenty-three years in Long Beach at the request of a man . . . that same tragic flaw that was Maud's own. And so, in murdering Bethesda, she murdered the last small dandelion-dream of a femininity she had grown to loathe."

"Long Beach!" exclaimed Gongor. "I am sick of Long Beach."

"So, Gongor, are we all," said Parturient. "But don't you see that Cronopios is on a new kick? Beyond ideology, what *is* there for him? If not the community of the Dionysiac Pack, then the solitary splendor of the artist! Long Beach, full of ambiguous designs, has physically embodied itself in *him*. For what purpose, other than the usual doomed desire, as characteristic of cities as it is of fathers, to create in its own image as best its poor powers (and its poor image) will permit? The hugger-muggery of these disasters has been his education into his role: to inquire into those other purposes, those ambiguous designs. *Now* he has the credentials. For has he not *accepted* the City, like a clubfoot or a malfunctioning kidney or a mother? Has he not *endured* it, like a spiritual marathon? Has he not *fed* it, like an insectivorous sundew flower, with fillet of his very own soul? And has he not, to the best of his inabilities, *destroyed* it, too? The destruction is especially necessary, for the artist must count the components before trying to foist upon them a new *Gestalt*. Then, out of his guilt and pain, he seeks to re-create the face of the City, as one reconstructs a shattered clock in order to escape the madness of an unregulated delirium. For Long Beach, like the clock, is a lie; but it is a necessary lie, which makes the madness supportable. And the artist must go on smashing and reconstructing *all* the clocks. Otherwise, there would be no Time."

Stanhope looked at Parturient wonderingly: "You *understand*," he said softly.

"Don't blow your cool, Cronopios," said Parturient. "Next you'll be adopting *me* as a father figure, and I have no desire to achieve a premature martyrdom."

But he *did* understand, thought Stanhope; he understood the meaning of the butchered loves and the vanished hopes so much better than, say, John the Ossified Man had understood them. On reading the memoir, John had said: "Half bastinado, half emetic. Too much construction, not enough erotics. A shockingly low sensory quotient. And *all* your characters talk in exactly the same way!" To which Stanhope could only reply: "So what? All Homer's heroes talked in Ionian hexameters." John had just smiled; and not at Stanhope, but at a snapshot of himself, under the lemon tree, with the simpering girl. "Do you know what?" John had said. "They are going to name the new pier at the World Trade Center for *me!* Pier J! Hydraulic filling has already begun; I watch them every afternoon, barging in the big boulders from Catalina Island." Stanhope had been disgusted. Either John's sense of reality had undergone an ossification akin to that which attacked his musculature, or, more probably, the City Fathers had suborned him with this cheap gesture. Did John so long to receive from the money-monks his absolving Saltine, that such a token sufficed to turn aside the stiff stiles of his anger and his intuition, permitting the City Fathers to spin him and pass through his witness without harm? Pier J! John had said: "Life, Stanhope, is a movie. Death is a photograph." And Stanhope had known that the Ossified Man had squandered his authority to criticize the manuscript. He had flung the pages in John's face and rushed wordless out of the trailer. It had been, in a way, like leaving one's youth. Because that leave-taking is inevitable, you cannot be accused of *abandoning* your youth, but still . . . youth *was* a ward of yours, of sorts, and you feel you might have done more by it, played more ball with it, humored its imaginary companion . . .

If, however, Parturient understood, Stanhope might not be condemned forever to lick the bitter lollipop of his seemingly inexhaustible desolation. He stood at the boat's rail and stared at the tide. "I sought," he told Gongor, "to abstract from my experience its salient features; to cast those features in the form of words and symbols; to exchange them for other words and symbols with other members of my species." He turned. "Let me wring just one more variation. On leaving my memoir with John, do you know where I went? I went to the Port Authority Building, to ponder once more the ceramic mural which disfigures it. And I decided: Dokhma Koan was tragically mistaken in thinking that mural banal—for the pathos of an artistic act inadequate to its aspiration can never really be banal. I was, of course, trying to comfort myself. I did not succeed. But, Gongor, I *will* succeed if your publishing house sees fit to purchase my manuscript."

Gongor stood up again, and stretched. "Oh," he said, "we're certainly willing to buy all rights to it. I want to show you something." He rummaged in a briefcase and extracted a large piece of pasteboard. "Take a look," he said. It was a sketch of the cover of a comic book. It depicted in lurid exactitude the mandala-star, the helicopter, the Ashramblers, and . . . *Captain Happen.* The title, spelled out in balloon letters, read: THE ADVENTURES OF CAPTAIN HAPPEN (AND HIS SNIDE-KICK, SWITCHED-ON BLADE)!

"But—" began Stanhope, horrified.

"Cucking Stool & Sons publishes nothing but comic books," said Gongor. "It is not only lucrative, but, as a cultural phenomenon, a powerful subversive force. We are prepared not only to buy your manuscript, Cronopios, but to offer you an editorial position, working directly with our team of artists."

Gongor's bald head was a moon-reflector. In fact, Stanhope felt himself tightrope-walking the haywired silver thread from skull-like moon to moon-like skull. Death reflecting the reflected light of death . . . so at last the course of pseudo-events catches up with and engulfs us. He looked away, toward the beach and the lights of the Pike. They were no help. The sea heaved black lions upon the sand, then tore them away once more. The black lions snarled, raged, cried, tried to claw their way to deliverance, but were dragged back.

Slowly, Stanhope said: "To make of those nights, that time, those

dead nights and that lost time of death-giving . . . a comic book!
But *surely* my people, my victims . . . indistinct in their complexity
. . . I mean, this vast moral calculus, as I have called it, by the progressive examination and obliteration of its symbols, works an awful
equation toward nullity, toward—"

"The cartoon!" said Gongor. "Exactly. The end of calculus, the
snake-eyed cube of meaning: the cartoon! That's why we're *respectable* today, Cronopios. Our editorial board would wow a philanthropic
foundation: Brown, McLuhan, Sontag, Podhoretz, Warhol, Leary,
Watts . . ."

"But Long Beach—" began Stanhope.

"Long Beach!" Gongor sneered. "I have seen the world, and it is
Long Beach. On a Friday night in any city in this nation, around the
bars and the movie houses and the all-night cafeterias, they are waiting, their hands in their pockets and their brains in their shoes. They
are waiting, slung in doorways, hung from street lamps, lying on the
hoods of automobiles, in six-packs, bored beyond tears, hurling
coarse images of brutality and violation at passers-by. They hate
everything, even sex. Queens, eunuchs, bullies, transvestites, dwarfs,
internal refugees, twitch-machines, the self-dispossessed, the living
dead, the plastic men . . . ! Waiting for what? They long in the neon
light for a purification by fire, a blinding apocalypse to redeem them
and give shape and point to their listlessness, their hatred. They are
waiting for an accident, Cronopios. *They are waiting for Captain
Happen!* Long Beach is no different from any place else."

"You lie!" cried Stanhope.

Gongor addressed Parturient. "This guy Svam Spade . . . I understand he's got a copyright on the name 'Captain Happen.' Where
can I locate him?"

"Tomorrow in Recreation Park somewhere," said Parturient. "He's
organized a Die-In at the Iowa State Picnic."

Sahasrara shuddered, and nuzzled Parturient's ribs. Gongor said
to Stanhope: "Well? Whaddaya say, kid?"

Stanhope shrugged, as even God must, occasionally. "All right," he
said. "I will sell you my manuscript. And . . . and I will write for
your comic book. Because . . . are you capable of understanding
this, Gongor? Because I still believe in work as a form of social communion." Then, beseechingly: "But you *must* not rob me of the horror
and significance of Long Beach."

Gongor threw up his hands in glee. "Work as a form of social communion!" he scoffed. "Kid, you really *are* the Last of the Rhomboids, aren't you?"

Parturient, compassionately, said: "This dying fall has gone on long enough."

"One more question," said Gongor, and he grinned. "Cronopios, I want you to tell me just one last thing." He paused. *"Why do you love Long Beach?"*

"I don't love it!" screamed Stanhope, gripping the boat rail. "I don't love it!" again. I don't love it, he thought, sobbing in the salt- and oil-scented air, the drifting silver threads of pseudo-eventuality. "I don't love it! I don't! I *don't!"*

"Ha, ho, ha!" said Gongor. He unzipped his sheared French rabbit battle jacket, and from an interior pocket whipped out his embossed leather checkbook and his gold-capped fountain pen. The cracking open of the checkbook was like a snapping of vertebrae.

Looking at him, Stanhope saw (as though Gongor were a periscope poking up and out of the present tense, this *tense* tense of a self-knowledge as indigestible as a glob of cold lamb fat, as a cutlet of frozen dream) . . . he saw: his future:

To be, forever, a banana peel on the stage of History.